THE PEARLS OF
COROMANDEL

THE PEARLS OF COROMANDEL

KERON BHATTACHARYA

ST. MARTIN'S PRESS ☙ NEW YORK

ISBN 0-312-14389-3

First published in Great Britain by Robert Hale Limited

First U.S. Edition: June 1996

10 9 8 7 6 5 4 3 2 1

Acknowledgements

The characters and events in this novel are fictional though the background is authentic, for which I needed help from many sources. I am particularly indebted to Barbara Dasgupta for her endless suggestions to improve the text and Jean Finlayson Stokes for crossing the 't's and dotting the 'i's. The staff at the British Library, India Office Library, Slough Library and Beaconsfield Library helped me assiduously with my research. The Friends House in Jordans kindly allowed me to attend their silent prayer meetings for which I am sincerely thankful. I am grateful to John Hale for his help with the publication.

For Shomick, Rishi, and Angela
for all those silent mornings they had to suffer
while I was writing this novel.

PART ONE

The Journey

ONE

I

David Sugden stood on the deck and looked at the deep blue Arabian Sea. There was nothing in sight – just endless ink-blue water. The ship, the SS *Bharat*, had left Aden five days before. Another six or seven hours and the yellow sandstone of the Gateway of India would be visible. He paced the deck restlessly for a while, then gritted his teeth and muttered a motley group of names: Ratan Banerji! Charles Garvey! Anil Saha! Khodadad Khan! Harmohan Joshi! He was impatient and angry – full of hatred. Singapore has fallen, he thought, and so has Burma. Millions have crossed overland to India to escape from the Japanese occupation. But for how long? The Lion definitely has her back to the wall. Is it the beginning of the end – the end of the British Raj?

Racial strife, according to the ship's news bulletin, was still rampant in the country – more rapes, more killings everywhere. The old man, Gandhi, was still walking thousands of miles to bring peace to the feuding sects. Or so he claimed. No, unlike John Sugden, his father, David did not believe Gandhi was a saint. How could he be a saint when he was inciting so many people to break the law? '*Karenge ya marenge*' – do or die, he had recently demanded of his fellow countrymen. That was a clear message to the ordinary, peace-loving Indians to take up violence.

David Sugden now sat down on a deckchair and started flicking through a few pages of his father's diary. He really did not understand his father. Gandhi brought so much pain and misery to his life and he still had nothing but praise for the man. John Sugden was humiliated by both the Raj and the Indians. Yes, the Raj as well. There could be no two ways about it. That was the reason for his premature death.

9

He turned a few more pages. Oh, so many times he had read this diary – especially that horrific account of the rape. I must be a masochist, he thought, as he started reading it all over again and was soon consumed with an immense passion for revenge.

II

Hari Mukherji was the only son of his parents. He had a sister, but she had married a long time ago and lived some distance away. The family was an extended one because his parents lived in the same house as Hari and his wife. They were quite elderly as Hari had been born to them late in life. For the last few years Hari's father had been suffering from acute rheumatism and most of the time he was bed-ridden. His mother, though in good health herself, had to tend to his father, which meant for all practical purposes that they stayed in their own room. This, in a way, gave Hari and his wife, Kamala, a bit of privacy which was hard to come by in India and spared them the frustration so often generated through overcrowding. Basically the family was in complete harmony. Both his parents adored Kamala, and she in turn looked after them as if they were her own parents.

It was a warm evening. The air was heavy as the monsoon had just come to an end. The months after the monsoon were always muggy in Bihar with humidity reaching near saturation point. One did not have to do any work – just sitting idly was enough to bring streams of perspiration trickling down the body.

Kamala as usual cooked the evening meal for the family. Father, mother and Hari, her husband, all had dinner before her which is customary in a Hindu household. Father once again was not feeling well; the humid summer evening had affected his rheumatism and he retired to his room immediately after. Mother followed him with medication and stayed with him in the room. Hari sat in the courtyard and smoked his hubble-bubble while Kamala had her dinner. Occasionally they conversed – Kamala shouting from the kitchen and Hari only responding with monosyllabic replies. This was his habit – he was taciturn by nature.

The night was very dark. But the stars were visible in the otherwise clear sky and a thin slice of crescent moon – or the moon for Idd as they call it in India – just about kept its presence. Earlier in the morning the *maulavis* had to observe the crescent moon before starting their ululation to signal the propitious start of the festival.

Hari's house was just on the outskirts of the Hindu colony. Though they were not really prosperous – not like the Banerjis, his in-laws – they had various orchards, mango-groves, a pond in which to culture fish; these they would have found difficult to afford inside the Hindu sector.

Initially Hari's mother did not like to be so near to the Moslems, but soon she adjusted to the environment and found them friendly. Moreover, Hari's working for the Raj added status to the family, especially in the eyes of illiterate Moslems. During the recent riot, for example, nobody had even attempted to lay a finger on them – not that it was expected – for Hari was a well-respected person.

Earlier that evening, because of the close proximity of the Moslem quarters, they had heard the din of the celebrations. But when night fell, the noise gradually died down, leaving only the sound of crickets from the pond and, later, Hari's hubble-bubble from the courtyard.

That evening when Kamala finished dinner, she prepared *pans* for Hari and her in-laws. She had never liked *pans* for they tended to make her mouth go red, which she never enjoyed. This had been in the past a major cause of argument with her mother-in-law, but Kamala being stubborn, dug in her heels and finally got away with it, though her mother-in-law still complained that it looked graceful for a housewife to have her mouth reddened with a *pan*.

Kamala took the *pans* to her in-laws first and then she came into the courtyard and sat next to Hari. He was in one of his uncommunicative moods. He took the *pan* but did not offer much in the way of conversation. Disappointed, Kamala decided to go inside and take up again the novel which she had been reading.

In Hari's house, as yet, they had no electricity. In the town centre where Kamala's parents lived, they already had the cable bringing power, which offered for the first time the security of a light that would not be put out in a storm. The poor Moslem quarters were not so lucky. It was expected to be a few years before the cable came as far as Hari's house. His family was eagerly waiting for this luxury to reach them.

It was very dark outside that night. The noise of a cricket continuously breaking the silence was only punctuated by Hari's hubble-bubble, although now that sound was becoming more spasmodic, meaning that Hari was deeply engrossed in his thoughts. Kamala tried to read by the hurricane lamp – Robert Louis Stevenson's *The Strange Case of Dr Jekyll and Mr Hyde*. This book among many others had been a wedding present from the Sahib, the local district officer. She had learnt English at school, so it was not difficult for her to read an English novel.

Soon the story engrossed her completely, for how long she did not know. Suddenly she became aware of a strange silence – Hari's hubble-bubble noise had stopped. For a moment or two she thought perhaps he had gone to the toilet. Rather unnervingly though, the silence continued. It was very unusual because all through summer evenings until he came to bed, Hari's way of relaxing was to sit in the dark courtyard and smoke his hubble-bubble. She wondered whether he needed to relight it and was just too lethargic to get up and go to the kitchen.

She placed a bookmark, closed the book and decided to go and see what was happening outside. As she was about to get up, much to her great dismay she saw a long distorted shadow on the wall. A man. Her heart jumped in fear and she screamed. But only for a moment. The man leaped towards her and put his hand over her mouth. Kamala saw him but there was no way she could recognize him even if she had tried. His face was painted jet black which made him hideous, almost like a monster. A stinking, rancid smell took her breath away.

She struggled to push him off, but all in vain. He was much too powerful. With his rough, muscular hand he held her mouth firmly and then with the other hand he took the end of her sari, tightly stuffed it in her mouth and tied it.

More men entered the room. She did not know how many. Maybe a dozen. All with painted faces, carrying big knives. In that cold hurricane light, their shadows criss-crossing the wall made Kamala shiver with fear. She started sweating profusely. She tried to scream but couldn't because they had gagged her so tightly, only a groaning noise came out.

Now they tied her hands and started ripping her clothes apart with animal force. In humiliation and fear, she lay with her top completely bare, in front of two dozen goggling eyes.

One man came forward and brazenly touched her breast. Such shame! She looked at them, begging them ardently with her eyes to spare her. Just to have pity on a young girl. Only eigheen. But their hardened faces filled with nauseating concupiscence. The man started molesting her breasts. Hard. Fearfully hard. She writhed in pain and struggled. But her tied hands were no help and her legs were held apart by two men as they laughed aloud. Devils' laughs! All of them joined in now and together tore at her clothes. The young innocent nakedness! They grabbed that nakedness with the poison of a reptile. She tried to tighten her body in revulsion but someone slapped her face. The pain came right through as she could taste the salty liquid of her blood slowly trickling down her throat. She struggled and struggled. A man pushed himself inside. The nauseous feeling nearly choked her. The first man ever, apart from Hari. The first man to enter without love. Without desire. The brute force of a penis desecrated the temple.

That was not all. Everyone now took his turn and tore apart her fresh young body in lascivious hunger. Another. And then another. And more. She did not know how many. She lay there in pain with the strong fishy smell of semen filling the entire room. Her body, her inside, like a sewer, flooded with filth. 'Oh God! How long will this last?' she cried in agony.

The darkness fell suddenly and took away her consciousness. All nightmares on this earth must have an end. And so had Kamala's. But it seemed to her that the time of that excruciating pain and humiliation was eternal. They pierced her with endless hatred which no one could obliterate – Not the Sahib! Not Gandhi! Not even God!

TWO

I

David Congdon was a well known hardware merchant in Calcutta. His grandfather had come to India from rural Lancashire and built the now well-established business from scratch. It had been hard work for the old Lancastrian, for in those days ships used to voyage a full six months crossing the stormy and pirate-infested

Bay of Biscay and rounding the Cape before reaching the British ports in India such as Calcutta or Madras. By comparison, David Congdon was lucky. Since de Lesseps had completed the construction of the Suez Canal in 1869, it took only a fortnight for a ship to make that journey.

For an Englishman David Congdon was dark skinned but his grey hair made him look distinguished. He had the manner of a successful man. And indeed he was successful. He lived with his family in a palatial building in Park Street, near the maidan. Naturally he was pleased with his life. But even the moon has its shadow. David Congdon also had one cause of resentment.

Of late he had been extremely happy because his young son, Stanley, was back in Calcutta after finishing his studies at Cambridge. Moreover, Stanley's friend, the newly-arrived ICS officer, John Sugden, was courting David's daughter, Martha. Balliol-educated John Sugden was a scion of an influential Quaker family from Pennsylvania, which was now settled in England.

'I like John Sugden,' David Congdon commented approvingly to his son about his new friend.

The young man, dark, tall and handsome, replied with delight, 'He's a nice chap. Not often do you come across such a genuine person.'

'If he's an Oxford man, how did you come to know him?' the old man was curious.

'I met him on the ship – on the way back from England.'

'So you haven't known him for long?'

'Not long at all. On the other hand it seems as if I've known him for years.' Stanley seemed pleased to have acquired a friend from England.

'If you're that friendly, why don't you ask your friend to stay with us and enjoy home comforts rather than be alone in an hotel room? He can't know many people in Calcutta.' The old man was keen for his son to build a firm friendship with this newly-arrived ICS officer.

Stanley hesitated – he was not sure how to put it to his father, then he decided to tell him the truth. 'I did ask him but his department isn't all that keen.'

The elder Congdon turned his face away, visibly hurt.

'He's taking Martha out – hope you don't mind.' Stanley mentioned it to cheer up his father.

The old man's eyes glowed once again. He looked affectionately at Stanley and said, 'I'm glad you're back now, Stan. These last few years I have been counting the days to your return.'

Stanley looked pleased, appreciating his increasingly important role within the family. 'Business is expanding rapidly, Stan,' the older man enthusiastically continued. 'Although your two brothers are already carrying the major burden, I need more managers of the right calibre whom I can trust.'

Fresh from England, Stanley was trying to learn every aspect of the family business. He did not want to lose this opportunity, so he asked, 'How is it that the business is expanding so rapidly, Father?'

'There're more demands for our hardware,' replied the old man. 'Morever with the Calcutta port silting up, the bigger ships are now diverted to Bombay or Karachi. So I am trying to expand business in those areas as well.'

Stanley was pleased to hear about his father's expansion scheme. He commented, 'I suppose with the railways improved it's no longer a problem to transport goods. That must be a real advantage for us.'

'You're right, son,' the elder Congdon appreciated his son's business acumen. 'You see, we're importing most of our goods from England – and then we have the task of distributing them throughout the country. A complex operation really.' David Congdon stopped briefly, musing over his problems, then continued, 'In many places where we don't have shops, we use local dealers through a distribution network. It requires extensive coordination – making sure the distributors have sufficient stock – the shelf-life's not too long – and that they're paying up.'

'Do you have many problems getting money from them?' Stanley enquired.

'That's the least of our worries unless someone goes bankrupt,' replied the old man. 'The distributors pay when they buy our goods. We also hold signed blank cheques from them – once we have worked out the amount they owe us for the goods dispatched, we fill in the figures.'

'That's very trusting of them.'

'In this country, they still trust a white man,' the old man commented with a certain degree of self satisfaction. Stanley turned his face away from his father. The old man noticed his son's reaction and remained silent for a moment or two, then with a sigh, added, 'You see, I'm getting old. I can't move about in the way I used to. We need more managers like you, Stan, to help us with our business.'

'Why don't you recruit a few?' the young Congdon asked.

'Expatriates, or for that matter local Europeans, are quite expensive these days. Then there's always the fear, once they know the ropes, that they will leave and start on their own in competition – or worse, take some of our clients in the process. I know quite a few cases where it has happened.'

'That's treacherous!' Stanley showed great surprise at this news.

'You can't trust anyone these days, Stan. Not even a European. That's the problem.'

'What about training a few educated Indians? Some of them seem capable.' Stanley, fresh from university, was now more open minded about Indians than he had been in the past. He had met a few bright ones at Cambridge.

But the old man was not convinced. 'No, Stan! They can't operate at a senior level. They have neither the personality and social graces, nor the necessary contacts.'

'The government seems to be finding a few – such as Lord Sinha.'

'Oh he's unique. In spite of being born an Indian, he's considered more English than an Englishman. Otherwise can you imagine, making a native the Governor of Bihar, taking him into the Imperial War Cabinet, inviting him to the House of Lords to have the privilege of his wisdom?'

'Aren't there any more like him whom we can groom?'

'A few. But they're quickly snapped up by the government. I tell you what though,' the old man suddenly seemed excited as he continued, 'if I could get someone like John Sugden into our business, he would be a great asset.'

'He'd never join your business and become a boxwallah, Father. He's an ICS officer with a great future ahead of him.' The young man tried to pour cold water on his father's enthusiasm.

'You never know,' the old man still pursued the topic. 'If something develops between Martha and him, then it'll be like a family business, won't it?'

'Stop daydreaming, Father,' Stanley, seeing the improbability of the old man's suggestion, shouted at him, then quickly regretted losing his temper and apologized profusely. David Congdon left the room hurriedly now. He was embarrassed for having let his son know his dreams.

II

Martha, Stanley's sister, was now deeply in love with John Sugden. He was so handsome – tall, slim, with blond hair and blue eyes. And so bright. It was the attraction of opposites because Martha was dark and though very pretty, she could not really be classed as intelligent. But she compensated for this with her gregarious and fun-loving demeanour. And that was what John Sugden found so attractive.

But John's time in Calcutta was coming to an end. At the very start of the cold-weather season, he was due to take up his post as the district officer in a small town called Raigarh, near Sripore, some three hundred miles away from Calcutta. Although there was a direct railway link between Calcutta and Sripore, it did not go as far as Raigarh. To get there required another half a day on a horse as the road was far too rough to use a motor vehicle.

Martha was extremely unhappy because of John Sugden's imminent departure. She made no bones about it when she found him alone one day in the Congdons' palatial home in Park Street.

'Everything's going to happen in Calcutta now the cold season is starting, and you will be gone.' Martha turned her face to the wall, for she was already feeling miserable at the very thought of John going away.

'I have no choice, Martha,' John replied rather guiltily. 'I'm hoping that around Christmas I will be able to come back.'

'That's another three months!' Martha sighed. 'So I won't be seeing you for a full three months!'

'You don't need to tell me! I feel just the same as you do.' John tried to express his own eagerness to spend more time with his newly acquired girl-friend. To appease her he added, 'Why don't you and Stanley come and spend some time with me in Raigarh?'

Martha did not seem too keen on the idea. She replied, 'Stanley's so taken up now with business, I doubt whether he would have the time.'

'I'll ask him, see what he says.' John sounded persuasive.

Martha, however, was visibly unhappy with this suggestion. She pouted in disappointment and said, 'If Stanley comes then I wouldn't have any time alone with you – would I?'

John was only too conscious of this fact but he could see no way out, so he answered, 'Stanley's a sensible friend, you know. He understands the problem. But I don't think your father would allow you to come on your own, especially since there are no Europeans in Raigarh.'

'I know! I know!' Martha wailed.

John tried to comfort his pretty girl-friend, saying, 'There's the Autumn Ball coming next week at the Grand, Martha. I sincerely hope you'll be able to come with me.'

'Is that an invitation?' asked Martha, still upset.

'Of course, yes! Who else would I be going with apart from you?'

'I don't know, John. I never take anything for granted,' Martha replied.

'You should,' John assured her and as there was no one else in the room, he held her and gave her a kiss.

II

The ball at the Grand was a major event. Although called the Autumn Ball, it signalled the start of the cold weather season. All the senior government officials with their families were now back from Darjeeling and Simla. The stalls in Hogg Market were full of people – European ladies, followed by scores of servants, scouring the shops for the coming cold weather season and replenishing their stock: cosmetics, underwear, perfume – everything. The departmental store, Hall and Anderson, at the corner of Park Street, was just the same. The Jewish tailors of Lindsay Street were working twenty four hours a day on the fittings for the fashionable and expensive dresses to be worn at various balls. Suddenly Calcutta came alive again with the memsahibs back in droves and their servants crowding round at Kaventer's for the daily supply of ham and bacon.

With the effervescent bubbling of the crowd, the whole atmosphere of the city changed almost overnight. The lights in the Metro, Lighthouse, Elite and New Empire – all the cinema halls – were glowing once again. Vying with one another to attract memsahibs, they were running the new films such as 'The Sheik', with Rudolph Valentino. The obvious sign of success in the competition was the proud boast of the 'House Full' board outside the cinema hall and then the advertisement in the *Statesman* – 'Seven Continuous House-Full Evenings – Book Now to Avoid Disappointment', with the last two words distinctly underlined.

John and Martha took this opportunity and went to see a couple of films, one in the Metro and the other in The Lighthouse. A new production of a Shakespearean play was soon to be staged at the New Empire by a well-known English company, but by then John would be away in Raigarh.

The Autumn Ball was organized by the Order of the Black Hearts of Calcutta. They were a strange group, mushrooming in every station throughout British India. Originally it had started because a few bachelors, feeling rather lonely on their own, had been eagerly looking for some fun and the obvious way, they thought, would be to organize a ball to bring all the bachelors and grass-widowers into contact with single girls. Since then it had grown enormously in popularity. Now even married couples were invited to take part in the fun. It was known that many romances and future marriages blossomed from initial encounters during these balls. With so many bachelors recruited to serve India, various dinner dances and grand balls were part of enjoying life in this distant post.

The start of the season was invariably marked by a fancy dress ball. In recent years these had become very popular in British India. The fashion had started with Lord and Lady Curzon, but soon it became a craze throughout the colony as more and more fancy dress balls were organized in every station, unleashing the creative energy of Anglo-Indians, especially of the women, who had nothing much to do during the day apart from keeping the peace among scores of feuding servants. To help the memsahibs with their creative ideas, various commercial organizations, specializing in the design and manufacture of fancy dress costumes, spread throughout the country.

John was invited to the ball. As one of the prime and eligible bachelors, a new arrival and an ICS-covenanted officer with an Oxford degree, he was among the most sought-after men in town for this kind of gathering. He did not, however, have an easy time getting the organizers to agree to an invitation for Martha. Compton-Smith, the man responsible for John Sugden's welfare in Calcutta during the induction period, was very much involved in this and he raised strong objections.

'You've just arrived – why don't you enjoy your freedom and try to get to know others? There're plenty of beautiful and interesting girls in Calcutta at the moment – Brigadier Johnson's three daughters have just arrived, then Judge Hobb's two – there're many more. You can book dances with whoever you like – and then if you fancy any of them, I will throw a dinner in your honour and invite her to our house. Don't get so easily tied to someone when the world is your oyster.'

Compton-Smith was not keen on Martha nor on Stanley. John believed the reason why Stanley, in spite of being a very eligible bachelor – handsome, a Cambridge graduate and wealthy – had not been invited was Compton-Smith's dislike of him. Really one would have thought the junior Congdon would be an obvious choice for the Black Hearts' Fancy Dress Ball.

But Stanley was not perturbed by this snub. 'You take Martha with you if you can – I don't like that kind of gathering anyway. I'd much rather stay at home and read Byron or solve some mathematical puzzles – I find them much more stimulating than trying to fit in with the pecking order of the civil servants and listening to their endless gossip.'

'I understand your misgivings, Stan,' John retorted, 'but we should not be bickering with each other while we are living in a foreign country.'

'But the Black Hearts clan is not my cup of tea.'

'The thing is that if you exclude yourself from all these gatherings,' John said, 'you will soon be too dry and lose the ordinary human touch.'

'Oh don't worry, John,' replied Stanley. 'My trips to the *Moffussal* are giving me plenty of opportunities to meet people. They may not be senior ICS officers or judges – they may be only traders – but don't forget, they're the people running Anglo-India.' Stanley paused for a moment then added remorsefully, 'Anyway, the question doesn't arise as I haven't been invited.'

'If you would care to go I can mention it to Compton-Smith.' John was still eager for his friend to attend the ball.

'Please don't try to hook an invitation for me. Take Martha – she seems keen to go with you.' Stanley Congdon rejected the idea with such determination that John Sugden did not press him further.

IV

John and Martha decided to dress up as Henry VIII and Anne Boleyn. Originally John had wanted them both to dress up as gypsies, but Martha refused. John could not understand her antipathy towards a gypsy outfit but he did not want to have a disagreement about such a minor matter. They made a trip to Youd & Co in Government Place near Dalhousie Square to arrange for the costumes. Youd & Co were prominent fancy dress makers in Calcutta and supplied oufits for most of the fancy dress balls. They were well known for making costumes for the professional stage, but these days the lion's share of their business came from this new fad.

The evening in late September was still warm. To mark the occasion for the ball, the Black Hearts decorated the huge edifice of the Grand Hotel with lights in every window and on the balcony. Just above the entrances a large illuminated hoarding was placed, on which **The Autumn Ball** was proudly emblazoned.

The Grand Hotel was quite a spectacle. The main ballroom on the ground floor had all the pomp and splendour of the Raj – polished marble floor tessellated with octagonal pieces surrounded by rectangular ones, elaborate chandeliers hanging from the very high ceiling, interspersed with noiseless, clean, white ceiling fans. An artificial fountain, suffused with light in the corner of the hall, gave a soothing cool ambience to the warm tropical evening. Then there were the wide staircases, leading to the main platform, where the band were eagerly waiting, holding their various musical instruments.

First there was a speech from Lord Ronaldshay, the Governor of Bengal and the chief guest for this special event. He spoke briefly, rather a serious speech for the occasion. But soon the effervescent nature of the event took over and the Anglo-Indian society of Calcutta started enjoying themselves to the music of waltz and foxtrot. Men and women in varied costumes of kings, queens, pirates, soldiers, beggars, danced as champagne flowed freely.

Suddenly a strange commotion started as someone with a black sense of humour appeared, bare chested and with a slightly hunched back, dressed in a loin cloth. 'Gandhi! Gandhi!' everyone shouted. 'Send him to prison! Send him back to South Africa.' One with a loud voice bellowed 'Send him to the gallows.' They pushed and shoved the new arrival. His very presence created hysteria among that fun-loving throng. The man was now so frightened by the heightened atmosphere of hatred among the guests that he hurriedly escaped from their attentions and came back as an Englishman, wearing a suit and tie, which appeased everyone.

Martha was enjoying herself, floating like a butterfly on the dance floor. John was somewhat clumsily keeping pace with her. He was obviously not an expert in ballroom dancing. In between foxtrot and waltz she pulled his hand and said, 'It's getting a bit too hot inside, let's just go across the hall.'

They made their way through the dancing crowd and excitedly moved towards the *kala jugga* – the dark corner – a secluded area surrounded by ferns and potted plants. John and Martha were not alone; a few others were already there, but no one lifted their eyes to look at the newcomers as they themselves were already far too preoccupied.

Martha sat close to John. He moved forward and kissed her. Then they kissed passionately holding each other. John put his hand on her firm bosom. She did not object – she was eagerly awaiting this very moment.

V

It was nearly midnight when they came out of the ball. Congdon's chauffeur was waiting just round the corner and brought the car to the entrance. John and Martha entered the car and the chauffeur drove off. But as he started, they caught sight of something which sent a cold shiver through them.

'What's happening there?' John rather edgily asked the chauffeur.

'A lot of trouble, sir,' the Indian replied. 'Gandhi is telling people to burn their foreign clothes.'

'He has a bloody nerve,' John muttered angrily and then ordered the chauffeur to drive the car towards the maidan. Martha, blissfully happy after the evening's enjoyment, suddenly became agitated and issued a gentle word of warning, 'Things could easily turn very nasty here. You're a newcomer – you don't know the strange ways of the natives.'

John, now filled with rage, decided to ignore Martha's warning. He had his eyes glued to the car window as the chauffeur drove towards the mob and parked the car close to the monument in newly-built Red Road.

It was an incredible sight: a huge conflagration. A makeshift raised platform had been built with stones and bricks, especially for the fire. In front stood a lean figure, easily recognizable from his loin-cloth and the bare chest. Although there were thousands in that crowd, there was no one quite like him – his rigid body, with stubborn determination exuded magnetic charisma which glowed in front of the flames.

John observed someone else standing next to Gandhi – a stockier figure whom he assumed to be C.R. Das, a local Congress chieftain. Gandhi was addressing the crowd. His voice was earnest, polite but firm – not filled with emotion and excitement nor trying to stir people by screaming and shouting – but enough there to bring frenzy.

He was speaking in Hindi and then in English, a lilting musical voice: 'We are fighting for our national existence, for the recognition of our elementary rights, freely to live and evolve our own destiny. It will be sheer hypocrisy on our part to extend a national welcome to the ambassador of the power that denies us our elementary rights.'

John realized he was referring to the impending visit of the Prince of Wales.

'Friends, brothers and sisters!' Gandhi continued. 'The British came here to buy our silk which used to be the envy of the entire world. They came and by devious means captured power by inciting us to fight against each other – creating dissatisfaction among Hindus and Moslems – brothers and sisters. And while we fought among ourselves – they demolished our own cottage industry. We don't produce the same silk any more because the Lion wilfully destroyed our silk trade.' He paused for a moment, allowing his lilting voice to echo through the dry air of the September night. Soon he resumed, 'Now the Lion is flooding our country with clothes made in Lancashire. But we are left with no choice because we do not make our own clothes any more. So the Lion is asking us to pay exorbitant prices for these foreign clothes. And with what? With blood and sweat we pay in spite of our poverty-stricken state so that they can keep their own people happy and prosperous.'

Gandhi now moved towards the rising yellow flame of the fire. His lean figure seemed mesmeric against the background of that burning pile. He raised his voice and stretching his arms commanded, 'Come friends! Take off your foreign clothes! Take off your clothes made in Lancashire and bring them to me so that we can make our sacrifice to erase the humiliation which some of our forefathers brought upon us. Let us move forward to a common goal – Freedom!'

The crowd roared, 'Freedom! Freedom!'

Gandhi allowed the noise to settle down and then continued, 'Freedom from foreign domination for which there is only one way – freeing ourselves from foreign luxury! From foreign goods! From foreign clothes! And replacing them with our own home-spun *khadi*!'

The crowd was now totally delirious in that electric atmosphere.

'Come friends!' he called again, 'Don't delay! Bring your foreign garments so that this funeral pyre can reach sky-high! Higher than the Grand Hotel! Higher than the Octerlony monument! Higher than the Governor's house! And send our message to His Royal Highness that his presence here is not welcome.'

The frenzied crowd roared as they brought more and more clothes to be sacrificed. It was an unusual sight, a moving sight, a frightening sight. Not like the sight of Nero burning Rome – but a strange surge of moral rectitude was exercised by a lean man casting a magic spell. Almost fifty thousand people bursting with an intense glow of unbelievable fervour queued there with expensive foreign garments which they wanted sacrificed to the fire to erase the experience of humiliation – the humiliation created by an alien power through enforced subjugation.

Sitting next to Martha in that chauffeur-driven car John froze at the prospect of fighting this stubborn man who could cast such a magic spell on so many and extract sacrifices. We have a major struggle ahead of us, he thought, as he asked the chauffeur to drive on, while Martha looked at him with fearful concern.

THREE

The road stretched ahead to the horizon, across the plains of India – absolutely flat except for the distant hills. The fields were chequered with ridges of raised soil, indicating the boundary of each plot. The peasants were assiduously tilling these plots with the help of their oxen, both men and beasts equally skeletal. Malnutrition must be endemic in this part, John thought anxiously, as he looked round. The signs of poverty were everywhere. The peasants were wearing next to nothing; a piece of loin-cloth, barely saving their modesty, only exaggerated their emaciated nakedness.

Strangely, amid all this poverty, some women, especially the young ones, looked beautiful. Wearing colourful skirts and blouses they exuded beauty in abundance – the beauty of the soil, uninhibited and free.

Young children ran across the road to have a closer view of him. They came running and then stood by the carriage. When it moved on, they ran behind it with their big eyes wide, full of simple enthusiasm. They chanted '*Gora!*' '*Gora!*' 'The white man!' Then the older ones, hearing the chanting, came out to look at him. They admonished the young ones for shouting '*Gora*'. '"Sahib – the master," not "*Gora*",' they told their youngsters. The young ones now chanted 'Sahib!' 'Sahib!' John smiled at them. Men left their tilling, tied their oxen to nearby trees and crowded round the carriage with the smile of friendliness. Not a trace of hostility anywhere, not in any pair of eyes – just a spontaneous welcoming invitation to their lord, their master, their Sahib.

Soon they came to the village boundary; beyond it lay rugged land with wild trees and bushes. In the next village, it was the same again – the same chanting of 'Sahib', the lord, the master. John looked at them with affection. *They are my people*, John thought. *I am their lord, their master. I must look after them, serve their interests to the best of my ability. They are relying upon me as a child does on his parents – a natural dependence.* Never before in his life had he received so much warmth from so many strangers. This was not Gandhi's India, he thought. This was British India, the India of the Raj. His heart now filled with immense untold pleasure. Gandhi was only a mole – an insignificant mole. His influence had only reached a few big cities, not the vast countryside. It would be their job, his job, to ensure that Gandhi's power did not spread all over the land. India needed Britain, India needed Englishmen, India needed him. Gandhi was only a destructive agitator, not a builder like the British. The more he thought, the more he was convinced that Gandhi would be a temporary phenomenon if only Britain would look after India with empathy and concern. Foremost in their thoughts must be the well-being of the Indians – it was their duty and responsibility – the responsibility they themselves had undertaken and they must execute it to the best of their ability. Gandhi must not be allowed to destroy the entire achievement of two hundred years of the British Raj.

The nightmare of Calcutta slowly lifted as John observed the ordinary people, the peasants in the villages, the traders in small towns. He took out the formal covenant from his pocket and looked at it intently: Agreement made on the Twelfth day of July, One thousand nine hundred and twenty one, between John Joshua Sugden of 13 Field Way, Chalfont St. Giles, Buckinghamshire of the first part and THE SECRETARY OF STATE FOR INDIA IN COUNCIL of the second part ... That if he shall during the said term of five years voluntarily relinquish the service of the Government except in consequence of ill-health certified to the satisfaction of the Government, he shall forthwith, on demand, pay to the Secretary of State for India in Council the cost of his passage to Bombay ... That'll never happen to me, he said to himself. I will never leave India. It is my own country, my own land, I am the Sahib, the master, the lord.

The carriage passed unhurriedly through the outskirts of the small town of Raigarh, John's new home. He had had an early signal of their arrival because some children had been waiting for him a mile ahead of the town. They chanted with joy: 'Sahib! Sahib!' John reciprocated by waving at them which encouraged the children even more as they vied with each other to come closer to the carriage to have a proper look at their lord. Some local pipers with bagpipes and drums, dressed in ceremonial golden robes, were waiting for him just on the outskirts. They now came in front and marched with the carriage, playing *Auld Lang Syne*.

From a distance John could see a massive arch, decorated with flowers – marigold, jasmine and many other Indian varieties. The message, picked out in red, white and blue flowers, was clearly visible: WELCOME. It was a delightful sight. He wondered what Gandhi would have felt, if he had seen it.

There was a congregation of the local Indians – a celebration to welcome him. As he got down some women brought conch shells and blew them while others ululated to signal the arrival of a favoured person, a near relative.

Suddenly John caught sight of a beautiful girl, about sixteen or seventeen, looking at him with both curiosity and enthusiasm. She was very light-skinned compared with the rest, almost like a southern European, a Spaniard or Portuguese, with an immense mane of wavy black hair hanging right down her back, billowing and undulating every time she moved. Her beautiful, wide, expressive eyes were decorated with kohl which made them look even darker. Her face beamed with health and beauty but hidden beneath her expression was a calm serenity which could take on a thousand tempests without being ruffled even slightly. She had a garland in her hand which she brought to John slowly and gracefully. He lowered his head to accept it. Everyone cheered and clapped. John removed the garland and placed it on her. She blushed. they all laughed.

'This is my girl, Kamala.' A little man with greying hair stepped forward. He looked like a senior clerk – his shirt was well tucked-in under a loin-cloth and over his shirt he was wearing a black alpaca jacket. 'I am, sir, your obedient servant, Chief Assistant – Ratan Banerji BA, Calcutta University.'

John could not resist a little chuckle at the way Banerji introduced himself. Banerji continued without pause almost like a parrot, 'She will be married soon to a local boy, Hari Mukherji. He also works in your establishment, sir, a clerk, also a BA, from Calcutta University,' Banerji now turned his head towards the crowd immediately behind him and shouted, 'Hari!' A pale-skinned, rather shy-looking young man moved forward. 'A very good boy, polite and diligent,' Banerji added. 'You will see it for yourself, sir. I sincerely hope you will be able to come to the wedding, sir.'

A pang of disappointment went through John for some strange, unknown reason. He was highly embarrassed. All this welcome has perhaps overwhelmed me far too much, he thought. The sight of Gandhi offering foreign clothes to the conflagration that night on the maidan was still vivid in his memory like a nightmare. The frenzied crowd bringing more and more of their expensive attire, running and screaming and competing with each other for the clothes to be burnt by Gandhi, so impatient had been their desire to obliterate everything foreign from their life – all that turmoil was so different from the calm tranquillity of Raigarh where they welcomed him by ululating and blowing conch shells. These two spectacles could almost be from different continents, different worlds.

For the moment, however, John was desperately looking for

some peace. But that was not yet possible because he had to hold a mini durbar of the town heads – the headmaster of the local school, the chief of police, local traders, the local doctor. They all brought the *nasrats* or gifts, acceptable under the *phulphal* rule which Queen Victoria promulgated to ensure that no British officer took bribes. But there were enough *nasrats* for John to feed a whole platoon for a month.

At last everything was over. It had been a very exciting occasion indeed, albeit exhausting. John was thrilled with the reception he had received from his Indian subjects. It's been a memorable day for me, he thought to himself.

FOUR

I

Raigarh was not a town of major importance because the railway lines did not go through this part of Bihar, but it was by no means an insignificant place. It had a thriving population of Hindus and Moslems, who earned their living mainly through trading agricultural produce from the adjacent hinterland. There were also some cottage industries, producing elaborately-designed copper pots and pans, mandatory for the religious rites which for the Indians had a strange fascination. This meant there was a ready-made demand for those products. Under normal circumstances one would have expected a saturated market for them since each family needed only one set for worshipping. This, however, did not quite happen because the producers soon realized the market's weakness and started churning out these pots in different shapes and sizes with a variety of designs. Each household was now tempted to acquire more than it needed and most of them amassed a considerable range, much to the satisfaction of the producers.

In the Indian context therefore, Raigarh was important. Moreover, the River Ganges touched the very end of the town. And for the Indians, wherever the sacred river carried her holy trail, the place became a destination for pilgrimage. The Ganges with her tributaries, occupying the heartland of India, also provided the necessary means of transport for the local produce. In spite of being slow, it was more convenient to carry these goods by river than to trudge through the dusty tracks of a rough terrain.

In the eyes of the Raj, however, Raigarh was insignificant because militarily and strategically it had very little to offer; and the surrounding area was on the whole peaceful unlike the Punjab and Bengal.

John was the only European in this part of the country; there was no one else within a fifty-mile radius apart from a missionary doctor of European origin: a Belgian or something. However, because he had acquired certain native habits and intermingled with the locals, the British administration, for all practical purposes, did not consider him a European. That did not discourage the locals from queuing in front of his house, for his wonder drugs had the reputation of curing all maladies.

The nature of the town, in a way, dictated John's duties and responsibilities. He was both the collector and magistrate. Under normal circumstances these would have been two separate posts, but the Raj did not think an unimportant place like Raigarh warranted such extravagance.

As a collector, representing His Majesty the King-Emperor George V and his Viceroy, John was responsible for collecting all the taxes and ensuring that no one escaped from paying the appropriate amount. This, on the whole, was comparatively easy, although some crooked merchants from time to time tried to play a trick or two which called for iron-fisted control so that no one else followed suit.

The task of a magistrate, however, was more cumbersome and messy. The Indians were always engaged in internecine battles among themselves – Hindus against Moslems, one landowner against another and then petty jealousies very often grew into tribal warfare. Although there had been occasional instances of dacoity on the whole the brigands left this territory in peace since, not all that long ago, a major leader of the dacoits had been captured by one of John's predecessors whose courage and valour were still legendary in this part of the world.

II

John's administrative staff were not insignificant in number. Compton-Smith was right though: they were very efficient. Ratan Banerji, his deputy, was an able administrator. He had all the local know-how. He knew exactly what most people had been up to; for example, he could tell without any difficulty whether a person was lying or not. This came as a great asset to John. Fresh from Britain, unworldly, without experience outside High Wycombe where he had spent all his childhood until his father remarried, and then, of course, Balliol, a through-and-through esoteric place, he was inclined to take people at their face value and believe whatever he was told. But Banerji soon put him straight and instilled doubts about almost everything.

Although John was confused most of the time by Banerji's analysis, the chance of making a gross mistake was largely eliminated, much to his great relief, and he began to consider Banerji an indispensable ally in this distant post. Banerji also took upon himself the duty of protecting the Sahib. If anything, this enhanced Banerji's position in the town and he was delighted to become an almost *de facto* DO.

III

One Wednesday morning Banerji appeared with a piece of highly decorated yellow notepaper with a patterned border and a picture of a woman with a conch shell at the top. Inside, there was a closely printed text in the vernacular. John was first of all perplexed; not knowing the ins and outs of the place as yet, he wondered how he was supposed to react to this note.

'My daughter's wedding, sir.' Banerji beamed with a smile.

'That's good news – when?' John asked enthusiastically.

'On Sunday, sir, this coming Sunday.'

'With Hari?'

'Yes sir. He is a very good boy, very diligent, also a BA from Calcutta University. With your blessing, he should go high up. He is intelligent, sir. Very intelligent!'

John smiled. He had already learnt that on these matters it was often safer not to say much, because if he supported Banerji's statement, he would be expected to give Hari a promotion almost forthwith and with it a pay rise. John was far from convinced that Hari merited such favour.

'Isn't she a bit young to be married?' John asked somewhat protectively.

'Not in India, sir. She is seventeen. My mother was married at twelve.'

'But that was a long time ago.'

'I want to see her settled, sir,' Banerji replied. 'I am already fifty. Only a few years left before I retire. And Hari is a good boy, sir. He will look after her.'

John smiled approvingly, but Banerji thought the Sahib was far from convinced about Hari's suitability as a bridegroom and tried to defend his future son-in-law. 'He looks a bit docile, but he is a nice fellow, sir. He will take good care of Kamala. Though she is my own daughter I must admit she is headstrong – very stubborn – needs careful handling.'

'I'm sure, they'll be happy,' John replied.

'Yes, sir. And Hari's family is not as high up as us. That is good for her. They will treat her with respect.'

'Wouldn't they otherwise?' John was surprised.

'No, sir. We Hindus are very strange. Torturing a woman after marriage is not unusual. And not just verbally, physically as well.'

'Gracious me! That's medieval!'

'Yes, sir. In some cases, the newly-wed bride even commits suicide to escape humiliation. But Hari's family is *bhadralok* – gentle and honourable – they will treasure my daughter.' Banerji wore a proud face of self-satisfaction.

'So what am I expected to do?' John was not sure about his role in this wedding. 'What does a district officer do on such an occasion – you'd better advise me?'

'Well, sir,' replied Banerji, 'we would very much like you to come to our place on the wedding day.'

'But is it the done thing?' asked John. 'Am I allowed to go to a Hindu wedding? Wouldn't people mind me, a non-Hindu, participating in your celebrations?'

The Indian was full of charm. He said, 'Leave that with your Ratan, sir. Absolutely no problem. We shall be very pleased to have you.'

John was not entirely convinced by his subordinate's reply. He asked, 'But what's the normal custom?'

Banerji kept quiet which was unusual for him. Having found the Sahib inexperienced, the Indian had inundated John with both wanted and unwanted advice in the last few months. From time to time John really had to put the stopper on him because, like most of his countrymen, he could easily get carried away once he started on something. After each of these outbursts of enthusiasm, which came all too frequently for comfort, if John did not support him. Banerji would sulk interminably until the next idea came upon him. John was wary, for he knew that he must handle Banerji judiciously. But this morning Banerji was not very forthcoming with his advice. Even solicitation did not work. John instinctively knew that going to an Indian wedding was not the done thing – an Englishman, a DO, was not supposed to go to such celebrations.

'Come on then, Banerji. Tell me what am I supposed to do,' John asked in a friendly voice.

After a lot of cajoling Banerji finally came out with the normal practice for a DO: after the wedding the bride and groom were supposed to come to the Sahib's bungalow for blessing and, for someone of Banerji's stature in the Raj, the Sahib should offer them tea.

'Fine, that will be done,' replied John with a sense of relief. 'I offer my invitation. In the meantime, I'll arrange to get a present for them. Perhaps something for the household would be useful. Where are the new couple going to live?'

Banerji seemed a bit embarrassed by that question. 'You know, sir, we Indians, we are very much family-oriented people. We are not like the Europeans that the bride and groom would live separately from the family.'

'We used to have the same custom, Banerji,' replied John. 'We Europeans aren't much different from you. Even now, those who are not very well off live with their family.' He then paused and said, 'Anyway you have plenty of room in your house.'

'No, sir! No! That's not the custom here,' Banerji said. 'Kamala will have to live with her in-laws.'

'I presume Kamala gets on well with her future mother-in-law,' John asked somewhat naîvely.

Banerji looked perplexed as if he had heard something completely alien. 'Sir, in India women don't have any choice in these matters,' he said. 'They always do what the *dharma* dictates. And the *dharma* for a woman is to live with her husband and his parents.'

'Don't get me wrong,' John hurriedly interrupted in case Banerji had misunderstood him. 'I respect your *dharma*. I was just curious, that's why I asked.'

The following day, Banerji came with another note. 'It is from my daughter, sir. She has written you a note.'

John was surprised. He did not expect a girl from a remote town like Raigarh to be able to write in English. He opened the note and read on –

'Sahib,
I would very much like you to come to my wedding.
Kamala'

Seeing the Sahib's utter surprise Banerji boasted, 'Sir, she went to the local school – would have passed her matriculation with distinction had I not prevented her from taking it.'

John now understood why those sparkling eyes looked so extraordinarily bright. 'But why did you stop her?' he asked, surprised.

'Too much education is not good for a woman – makes her rebellious. The *dharma* wants a woman to be docile for a happy marriage.'

John did not want to get into any futile argument with Banerji; but he did want to give further thought to the question of whether he really should go to the wedding. 'I'll let you know tomorrow, if that's all right with you.'

'Of course, sir.' Banerji left the room silently.

It would indeed be a great experience to witness a Hindu wedding, John thought. Still he found it difficult to make up his mind. He wondered whether to seek advice from someone outside. The only people who could really help him were Stanley and Martha, both in Calcutta, or Charles Garvey, his superior officer in Sripore, which meant a day's journey. He had a vague suspicion that both the Congdons and Garvey would dissuade him from attending the wedding and he very much wanted to go.

IV

When John arrived at Banerji's house in the mid-afternoon on Sunday, the place was teeming with people. Some children had seen him a long way ahead and had already alerted the household, screaming 'the Sahib is coming'. Banerji wearing a *dhoti* and silk *kurta* looked slightly perturbed as if the responsibility for the whole event had somewhat overwhelmed him. Hari was not there. Apparently according to the Indian custom, the groom with his relatives and guests would come in the evening in a procession.

John sensed that the people were a little nervous about his presence, but soon with the excitement of the occasion everyone forgot that a European was among them and began to feel more at ease with him. Even Mrs Banerji lifted her purdah and started treating him as if he were one of her relatives, although she could not actually converse with him, for she spoke no English. But she made up for her inadequacy with gestures, postures and the help of others who could speak a word or two of the *bilayati* language.

Banerji's mother, an elderly woman in her eighties, came out to see the Sahib. She had no inhibitions and behaved as if she were his own mother. She suggested the Sahib wore Indian clothes, for then he would find moving among the crowd easier. Now Banerji came to the rescue. He did not want his promotion prospects jeopardized by his mother's over-enthusiasm – trying to make an Indian out of a revered DO. But John took up the suggestion in the right spirit and readily agreed to change his European clothes for the Indian ones.

A silk *kurta* and *dhoti* presently came for the DO. One of the boys helped him to put it on and they all cheered when John came out wearing his Indian clothes. Someone gave him a garland, which he put round his neck smilingly. 'He looks like the groom!' the old woman shouted, making Kamala blush and run away, which embarrassed John. Mrs Banerji tried to lighten the atmosphere by offering him a cup of tea.

The people were all jostling, shouting, screaming and laughing. It was quite an unforgettable scene. Someone brought a chair out for John. He sat there, observing his surroundings. From time to time one or other of the guests came trying to make conversation with him in their inadequate English. Banerji, in between organizing various necessary rituals, came to tend to the revered district officer to ensure that everything was all right and that the Sahib was still enjoying himself.

On the adjoining land, Banerji had put up a *samiana* – a temporary structure, covered with tarpaulins, where the cooking for the couple of hundred guests expected that evening was going on in make-shift earthen ovens. The aroma of exotic food pervaded the entire house. Occasionally it was mingled with the smell of smoke from damp wood, which, if anything, added to the general ambience.

It wasn't long before a horde of servants came with the presents from the groom's family: those offered to the bride – elaborate jewellery, exotic and expensive silk sarees, new furniture for the couple, tea-sets, dinner-sets, bric-à-brac. The presents were all put on display in one corner.

Now it was time to throw saffron on the bride to prepare her for the wedding. Everyone threw saffron at Kamala. Soon she looked completely yellow – covered with saffron. Seeing the sight, John could not help laughing and that encouraged others even more. Someone asked him to throw saffron at her, and he was tempted but Kamala looked at him disapprovingly, so he promptly declined. The excitement of the wedding ceremony was now in full flood.

In the evening the bridegroom arrived with his guests, nearly a hundred people in a procession with the pipers heading the group, playing, 'For he's a jolly good fellow·....' It was quite a sight, especially as everyone carried a torch, flashing it to attract attention of the bystanders who queued on each side of the road to watch the procession go past.

The evening wore on. The priest who would conduct the wedding came in a strange robe – a yellow cloth with red writing in Hindi: 'Hare Krishna Hare Rama'. Kamala was dressed like a princess with a beautiful red sari, elaborately ornamented. Her face, powdered and glazed, was decorated with sandalwood paste and on her head she wore an artistically-carved wooden crown, painted white and liberally adorned with sequins.

Hari was wearing a fine silk *kurta* and *dhoti*. His face was also decorated with sandalwood paste, though not so elaborately. On his head he wore a crown, but different in design from Kamala's – more like a Roman one – white and beautifully carved.

The bride and groom now sat next to each other holding hands in front of the ceremonial fire. A small crowd gathered round them, mainly parents and near relatives. John was given the special privileged status of a near relative and he stood with them watching the ritual. The couple, led by the priest, started chanting mantras which would for ever secure their life together.

It was quite some time before this ritual was over. Next the groom stood alone on the floor and four young men carried the

bride on a beautifully decorated wooden plank, moved her round
the groom seven times and then brought her in front of him.
Everyone was bubbling. Someone suddenly shouted something.
They all laughed. The man nearby translated it: which among these
two would hold the power – the bride or the groom? The relatives
of the bride shouted in full-throated voice – the bride! The groom's
relatives opposed it by shouting down the bride's friends – all
good-humouredly. The men, carrying the plank on which Kamala
sat, tried to lift her up well above the groom's head to show her
prowess. They all giggled, nearly falling over each other.

Suddenly the seriousness came back as one of the major rituals
of the wedding was about to take place. Someone spread a canopy
over the couple's heads. This was meant to be the time when the
bride and groom exchanged their first glance and Madan was
supposed to be waiting in the wings to shoot his blessed arrow of
flowers and chain the couple for ever in love.

John stood in a corner, excitedly observing the ritual. All the
guests and relatives were looking at Kamala expectantly to ensure
that Cupid's arrow struck at the right spot. But she took her time,
keeping them waiting, though Hari had already fixed a loving stare
on her. Slowly and shyly she now lifted her eyes. No! No! That
can't be true! Surely not! For a moment John froze as if he were
engulfed with some unearthly sensation of both heightened
pleasure and extreme anxiety. It seemed to him that those intense
eyes were looking at him and not Hari. Please, Kamala, no!
You're making a grave mistake! His heart pounded as he moved
aside. Soon he realized it must have been his fertile imagination as
everyone cheered, observing the blessed looks being exchanged
between the bride and groom. He felt like a fool and at the same
time greatly relieved by the cheering of the crowd.

The evening settled down now and became more relaxed. The
tension of the early part of the ceremony had evaporated after the
celebrated exchange of gazes. The bride and groom were asked to
play various games with *cauris*. These were meant to be a test of
the bride's shrewdness in combating the supposed superior
intellect of the groom, so that she could take on the dominant
husband and survive without allowing him to walk over her.

John was whisked away by Mrs Banerji, who held him by his
arm as if he were a near relative. He was taken inside where a
dining-table was set especially for him. He was about to protest at
this special treatment but promptly he realized that this was

perhaps the best arrangement. Delicious Indian dishes began to arrive in numerous varieties. With the help of an interpreter Mrs Banerji repeatedly asked, while fanning him with a small punkah, whether he wanted European dishes, because they could easily be made available. John was enjoying this meal so much that that was the last thing he had in mind and he expressed that to Mrs Banerji. She seemed delighted that the Sahib liked Indian food. And it made John feel closer to her.

As the night fell, the bride, groom and their friends all sat down and started singing local songs to the accompaniment of an old harmonium. This was to go on all night. The real marriage was not to be consummated until the bride and groom arrived at the groom's house on the third day to spend the night in the nuptial bed, decorated with flowers to remind them for ever of the ecstasy of their first love-making.

John now left the crowd to their merriment. How different an Indian wedding is from a European one he thought as the carriage was driven towards his bungalow. Then his mind wondered whether all these festivities and rituals made a marriage happy. He prayed to God for Kamala's happiness, for she had looked so radiant tonight.

FIVE

I

Sripore was a pleasant, well-laid-out place, typical of the majority of these towns in British India. The railways provided the lines of demarcation between on the one side, the establishments of the Raj, so to speak the rulers, and on the other, those who were ruled – in the common Anglo-Indian expression the 'natives'.

The houses in which the Indians lived were often mud huts. A sprinkling of brick-built houses, indicating affluence, were inhabited mainly by the landowners or wealthy traders. The

Indians had their own segregation within the town with the Brahmins occupying the best land near the temple and water supply, and the untouchables, who were never allowed inside the temple or to fetch water from the pond, living on the outskirts.

The Eurasians occupied a very strange position in Anglo-Indian society. They were neither accepted nor totally rejected. They provided vital services for the Raj, especially in running the railways. In a town they were normally found next to the railway lines, but in the European sector. In that respect Sripore was no exception. The Eurasian settlement was separated from the Europeans by a maidan which was partially enclosed by office buildings, then a wide mall led from there in to the civil lines or the main European quarters. The roads in this part were properly built with grass verges and a company *bagh* – a beautifully-laid-out park with a band-stand inside. Beyond that stood the church, the station club and finally the elegant bungalows with manicured gardens for the senior officers. Further along the mall were the police lines and then the military cantonment with its own church, market and parade grounds.

Charles Garvey, John Sugden's immediate boss, was stationed in Sripore. He was tall, stout and red-faced – the colour a pale Englishman often acquired after living in a sunny climate for years. A butterfly moustache added to his domineering appearance. Charles Garvey had also been to Oxford, though many years ago. He had come to India soon after his graduation and stayed on. An old hand in administration, he knew all the ins and outs of the way the Raj ticked – knew the right people and belonged to the right clubs. His next promotion was likely to be to Patna, the provincial capital, perhaps followed by a brief period in Calcutta and then Delhi – nearest to the Viceroy. By then he would have to consider his retirement home in England, perhaps in Surrey or Sussex, spending the rest of his days in the tranquillity of England's green and pleasant land, where the sun is mellow and the landscapes are picturesque like a painting by Constable or Turner – very different from the dusty and sweaty plains of India. Charles Garvey was already looking forward to those days. Every time he had had a furlough and had been to England he had found it harder to slot back into the groove on return.

Garvey had never liked India or Indians much. For him it was a job to do, but he did it with efficiency, honesty and integrity, like a professional, a true Englishman. He knew the Raj demanded high standards of behaviour from its officers to set an example to the Indians and he adhered to these standards both for himself and his officers. He had no doubt in his mind that this was the only way the Europeans could claim moral superiority over the Indians – by proving to them that the Europeans were efficient, capable, technologically superior and at the same time honest and upright. The Garveys of Anglo-India were the necessary pillars of the British Raj – and he himself was very much aware of that fact. He would never allow the Raj to crumble either through his own folly or that of his subordinates. But in spite of it all, he was not a ruthless administrator, more a man of compassion. He firmly believed in the dictum of the Empire that a civil servant was there to serve India and he took it as his God-given duty to do so.

Just before coming to Raigarh John Sugden had visited Sripore. On many occasions since then he had been a welcome guest in the Garvey household, for Mrs Garvey took kindly to this new recruit of her husband's, especially when she came to know of John Sugden's tragic experience in finding his mother trapped in a blazing house fire the morning after he had been out celebrating the victory over Germany in the Great War.

II

John gradually settled down in Raigarh as the months wore on. At first he liked everything there: the relentless sun which rose every morning like clockwork and for the next twelve hours scorched the earth mercilessly, then the tranquil river, the Ganges, which was supposed to wash away sins of all Indians. During the monsoon, however, the river became more violent – her billowy waves surged thunderously as incessant rains conjured up tricks with the wind. But the farm workers were not aggrieved by this. They snapped up their eagerly-awaited water ration to grow the much-needed crops that would keep them alive for the rest of the year. In autumn the flow waned as if like a human being the river became mature – the violent force of sexual hunger no longer clamoured at the door with the same intensity and allowed her the freedom of being distant – spreading calmness even to those who came along the river-bank for an afternoon stroll.

On many an afternoon John enjoyed that stroll, looking into the distance at the hills of the Himalayas, some small – very small – almost like hillocks, others more significant, rising up to several thousand feet, though the really big mountains of this range were further up north in Nepal. On a few occasions he ventured on to a couple of hills, scaling the heights, trotting like a mountain goat from one crag to another and finally arriving at the summit where invariably the Hindus had built a temple to invite their god to descend from his heavenly abode.

John was mesmerized by everything around him but nothing fascinated him more than the people, dark skinned, lean but beautiful, who often looked at him from a distance with awe and saluted when he came closer. The endless, scantily-dressed children courageously came a little nearer than their parents and watched the Sahib with a fixed stare. Once they caught John's eyes their faces lit up, smiling with their dazzlingly white teeth and they nodded their heads with welcome. But the most delightful sight was watching the young girls who, walking freely across the field, would smile shyly once their stolen glances were discovered by some chance observation.

For a few months John was totally immersed in his new surroundings and enjoyed every moment. But slowly a kind of ennui set in as he became restless. The river did not bring the same excitement as it had on his early encounter; the dazzling, incessant sun suddenly became monotonous as John craved for a little mellowness or cloud or a drizzle which one so often faces in England. Even the Ganges and the Himalayas with their endless mysteries failed to offer him that feeling of tranquillity for reflection in his soul.

To make matters worse, he gradually became tired of seeing dark Indian faces every day, everywhere. The novelty of India was beginning to wear off and he very often desperately wanted to see a white European face, one of his own kind, who might offer him security and nearness. He had never experienced this feeling before, nor even thought that he would actually face this kind of emotion. Although he made a few journeys to Sripore, to the Station Club, played billiards at midday and polo in the afternoon and had his gin and tonic when the dusk set in and dinner with the Garveys in the late evening, as soon as he came back to Raigarh, all these seemed so distant and remote that once again his gloom descended. He was surprised to find that he was longing for his Oxford days, chatting at George's Restaurant with the aesthetes – nothing substantial, nothing significant, but intellectually invigorating. He now had no doubt that he was missing England.

Homesickness? Yes! But his furlough was not due for another four years. So there was no possibility of his leaving India for England even on a short holiday.

In desperation he wrote a brief note to Stanley, inviting him to come and spend a few days with him in Raigarh. It was a heartfelt plea and Stanley's sensitive antennae spotted that immediately. His response was quick. He promised to come for a few days in a week's time and also, much to John's excitement, mentioned that he would bring Martha with him. The news thrilled John, and he looked forward eagerly to the time when Stanley and Martha would come to Raigarh.

III

'Hello old boy!' Stanley's cheery voice greeted him from the railway carriage. John's eyes lit up at seeing his friends getting down from the train. John had been waiting for them for over an hour at Sripore station with his carriage. The train had arrived late. He went eagerly forward to greet his friends. Martha, rather shy, stood behind Stanley. John moved forward to greet her with an affectionate embrace and kisses on her cheeks.

'What's the news of Calcutta?' John asked eagerly.

'Lots and lots of activities are going on now.' Martha's voice was full of youthful excitement. 'The cold-weather balls are in full swing; new Irish colts running flat races, a theatre group from Stratford-upon-Avon's soon to open at the New Empire; and then there are all the picnics.'

'So I'm missing everything!'

'You must come to Calcutta soon, John,' Martha boomed.

'You're only making it worse for him. Now he will miss Calcutta all the more.' Stanley tried to admonish his sister for her over-excitement.

'No! No! I would like to hear what's happening in Calcutta,' John said. 'Life is so dull here – I'm finding myself almost choked for lack of company. If I remain like this for long, I'll go completely barmy.'

'You need a holiday, old boy. Perhaps Martha's right – a few days away from it all.'

'I don't see any way of taking time off now. I'm too busy.' Heaving a sigh of sadness John added, 'I'm afraid I have to bear it until summer. The life of a DO, in spite of all its glamour, is one of sheer endurance – nothing else.'

'That's life, my friend, for every European in this country – no matter your profession. More than half my time's spent in the Moffussal, rushing through dusty bazaars in small towns – facing flies, mosquitoes – you name it.' Stanley tried to console his friend and at the same time impress upon him that his job was not at all cushy in case John had the wrong idea about the difficulty of running a business in India.

'That's the problem,' John whole-heartedly supported his friend. 'The Indians see the Europeans having a good time with all their money, servants and power: they don't see the effort that goes on behind – the gritty determination to make one's living in a totally alien environment. But if you say that to Gandhi, he'll ask you to get out.'

'Why should we?' Stanley raised his voice in sharp protest. 'For generations we've put down our roots here. We've developed trade and business from scratch while the Indians lazed away doing absolutely nothing. My great grandfather, my grandfather, my father, we all put in our life's work and earned every bit of whatever comfort we have now – and that's not much in recent years with Gandhi's agitation.'

'I'm afraid Gandhi won't accept that argument,' replied John.

'But he has no right to tell us to leave India,' Stanley said. 'In fact we have more right to this country than the Indians because we have made India what it is today.'

'I know you're right,' replied John, 'but Gandhi would simply say, it doesn't matter how long you live in this country, it's not yours. It'll never be yours.'

'Yes! And that's exactly what my argument is all about.' Stanley was now fuming with passion. He continued, 'When we came to India, the country was highly fragmented – run inefficiently by the local chieftains. Major suffering was the order of the day for most people – tyranny, famine, disease, dacoity – everyone lived in absolute terror. If it was not the zamindar taking the last pice out of a native, it would be the thugs, who would wait in the dark corner to strangle him, robbing him of whatever earthly treasure he had on him at the time. And they were indiscriminate in their killing – not just the rich – they killed everyone, even the poorest of the poor, such was their greed.'

'It must have been awful,' said John. 'Every Indian should be grateful to Sleeman for the sheer relief of travelling without fear.'

'See! This was India!' Stanley was still passionate. 'And now Gandhi claims we're exploiting the Indians. It's the Indians who're exploiting the Indians – not us.'

'But who'll convince Gandhi?' asked John.

'Gandhi's an opportunist. Can't you see? Now he's shouting foul play over the *Moplahs*.'

'But the *Moplahs* are a different case, Stanley,' the young officer tried to set the facts straight.

'Why? Because of eighteen hundred killed? Of course it was necessary. No government could stand still and allow the rebels to run the country.'

'I agree with your sentiment, Stan,' replied John, 'but the current mismanagement by the railways can't be condoned.'

Stanley was suddenly taken aback. He had not known about that. 'What railway mismanagement?' he asked enquiringly.

'The police had about a hundred captured rebels in Calicut and they sent them to Madras in a closed iron wagon. Sixty six of them were found dead from asphyxia when the train arrived at Podamur.'

'Good heavens! How could that happen?' asked Stanley.

'A pure cock-up on someone's part. No doubt heads will roll soon. For the time being it has given Gandhi more ammunition against us.' John paused as the carriage passed the gate of his bungalow. Then in an apologetic voice he added, 'Let's not discuss politics any more; we're boring Martha. I'm sure there're other things to talk about than Gandhi.'

'No! No! Please!' Martha protested. 'I don't often join in this kind of conversation because I know so little about politics. But I'm interested. I always like to know what Gandhi's going to do next.'

'We know *that*,' Stanley spoke bitterly. 'Burning more clothes; creating more trouble. People, following his example, are burning British-made clothes everywhere. Some hooligans even set fire to shops selling Lancashire fabric.'

'That's absolutely awful.' John spoke with determination. 'Gandhi must be controlled; if necessary, punished. We can't allow India to disintegrate – all our work over the last hundred and fifty years to be completely ruined – because of just one man and his antics.'

They both agreed whole-heartedly with John's statement – Gandhi must be stopped – but the question was how?

IV

The next day John woke up feeling light and agile. He had not felt so happy for a long time. The previous night they had chatted long and late over Scotch and soda, discussing every possible topic under the sun: Indian politics, Britain, Lloyd George, Baldwin, the Great War – and of course the nostalgic Oxford and Cambridge days, which seemed a distant dream for both John and Stanley.

The morning was bright and sunny. John decided to take a day off and planned for all of them to go to some picturesque spot in the hills. Martha started organizing the things to be prepared for the picnic with Ibrahim, the *khansama*, and Jadu, the *khitmatgar*. As they were having a leisurely breakfast on the veranda the postman appeared on his bicycle over the brickdust path by the lawn – his routine trip, but this morning he was holding a telegram. John waited eagerly. Who on earth would be sending him a telegram and for what reason? His impatience disappeared when he saw that the telegram from Calcutta was for his friend. Stanley took the telegram and hurriedly opened it.

'What is it?' Martha asked anxiously.

'I'm afraid we have to go,' Stanley replied.

'What do you mean?' John was dismayed by this totally unexpected news. 'Is your father ill?'

'No, nothing personal. I have a business problem.'

Martha's face fell immediately. She had been so looking forward to a few days with John. Since their first meeting they had hardly had any time together except for those few summer months when John had arrived in India. Stanley could see Martha's disappointment, not to mention John's.

'Do you really have to go, Stan?' Martha asked rather sadly.

'I see no option. Not only is there a problem in Calcutta, but I then have to go to Allahabad and Lucknow. A lot of money and goodwill's involved,' Stanley replied rather guiltily, knowing what was going through his sister's mind.

'Isn't it possible for you to spend another day and then, say, go to Allahabad direct?' John asked tentatively, wondering how he could prolong their stay in Raigarh.

'No! I'm afraid I have to go to Calcutta first before I can go to Allahabad. One of those things: it simply can't be avoided.'

'So when do you propose to go?' John asked.

'By this evening's train, if that's possible,' replied Stanley. 'I think this time of year the Kalka Mail has an additional stop at Sripore. If we could get that, we should be in Calcutta first thing tomorrow morning.'

There was a silence now: the morning's pleasure spoilt by the unexpected change of plans made everyone withdraw into their own world. John finally spoke in a tentative voice, 'Even if you have to go, Stan, can't Martha stay for a few more days?'

Martha looked at Stanley expectantly. He 'um'd' and 'ah'd' for a while before making up his mind. Finally he smiled and spoke in a relaxed voice, 'All right, but only for a couple of days; I think I can tackle father for that period. But please! No more than two days!' Then he looked at Martha and said, 'You must be back in Calcutta before the end of the week.'

'I promise you that, Stan,' John spoke with obvious pleasure in his voice.

Martha could not hide her excitement. She jumped up and embraced her brother, which made Stanley slightly self-conscious.

'I'd better not go out this morning,' Stanley said to his friend, 'but don't let me spoil your fun. If you two want to go out, you can. I have to write a couple of letters and also repack my case.'

'No, Stan!' replied John. 'It's not often that I see you. I'm sure Martha won't mind if we don't go for a picnic today.'

'I don't mind in the slightest.' Martha was so delighted that she could stay a couple more days in Raigarh, everything else seemed totally irrelevant.

Stanley departed that evening for Calcutta. John went with him up to Sripore. At first Stanley had tried to dissuade him, saying he would be perfectly all right with the *saice*, but John would not listen, for he did not want to lose this opportunity of talking to his friend even if it were only for a few more hours. Martha was far too tired to make another trip to Sripore over the rough terrain, so she stayed behind, which seemed the best arrangement for everyone.

V

The following morning when Martha woke up John was already sitting on the veranda, smoking a cigarette.

'Good morning!' Martha came and sat opposite, taking a cigarette from the packet, which he helped her to light. 'Did the train come on time, or did you have to wait?' Martha had been asleep when John had come back the previous night.

'Perfect timing!' replied John. 'We arrived there at nine o'clock, just had enough time for a quick drink at the Station Club. The train came at ten. It all went like clockwork.'

'So what time did you come back last night?' Martha asked.

'About two in the morning.'

'You must be awfully tired, John. Perhaps you would like a little siesta this afternoon?'

'Good Lord, no!' replied John. 'I don't like sleeping in the day. Very old-fashioned and very British in that respect. I was hoping we would go for that picnic we missed yesterday.'

Martha stood up in excitement. Although she was no younger than John, in many respects she was still very girlish and this appealed to John a great deal.

'That'll be just wonderful!' Martha spoke eagerly. 'Let me get the things ready then we could go bright and early.'

'Listen! As it's only the two of us, let's not bother with the servants – we could go on our own. I don't think we have much to carry between us.' Although the Indian servants were surprisingly unobtrusive, John, comparatively fresh from England, was still not quite accustomed to always having them around.

It was nearly ten o'clock when they rode towards the hills. It was a beautiful day and they rode slowly, enjoying the sun. A winding path between small hillocks went right up to the top of the highest peak in that region – Nag's Head. Local legend had a story attached to this hill. Basuki, king of serpents, was apparently holding the earth on his head. Once, when he was very tired and trying to reposition the earth to the other side of his head, the violent jolt caused an earthquake and hence a new hill arose in the Himalayas, Nag's Head. Every year on 15 April the locals came with fruits and flowers to worship Basuki and pray that he would not change the position of the earth and create another earthquake. John told Martha the story which he had come to know from his servants.

'Do you believe it?' Martha asked jokingly.

John pulled a face and in a gruff voice replied, 'Of course, yes.'

Seeing his face Martha giggled so much that she nearly fell from her horse.

'Now! Now! Don't get over excited,' John teased her. She

blushed for no apparent reason and he did not fail to notice. Although he made no further comment, for he did not want to embarrass her, it gave him pleasure all the same.

They soon stopped by a waterfall which created a lake up on the hill. The surrounding area was tranquil and beautiful. There was a little greenery – a few trees and mountains shrubs grown with the assistance of the water from the fall. Amid the parched grey mountains the small patch of grass and greenery looked like a little oasis. They spread a mat and sat down. Martha opened the basket and brought out sandwiches and beer.

They stayed there after lunch, leaning on each other, holding, kissing, cuddling – two young people very much in love. On that remote lonely mountain of the Himalayas, John suddenly felt he had a friend, a companion, on whom he could rely to get through these years of loneliness. He felt happy and elated.

In the late afternoon they got up and trekked back, for they did not want to stay on beyond dusk. On the plains of India darkness falls very rapidly after sunset – one moment it's sunny and the next pitch black. The mountain roads could be hazardous at night with all the pot-holes, sharp ridges and steep inclines and a fall would mean certain death.

They were back in the bungalow before the darkness became opaque. Ibrahim's cooking was already giving off a delicious aroma. They sat on the veranda in the dark, sipping gins and tonic. John was delighted that Martha had stayed on. The last few months he had felt very lonely in Raigarh. The thought of facing that life again in a few days' time made him despondent. He knew that there was only one thing that would make his stay in Raigarh tolerable – but would Martha agree to it? He gathered enough courage to ask her that question – perhaps a little awkwardly.

'Suppose I asked you to marry me, Martha. What would you say?'

'Is that a question, a conjecture or your way of proposing?'

John laughed aloud to release his nervous tension and then smilingly added, 'You're getting as bad as those Oxford and Cambridge ladies. I think it's Stanley's bad influence on you.'

'I don't need Stanley's influence,' replied Martha with a smile. 'I can stand up for myself without any assistance, thank you.'

'I'm sure you can. That's why I find you so fascinating.' John spoke with a glint in his eyes.

'That'll wear off soon if you know me better,' Martha said. 'I'm not as docile as I look.'

'You don't look docile at all,' John responded good-humouredly. 'Moreover, I don't like docile women. I like free spirits. My mother was very much that way inclined.'

'Isn't she alive?' Martha quizzed, perhaps she was a little surprised.

'No, she died in an accident.' John spoke with a distinct trace of sadness in his voice and then added, 'My father's remarried.'

Martha felt uneasy. She wanted to know in what kind of accident his mother had been involved but thought it impolite to ask. Fortunately Jadu came to the veranda in a moment or two and broke the awkward silence which had developed between them. The *khit* asked the Sahib whether he should set the dinner on the veranda.

'No! Let's go to the dining room,' Martha suggested. She knew that she wanted a more intimate talk with John and the veranda was not the right place for it.

At the dinner table, however, John and Martha were unusually silent – both were engrossed in their own thoughts. After dinner they moved into the lounge and sat close to each other. Jadu entered and served the Sahib with a brandy and the Memsahib a port. John gently started caressing Martha's hair. She absorbed this affection, leaning on his arm. After a while rather nervously he repeated what had been foremost in his mind: 'You haven't yet answered my question.'

'What question?'

'Will you marry me?'

Martha remained quiet.

'You don't have to give an answer right now. Think it over.'

'There's something you ought to know, John,' Martha murmured distantly.

'What?' asked John.

'Can I speak to you in confidence?'

'Of course, darling! No one will hear from me, I promise.'

Martha hesitated for a while and then said, 'Not many people know, but we're Eurasians – in a way, therefore, second-class citizens. Because we have money and education, we're not classed as such. On the other hand, if you marry me, you may find your career blocked.'

John was not as much shocked by this news as he would have been had he not heard it before. Compton-Smith seeing his intimacy with Martha, had warned him about the consequence of any Englishman falling in love with a Eurasian.

'I knew that already, Martha. I was warned early on.' John spoke in a clear and honest voice, and then added, 'If I were asked to sacrifice my civil service career for you, I would do it unhesitatingly.'

Martha was quiet. Her heart was throbbing fast. She knew what she wanted and so did John. He pulled her very close and kissed her passionately. Martha responded and they stayed like that for a very long time.

The night was dark. It was already quite late. Even the noise of the crickets had stopped. John and Martha were in close embrace, just feeling each other. Slowly and gently he started unbuttoning her blouse. She protested a little. 'Only this bit and no more,' he tried to reassure her. She held his hand to stop him but soon felt completely dazed. He realized that her grip on his hand was no longer very firm.

A little desire was clearly expressed in that soft touch of hers. He fell to kissing her more vigorously and at the same time began to unbutton her blouse. This time she did not protest. When he began to struggle in his effort because he had no idea how to take a woman's blouse off without ripping it apart, she helped him so that he did not ruin the blouse. He looked at the firm dividing line of her cleavage and placed a deep sensuous kiss upon it. She pulled his face up and started kissing him passionately. He now put his hand right through her bra and then slowly and eagerly touched the left bud. She shivered violently. He started undoing her bra but he did not succeed. 'You are a novice – aren't you?' she said with a smile.

This offered him encouragement. He smiled back nervously and said 'This is so difficult, I don't know how you manage to put it on.'

She undid her bra. He pulled it away from her body. Martha was a big woman. Two large breasts and yet so firm came out of captivity. The buds were darkish brown but so taut that they created immense passion in John. He brought his pink sensuous lips on one of those dark buds. She shivered and shivered and now began unbuttoning John's shirt. He took it off and then his trousers. He was completely naked. He unbuttoned Martha's skirt. She threw it on the floor. John now started to pull down her corsets, suspender belt and stockings. She took them off too. And finally her knickers. When he touched them, she said – 'Not here'.

John took her hand and rushed her through the corridor towards the bedroom. Martha looked round, afraid that a servant might still be awake. There was no one to be seen – it was far too late for them to be up. In John's bedroom he tried to take off Martha's knickers once more but she resisted again. Running away from him she just jumped on the bed and wrapped herself with the sheet. John, panting with excitement, was puzzled for a while.

'You want to – don't you?'

She looked intently at him. He moved towards her. She pulled him nearer and started kissing him violently. He drew the sheet off her and lay next to her. She now allowed him to take off her knickers, then pulled the sheet on top of both of them. But only for a while. Suddenly John gave a shrill cry that pierced the dark night.

'What's happened?' Martha was alarmed.

That stench, John could smell it, that stench that he had smelled from High Wycombe station on the morning of his mother's death. The billowy dark smoke covered the entire sky. John shivered. A cold stream of nervousness went through his spine. He started sweating as if he could feel the intense heat of that fire, as if his mother was being burned alive in that very room. He could see his mother's corpse, completely charred, lying in the morgue. Two huge gaping holes right through her skull, where she had once had those lovely affectionate eyes.

No, he could not do it. Not again! Perhaps never! It was his love-making that night that had caused the death of his mother. Had he been there to protect her from the murderer's claws instead of enjoying pleasures in the arms of that girl, no one could have taken her life. 'No! No!' He screamed and screamed. Martha was shaken to the core. John, desperately gasping for breath, leapt away from Martha and ran out of the room. Martha, naked and bewildered, had no idea what had gone wrong.

After a few moments, she wrapped her body in the sheet, then stealthily came out of John's room and hurried towards the guest room next door where she was supposed to sleep. Her face was burning with rage and indignation. She could think of no other reason for John's strange behaviour than his subconscious rejection of someone of mixed blood. Martha could have died of shame at that very moment. The thought of spending the rest of the night under the same roof as John mortified her. But for the time being there was nothing she could do except wait for the morning, when she could run away from this humiliation. She waited impatiently in her bed, counting every moment, longing for the morning to come.

SIX

I

The morning sun rose as usual without any hesitation or modesty. John stayed in bed long and late, wide awake though he had not had a wink of sleep all night. Very early on in the morning Martha got up, packed her case, then called Jadu to arrange for the *saice* to take her to Sripore to catch the train – the Delhi local – very slow, stopping at almost every station, but she wanted to get away as soon as possible. Emotionally, she could no longer cope – the whole experience had been devastating, especially as her heart was still deeply enmeshed in love.

From the very first day that she had met John, his honesty, integrity, forthrightness and kind sensitive approach to human problems had appealed to her growing sense of awareness of the outside world, the human world. But she had failed to realize that deep down at the subconscious level, where a human being is no longer guided by the logicality of the situation, the evenness, the knowledge of what is right and what is wrong – but is overwhelmed with the dark forces of pathological nightmares, prejudices, confusion – in that private world, John was filled with complex problems. Martha had neither the maturity nor the worldly sense to understand the deep intricacies of human behaviour.

She now firmly believed that when the crunch came, John's deep-rooted prejudice against a Eurasian girl had finally overpowered him, that he could not free himself from it, such was the depth of his abhorrence of the idea of a mixed marriage. She found this so humiliating that she wanted to get away from it all. Raigarh was a nightmare to her now. She wanted to turn her back on last night's bitter humiliation and open her eyes somewhere else. In some other place. Even in Sripore. So she waited alone at the station for the slow Delhi local to come and take her away from the past.

While Martha was arranging to leave Raigarh, John, in a daze, heard every noise. He himself could not forget even in the stark daylight the devastating experience of the previous night. Something had gone radically wrong, no doubt, he thought remorsefully. He had to face the fact that at the age of only twenty-four he had become impotent. But how to get out of this abyss?

The days passed in absolute gloom until one day he could stand it no more. He took a long ride to the hills to shake off his nightmare. To distract his mind, he decided to turn his attention to learning Hindustani, which was part of his service contract. The Raj insisted that all newly-recruited officers in the civil service must pass a test of proficiency in the local language.

He asked the pandit to come to his place three or four times a week and with his Balliol intellect galloped through Hindustani. He tried to master the language much more deeply and to read the original texts of some of the Hindu philosophical treatises and literature: the Gita, the Mahabharata, the epics of Kalidasa – often with the help of Max Müller's translations which made understanding easier. He directed his intellectual quest towards fathoming the wealth of eastern wisdom.

II

Every week-end John religiously visited the Station Club in Sripore – very often dining with the Garveys. Mrs Garvey took a keen interest in the welfare of this young intellectual who, her husband predicted, would one day reach one of the top jobs in India, perhaps the governorship of a province. She knew that he was disturbed of late by something. But like all newcomers in India, he had to go through the painful process of adjusting to the country: the heat, the dust, malaria, mosquito bites, loneliness and missing near relatives. The problem was even more acute for those who like John, served in a distant, remote region. With only one thousand officers running the administration of a vast country, loneliness for some was unavoidable. The Raj also thought that the best way to find out whether a person had an aptitude for the job was to throw him in at the deep end. If he could swim out of the crisis, the Raj would then have a leader with the experience and ability needed to cope with all the crises in the country, especially during this period of heightened tension.

Mrs Garvey, aware of the problems of a young officer in India, became motherly towards John. At the Station Club she always introduced him to all the bright prospects – distant cousins, nieces and sisters, who, during the cold weather season, crowded the local balls, injected life into endless picnics and showed up enthusiastically at the dramatic society – whether to act, organize, or as part of the audience. Soon she found that most of the time John was ill at ease in the company of over-enthusiastic, boisterous or vigorous women. Perhaps a reflective type would be more suitable for him, she thought. But even when she introduced him to such a woman, the relationship progressed no further than a polite, preliminary courtship. It seemed to her that John was not really interested in women.

'It's so unnatural – a young man, not interested in women,' she complained to Garvey one day.

'Perhaps he's the academic type,' replied Garvey. 'Anyway, it may not be bad for the Empire. We don't encourage young officers to get married too soon.'

'It seems so unhealthy!' Mrs Garvey complained.

'You must understand, dear,' Garvey spoke with the pragmatism of a seasoned officer, 'it's damn difficult for a man to live in that God-forsaken territory. And if you add a woman, we'll be forced to find him a more amenable place – or he'll simply leave.'

'All the same,' Mrs Garvey replied, 'you must look after the interests of your subordinates.'

'Oh Eileen!' Garvey spoke somewhat irritably, 'can you imagine the problem – compounded all over India? It might cause the biggest drain of our best officers and we can't afford the sacrifice. The longer he can stay without a woman, the better off everyone will be, including him.'

Mrs Garvey, however, was not pleased with her husband's logic and invited John to dinner with other prospective marriage candidates from the locality. Although John was no longer looking for a woman companion, he enjoyed the informal atmosphere of these evenings and was grateful to Mrs Garvey. In a way these occasions took the edge off his loneliness.

III

One evening when John went to dinner at the Garveys, he found the whole atmosphere rather tense. They were all on the veranda. Garvey was sitting on an easy chair, Mrs Garvey on the wicker settee, mournfully leaning on one side and looking blankly at the sky. John came and sat on the rocking chair. Dusk was already down and the *khit* brought gin and tonic. Garvey lit a big cigar, puffing the smoke into the still air in silence. Garvey was distant and reflective, which was very unlike him. John could tell from Garvey's manner that something was wrong, but he waited patiently while Garvey took his time.

'I've bad news, John!' Garvey said.

John remained silent, allowing Garvey to harness his emotion.

'Compton-Smith's dead.'

'What! What happened?' John found it difficult to believe the news.

'Killed!'

'By Gandhi's men? By Congresswallahs?'

'No! A tragic accident!' Garvey took a sip of gin, puffed the cigar and then continued, 'One evening he had to go and meet a new recruit at Howrah Station. On the way back just by the bridge he found a little Indian boy struggling in the river. A crowd had gathered around – everyone screaming and shouting, but nobody had the courage to go into the river because the tide was expected any second.'

'So, what happened?' asked John.

'Compton-Smith, without even a moment's hesitation, jumped in the river to save the boy. He swam fast, grabbed him, but before he could reach the shore, a violent wave, almost twenty feet high, crashed upon them.'

'Good Lord! And then?' John asked anxiously.

'At first it seemed they both managed to overcome the terrible thrust, but it was too much for Compton-Smith. Although the boy reached the shore safely, Smithy was swept away. His body was found later thirty miles downstream.'

John was far too shaken by the news of the tragedy to utter a word. Compton-Smith must have been a real gem of a man, he thought. Of all the people he knew, Compton-Smith was more racist than anyone else. Hardly a second passed without him calling the Indians names – and very often openly, which had acutely embarrassed John during their early encounters. Niggers, coons, wogs, nigras – he complimented even the senior Indian officers with such epithets. And he did not hide his racist feelings – nor his distaste for Indians and India. For him, India was simply a place to work, to earn his living. And a bloody place too – with all the discomfort, disease and turbulence. Unlike many others, he did not warm towards India – just took it as the duty of an officer serving the Raj. By choosing to come to India, he had accepted a profession and he was determined to execute his duty to the best of his ability. And he did so with courage.

'What about his widow and family?' John by now had recovered sufficiently to ask the most pertinent question.

'Of course, they're all shocked. At first his wife had to be put under heavy sedation; now she seems to have recovered.'

'Are they going to stay in India?'

'We don't know yet,' replied Garvey. 'Of course we'll pay for the passage if she wants to return. She'll have just the normal pension though – nothing more. It's likely that Smithy will posthumously receive a medal of some sort for his courage, but in terms of cash, that would add nothing – nothing at all.'

'Just an addition to the heroic history of those who are serving the Empire with their last drop of blood.' Even John was surprised by the bitterness of his own statement – even a bit embarrassed. Englishmen were not given to showing sentimentality.

The following morning John wrote a short letter to Mrs Compton-Smith. It read:

Dear Mrs Compton-Smith
I was shocked to hear about Geoffrey. I did not know him well but during my first months in India he was kind and generous to me. We are proud of the way he gave his life – not for the cause of the Raj, but for humanity. I am honoured even to have been associated with him. If there is anything I can do in my personal, humble capacity, I shall be delighted to have the opportunity.
With kindest regards
John Sugden.

He received a letter almost by return post. It read:

Dear Mr Sugden
Many thanks for your kind letter. Geoffrey always tried to do his duty to the best of his ability. He always maintained that we, the British, must show to the Indians our basic superiority as a race. Only by establishing that superiority over them could we morally claim to run this country for their benefit. In spite of all his shortcomings, he tried to uphold British tradition and morality during this turbulent time in India.
With best regards
Sylvia Compton-Smith.

PART TWO

The Turmoil

SEVEN

I

After the sad experience of losing a colleague John needed something to occupy his mind. He now made even more effort to learn Hindustani and in due course passed his test with flying colours. In the summer months he did not go out much except for his regular visits to the Station Club in Sripore. Mrs Garvey was away in Simla and invited him to go there for a holiday, but he declined, claiming pressure of work in Raigarh, which was partly true.

He made a brief visit to Calcutta and while there contacted Stanley's office and arranged to meet him for lunch at Firpo's. Their friendship was still intact and they nostalgically talked about the good old student days. After lunch they went to the Saturday Club and drank right through the afternoon so that by the evening the two friends were totally inebriated. During that entire time though, John never once asked after Martha, nor did Stanley extend the invitation to dinner at their palatial home in Park Street that only a few months before would have been natural.

At the start of the cold weather John decided to make full use of the season and visit the outposts of his district. He took some of his staff and servants and camped in faraway places. This was the routine programme for every officer in the civil service – the Raj on the move – to ensure that even in the remotest part of the country justice was meted out and that there was no tyranny whether from Europeans to Indians or – the more likely situation – from Indians to the vulnerable sections of their community. Justice and fair play were the watch-words for the Raj and duty for the likes of John Sugden was to implement them even in the distant corners of the country.

The experience gained from this cold weather trip was a real eye-opener that John would not readily forget. Men – common, ordinary men – came in droves to seek justice. Some of the complaints were minor – litigations between brothers and cousins over the ownership of a mango tree or some such ludicrously trivial matter. But there were others – really horrific stories – the local *zamindars*' torture, the incursions by the dacoits, looting, arson, rape and murder – the news of which never travelled beyond the boundary of each village concerned for fear of reprisals. Now they all came to the Sahib, their lord, begging him to save them from the tyranny of the strong and powerful. John was not able to mete out justice in every case, but in spite of that the cold weather trip established him as someone to whom people could come and air their problems without fear. They firmly believed that the Sahib would take suitable corrective measures to forestall any future acts of tyranny.

On one of the trips, John was camping on the outskirts of a small town called Rajpore on the bank of the Ganges. His platoon of servants was there with him as was customary to make life comfortable. But comfort was a far cry from anywhere in India and at these relatively small stations even the British-built dak bungalows offered only rudimentary facilities. But that was the way of the Raj and no officer so much as dreamt of complaining about such inadequacy.

On this trip, however, when a little diversion presented itself, John was delighted. He came across a European, rather wiry and weather-beaten, with a grizzly beard and easy, amicable manners.

'I'm Father Fallon. I've heard a lot about you,' the man shouted from his mount. 'Sorry, I've to rush – need to attend to a patient very urgently – otherwise he'll die – perhaps he'll die anyway. I can't undo God's work – but I'll try my best.'

John could not help but be amused by this rather matter-of-fact statement from a Christian missionary.

'Why don't you come to my hut for dinner this evening?' the father added convivially.

John accepted the invitation with alacrity. He was desperately looking forward to talking to a European, for since the start of the cold weather trip, he'd not had such an opportunity.

He had of course heard quite a lot about Father Fallon, the mad missionary. Fallon, a French speaking Belgian from Brussels, had originally come as a doctor to work in a British hospital. That was many years ago. Soon the young doctor, observing the infinite hardship among the deprived and down-trodden, decided to leave his secure employment. Ever since then his entire time had been spent on looking after the poor who had no one else to fall back upon.

Perhaps because of his eccentricity, Father Fallon also gained considerable notoriety, mainly founded on rumour, about his adopting various strange, native habits. The Raj looked upon him with suspicion because he did not fit into the norm – even a missionary norm. They considered him a potential troublemaker, not least because he often clamoured for money to buy medicines for people facing epidemics of one sort or another. The Raj had nothing against the work he was doing; it obviously needed to be done. It was his smug attitude towards Europeans, his avoidance of the Club and chukkas that irritated them. 'A good man, but he's no longer one of us.' That was Garvey's assessment of Fallon.

II

Father Fallon lived in a small, neatly-built, unpretentious bungalow on the edge of the town. Of course, unlike John, he did not have a big establishment of servants. The old missionary had only one person who cooked for him, kept his place tidy, carried his medicine-bag when needed and even on a few occasions helped him to perform emergency surgery. Buraji was Fallon's Man Friday. The Indian was totally committed to the old Belgian and served his master with utmost loyalty.

That evening when John went to Father Fallon, Buraji was already waiting with a hubble-bubble ready for the new sahib. Welcoming John, Fallon took the hubble-bubble from his servant and offered it to the young man.

'I've never smoked one before,' the young European confessed with boyish enthusiasm.

'Do you know, this is India's best invention since Arabic numerals,' replied the missionary with a smile. 'When you inhale, the smoke comes through water which absorbs all the harmful elements from the tobacco.'

'I say, you're being scientific about it, aren't you? Perhaps you advise all your patients to smoke a hubble-bubble.'

'It's quite costly, you know, by Indian standards,' the old Belgian was informative. 'Ordinary folk can't afford such luxury. They smoke *bidis*, stink the whole place out and ruin their health.'

'Then who smokes hubble-bubbles?' asked John.

'Oh, the upper class!' replied Fallon. 'They keep half a dozen of them – one for the Brahmins, one for the *Kshatriyas*, one for the *Vaishyas*, one for Moslems and Christians – if they ever entertain them – and a couple of spares.'

'What about the untouchables? Aren't they allowed to smoke a hubble-bubble?' John asked jokingly.

This incensed the Belgian missionary. He replied forcefully, 'You should know, Sugden. You've already been here more than a year. The untouchables are allowed nothing. Nothing at all. Don't you remember that recent event, reported in a Calcutta newspaper?'

'These days I hardly have the time to read a newspaper, Father. The only thing I read about the untouchables has to do with Gandhi. And I find him nauseating,' John replied.

'Don't make such a snap judgement about Gandhi. He is a great man.' Fallon made no bones about his own assessment of the Indian leader.

'Tell me the story – then we don't have to argue over him,' John tried to avoid any disagreement so early on in their discussion.

'As you wish,' Father Fallon smiled and continued, 'A few of the untouchables have now broken through the ranks and educated themselves to respectable professions. One such person is Deb Biswas, a lawyer in the Calcutta high court.'

'That must be quite an achievement for an untouchable!' John was genuinely surprised.

'Absolutely!' the Belgian replied. 'But the servant in the bar library, a caste Hindu, thought differently and refused to offer him water even in the hottest months.'

'Surely, he can't do that.'

'Oh, yes he can! And the worst part of it was that when Biswas complained, the Bar Council ruled against him. Can you imagine anything so obnoxious?'

'What happened then?' The young officer was now curious.

'Fortunately there're a few Hindus with more sense,' Fallon continued, 'Chatterjee, an educated Brahmin and the editor of a local newspaper, came to Biswas's rescue and offered to do the servant's job free.'

'Isn't it appalling – I mean the whole fabric? It must be degenerate to create such systems which humiliate people.' The young officer voiced his strong feeling against Hinduism.

'A reign of tyranny if you ask me,' the Belgian concurred and then added, 'The problem is that these people have no voice – absolutely none – no education, nobody sufficiently eloquent to speak on their behalf, nothing.' Suddenly Fallon became passionate. 'Do you know that an untouchable isn't allowed to walk through a village in case a Brahmin happens to touch – not merely him – but even his shadow. Just imagine! Even a leper in medieval times was never so humiliated. But sadly, the Raj doesn't do anything at all to help them.'

'What can we do?' John spoke defensively. 'After all, it's a religious matter. We can't just tinker with their religion because we happen to administer the country. And with Gandhi breathing down our necks, it's not an easy task.'

The Belgian, however, was not prepared to allow the young man to get away so easily. He said, 'Do you know, since Lord Bentinck abolished suttee in 1825, the government hasn't tried a single reform? Not one!'

'The policy of the Empire is not to interfere with the local customs. We are not here to reform,' John replied. He was convinced that for the smooth running of the country the policy of the Raj had to be so.

Fallon was not happy with this reply. He said accusingly, 'If you're not here to reform, to educate, to enlighten people from their dark prejudices – what are you here for? Power? Money? Exploiting the natives?'

This incensed the young Englishman. 'Of course not,' he replied. 'But reforming India is a monumental task. Just think of the impact of Bentinck's abolition of suttee. Then we had to face the social problem of widows whom nobody would marry – unwanted pregnancies, murder of newborn illegitimate babies, increase in prostitution – the whole gamut. Even now, after nearly a hundred years, the repercussions of that single change are very much in evidence.'

'But does it mean you condone suttee?' asked the priest. 'Would you allow a crowd to burn a woman alive?'

The thought sent a cold shiver down John's spine. For a few moments he was speechless; then he recovered a little and mumbled, 'No, I'm not saying that. But in solving one problem, you can't allow others to mount up in different directions. It's safer not to get too involved in social engineering on a mass scale.'

'We missionaries are here to do that for you,' the priest

commented. 'We could educate people – if only you would allow us to get on with the job and give us a free hand.'

'Not after our experience of the Mutiny, Father.' John knew that the over-zealous actions of the missionaries had sparked off the Mutiny in the first place.

'I'm not so sure about those stories.' Fallon tried to defend the involvement of the missionaries in the Mutiny. 'Even if those stories were true, is it right for you to allow the untouchables who make up a sixth of the population to suffer such abject humiliation for fear that you might have a mutiny on your hands?'

'But Father! With all your efforts, you're not achieving any real results.' John was determined to show the fallacy in the Belgian's argument. He continued, 'I have a servant, Albert David, a convert from the untouchables, but his status hasn't changed. He isn't allowed inside a Hindu village even now. Both Hindus and Moslems refuse to work alongside him. The Christians don't even sit next to him in church. So all that's happened for him is that he calls himself a Christian. Nothing else! Nothing else whatsoever!'

'That's a start. Everything here changes slowly as you know. But one doesn't have to be a missionary – Gandhi is bringing about great changes in the social structure.'

'Oh, please! Don't talk to me about Gandhi!' John spoke with a strong feeling of disgust written all over his face. He said, 'Gandhi is a hypocrite! A demagogue! And all this façade of wearing loin-cloths, abstaining from sex, a day of prayer in silence! I think the man's a lunatic or perhaps even a devil.'

'You dismiss him too readily, Sugden. There's a lot of good in him.' The father was positive in his support for Gandhi which annoyed John, who said,

'Do you know I saw him in Calcutta, stirring up a frenzy – almost like witchcraft. People were screaming, shouting, and then bringing piles and piles of expensive foreign clothes to be burned on a bonfire.' Even now John could distinctly remember the frightening scene in Calcutta.

'There's a reason,' the Belgian tried to assure the young officer. 'It's the British who first destabilized the Indian economy and destroyed the cotton industry, and now Gandhi's trying to free them from this dependence.'

'We are not discussing history, Father,' John was irritated. 'We are talking of today – this present moment.'

'Don't misunderstand me,' the Belgian said. 'I'm not

supporting his law-breaking. There's another side to him – can't you see? He's trying to bring about a social revolution by removing the drudgery of the untouchables – lifting their status – calling them *Harijan* – Children of God.'

'What good will that do?' the young man protested. 'I call my gardener Albert David, he still remains an untouchable.'

'Gandhi has a way of doing things,' the priest said. 'By calling them Children of God he is trying to bring about a psychological change in people's minds.'

'What psychological change?' John asked somewhat brusquely.

'Well, after some time people will start believing that the untouchables really are Children of God and then we will have a social revolution.'

The young man was not convinced. He said, 'We know Gandhi's trickery only too well. He's a devil, the Satan incarnate. He calls his burning clothes *satyagraha* – seeking truth. What truth! In Chauri Chaura his followers burnt alive twenty-two policemen – so much for his non-violence!'

'But he called off the strike the next day.'

'That's not the point. He's creating such a frenzy among the people – whether in Chauri Chaura or Amritsar – violence is bound to break out.'

'You are wrong about him, Sugden.' The Belgian tried to defend Gandhi. 'Don't forget – his main intellectual weapon is not just Hinduism. He's influenced by Tolstoy, by the teachings of the Sermon on the Mount, by George Fox and the Quakers.'

This was too much for the young man. He almost shouted at the missionary, 'Father, my mother was a Quaker. She was descended from Tom Lloyd, the Quaker hero, who resisted the tyranny of Governor Blackwell in Pennsylvania. His blood is flowing in my veins. I know the beliefs of the Quakers – you don't have to tell me. When the Quakers were persecuted for their beliefs they never preached violence under the guise of seeking truth.'

'Be realistic, Sugden,' the father tried to appease the young man. 'You have only one thousand officers running the administration of a huge country of three hundred million people.'

'But we are running it efficiently. Much better than the Indians had ever done.'

'I know – but consider your own situation – a young Englishman still in your twenties, thousands of miles away from home, living in a remote part of the country with no other European to talk to, share experiences with – not even the company of a woman. Your only contact with Europeans is at the Station Club and no doubt you hope that one day you may meet someone willing to share life with you in India.'

'That doesn't bother me. That doesn't bother me in the slightest,' the young man replied.

'Even if it doesn't bother you, for many this is a life of extreme misery.'

'You exaggerate, Father.'

'No, Sugden, no!' replied Fallon. 'You ask any Englishman working in a remote place and he will tell you about his loneliness. And for what?'

'There is no real solution to that problem, Father.'

'Yes, there is,' Fallon spoke determinedly. 'No one frowned upon intermarriage before the Mutiny. The offspring were as proud of their parentage as any Englishman. Think of Lord Liverpool! But now? Yes, they'll permit you to have local women. Fornication is permitted – but not marriage. If by chance you become emotionally involved – you've had it.'

'There are so many problems in an intermarriage, Father.'

'How can you possibly have the moral strength to survive the exigencies of this country when you're being asked to behave unnaturally – fornicate but not marry.'

'Nobody in the Raj is encouraging fornication, Father,' the young man replied. 'You Roman Catholic missionaries remain celibate all your lives. Why should it be impossible for us to do the same until we find the right Englishwoman?'

'Tell me, Sugden, why can't we adopt a freer attitude towards intermarriage? After all, it didn't bother us in the past.'

'I don't believe in intermarriage, Father,' the young man was firm in his conviction. 'There's so much cultural dfference between Europe and India. The Indians are still living in the middle ages. People are naïve, extraordinarily naïve – full of superstition. The world doesn't seem to have changed for them since the time of Marco Polo.'

'It's changing very fast now, John,' the Belgian warned. 'And you need an accommodation with Gandhi. He's a moral reformer – can't you see? He's basically a Christian in a Hindu robe.'

'I don't believe it, Father. But let's not talk about Gandhi any more. I'm thoroughly sick of him.'

Fortunately just at that moment Buraji interrupted their heated discussion. He knew his master only too well. If the master felt passionately about anything he could easily get carried away. Buraji did not want him to upset this new officer of the Raj. 'Dinner is ready, Father,' he announced politely.

John was glad of this interruption, for he did not want to spend the rest of the evening arguing with Fallon about a topic on which they could never agree.

That night, however, when John was riding back he wondered more about Gandhi than he had ever done in the past. Was there really a Christian in Gandhi? No! Not at all! He was convinced that Father Fallon was wrong. Gandhi was a trouble-maker who must be pacified for the good of India. On that score he had no doubt. The Raj is here to stay for a long time yet, he thought – definitely the rest of this century, perhaps even the next.

EIGHT

I

One morning, soon after returning to Raigarh from his cold weather trip, John saw a horse-drawn carriage gently rolling along the brickdust path leading to his bungalow. An Indian gentleman, neatly dressed in a suit and tie and wearing a trilby hat – rather unusual for this time of year except on formal occasions – peeped out of the carriage window. The fact that he was dressed in that way did not surprise John, for the educated Indians on the whole were more fond of dressing formally than their European counterparts. Somehow they believed that formal clothes gave them status and dignity and separated them from the rest; at least so it seemed.

The *darwan* at the gate and Albert David, the gardener, saluted him with a degree of awe which they normally reserved for a European officer. The man got down from the carriage and in an unhurried but rather mannered trot climbed the steps.

'Good morning, sir.' The man smiled widely.

'Good morning. Please, come in.' John was surprised to see Anil Saha. He was a man in his late thirties, a small but paunchy fellow, corpulent like most Indians in senior government positions, but smooth – oozing charm almost to the point of embarrassment.

'Sit down, Saha. What can I offer you to drink?'

'Well, sir, as they say back home, no alcohol before sundown. Tea would be just fine.' Some of these Indians referred to England as 'home' in the same way as an Englishman would do. Their stay in England in most cases, though, did not extend beyond studying for, and taking, civil service examinations. 'Well, it is a nice day, sir, so I thought I would come and say hallo to you.' Saha tried to explain the reason for his visit. Then with a broad smile he added, 'After all, it is a very remote place – this Raigarh. No civilized company here – not like Sripore. For an Englishman, an intellectual such as you, sir – it must be awfully dull to live here.'

'I don't mind it at all, Saha.'

'But, sir, there is not even a library or a cinema – not even a club where you could go to meet Europeans.'

'I quite enjoy my own company,' replied John. 'I'm not sure whether I would like it any other way. There's a nice tranquillity here. I like it in Raigarh.'

'You must be a poet, sir,' Saha commented respectfully. 'From the first day I met you I had an inkling. A poet always recognizes a poet. I also write poetry, sir.'

Somehow John found Saha more interesting this time than on previous occasions. 'Do you write in your own language?' he asked the Indian.

'Oh no, sir – not in the vernacular,' the Indian replied. 'In the vernacular, sir, there is not much literature in existence – whatever there is is all dull and boring. Moreover, I have never learned to read in the vernacular – always English. That's why I find myself at ease in the company of Englishmen.'

'I'm sure there're some good books in the vernacular,' John said. 'You have your Nobel laureate, Tagore. Even some of the old Sanskrit epics, like the Ramayana and the Mahabharata are works of merit.'

'Of course, sir, of course. You are right a hundred times. You are such a knowledgeable man, you have even read Indian epics.' Saha seemed pleased with John's knowledge of old Sanscrit books.

John smiled politely and that encouraged Saha. He continued, 'You see, sir, now we are having an intellectual conversation. The Indians don't know how to conduct an intellectual conversation. They become too serious and lose their temper. They cannot differentiate between an argument and a quarrel, sir.'

John nodded his head indulgently.

'I say, an argument is a method of intellectual discussion to establish truth,' Saha continued, 'whereas a quarrel is a different thing – it is just losing one's temper – isn't it true, sir?'

'Yes, I think you have a point,' John replied.

'You see, sir, that is why I like the company of Englishmen,' the Indian carried on charmingly. 'You possess such sharp brains. You understand an intellectual matter so quickly and easily. What you understood in a second, I would have had to hammer at for hours with an Indian, and even then he would not have been able to grasp what I was saying.'

John did not reply. He was beginning to feel a bit bored with Saha.

'Don't get me wrong, sir,' Saha continued, 'I don't discuss these things with Indians. Socially, I don't mix with them at all. I have a few European friends, like you – I can call you a friend, can't I, sir?'

'Of course you can.' John was getting more and more exasperated with this conversation, especially with Saha's use of the word 'intellectual' in every other sentence. Still he could not really be impolite to a fellow ICS officer.

'Sir, Gandhi is destroying everything in this country. Don't you think?' the Indian asked.

This was a topic close to John's heart. 'Yes, I think you're right,' he said and then somewhat ambivalently added, 'but having said that I must admit he's doing an awful lot of good work with the untouchables.'

'Of course yes, sir,' Saha agreed whole-heartedly. 'It's a shame – this untouchable business. The problem with the Indians is that most of the time they do not know how to behave themselves.'

John did not reply. His mind was still preoccupied with the fact that he had publicly supported Gandhi and he had no idea how he could have done it. Saha, however, was full of loyalty for the government. He continued, 'I tell you one thing, sir – the Indians don't like Gandhi. They don't like his anti-Raj campaign. The Indians would like to stay under the British Raj forever.'

'I fully agree with you, Saha.' John was pleased by the Indian's remarks. 'Even if Mr Gandhi thinks differently, we need to be here, at least for the time being. I don't think the Indians are ready to take over the administration yet.'

'You are a hundred times right, sir,' replied Saha. 'The Indians will never be ready. If they get the power, they will spoil the whole thing – fight among themselves – Hindus and Moslems, Sikhs and Jats, Bengalis and Biharis. They will destroy everything. They need us, sir.'

John was amused. Saha obviously considered himself an Englishman. Still, we need loyal Indians to run this country, he thought.

II

The following day when John travelled to the Station Club in Sripore, the reason for Saha's visit to Raigarh became clear. Everyone had gathered round the bar and a heated discussion was going on which was obviously ruffling a few feathers. The intensity of discussion was apparent from the many red faces full of anger.

'They'll come here over my dead body. I'm not having coons in this club.' Bill Wright, a local officer with the reputation of calling a spade a spade expressed his views in no uncertain terms.

'Bill's right,' said Paul Smith, a trader who had been admitted to the club only recently after a considerable amount of deliberation and soul-searching. The club had hitherto been against admitting boxwallahs; but under Garvey's guidance the committee had made a major concession and admitted Smith. 'They reek of mustard,' Smith continued, 'I tell you, they do – I have to deal with them every day. They'll come here, chew their betel leaf and spit everywhere. Ooh! The whole place would be absolutely horrible! It wouldn't remain British any more. It would be like a bazaar.'

George Selsdon, a lawyer, known for his moderate views, joined the argument in a sensible way, 'I think what we have to consider is the fact that many of us come over here to relax. Especially when we have had a few drinks we discuss things which could easily be regarded as sensitive – both militarily and politically. We can't be on guard all the time. Not only that, considering some of the recent terrorist attacks, it would be inadvisable to have Indians among us in this club.'

'That's the crucial point,' Smith shouted. 'Once you allow one

Indian in, they will all crowd into the place: Gandhi's agitators, terrorists, everybody. The *darwan* wouldn't be able to distinguish between the bona fide members and others because all Indians look alike, anyway.'

'Come on Paul!' Garvey said, 'let's discuss this matter sensibly. The *darwan* himself is an Indian, he wouldn't have the same problems that you and I might have. Anyway, I don't know about you, but I have no difficulty in differentiating between Indians – I never mix up my *khansama* and *khit*.'

'The point I was making,' Selsdon raised his voice, 'is that really and truly we can't trust Indians. If the Raj really has confidence in them, why don't we see more of them in sensitive political and diplomatic posts? The native officers are still crowding Land Revenue – why? Because there they have no access to confidential information. And if that's the case, which I believe it is, we will jeopardize our own safety and security by allowing them into the club. It'll be just too darn difficult to keep sensitive issues away from Gandhi and the terrorists.'

'On the other hand, you have to consider the reality.' Raymond Lichford, the editor of the local newspaper and a well known liberal, supposed to be a friend of Gandhi's supporter Guy Horniman of the *Bombay Chronicle*, raised his voice of wisdom. 'It doesn't matter for how many generations we have been living in India, this is their country. The fact is – that if we are to live here, we must make a gesture of goodwill – the kind of goodwill the Prince of Wales suggested in his speech last year.'

'Rubbish!' snorted Smith. 'The Prince of Wales suggested no such thing.'

'Calm down, please, Paul!' Garvey maintained his dignity.

Smith took no notice of Garvey's interruption and continued, 'Sorry! But we don't even allow half-castes into the club. They're more deserving than the natives. After all, the half-castes know our manners; they know how to behave. At least they're civilized. But not the wogs. They'll come over here, bring their women, stink the place out, pick their noses and blabber in shitty vernacular.'

'Watch your language, please, Smith!' Garvey once again reminded the trader that he would not allow this discussion to get out of control. 'The problem is,' Garvey put his cards on the table, 'we have instructions from the Governor, based on the Viceroy's own request, that the European clubs must open their doors to a token membership of one or two Indians. We want to show our willingness to cooperate and mix with Indians at all levels.'

'Never!' The rejection came almost unanimously from the gathering.

'I'll never swim with a wog in the same pool,' vowed Smith.

'One thing you must consider,' the sensible voice of Selsdon once again filled the room, 'they are more prone to disease. It's not their fault, but the conditions in which they live make them more susceptible to spreading disease – be it malaria, cholera or smallpox. By allowing them in we will expose ourselves to an acute health hazard. It's bad enough living here with all the problems – why bring more?'

'For heavens' sake, Selsdon!' Raymond Lichford now lost his temper. 'You have a score of Indian servants doing all the menial jobs – cooking, washing, everything – if you're to get any disease from an Indian, you don't have to come to the club, you'll get it from your servants.'

Raymond Lichford's comment created a near commotion in the club and in a most un-English fashion they now started shouting at each other. Garvey unsuccessfully tried to bring about some order by raising his voice above everyone else's, but it was not an easy task. John Sugden, who until now had been listening to the debate in silence, tried to come to his boss's assistance.

'I suppose the kind of person we are thinking of admitting into the club is someone like Anil Saha,' he said tentatively. John had certainly not intended proposing this name, but it occurred to him that, in this impasse, a name would bring reality to this squabble over whether to admit an Indian or not.

John's statement had a strange effect on the agitated members of the Station Club. There was a moment's silence. But Paul Smith, the trader, was not subdued by it. He yelled, 'Not that slimy bugger! I can't stand him. He melts every time you talk to him.' Then in a mocking voice he mimicked, 'Yes sir, no sir, three bags full, sir!'

They all laughed at Smith's comment and this brought light relief to the atmosphere. Tactfully Garvey decided to end the meeting on that note of amity. The issue, though, remained unresolved. Garvey suggested that the question should be formally discussed at their next annual general meeting. Everyone agreed to his suggestion and felt happy that at least for the time being a definite decision had been averted.

NINE

I

Reading his father's diaries after his death, David Sugden found the following notes on the causes of racial violence in India: 'Towards the end of last century, some of the liberal elements of the Hindu intelligentsia decided to form a political wing to voice the measures required for the country's well-being. The Raj welcomed this new approach. On the initiative of a retired English civil servant. Allan Octavian Hume, a new party was formed in 1885 – the Indian National Congress.

'The pressure for independence, however, was building up within the country through various terrorist movements. This prompted the British Government in 1909 to ask Viscount Morley, the then Secretary of State for India, to produce a report on the question of Indian representation and how it could be constituted. Under the influence of Ameer Ali, a professor at the London School of Economics, Lord Morley proposed a separate electoral roll for the Moslem population so that their voice was not swamped by the Hindu majority.

'Mohammad Ali Jinnah, a new star for the Moslems, was rising fast at the time. A successful lawyer, he had been an ardent Congress supporter until a major political phenomenon from South Africa in the form of Mohandas Karamchand Gandhi suddenly landed on the Indian scene in 1915. Before Gandhi's arrival, Jinnah had enjoyed the support of both the Hindus and Moslems and had been tipped by many as a future leader of the Congress. He was calm, cool and eloquent – all the essential qualities needed to influence the middle class.

'But the scene started changing very rapidly once Gandhi entered the arena. Overnight he transformed middle class agitations of the intelligentsia into a mass movement, bringing all shades of colour into the Congress fold, especially the so-called lowly-bred – the untouchables. This created an immediate problem for someone like Jinnah – a man with ambition, charisma, ability and intelligence.

'Although Jinnah tried to seek a new role for himself, he soon found that every known avenue had been blocked by Gandhi. Unless one became converted to Gandhism – going round cleaning public lavatories, eating with the untouchables in their mud huts and of course joining the non-cooperation movement, which Jinnah's law-abiding mind could never accept – there was no longer any scope in the political field. Westminster-style oratory in small middle class gatherings no longer paved the way to leadership.

'On 9 February 1921 the Duke of Connaught, son of Queen Victoria and uncle of the Emperor George V, proclaimed, "The principle of autocracy has been abandoned. The gradual development of self-governing institutions with a view to the progressive realization of responsible government in India as an integral part of the British Empire will henceforth be pursued."

'Jinnah, like all other political leaders, now became aware of a distinct air of change. The question for him was whether to play a pivotal role, especially as the Raj looked upon him favourably for not joining Gandhi's non-cooperation movement. It was a challenge – and he decided to accept it.

'With Gandhi dominating the Hindus, it became obvious to him that his real power base was the Moslems; and separate electoral registers were imperative to offer him any significance. Jinnah began to argue the case for the Moslem minority and the unfair treatment that they might receive in the event of a Hindu Raj. The pressure brought upon the government soon yielded results and the Viceroy accepted the principle of separate electoral registers.

'The strong racial antipathy which already existed among the people was further exacerbated by this new move from the government. But Jinnah was not content to rest on his laurels. He spent long and arduous hours with Moslem scholars, religious leaders and the intelligentsia and worked out a detailed paper insisting that ethnically the Moslems in India were a different race and had nothing in common with the Hindus.

'Right-wing Hindu and Moslem organizations now began to mushroom very quickly against this backdrop. Two such organizations were the Islamic Front, led by a London-trained barrister, Khodadad Khan, and the Hindu League, led by an extremist, Harmohan Joshi.'

II

'Sir, Khodadad Khan is coming to speak in Raigarh.' Banerji spoke nervously.

'No! Good Lord, why? Why Raigarh?' John was concerned.

'They are now holding meetings in every small town round here, especially where there are a lot of Moslems. What should we do, sir?'

John was thinking hard. He knew that a sensible decision had to be made – and quickly. Being independently-minded – and proud – he did not want to rush to Garvey for advice at every hint of trouble. He was aware that the situation in India at the moment was so explosive that even the slightest error could spark off major disorder, and that had to be avoided at all costs. He remembered vividly how when he was young he had once been trapped in the midst of a violent riot in High Wycombe. It was during a parliamentary election when serious trouble broke out between the Tories and the Liberals. The supporters of the Tory candidate, Sir Alfred Cripps, and those of his opposite number from the Liberal party, a man called T.A. Herbert, fought openly over the hot election issue at the time, the Liberal party's open trade policy – allowing cheap furniture to be imported from abroad – which the Tories feared would ruin the local furniture industry.

To make the issue more real to the electors the Tories had opened a dump shop where they put imported cheap furniture on display and hung big posters outside describing what life would be like if the Liberals were to get in again. But the Liberal supporters were not prepared to accept this unfair propaganda from the Tories. They promptly set fire to the shop. That was bad enough but the worst part was when the mayor of the town read the Riot Act and called in the police.

The sight of the police sent the entire town completely berserk and led to widespread violence. Many, severely wounded, were taken to hospital. And that was in a civilized, law-abiding country like England. But here in India, John thought, the people are so volatile that even the slightest provocation could ignite the fuse. He had no doubt in this mind that the presence of the police at the outset would only add fuel to the fire and could easily spark off a major riot which in no circumstances must be allowed to take place.

'My intuition tells me to do nothing,' John replied to his subordinate after a long pause.

Banerji was totally baffled by this decision. 'What about law and order, sir?'

'We have to instruct the police to remain alert. The sight of police often creates more trouble. Gandhi has taught them one thing – not to be frightened of the police.'

'True, sir,' Banerji said. 'Gandhi has made the Indian police absolutely toothless. Think of Chauri Chaura, sir. A few years ago, no Indian would have dared to lift a finger against the police – and now a mob could go and burn alive twenty-two policemen in one fell swoop.'

'But we've arrested the damn lot – one hundred and seventy two murderers – and they will all be charged. Gandhi or no Gandhi,' John replied angrily.

'He is encouraging the *goondas*, sir, the rogue elements.'

'That's the most unfortunate part. If the police have no authority, who can stop the hoodlums?' John expressed his concern about Gandhi's tactics.

'You see, sir, now that Gandhi has started it, Jinnah is following his example by bringing the fighting on to the streets.'

'You're right, Banerji,' John agreed with his subordinate. 'The problem with Gandhi is that his non-violence is in itself violent. In spite of whatever he says, his hands are blood-stained – even the killings at Amritsar wouldn't have happened without his incitement.'

'True, sir! That is very true! We obviously need more police to control these meetings.' Banerji had seemingly forgotten the Sahib's reluctance to bring in more police.

'No, Banerji, it wouldn't work that way. We have already had enough evidence to show that the presence of a big contingent of police to control an unruly mob is not the best way to go about it.'

'But, sir, if violence breaks out – what do we do then?' Banerji asked nervously.

John was thoughtful. 'Leave it with me,' he replied to calm his subordinate, but he had no idea what course of action he should follow.

III

The problem for John, however, did not stop with Khodadad Khan. The Hindus, not to be outdone by the Moslems, invited the extreme right-wing fascist party, the Hindu League. Hearing about the Moslems flexing muscles in Raigarh, their leader, Joshi, immediately accepted the invitation.

The whole situation now became very tense. The young officer started having nightmares when he came to know about Joshi's past. Before the war, Joshi had had contacts with Sinn Fein and had been in Europe to buy arms for the nationalist struggle. Guns had soon been found filtering through to the terrorists in India. When the British police had finally tracked him down in France, the fear of Joshi's absconding was such that he had been put in a specially guarded boat to take him from Calais to Marseilles before shipping him back to India to face the notorious Nasik Trial. But now released, he had decided to take up the cudgels on behalf of the Hindus.

The bad news about Joshi, however, was yet to come. Soon John learned that Joshi had not only accepted the invitation but prompted the Hindus in Raigarh to organize the meeting on the same afternoon Khodadad was due to speak. Joshi's extraordinary desire to show his strength left no doubt in John's mind that the whole situation was about to take a nasty turn. In a rare bout of fear, he rushed to Charles Garvey for advice.

'What do we do now?' John asked anxiously.

'We cannot have two meetings on the same day. That's really asking for trouble,' Garvey replied. 'Joshi is both crafty and dangerous. This may be his ploy to crush Jinnah's plan of consolidating Moslem opinion through India.'

'But surely a clash between the Hindus and Moslems would only further Jinnah's cause?' John was puzzled.

'Joshi does not see it that way, John. He thinks if he could bring Hindu fanatics to work against the Moslems and stir up trouble, soon the British government would have to put both Jinnah and Joshi behind bars, and that would destroy the Moslem League.'

The young officer could see the obvious solution to the problem. He said, 'Why don't we offer Jinnah the same treatment as we have to Gandhi?'

'What do you mean?' Garvey was unsure of what his subordinate officer was trying to suggest.

'I mean why don't we arrest Jinnah?'

'On what grounds?' Garvey was clearly surprised.

'For inciting people and creating racial tension. Exactly the same charge as we brought against Gandhi,' John replied.

'But he hasn't done anything – it's Khodadad who's organizing meetings in various towns.'

'It's the same,' said the young man, somewhat naïvely.

'No, not the same,' replied Garvey, and then added, 'moreover – now that we have put Gandhi behind bars, we must give Jinnah a bit of leeway. We might as well create some division among the Hindus and the Moslems, some clash which would dissipate their energy.'

This statement from his superior officer confused the young man. 'But that's dishonesty, sir!' he said.

'There's nothing like a civil war to weaken a nation,' the experienced functionary grinned. He was well versed in how to handle the affairs of the Empire. He added, 'If Viscount Morley has unwittingly sown a seed, we may as well use it to our full advantage.'

'That's playing with fire, sir,' the young man could not hide his concern. 'For all we know, it could easily start widespread riots which would be beyond our ability to put down.'

'Sorry for sounding so callous, old boy,' Garvey replied. 'The general belief now is that we don't want another Amritsar. Not at any price.'

John was not happy. He pleaded, 'But, sir, that's exactly what will happen if we allow Jinnah to have his own way.'

'No, John, no,' the senior officer tried to make his subordinate understand the real power politics. 'Small skirmishes between the Hindus and Moslems won't do any harm to our interest. If anything, it'll weaken Gandhi's power.' Then, sotto voce he added, 'The bugger has equal hold over the Hindus and Moslems. We have to put an end to it if we want to survive in India.'

'Suppose it brings deaths?' The young man was agitated.

'That's where we would come in,' Garvey replied. 'We must not allow it to get completely out of hand.'

John looked totally nonplussed by Garvey's theory.

'Don't look so baffled, old boy!' Garvey tried to soothe the anxiety of the young officer. 'Can't you see Jinnah's actually supporting us? Edwin Montagu has put in so much hard work on India – and you have to admit his scheme is fair. But Gandhi won't accept it. He even urged the Indian Council members to resign from their posts. We don't know for sure whether Lord Sinha's resignation was due to pressure from Gandhi.'

'Surely, a man of Lord Sinha's stature would not have left us because of Gandhi's threats,' the young man replied with conviction.

'The rumour is flying around that Sinha resigned in case he had to arrest Gandhi in Bihar at the time of the Prince's visit.'

John was subdued by Garvey's words, but he was still unhappy. He said, 'Gandhi had to be restrained no doubt, sir, but supporting Jinnah will only create problems.'

Seeing John's concern, Garvey laughed smugly and said, 'It's like homoeopathy, my boy! You prescribe a small dose of poison to fight a bigger disease. As long as you can keep the dosage under control, it's actually working for you.'

By now the young officer was completely disenchanted. 'Sir, pardon my impertinence,' he said, 'but I firmly believe this policy is wrong.'

'Wrong!' Garvey replied. 'No! No! This is the most effective way of controlling Gandhi.'

John was upset by what he had heard from his senior officer, but he was conscious of his duty. He said, 'The Indians are passionate. They can be easily overwhelmed by even the slightest provocation. I know I can't arrest Jinnah or Joshi or Khodadad, but I have to stop these meetings.'

'On what pretext?' Garvey asked. 'If you try to stop them, almost immediately there will be a riot.'

'I'll talk to the organizers,' John said.

'That you can do. In fact it may not be a bad policy to do so.' For the first time Garvey sounded constructive. 'Tell them, unless they arrange the meetings on two different dates, you'll impose a curfew and bring in the PC 144.'

Yes, that might do the trick, John thought; use the threat of a curfew and the PC 144 which prohibited any assembly of four or more people. Garvey's suggestion at least temporarily eased his sense of foreboding.

The adoption of the tough policy against holding meetings on the same day brought about the intended result. Both Khodadad and Joshi backed down, agreeing to different dates for their meetings. The tension, however, continued unmitigated in Raigarh. Rival posters appeared next to each other in inflammatory language. A few skirmishes had already taken place with each faction blaming the other for ripping their posters. The Islamic Front supporters with their green festoons and caps and the Hindu League volunteers with their saffron banners roamed the streets, chanting 'Death' to each other. Although tension mounted, John managed to keep a modicum of peace during these days using a low-profile police presence.

IV

On Saturday afternoon Khodadad was due to speak, and on Sunday it was Joshi's turn. A huge crowd of Moslems had assembled to listen to Khodadad. Much to John's annoyance, Ibrahim wanted to have the afternoon off to listen to his leader. Following Ibrahim's example Jadu also asked for time off to listen to Joshi. John agreed to both, albeit reluctantly, for he thought more harm would be done by trying to stop them.

In the football ground a temporary structure had been assembled to prepare a makeshift rostrum, decorated mainly with green festoons – the Islamic colour. Microphones were installed so that the messages could be clearly heard even by those arriving late and who could not secure a ringside position. Khodadad, a highly sophisticated and articulate man in his early thirties, tall, slim, slightly balding, dressed in the North Indian clothes of *sherwani* and *churidar*, took the rostrum amid a great cheer from the crowd.

'Friends! Moslems!' His voice trembled slightly as he spoke. 'Let us not be misled by Gandhi's trickery. In spite of all his so-called sympathy for the Moslems, when he talks of *swraj*, he talks of *swraj* for the Hindus in which we, the Moslems, will be more down-trodden than we have ever been in our whole history.'

The crowd roared, 'Islamic Front *zindabad* – Long live the Islamic Front!'

Khodadad continued, 'We ruled India before the British came – why? Because we are natural rulers of this country. We ruled it for eight hundred years while the mighty Raj has ruled Hindustan for a mere sixty.'

The crowd cheered vociferously, waving green flags. Khodadad allowed them to calm down before he continued, 'We are not going to kowtow now to the Hindus because they are greater in number.'

The crowd shouted, 'No! Never!'

'We are superior to them in every respect – both culturally and physically.'

The crowd screamed, 'Allaho Akbar!'

'We have behind us the great tradition of Islam, a great culture that flourishes throughout the world – in every continent – in Africa, in Asia, even in Europe. The Islamic empire once spread to Spain, Portugal, Russia – everywhere.'

The crowd roared, 'Islam! Islam!'

'We are not going to serve the Hindus, whose supreme god, Shiva, is a drug addict. And the goddess Kali – the naked black woman, drinking blood like a vampire – shows the cannibalism that still exists among them.'

The crowd shouted, 'Kaffir! Kaffir!'

Khodadad continued, 'Don't get side-tracked by Gandhi's so-called *ahimsa* – non-violence. The scripture he quotes constantly, the *Gita*, asks them to kill even relatives – grandfather, uncle, cousins – everyone – for power. Do you hear that – their religion asks them to kill their blood-relations for power? Do you think they will spare us if they ever rule Hindustan?'

The crowd screamed, 'We won't accept the Hindus.'

'Brothers! Don't be fooled by Gandhi.' Khodadad was now more eloquent than ever. 'We have nothing in common with the Hindus. That great son of Islam, Jinnah, has shown with his research that we are ethnically different from them, as the Europeans are. A Hindu is no closer to us than a European. In fact we have more in common with the Europeans than with the Hindus. So let us all unite our voices and say – we want Moslem rule back in India!'

The crowd roared – 'We want Moslem rule back in India!'

John had the police neatly positioned to tackle the highly charged crowd if need be. Fortunately his fears did not become reality. Apart from the crowd chanting slogans and roaming through the streets with Islamic Front banners, the afternoon, much to John's great relief, ended in relative peace. But he still had to think of Joshi's meeting.

TEN

I

Joshi's meeting was almost a repeat performance of the previous day's. His inflammatory speech about the conditions in which the Hindus had had to live during the Moslem rule, paying *jizya*, the tax which had been imposed only on religious grounds, fanned the high-pitched tension already generated by Khodadad Khan.

Just as the Moslems had done the previous day, the Hindus now marched through the streets with their saffron banners, chanting, 'Death to Jinnah! Death to Khodadad'. John was worried in case it provoked the Moslems. The very last thing he wanted was a riot on his hands. But fortunately the Moslems had calmed down and the shouting and screaming and hurling of insults by the Hindus did not provoke sufficient hostility for them to come out on the streets and take on their enemy. Not only John, but Banerji also breathed a sigh of relief when the tensions of the previous two days waned to a calmer atmosphere.

Though on the surface the disturbances subsided, the discord continued for longer than John had expected. Even in his own household he had a problem; Ibrahim and Jadu were at loggerheads – hurling insults at each other at the slightest provocation. Once when it came to fisticuffs, John, in no uncertain terms, warned them both that for such behaviour they would not only lose their jobs but might well end up in prison – he would not hesitate to put them behind bars if the situation warranted it. This put sufficient fear in their minds to restrain them from any future fracas. But the tension continued all the same.

The atmosphere in Raigarh was even worse – like a keg of gunpowder just awaiting the fuse to spark it off before a violent explosion blew the place to smithereens. John waited nervously for normality to return. For the time being, however, he was grateful that at least this level of peace could be maintained.

II

Holi, a major annual festival for the Hindus in Bihar, is a month-long affair. The celebration is to commemorate the love between Lord Krishna and Radha during their younger days in Brindaban, the lovers' paradise. This year, as in other years, the Hindus prepared themselves elaborately. The main activity was to jet thickly coloured water at one another at random – just for fun.

With the tension already high from Khodadad's and Joshi's demonstrations, John decided to take precautionary measures to ensure that the festival did not become a cause for a major riot. He issued strict instructions that on no account should this coloured water be thrown on anyone wearing clean clothes who did not wish to be part of the celebrations – neither a Moslem nor a Christian. Banerji had some posters printed in both English and the vernacular and had them hung in appropriate positions in the town. Warnings were also issued that any violation of this civil code would incur a stiff penalty – possibly even a prison sentence.

Both John and Banerji remained tense throughout, hoping the festival would pass without any severe disturbances. For a time, it seemed that the measures taken were yielding results. The main celebrations progressed without incident. If anything, they brought together the different ethnic groups as the Hindus offered sweetmeats to the Moslems who, for their part, merrily joined in the festivities. An altogether friendly atmosphere prevailed right through Raigarh much to John's relief.

The very last day of the festival that year fell on a Monday. The youngsters, who normally threw themselves into the celebrations with more vigour than anyone else, should have been exhausted after nearly a month of continuous merrymaking, but they showed no sign of wilting. They assembled on various street corners with their motley range of metal syringes and buckets filled with coloured water and indiscriminately squirted water at passers-by.

It was afternoon and everyone had gone home for lunch, leaving the hot, deserted street stained with a diversity of colours. A local Moslem trader decided to take the opportunity of this lull to set up his bullock cart and carry a cargo of cotton dresses to be delivered to the nearby market. Under normal circumstances he would not have taken the risk, but this year the Hindus had been behaving admirably, perhaps due to the Sahib's stringent measures. He had already taken a few cartloads during the festival without any incident.

The first part of the journey was uneventful. This gave him the courage to go through the Hindu quarters, so cutting down his journey by as much as three miles. After turning the corner by the Hindu temple, he caught sight of some boys chatting idly in the street. That did not bother him particularly as he had noticed the Hindu boys had been exercising considerable restraint this year.

But drawing nearer, he sensed a certain danger. Something in their expression prompted him to think that not everything was right. Frightened, he tried to turn the bullock cart round. But before he could manoeuvre it successfully, the boys, encouraged by his fear, chased him and emptied all their buckets. The thickly coloured liquid: blue, green, orange, red, were fast absorbed by the cotton goods. The trader was in tears. He prayed to the boys to spare his merchandise, because they were to earn him the whole year's livelihood for his family. His cry unfortunately fanned the boys' excitement as they poured on more and more colours.

One boy, remembering some of the phrases he had learned during Joshi's meeting, shouted, 'Death to Moslems'. Now they all shouted, 'Death to Moslems'. That was the last straw. The man could stand no more. In a rage he picked up a bamboo stick and tried to attack the gang leader.

Seeing a Moslem attacking a Hindu boy, men from the nearby houses promptly came out with whatever weapons they could lay their hands on. Soon a dozen or so men appeared with sticks, knives or pickaxes. The Moslem, suddenly realizing the extreme danger facing him, tried to run away. But he was not fast enough. Someone chased and grabbed him from behind; the others followed. One of them punched him on the face. Blood streamed from his nose as he prayed, 'Please! Please! Forgive me, *babu*. Please, spare my life. I have ten children. They will have no one to look after them.'

'What about our children you are trying to kill – you mother-fucker, son of a whore!' someone shouted.

'I did not try to kill him, *babu*. Allah's *kassam* – on God's oath!' he prayed. 'I know I lost my temper, *babu*. But you look – you yourself look!' He frantically tried to undo his merchandise to show how it was all spoilt. 'My whole year's livelihood's gone, I don't know how I am going to feed my children.'

'You hit him because he is a Hindu,' the man shouted at him accusingly.

'No *babu*, no! I have many Hindu friends. Believe me, I have! I have!' The trader nervously tried to remember a few Hindu names to give his claim credence.

The attacker did not even listen. He thumped the Moslem hard. The poor man fell down. Soon the Moslem grabbed the man's feet and desperately pleaded, 'You are my father, *babu*! You are my lord! For my children's sake, *babu*! Please spare my life! Please let me go!'

Someone suggested he had had enough punishment for whatever he had done and should be allowed to depart. For a moment, it seemed, everyone agreed. But as he was about to get back on to his bullock cart, a man from behind came with a knife shouting, 'You don't have to feed your children any more – I'm your Allah – I'm saving you from it,' and stuck the knife right through him. Blood came pouring from the gash. The Moslem once again held the man's feet and begged for mercy. 'If I die, they'll all die. Please don't kill me. I'll do anything you want me to do. Take everything I have. Just spare my life.'

His shrill, desperate voice, pleading for mercy, pierced the air but it stirred no remorse in his assailants. They now all joined in and butchered him to death, leaving his body lying on the road in a pool of blood.

The police soon arrived on the scene. They went from house to house, asking whether anyone had seen the killing. Everyone was frightened and uttered the same excuse – they had been indoors; they had been busy doing something or other; they had seen nothing; heard nothing. The boy who had been attacked by the Moslem could not be found anywhere.

When John heard the news, for a brief moment he almost panicked. He did not know how to respond to this mob rule – should he show strength, or would it create more problems? But he could not possibly allow the killing to go on – and such violent, ruthless killing. He asked the local police chief to keep the area under constant vigilance.

The news of two further killings was reported in the evening, this time from the Moslem quarter. Two Hindus, who had needed to go there on some business, had also been battered to death. The police patrol now moved to the Moslem area. Once again the local households denied any knowledge of the murder – they had seen nothing, heard nothing, did not know who had murdered the men.

The situation remained tense the following day, although no further incidents took place. The police imposed a curfew except for a couple of hours in the morning for the families to get their basic necessities. The PC 144 was also imposed.

That was Wednesday. On Friday life became downright dangerous in Raigarh. Dr Hassan, a Moslem who knew Banerji well and had heard about the riots, came to see whether his friend was all right. The doctor was anxious because Raigarh had a predominantly Moslem population. Banerji, surprised and touched by his friend's concern, asked him to stay on, though he was frightened in case the Hindus should come to know about his Moslem friend and attack his house – the anti-Moslem fever in the area was rising high. Finally to get out of the dilemma he decided to give Dr Hassan a police escort to take him out of town though he was not certain to what extent his friend would be safe even then because so much racial tension still existed. But at least it will relieve me of my responsibility, he thought.

His worst fears, however, came true. On Friday when the doctor was returning with the police escort, both men were ambushed on the road. The policeman, tied up with rope, was left, but the doctor's mutilated body was found dumped in a ditch.

III

It was not long before the news leaked out to the Moslem community that Banerji had been an accessory to the murder of his own friend – the friend who had actually come to see whether Banerji was safe.

'How could you possibly murder your *dosht* – the friend with whom you have shared your meal? *Nimakharam*!' they shouted in unison.

Their anger was not assuaged just by shouting. Posters appeared everywhere in the town – BANERJI IS A RACIST, ANTI-MOSLEM PIG! HIS HANDS ARE STAINED WITH MOSLEM BLOOD, HIS FRIEND'S BLOOD. BEWARE OF THOSE WHO TAKE THE VEIL OF FRIENDSHIP AND PUT A KNIFE IN YOUR BACK! Those posters alone were enough to put the wind up Banerji. But that was not all. Fresh posters appeared – KHOON KA BADLA KHOON CHAI – WE SEEK BLOOD FOR BLOOD: DEATH FOR DEATH.

The truth was that the Moslem community was deeply hurt by the news about Banerji. All these years, in spite of whatever Banerji's own racial feelings might have been, he had kept a general level of decorum in his behaviour towards the Moslems – one of fairness and justice. He was not like other Hindus who automatically looked down upon the Moslems as inferior beings. Nor did he believe that because they were Moslems they must be treacherous. In Moslem circles Banerji had been well respected. But now attitudes changed. The hurt feelings of the Moslems turned into passionate rage as they cried, 'Justice must be meted out to the murderer.'

The Moslems now planned a major demonstration to protest against Banerji's behaviour. The curfew and the PC 144 had been lifted a few days before when the atmosphere in the town had become calmer. A curfew was always necessary to bring a very tense situation back to normality; however it was never allowed to continue longer than necessary. John toyed with the idea of imposing a fresh curfew to prevent the possible outbreak of hostilities, and decided to seek Garvey's advice on the matter.

IV

'You're on a sticky wicket, old boy!' Garvey sounded concerned.

'What do you think I ought to do?' asked John, who was very nervous.

'Buck up, old chap! You can't quit in these matters you know. You have to damn well fight it through. And that's the essence of it.' Garvey tried to raise the young officer's spirits.

'It was all right until this incident with Banerji took place. I don't understand why on earth he allowed that man to go with just one policeman. That was really asking for trouble.' John was upset by Banerji's sheer stupidity.

'Some of these Indians have no common sense whatsoever,' Garvey tried to console him.

'But what do I do now? Do I go for a new curfew?' John asked anxiously.

'No, that won't work. It'll only create hostility among the Moslems. They'll immediately see it as proof of our support of Banerji.' Years of experience in India had taught Garvey when not to stoke a fire.

'But the man can't be thrown to hungry wolves.' John was irritated with his superior officer's apparent lack of sensitivity to the crisis he was facing.

'I'm not suggesting that, John.' For the first time Garvey sounded impatient. 'Don't become emotionally involved in the situation. That won't help anyone. What I'm advising is for you to ensure that peace is maintained at all costs.'

'But how do we do that?'

'It won't be achieved by supporting Banerji,' Garvey cautioned the young man. 'Of course, we don't want any harm done to him – no more than we want any harm done to any of the Moslems. They must also enjoy our protection. We can't afford to be seen as partisan in this religious conflict.'

'So what do you suggest?'

'I suggest you try to ride the storm.'

'You mean by doing nothing?' John was surprised. 'No! That way the whole thing will go out of control. We won't be able to maintain law and order any more.'

'Of course, we have to maintain law and order, old boy,' Garvey interrupted him. 'But there are various ways of doing it. One is by imposing a curfew – but that will immediately make them think we are trying to prevent their right to protest over a justified grievance; might even indicate we're scared of them.'

'So what is your advice then, sir?'

'Well, we have to show our strength. Strength must be matched with strength. We must show the muscle power of the Raj.'

'But how?' John did not understand what Garvey was trying to suggest.

'We'll flood the whole place with armed police,' replied Garvey. 'That'll do the trick.'

John was not altogether happy with the suggestion but he acquiesced to it. 'All right,' he said, 'if you can supply enough police, I'll follow your advice; I don't have a sufficient number to control that crowd.'

'That's not a problem,' Garvey assured him and then enquired, 'What's Banerji doing at the moment?'

'He's frightened to death.'

'Just give him a few days' leave. Ask him to stay at home until the trouble blows over. The sight of him moving in and out of the office is not perhaps conducive to bringing about peace.'

'Yes, sir. That's a good idea. I should have thought of it myself.'

John began to see the wisdom of his senior officer's suggestions.

Before John's departure Garvey touched his shoulder to reassure him. 'Keep your chin up, old boy!' the old functionary said. 'Don't forget, we're British, we'll win at the end of the day. We always win, whatever obstacles we face – that's our way, our tradition.'

This last bit of encouragement from Garvey helped to lift John's sagging confidence. He now felt sure that he would be able to combat whatever threat Khodadad and Joshi might impose.

V

The morning was abysmally hot when a strong police contingent arrived in Raigarh. Men, fully uniformed, carrying bayoneted Martini rifles on their backs and pistols holstered by their sides rode through the town. People gazed at them in awe. They had no doubt in their mind what the consequences would be if any violence broke out.

In the afternoon a large assembly of Moslems gathered in the football ground. The Hindus, not wanting any trouble, especially with so many police present, stayed indoors. This meeting, however, was different from the previous one, for this assembly was spurred not by the fanatical stirring of Khodadad, but by a subdued feeling of rage – a sense of injustice caused by the actions of a trusted Hindu friend. All the speeches ended on the same note of shock and grief.

The meeting closed with the burning of Banerji's effigy. Before this the crowd showed their venom by kicking it and chanting, 'Death to nimakharam – a betrayer of friends.' Apart from this, nothing untoward happened. People slowly dispersed and walked home in small groups. And to John's great relief they did not stage the threatened march to Banerji's house, which certainly would have caused riots.

John felt really indebted to Garvey for his invaluable advice. Garvey had been shrewd enough to know that the opposition could not be tamed simply because the Raj was strong; that strength must be displayed properly and unequivocally. Without doubt, the presence of the armed police patrolling the street had ensured peace that day.

ELEVEN

I

For a few days everything in Raigarh remained as if nothing had happened. The murders and agitation now seemed like distant nightmares. John and Banerji breathed sighs of relief. It had been a test of nerve for both of them and they had managed to scrape through by a whisker. Had conditions deteriorated further, they would not have known how to cope. For the time being, however, they enjoyed peace and felt as if the pre-riot days had returned.

John began to relax, at least temporarily. He could see the worst was over, although the existence of general tension still concerned him. But what could he do apart from trying to instil a semblance of normality in the daily routine of the Raj?

But the longer the peaceful period continued, the more he realized it was hanging by a very fragile thread. Deep down, the wound that had been opened was nowhere near healing. There existed an enormous amount of antipathy between the Hindus and Moslems. They no longer trusted each other as they had done before. If Jinnah had started the agitation for the Moslems, there was no doubt that Joshi completed it, almost as if he had assisted Jinnah's cause by stirring up the Hindus.

Things were not meant to be easy for John. As time went on some new faces appeared in the Moslem quarters, who often spent long hours in the chai khana, drinking tea and chatting to people. Soon they were seen being invited into people's homes. Nobody knew why they were there, for they were not engaged in any kind of employment as such, though they seemed to have plenty of spare cash to sprinkle about. There was something – something strange about them. They looked far more intelligent than the kind of people they were seen with – and then they had that carefree manner which comes with bags of self-confidence. The people of Raigarh lacked such self-confidence.

It was Banerji who first spotted them.

'I do not feel happy about these newly-arrived men roaming round the street, sir.'

'What's wrong with them? Who are they, anyway?' John enquired.

'They are not locals, sir. They look like miscreants – as if they are up to something sinister.'

'You mean dacoity?' John was concerned.

'No, sir. Not that sort. They look far more intelligent than dacoits,' Banerji replied, looking perturbed.

'Then what kind of sinister motive do you think they have?'

'I do not know, sir. It is only a feeling. I think they might be some kind of political activists – perhaps from a right-wing organization – I do not know, sir. But I do not like it.'

'Why on earth would anyone send political activists here of all places?' asked John. 'What do you think they would do anyway?' He could see that Banerji was frightened though for no apparent reason.

'I do not know, sir. I suppose they will start some trouble.'

'It's only your guess, Banerji,' John dismissed his anxiety.

'No, sir. I know this place. I am certain they are trouble-makers.'

'I'm afraid we can't do anything just on conjecture,' John replied firmly. 'There has to be much more than suspicion before we take action, otherwise we'll look complete fools.'

Banerji was unhappy with the Sahib's apparent lack of concern. He pleaded, 'Can't we arrest them? At least for questioning – to find out what they are up to?'

'On what charge?' asked John. 'We don't know that they're here to incite racial hatred.'

'I am absolutely certain, sir,' replied Banerji. 'They don't look the right sort of people.'

John was not convinced that Banerji's fear had any real foundation. He tried to reassure him by saying that, with the Rowlatt Act now repealed, he did not have the legal power to arrest anyone unless he could bring a charge against the culprit.

II

Banerji remained silent for a few days, but his mind was unsettled.

He was extremely unhappy with the way things were developing locally.

'Something is seriously wrong, sir,' Banerji complained again within a few days.

'What now, Banerji?' John asked.

'Some of these Moslems are getting obstreperous, sir.'

'It's all your imagination, Banerji,' replied John.

'No, sir. I have lived here a long time; they were never like this before.'

'It's not altogether a bad thing,' John tried to be rational. 'They used to be so down-trodden in the past. I know it won't help the Hindus, but a bit of a boost to their self-confidence won't do any one any harm.'

'You do not understand, sir,' Banerji said. 'I am sure they are up to something.'

John was irritated by Banerji's strange fears and responded sternly, 'If we arrest them because they might be up to some mischief, there'll be one thing for sure – riots. And we simply can't afford it.'

'Things are not right, sir,' Banerji persisted.

'I'm afraid we can't take any action just on suspicion,' John spoke firmly and then added, 'If you want me to do something you will have to produce concrete evidence.'

Banerji was quiet for a few more days. Then he came up with another story: that he had been followed at night by a few lads.

'Strange, sir. Not locals – I have never seen them before.'

'Point them out to me and we will pick them up for questioning. At least we can bring harassment charges against them,' replied John.

'Always someone different, sir – and I do not know any of them.'

'Are you sure it's not a figment of your imagination?' John could not hide his annoyance.

'No, sir, no! I am speaking the honest truth,' Banerji replied.

'Perhaps you're still edgy from the last riot. Would you like to take a few days off and go somewhere?'

'No, sir. I cannot go anywhere now. The harvest is coming soon – I have quite a bit of land round here.'

'There you are, rich man!' John teased him to lighten the atmosphere.

But Banerji did not respond. Wearing a serious face he said, 'With *Idd* coming soon I am very worried, sir.'

'You mean the Moslem festival next week?' John asked. 'Yes, I have been invited to attend the festivities.'

'You are not going though – are you, sir?' Banerji tried to be possessive.

'Why not? I go to your festival – don't I? I can't just turn round and say, sorry, my chief assistant is a Hindu, I'm not going to your festival.'

Banerji was hurt. He failed to understand how the Sahib could attend Moslem festivities and have fun with them when they were acting against him.

John could see from Banerji's eyes that he was offended. To reassure his subordinate he said, 'It's only for a brief period, to observe protocol. Don't worry, I shan't be spending the whole day there.'

Although John ignored Banerji's dismay, he too was aware of the new tension between the Hindus and Moslems and decided to keep the police on alert in case any trouble broke out. From his experience so far in India, he had found that there was more likelihood of racial disturbances during a religious festival than at any other time.

TWELVE

I

Every Sunday morning, since John had nothing much to do, he stayed in bed rather late. Occasionally to break the motonony he made a trip to the Station Club, but in those weeks he travelled on Saturday and spent the night at the Dak bungalow – the guest house in Sripore.

There was a small Anglican church not very far away, which he sometimes attended. As it was not like the Quaker meeting-house, that he had often attended as a child with his mother, the church did not evoke in him the same kind of feelings. But the Raj often expected its officers to attend church services to show to the locals that the Europeans were also religious and not godless. But since the riot John's mind had been preoccupied with the current problems and he found it more restful to spend his weekends alone – just lazing in Raigarh. In the afternoons he often went riding to the hills and the surrounding valleys which gave him a feeling of peace and tranquillity and soothed his nerves.

This Sunday was no exception. He was in bed, half daydreaming, when he heard a commotion at his front door. He could hear Ibrahim's determined voice, 'Sahib does not see anyone at this time on a Sunday. I will tell him that you called.' But the other voice was insistent, almost praying Ibrahim to let him in. There was a sense of desperation which John could detect even in his half-woken state. It was Banerji.

There must be an emergency, he thought. Ibrahim, like all other Moslems since the riot, was suspicious of the Hindu clerk. Whereas previously he would have allowed him in without even a murmur, now he realized that Banerji did not carry as much authority as he pretended to.

John, now fully awake, hurriedly picked up his dressing-gown and came out, rubbing his eyes. 'What's the matter, Ratan?'

Banerji immediately rushed towards him and broke into tears.

'What's the matter?' asked John, astonished by this outburst. The Indian could not utter a word. He cried tremulously, leaning his head on John's chest, tears rolling down his face. John, perplexed, asked Ibrahim to bring some tea and helped Banerji to sit on the wicker settee on the veranda.

Ibrahim soon brought the tea for them.

'No, sir! I cannot drink. I am feeling sick.' Banerji sobbed. It was obvious he had difficulty in breathing. Soon he started howling again. This time John was irritated. In a stern voice he said,

'Come on Ratan! Pull yourself together, man! Tell me what's the matter, so that I can help.'

'It's Kamala, sir.' Banerji's voice choked in tears.

'What's the matter with Kamala? Isn't she well?' There was anxiety in John's voice.

Banerji, his eyes bloodshot with tears, face distorted with pain, pathetically shook his head.

'What has happened? Tell me quickly!' John implored him.

'The Moslems, sir. They raped my daughter.'

'What?' John could not believe his own ears. A sense of cold fear engulfed him as Banerji's words sank in. Oh God! he thought. But why! Why! Why! Within a few seconds, however, he regained his composure and calmly asked the Indian, 'Where is she? At Hari's?'

Banerji nodded, still crying. 'We have to get a doctor to her as fast as possible.'

John called Jadu and asked him to take the carriage and fetch Father Fallon. 'Tell him it's an emergency. Don't come back without him under any circumstances. *Jaldi jao* – go quickly!' he commanded. Realizing the urgency of the situation, Jadu disappeared fast.

'Why don't we have this tea – then we shall go to Hari's,' John's voice was full of sympathy and concern for his subordinate. Anxious though he was to see Kamala himself, he thought Banerji was suffering from such intense emotional strain that a little diversion would help him.

II

Within a quarter of an hour John rode to Hari's house. A large crowd had gathered outside – men, women and children.

'*Hat jao* – move away!' he shouted, which made them quickly retreat to a few yards behind the trees and bushes. Inside the house there was a wailing crowd sitting in the courtyard – Hari's mother and some of her friends were uttering some repetitive, incomprehensible words and howling at the same time. Hari was sitting nearby, completely numb. As soon as he saw the Sahib, he turned his face in shame.

'Where's Kamala?' John asked. Hari stood up, a broken man, and silently led him to the bedroom.

Kamala was lying in bed with a white sheet covering her up to the neck. Her face was badly bruised and swollen. She turned her face and looked at him – a blank look – pale and cold, as if life had gone out of her for ever. It froze John's heart. He did not know what to say. He could not bring himself to utter a word of kindness or concern. After all it was he who was responsible. He was supposed to be there to protect her. Her and everyone else. How could he now utter hollow words full of false promises – offering care and protection? How could he look at her again?

But unlike Hari in the courtyard, full of shame, the Englishman's face was now filled with rage – a deep sense of guilt engulfed him for allowing such degradation to happen.

Fortunately Father Fallon came fairly soon and eased his anxiety a little. Fallon was cool and composed as always. He immediately assessed the situation and asked everyone to leave the room. Some of the women did so rather reluctantly, for they wanted to know the gruesome details of what exactly had happened to Kamala. But in John's presence they quickly had to obey the missionary doctor's orders.

'You can stay if you like, John. I may need help,' Fallon suggested.

'No!' A sharp and determined reply came from Kamala which took both the Europeans by surprise. John hurriedly left the room as if that piercing 'no' in some way accused him of his part in her humiliation.

Father Fallon took some time. Nervously John waited outside. When Fallon came out, he looked very distraught.

'Bastards!' he muttered in an enraged voice. 'At least eight men tortured her. Inhuman pigs!'

'How bad is it?' John asked, worried.

'It could have been worse. No permanent injury – as far as I can see, but she will require hospital treatment.'

'I'll arrange for her to go to Sripore hospital. They have much better facilities there.'

'I'm afraid I have to rush, John,' Father Fallon somewhat guiltily announced. 'There're quite a few urgent cases I have to attend. Moreover, there's nothing else I can do really. I have given her sedatives. They will make her sleep.'

'Thank you for your help, Father.'

Fallon gave a sad smile. On any other day he would have said, 'It's my job to help people', but today those words seemed so empty that he could not bring himself to utter them.

John decided to take Kamala to Sripore himself. He knew that that was the only thing he could do to even partially atone for the stupendous sin that had been committed against this young girl. Until now she had had so much happiness; in just one night it had all been obliterated from her life through humiliation, pain and suffering. But little did the young officer realize that the humiliation, pain and suffering he saw at the time was merely a wisp of smoke from a colossal volcano.

John stayed at the hospital for a while until the preliminary examination was over. Fortunately Kamala's injuries were superficial, though she had been badly mauled. That news at least offered him some relief.

III

On the way back he decided to call in on Garvey.

'Why are you here?' Garvey asked coldly, as soon as he saw him.

'Someone was raped in my locality last night. I brought her here to the hospital.'

'That's not your job. You're not an ambulance driver – you're a DO. You're behaving like a stupid fool and I don't like fools.'

John kept quiet. It was pointless arguing with Garvey. The old functionary knew only the rules – not the finer points in life.

'If I were you, I would go back double-quick.' Garvey spoke with urgency. 'A major riot has broken out in Raigarh. The Hindus are on the rampage: looting, burning, killing. Take some extra police with you and let me know the situation tonight. You may well have to be ruthless. The riot must be stopped. And go now!'

John ashamedly went back to his carriage and drove to the police chief to organize more policemen. He realized that in his eagerness to help Kamala, he had somehow neglected his responsibility as a DO. But the event had been so overwhelming that he had responded as any normal human being would have done. But now he was filled with remorse at the news of this fresh riot.

The scene when John arrived in Raigarh that evening was absolutely devastating. Literally every house was burning. The sky which normally would have looked dark at this late hour was deep orange, covered by billowy, black smoke ascending in spirals. There were dead bodies everywhere on the street, which looked just like a battlefield – cold corpses mutilated and strewn about, were lying in pools of coagulated blood, arms and legs stretched, faces completely horror struck, some bodies had been decapitated, or their limbs cruelly severed with a ruthlessness that a man would not use on a pig. A nauseating smell of rotting carrion had already begun to fill the air. The damage that had been done – not just in terms of property or community relations but also in suffering and pain – was enormous. John realized there was no room for sentimentality now. His most urgent task was to quell the riot as swiftly as possible whatever the price. Anything would be preferable to allowing this carnage to continue unabated.

As John rode through the street he could hear noises of battle coming from both the Hindu and Moslem quarters. '*Har Har Mahadeo!*' the Hindus were screaming, followed by '*Allaho Akbar*' from the Moslems. The young man's heart suddenly filled with complete revulsion against India, against Gandhi, even against the Raj.

This was no time for reflection. John ordered the police to open fire on sight on any miscreant, whoever he may be, who was trying to kill, maim, rape or set fire to any property. 'Set an example,' he told his police officers, 'so that this madness is never repeated again in these parts. So that people here know what the punishment will be if they flout law and order in future. We are here to govern, and govern we shall, in the best way we know. Nobody will be allowed to disrupt it. Not even Mr Gandhi.'

THIRTEEN

I

The tough action John took that evening, so uncharacteristic of him, nonetheless quelled the riot the following day. A few skirmishes continued for the next forty-eight hours, but for all practical purposes the riot was over that very evening when John told his men to open fire. 'Shoot on sight if you find a miscreant,' he ordered. 'No sympathy, no emotion, no kindness.' Whatever sympathy he once had, and he had had plenty, had been killed off during his time in India by Gandhi and his agitation. We are not wanted here, he thought. Fair enough! It's strictly speaking not our country. But what a way to go about it – killing each other. And in that way! John would now never be able to forgive Gandhi and Jinnah for causing this utter humiliation to Kamala. An innocent girl and so full of life – she had to go through hellish nightmares as a pawn in the power struggle.

The casualty figures were heavy – one hundred and eight killed of which eighteen died of bullet wounds from the police; the others were just hacked to death like those whose mutilated, decapitated bodies John had witnessed on the way back from Sripore.

The Raigarh incident was horrific enough for it to gain national attention. Despite the mass killings, it was the fact that eighteen people died of bullet wounds from the police which agitated prominent nationalist newspapers. The headlines did not unduly perturb John. He knew from past experience that newspaper reporters, like vultures, marked time in near passivity until a calamity occurred and when it did, they promptly grabbed the opportunity and reported in infinite detail – exhibiting their prowess in describing horrific incidents. In India in the early twenties horror-seeking reporters had endless opportunities as monstrous events took place in abundance.

But even for them the Raigarh incident was special, owing to the fact that an officer of the Raj was so deeply embroiled in it. These newspaper reports were so sensationally written that they immediately fanned anti-Raj feeling among the public. Political parties, always eager to make capital out of any event, soon instigated demonstrations in Patna and Calcutta, demanding John Sugden's immediate removal from his post. The brutal officer of the Raj who needlessly killed so many must go, they said.

This did not upset John as much as a new twist of events when the local Congress chief, Jay Prasad, sought an interview with him. Apparently Gandhi, who had been released from prison only a few days before, wanted to visit the riot-torn town of Raigarh. The young officer was already stretched to the limit of his patience and this was the last straw. He could take no more. All the same, acknowledging Gandhi's power to incite mass revolt, he granted Jay Prasad an interview to discuss Gandhi's proposed visit, though in all honesty he would have preferred no further disturbance in the area. Gandhi's presence at this moment, he thought, would only provoke mass hysteria.

'I have no objection to Mr Gandhi's visit,' John said curtly when he met Jay Prasad, 'but there is to be no demonstration, no riots. I won't hesitate to put down another riot with the same ferocity as the last one.'

Jay Prasad calmly listened to John and then replied, 'Mahatmaji preaches non-violence as you know, Mr Sugden. And so many deaths in a comparatively small town are a matter of national concern.'

John was not prepared to listen to this diatribe from the Indian. He said, 'If you Congresswallahs had kept out of it, this would never have happened.'

'With all due respect, Mr Sugden,' Jay Prasad replied firmly, 'the Congress had nothing to do with it, and I will not allow you to make baseless allegations. I know the British government is eager to lay every bit of blame on the Congress.'

'But Gandhi's hands aren't clean,' John said accusingly. 'His people, the *satyagrahis*, the non-violent vanguards of Christ's message as he proudly boasts, burnt to death twenty-two policemen in Chauri Chaura.'

'There was provocation from the police, Mr Sugden. But those deaths were very unfortunate.' Jay Prasad maintained his cool.

'So when Gandhi commits violence – it's just unfortunate! That's what you are saying!' The young officer was pungent in his questioning.

'Mahatmaji immediately called off the *hartal*, as you know,' Jay Prasad replied defensively and then added, 'To ensure that no further killing took place, he went on fasting for five days.'

'I'm not interested in his penance and fasting,' John rudely dismissed Jay Prasad's claim and then showed his unhappiness about Gandhi's visit in no uncertain terms by saying, 'Everything is peaceful now – what's Gandhi's reason for coming to Raigarh?'

'Mahatmaji has concern for the people here. He has a major hold both on the Hindus and Moslems. He is the only leader, the only man in the country who can unite them.'

'Rubbish!' John snorted at Jay Prasad. 'He's coming here to seek publicity. More newspaper coverage, more pictures of him walking through the town, talking to Moslems and Hindus, asking them about atrocities – that's what he's after.'

'No sir,' Jay Prasad replied arrogantly, 'Mahatmaji does not court publicity.'

This incensed the officer. He shouted, 'Gandhi doesn't have to come to Raigarh if he really wants to see the devastating effect of this racially instigated riot. He can see it in the Indian hospital in Sripore! A girl, a young girl, only eighteen, married, very happily married, the wife of one of my subordinates, whose wedding I attended – she is now lying in the hospital in pain. Eight men brutally raped her – one after another – can you imagine anything more horrific?'

'These things have been happening recently with Jinnah inciting racial violence and the British government supporting him to discredit Mahatmaji and the Congress,' Jay Prasad tried using a political excuse and then added, 'In fact, if you don't mind me saying so, Mr Sugden, these riots are all your doing. If you really want peace, the best thing will be for the government to let the Congress run this country.'

'What!' John snorted. 'I don't believe you can run this place. The moment we leave, violence, rape and killing will wreck not just Raigarh, but the entire country. You don't have the ability to run this place! You have no ability to build! None whatsoever! You know only how to destroy. Gandhi knows only how to burn foreign clothes.'

'I'm not here to listen to a lecture,' Jay Prasad interrupted him sternly. 'Mahatmaji will come to visit Raigarh next week. If you want to stop him, you will have to arrest him. But he warned – if you try to do that, the whole place will explode. You are not a very popular person in this country any more, Mr Sugden.'

When Jay Prasad left that day, John realized that the cunning Indian was right. John really did not have the power to stop Gandhi. Nobody had the power in India to stop Gandhi. Although the government with much trepidation imprisoned him from time to time, the Raj was afraid of him. He could do anything he liked – literally anything – including sending the Raj off back to Britain tomorrow, lock stock and barrel. If John had once thought that the Raj would continue even into the next century, he had to revise his opinion now. It could be a matter of a few years – might only be months – before Britain had to quit. But leaving power to Gandhi and Jinnah! The very thought made him shudder in fear as he envisaged the calamity that would follow in the aftermath.

II

The next Sunday morning Gandhi's people organized a prayer meeting in Raigarh. The Congress workers had come the previous day and put up a temporary structure as a dais and fenced off the football ground for crowd control. John had to admit that the work was done more efficiently than he would have supposed the Congresswallahs to be capable of.

Following Garvey's advice John kept a low profile. 'While Gandhi's in Raigarh, there will be no riots,' Garvey said grudgingly. 'The man has the devil's power to keep people calm and peaceful. So the police presence is really superfluous. But we don't want him to think that he runs the place, for he doesn't. We do!' John was unhappy not to have more police, but he obeyed the instruction.

The morning was warm. And when the sun came out at seven o'clock the place was crammed with people. Not just Hindus – but Moslems, Christians, untouchables – everyone was there. The overspill of the crowd spread to the nearby streets, on to the roofs of the houses, verandas, and up in to the trees. There was nothing but a sea of human faces eagerly awaiting the man they trusted – their Gandhi Maharaj.

About ten o'clock in the morning when the sun was blazing hot, Gandhi finally arrived in a carriage. Everyone by then had been waiting for hours in the hot sun – just for the privilege of seeing their revered leader. The crowd became excited as he got down from the carriage. People started pushing and shoving one another to get a better view. Soon the specially recruited, Gandhi-capped Congress volunteers, already well accustomed to controlling large crowds, made sure that people did not become too unruly for their leader's safety.

As Gandhi climbed up to the rostrum, the crowd roared, 'Mahatmaji *ki jai* – triumph to Mahatmaji! Gandhi Maharaj *ki jai!*' A thin, unassuming figure stood there wearing only a loin-cloth, but majestic in his authority, mesmeric in his presence. Hindus, Moslems, Christians – they all joined in wishing victory to their prophet – their Mahatmaji. Even John was spellbound by the spectacle, especially in such a riot-torn town.

The Mahatma held his hand high to calm the crowd. He did not make a speech but instead read selected passages from the Gita, the Koran and the Bible. And then at the end he chanted a devotional song, almost like a hymn, in which everyone joined. It was a glorious sight – Hindus and Moslems forgetting for once their caste, creed, religion, prejudices, taboos – just sitting together and adding their voice to the chant of their king – for peace, for friendship, for love.

In spite of all his previous misgivings, John was impressed by this little man and his charismatic power. He remembered what Father Fallon had said to him the other day. 'Gandhi is not just a political leader, he is a social leader, a religious leader – he's their king in the true sense of the word – not a distant monarch who never set foot in India. Gandhi is their emperor who gives them confidence, power, sympathy and love.' How could anyone quarrel with a man like him? Or incarcerate him? That would be incarcerating life itself! John now began to suffer from utter confusion.

III

Raigarh became quiet after Gandhi's visit, as if he had brought a sense of shame to both the Hindus and Moslems. Somehow he transmitted to them this superior spiritual aura, a kind of atavistic belief that men, all men, are here for a common goal, a common purpose, sharing each other's joy and sorrow, hope and disappointment, pleasure and suffering. It was almost a miracle.

John had heard from his mother the stories about the Quaker, George Fox – how he preached of the inner light and shared with people the experience of his direct contact with God. Gandhi in a way gave John that very experience as if George Fox himself, resurrected, were sharing his inner light. As if Gandhi were only a form, a medium, through which to reach the ultimate goal.

Although the situation eased in Raigarh and everything returned to normal – people once again laughing, joking, Hindus and Moslems sharing the common niceties of daily life – John remained highly perturbed. Ever since his arrival in India he had only one target, one aim – to uphold the Raj: its supreme influence, its extraordinary efficiency, its superior intellectual and spiritual aura. Now it all seemed so pointless. If a seemingly ordinary man, not Lord Reading, the Viceroy, nor Edwin Montagu, the Cabinet Secretary, not even His Royal Majesty, George V, King and Emperor, but a man draped in a loin-cloth like the poorest of the poor, could instantaneously bring peace to this enormous, feuding population of three hundred million people and capture the soul, the inner spirit of every human being, he must be the king, not anyone else. Definitely not the British Raj. And if that was the case, what was John doing in India? Why should a Balliol graduate sacrifice his young life away from home, family, known environment and security and waste it in a distant land of heat, dust, mosquitoes, disease and every conceivable inconvenience, if there were to be no purpose in it at all? Suddenly his entire dream of serving India, serving the people of India was shattered to smithereens from which he could not salvage even the minutest speck to treasure as a happy memory.

IV

'Get that silly idea out of your mind, old boy. We are here for a purpose. We're needed here,' Garvey boomed in his usual domineering fashion.

'I am no longer sure, sir. I no longer feel confident that our presence in India is really necessary,' John Sugden feebly responded to his superior officer's assertion.

'What do you mean? What you are saying is almost seditious.'

'I know, sir, I know,' John sounded weary. 'When I saw Gandhi in front of that crowd, reading from the Gita, Koran and Bible, and they, enthralled, mesmerized, absorbing every word he uttered, it seemed as if the Messiah had once again come down to take away all the suffering of this earth by the sheer magic of his power, I feel weak and powerless, sir. I've just lost my zest to live here and fight him.'

'But you don't understand! He's an evil force! You yourself saw how he created frenzy in Calcutta, stirring up that mob to burn clothes in the maidan. How could a man like him be compared to the Messiah? That must be the biggest joke you're telling me, John.' Garvey was surprised by his young subordinate's despondency.

'I know, sir, I know,' the young man replied. 'I was extremely unhappy about him then. But now I can see what he is trying to do. He is bringing confidence into India – into the spirit and soul of the common people. He is saying – ignore the Raj; be independent of them in all aspects of life. He is saying – don't just fight to remove the rulers, but show them, demonstrate to them that their presence in your life is completely superfluous. By burning Lancashire-made fabrics and making people spin their own clothes he is bringing to them both the pain and the pride of being an independent nation – a nation which could stride alongside Britain – not as a servant to a master but as an equal.'

'You're just talking rubbish now.' Garvey was not prepared to listen to this kind of statement from a young officer.

'No, sir, I am convinced,' John replied with sadness written all over his face. 'If any one is holding a ray of hope for ordinary Indians – it's Gandhi, not us.'

'What are you talking about?' Garvey blurted out. 'You know it's Gandhi who created the entire problem. He's the main instigator. He taught people to defy authority, defy the police, defy law and order. What's more, he made that act of defiance religious, pure, godly. Everyone now thinks there is pride in defying the police, undermining authority. He is making villains out of ordinary, law-abiding, peaceful citizens.'

'Yes, you're right, sir,' replied John. 'But only because he is declaring our law, our morality, even our civilization unjust.'

'But what has he got to offer instead?' Garvey snorted. 'His people are still prejudice-ridden. There are fifty million people, one sixth of the population, deprived of basic human rights, who don't even have the opportunity to enter a temple and worship. Can you imagine this happening in any Christian society?'

'But he is doing more than we are to improve their lot,' replied John.

Garvey was taken aback by his junior officer's statement. Somewhat defensively he said, 'You know we can't meddle in their internal, quasi-religious matters.'

'If we, the Raj, the protector of human rights, shun that responsibility, and one of their own people takes it upon himself to do something about it – what are we here for?' John uttered these words as if he was asking that question of himself.

Garvey was surprised by the intensity of John's passion. But he was a shrewd administrator – skilled in man-management. He thought it prudent not to provoke his young subordinate any more. He tried to lighten the atmosphere by saying, 'I see these riots have really affected you. Take a holiday, old boy. Go to Calcutta and have some fun.'

John realized that in his moments of despair he had perhaps revealed far too much of himself. Garvey after all was his superior officer – a well-oiled wheel of the Raj. Garvey could perhaps accept a temporary lapse in his subordinate's loyalty, but not a full-blown rebellion. Wisely John decided to change the subject and he started talking about Anil Saha and his silly habits. They both now became less tense and peace was restored.

V

While John was confused about the role of the British Raj in India, he was also concerned about Kamala. He had not visited the hospital in spite of a certain inner urge to go and see her, because of propriety. But he did contact the senior administrator in the hospital from time to time to enquire about her recovery and the report so far was satisfactory.

A major shock, however, was not very far off. One day when Hari came to his office to get a few official papers signed, John asked rather jovially, 'When does your wife come home, Hari? I hear that she's recovering well.'

There was an awkward moment as Hari dropped all his papers on the floor. His face, normally pale by Indian standards, blanched completely and he darted out of the room. John was highly surprised – not just by his disrespectful behaviour, but the way he reacted as if he had seen a ghost.

Banerji soon entered. John could not hide from him his annoyance. 'What's the matter with Hari? I asked him about Kamala, he dropped all the papers and ran out of the room. Is he still suffering from the incident?'

'There's a problem, sir.'

'What problem?' John asked.

'About Kamala, sir,' replied Banerji.

'What about Kamala? I understand that she's recovering well. Of course, after that terrible ordeal, it'll take her some time to get back to normal. That's inevitable.'

Banerji heaved a sigh, rather a sad one, and then continued, 'You see, sir, Hari can't take her back.'

'What do you mean – Hari can't take her back?' John was surprised and shocked.

'You see, sir, she won't be able to bear any children for him now.'

'But I understand she's all right. Nothing damaged physically.'

'It's not that, sir,' Banerji was hesitant. 'You see, sir, in our custom if a woman sleeps with another man, she is no longer accepted by society.'

'What're you talking about?' John was utterly amazed by Banerji. 'She hasn't slept with anyone,' he shouted. 'She was bloody well raped by the bastards!'

'It's the same thing, sir,' replied Banerji. 'In the eyes of our society, she has lost her purity.'

'Good God!' snorted John. 'I've never heard so much rubbish in my life.'

'The thing is, sir, if Hari accepts her, he will be ostracized by the community; nobody will come to his house, talk to him or invite him to any gathering.'

'But he's her husband. He has a commitment to her. He just can't shake her off like that!' said John passionately. 'And anyway, it's his bloody fault that he couldn't protect his wife – not that I am blaming him for it – but if anyone's to be blamed, it's him.'

'I know, sir,' Banerji replied calmly. 'But our society is very orthodox – it is not like yours. You are much more free than we are. You do not have the same superstition, the same taboos that we have.'

'I suppose you have to take her back now. Poor creature!' John's voice was full of empathy. 'Will she be able to marry again?' he asked.

Banerji became mute for a while then mumbled almost inaudibly, 'There's a problem, sir.'

'What do you mean?' John was beginning to get anxious, sensing he was about to hear something abominable.

'You see, sir, I have two other daughters. I have to think of their families, their problems.'

'I don't understand you, Banerji.' John was completely baffled.

'Well!' Banerji hesitated again. 'If Kamala comes back, I will be ostracized by the community. Nobody will ever come to my house or share a meal with me.'

John, alarmed, shouted, 'Now! Now! I'm getting totally confused. What are you saying, Ratan? Neither Hari nor you will have her back?'

Banerji, highly embarrassed, remained silent.

'So what is she going to do?'

Banerji took time to consider his reply, then feebly answered, 'I don't know, sir. Perhaps she could get a job as a maid somewhere, in some distant village where they do not know about the incident.'

'Come, come, Ratan!' John said passionately. 'You're an educated man. She's young, she's beautiful, and she doesn't know the ways of the world – where would she go alone? She would need someone to look after her.'

Banerji did not reply. Suddenly a thought flashed through

John's mind which made him tense with revulsion. 'You dirty swine! You son of a bitch!' he screamed. 'I know exactly what you want your daughter to do – to go to a distant village and become a whore – don't you? Good Lord! You're her father. Don't you have any affection – love for her? How could you force your own flesh and blood to become a street woman?'

Banerji remained silent – almost like a dumb, inert, stony Buddha.

'I beg you, Banerji! I beg you! Don't do this to your daughter!'

Banerji this time spoke rather philosophically. 'Sir, in India we believe in destiny. They say God comes on the fourth night after a child is born to write on her forehead her destiny. We offer Him sweets, keep a lamp burning, so that He can see what He is writing. But none of us has any power to change it. We cannot change our destiny. I cannot change Kamala's destiny even if I try.'

John was horrified by Banerji's repulsive philosophy. But he slowly recovered and then in a sad voice said, 'All these years I often wondered why a race so talented as yours with so much knowledge, wisdom and ability could come under our domination. Or for that matter under the Moslems for nearly a thousand years. Now I know – I know for sure. In spite of all your intellect you haven't been able to shake off your basic insecurity. You are turning away from life in the fear that death will otherwise punish you. You are spending your whole life in fear and nothing else. And that's your downfall. Deep down you are a very sick society. I no longer envy Gandhi. He has an awful lot to do to make this country civilized – civilized enough to see life in the spirit of human love – in the spirit of Christ.'

VI

That afternoon John rode to Sripore to see Kamala in the hospital. Her eyes lit up on seeing him, but only for a moment. A blanket of sadness soon engulfed her face.

'I have sad news for you, Kamala,' John nearly choked as he uttered the words.

She turned her face and looked blankly at the sky. And then with a sigh she said, 'I know! I knew it that very night when it happened. It's no one's fault – just my destiny.'

John hesitated for a moment and then rather nervously asked,

'Why don't you come and stay at my house? Ibrahim and Jadu are always quarrelling. I could do with someone like you to keep things in order.'

Kamala looked at John – a look of affection mixed with gratitude. Then slowly she murmured, 'Sahib, you are a kind person. But why should you take me in? If my destiny is to become a street-girl, you may, by taking me in, bring God's wrath upon you.'

'Listen!' John said firmly. 'I didn't give you all those books to read so that you could come back at me with this life-denying Hindu superstition of "destiny". I'm appalled by your father – but I'm definitely not accepting it from you.'

Kamala remained silent for a very long time. Then suddenly her eyes glistened with tears as she murmured, 'Sahib, you are kind. You are very very kind. I have never met anyone like you before.'

PART THREE

The Seven Steps

FOURTEEN

I

Kamala found it rather strange to live under the same roof as the Sahib. It was not the first time she had been in his bungalow. Soon after her wedding she had come here once, of course with Hari, when the Sahib had invited the newly-married couple to tea. But that was different. Coming here as a visitor and living here – there is a gulf of difference – so she thought.

It was a very large bungalow – much larger even than her own father's place. In front of the house an extensive lawn, kept beautifully green, was surrounded by high brick walls. A red brickdust path from a heavy iron gate divided the lawn and led on to the portico, on both sides of which were wide verandas. On the left where the veranda was sometimes used as an outdoor lounge-cum-dining room there were wicker settees and chairs, a large coffee-table, a couple of rocking-chairs enveloped in tiger hides and a chaise-longue which the Sahib often used in the evening to relax; a little further up stood a dining-table and chairs. To add to the general ambience of the place the Sahib had placed flowerpots with a great variety of flowers. These many-coloured blooms made the veranda look almost like a pretty garden.

Through the entrance there was a spacious hall and beyond it the lounge, which was expensively furnished with leather settees and chairs, marble coffee-tables, almirahs with glass panels adorned with much bric-à-brac and many foreign paintings on the wall. In the farthest corner of the room was a bar, which displayed colourful bottles of wines and spirits. The sight of the bar frightened Kamala a little. Coming from a Hindu household she was not used to seeing people drinking openly.

Beyond the lounge there was a sizeable library with a wide range of books – novels, encyclopedias, books on travel, poetry, science and literature, books by all her favourite authors – Kipling, Robert Louis Stevenson, Alexander Dumas, Victor Hugo. The books were all neatly dusted, as were the oak tables and chairs in the library.

Next to the library was the Sahib's bedroom which Kamala had seen only from a distance. Adjacent to his room was a spacious guest-room with a bathroom ensuite. The room was expensively furnished with a four-poster, a dressing-table and chairs, wardrobes and of course paintings on the walls.

To the left of the lounge was the dining-room with a large rosewood dining-table and chairs which could accommodate as many as twenty or so guests. And next to the big table, for daily use, were a small dining-table, also of rosewood, and chairs. Only on important occasions, when many guests were invited, was the big dining-table set.

The dining-room overlooked the large garden, which was beautifully tended with a wide range of flowers and a rock-garden and decorated with marble statues of semi-naked European men and women. Beyond the garden there were various orchards but they were quite long way away.

The kitchen was next to the living-room. It was enormous, though not readily visible from outside because of the portico on the one side and the dining-room on the other. Although sandwiched between the walls, the room was not dark, for it had a skylight and dormer windows. To the left of the dining-room there were four other guest-rooms, all with bathrooms ensuite, but these were not used much because the Sahib rarely had visitors.

Beyond the guest-rooms was a long corridor which led to the servants' quarters where twenty-four servants and maids who were engaged to perform various household duties lived. They of course had a separate entrance so that they did not have to use the main entrance under the portico. A little distance away from the servants' quarters were the stables, where half a dozen horses were kept. And beyond the stables was the cowshed. The whole set-up was luxurious and very different from the way Kamala had lived.

When Kamala had first arrived the question of where she was going to stay had to be resolved. The Sahib did not want her to live in the servants' quarters and had been quite adamant about it. Kamala therefore decided to settle herself in one of the guest rooms next to the corridor leading to the servants' quarters – or as far away from the Sahib as possible without disobeying him, for she did not want to be in the way of the Sahib nor of the servants. This seemed a satisfactory arrangement even for the servants because, although they did not dare to say anything, they would not have liked Kamala to live with them. First, she was a Brahmin, and second, for whatever reasons, no one felt quite safe with her living close by after the recent incident.

Until her ordeal Kamala had always led a very sheltered life, first at her parents' well-to-do establishment and later at her husband's, not so affluent but comfortable all the same. Both these households, however, were orthodox and brahminic. Banerji and Hari, in spite of their English education, had never discarded their roots. Every morning they spent hours sitting in front of the images of Hindu gods and goddesses, saying prayers, chanting mantras, offering fruits and flowers in the same way as they did to the officers of the Raj – to gain favours – either in this life or at least in the next.

Coming from that background, Kamala had been so accustomed to worshipping that at first she felt uneasy in a Christian household where they had no image of any kind to worship. John being rather godless in that respect did not even attend church, at least not regularly. And the Indian religious festivals were to him a source of great amusement. Not that he had any disrespect for them but these religious practices were totally alien to his culture.

But within a few days Kamala found Jadu had some images in his room and soon sought his permission to go there every morning and say her prayers. When John came to know of this he was rather amused and in a way surprised by the fact that in spite of all her suffering she had not lost her faith in God.

'You surprise me, Kamala,' John said to her one day. 'How could you still have faith in God?'

'Please don't say that, Sahib,' Kamala replied. 'God is the supreme power. It's only for Him that we live on this earth. And see how He provides everything for us – the beautiful sunshine, cool water, blue sky, crops from the soil, fruits in the tree, flowers in the garden.'

'How can you be so forgiving?' asked John.

'Who am I to forgive, Sahib? I only lead my life in the way God wants me to.'

'But you have had to face such abuse. And not only that – your close relatives – your husband and parents have disowned you through no fault of your own.'

Kamala fell silent for a moment. She looked sad. Then in a distant voice she said, 'You don't know Hindu society, Sahib. My husband and parents have no choice. Our society does not accommodate a misfortune such as mine. They think it came upon me because I must have committed some grave sin in the past – perhaps in my previous incarnation – for which God's punishment was due. And if God decides to punish me, they are not to make it easy.'

'Rubbish! Absolute rubbish!' John snorted. 'I don't believe in the kind of God who could mete out that kind of punishment.'

'Oh, please, Sahib!' Kamala rushed and put her soft hand on his mouth and implored, 'Don't be blasphemous!' But that was a spontaneous reaction for which she blushed and hurriedly ran away.

That evening John asked Jadu to get whatever images Kamala would like and set them in her room so that she did not have to go to him for her prayers.

II

At Kamala's insistence Jadu arranged a small kitchen for her next to her room. And this made her immensely happy, for she now had something to do rather than sitting about feeling depressed and watched her day slowly drift aimlessly by. Often though she told the Sahib that she accepted her destiny and with it all the humiliations, in her moments of despair she knew in the bottom of her heart that that was not the truth. Like all other women, she also wanted a husband – she also wanted children – she also wanted to watch them grow as all human beings do to be fulfilled.

Then there was another thing. Although she had never been madly in love with Hari, they were compatible enough to live in relative peace and harmony. In a strange way she often pitied him because he was such a weakling – not like the Sahib who was so strong that he could defy everything, every authority if he thought the defiance to be justified. But then the Europeans could afford to be strong. They were basically so independent, so full of confidence in their righteousness, so definite in their judgement. Imagine an Indian shouting 'rubbish' as the Sahib had done the other day when she had talked about her destiny bringing all her misfortunes.

In spite of everything she was still fond of Hari. She had missed him ever since the ordeal. And the worst part of it was that she missed him in bed. Sleeping alone all night, every night, became too much, especially as every so often she suffered from hellish nightmares – the nightmares of dark forces – grabbing her, holding her and then forcibly devouring her. She would cry in pain and agony, pleading with them over and over again to leave her, to have mercy on her, but the ruthless brutes would not listen. Some nights her heart-rending cries were so intense that even the Sahib would wake up and ask one of the maids to go and attend to her.

After a while the Sahib suggested a maid should sleep close by, which Kamala firmly refused because she did not want anyone else to know all her secret feelings, her acute tragedy, her passion. But the Sahib was not happy. He asked her to move to the guest room nearer to him, so that if ever anything were to happen, he would at least be able to help her readily. She gave this proposal a lot of thought. And finally she decided to say 'yes', for she trusted the Sahib. Moreover, the Sahib roused in her a strange sense of strength, a completely inexplicable strength which she so badly needed.

Under normal circumstances of course it would not have been respectable for her to live like that – so close to a man with no one to keep an eye on them. But she knew that she now had no honour left. And as for the Sahib, no blame ever touched the Europeans. Many of them had Indian women living with them until they were married.

III

From the time Kamala started doing her own cooking, John was tempted to sample her culinary talents. One day just as a joke he teased her that she was preparing all these marvellous Hindu dishes and not sharing them with him. 'The lovely smell of your cooking is really whetting my appetite – aren't you ever going to invite me to share it with you?'

'Oh Sahib, you make me feel mean! Of course I will!' replied Kamala. 'But these are very ordinary Hindu dishes, nothing compared with Ibrahim's – not rich and spicy.'

'Do you know, my mother always cooked plain dishes and I loved them as a child.'

'Perhaps when you go to England on furlough she will cook lots of lovely dishes for you.'

John heaved a sigh and then said, 'I'll never again have that opportunity I'm sad to say. She died a long time ago. My father's remarried now.'

Kamala remained silent for a while. Then with grief in her face she said, 'For men it's always all right. Nothing ever touches them. For women – they go through agony after agony.'

John sensed her sadness. He also remembered how he had felt when his father for the first time mentioned marrying Joyce Wilson, the Quaker woman from Chalfont St Giles whom his father had met through his mother at the Friends' Meeting-House in Jordans, and who came to comfort the old man after his mother's death.

'Yes, I was very upset when my father remarried soon after mother's death, especially as she died in strange circumstances.'

'Why! What happened to her?' asked Kamala. She was surprised.

'That's a long story.' John tried to avoid the subject, but Kamala was insistent, for she felt the Sahib had an unhappy memory somewhere in his life and she wanted to know. 'Won't you tell me?' she asked.

John paused for a while and then replied, 'She was burnt to death.'

'Good God! Did she commit suicide?' Kamala was shocked by his words.

'We believe she was murdered,' replied John.

'Whatever for?' cried Kamala. She could not imagine murders taking place in a country like England.

'We don't know for sure,' John said sotto voce, wondering whether to share with her his deeper thoughts and feelings. For a long time he had not done so with anyone. After a while he said, 'Do you really want to hear?'

'Please tell me!' Kamala implored.

John took his time. Kamala waited patiently, looking at him with a certain sadness. 'Well, you see,' John started somewhat awkwardly, 'my father in those days was a conscientious objector which mean he did not believe in war and refused to fight for any-one – even his own country.'

'So what happened to him?' Kamala asked with deep concern.

'Many people, especially those who lost their children in the Great War, felt strongly against him and he was threatened.'

'Oh no! And then?'

John paused again to harness his emotions and then he haltingly told her how on Armistice night when he was out celebrating, his father was out as well with friends and his mother was alone, someone set fire to the house and had murdered her.

Kamala was completely overwhelmed with the story of this tragedy.

'Oh, how horrible! How cruel!' She could not find any other words.

John became very silent. For a moment his eyes filled with tears and so did hers. There was now a bond between them as Kamala could see the strong Sahib was not without his share of suffering. She stood up, crossed the floor, came near to him and held his hand consolingly. He smiled, rather embarrassed, got up and hurriedly said, 'Let's see what you have been reading recently.'

IV

Soon, sharing her cooking with the Sahib became a regular event in Kamala's life. John thoroughly enjoyed some of the delicious Hindu dishes, which did not please Ibrahim. On the other hand it saved him some work and gave him more free time at which he was not unhappy. There persisted in Ibrahim, however, a sense of envy because he could detect the Sahib's strong affection for the Hindu woman. He wanted the situation to return to the earlier arrangement whereby he and he alone looked after the Sahib.

Ibrahim did not have much respect for Kamala. He knew eight or ten men had had her that night, for which he felt absolutely no sympathy. How could the woman have been a good wife and daughter if her husband and father for whatever reasons had ditched her, he thought. He could see she was playing up to the Sahib with all those stories of nightmares. Ibrahim had no doubt in his mind that she fabricated these stories to move to the room next to the Sahib. Obviously, she had her eyes on Ibrahim's job, and he was not going to let her have it. *Haramjadi*! No doubt the pig's daughter was not merely cooking for the Sahib but also playing naughty games – *besaram khanki* – the shameless whore – pushing him out of his job. Ibrahim was now prepared to do anything to get rid of Kamala from the house.

In Ibrahim's present state of mind, Jadu was no help. Anyway Jadu had never much liked that Moslem son of a bitch. And now he could sense that the control of the household was gradually shifting from Ibrahim to Kamala. The situation pleased Jadu mightily and soon he started telling all kinds of stories against Ibrahim. He even suggested that Ibrahim had been the main instigator of the recent turbulence, for he had been to Khodadad Khan's meeting and then moved around with those ruffians who had been here just before the riot and had since disappeared. This was far from the truth, for although Ibrahim had attended Khodadad's meeting just as Jadu had attended Joshi's, he had never ever betrayed the Sahib's position by associating with any riotous elements. He liked the Sahib and would not be a traitor for money or anything else. But that did not mean he had any loyalty for Kamala.

It wasn't long before Ibrahim started spreading rumours that ever since the Sahib's arrival in town Kamala had been sleeping with him. The people in Raigarh had been waiting for a scandal of this sort. They were on the whole regular people, believed in regular things. From birth to death, everything had its rhythm. It had to keep its beat – move logically. There were riots – very unfortunate – but it happened from time to time. Some killings, some rapes – wretched souls! Then as the dead bodies were cremated, so the raped women went to the next village or the one after and became whores. After that, occasionally the town elders who had fancied these women in the past would go and visit them, of course unbeknown to their wives, and would shower them with sympathy for their misfortune. Now that was accepted. But for a raped woman to end up in the Sahib's bungalow was completely unheard of. And of course it could never be right.

V

One Sunday when John was having lunch and Kamala was standing at a respectable distance to attend to him, he suddenly asked, 'Why don't you come and join me? I don't like having meals on my own.'

Kamala did not readily reply, for she did not want to disobey the Sahib. A few moments later she said, 'Sahib, in our society, we don't do that. We don't eat with men.'

'What's wrong with men? They are just as good as women,' John remarked with a glint of amusement in his eyes.

Kamala laughed and bantered back, 'No! Men are better, Sahib. That's why we don't eat with them.'

'Not that much better! At least, not in our society!' replied John and then added somewhat seriously, 'In a European family they always try to have their meals together – especially on a Sunday. It's a very special day – Sunday – and nobody's allowed to eat on his own.'

Kamala was worried. She said, 'Sahib, if I start eating from the same table as you, people will talk. Even your servants won't be happy to see a sahib and a native woman eating together.'

'Don't talk rubbish!' snorted John. 'Don't you ever say that to me again. I don't want to hear it. You're Kamala to me, a beautiful Indian girl, who smiled at me and welcomed me the very first day I arrived in Raigarh.'

'Oh, you still remember that!' Kamala's voice melted with affection. Then she added, 'For nearly a week we were so excited, doing all the preparations for your welcome celebrations. Then my father asked me to arrange a garland for you. Oh, I was so thrilled!' Kamala's face suddenly had that intensity of radiance which since the riot had been totally absent. John was pleased to see her happy and relaxed. After a pause she suddenly murmured, 'If it would really please you, Sahib, I'll eat with you.'

'Please don't do it because I've asked,' said John. 'Do so only if you would really like to.'

Kamala smiled beautifully and then said, 'Yes, Sahib. I would really like to.'

FIFTEEN

I

That autumn John Sugden felt much happier. Since his mother's death he had been unhappy. He had been seeking something – something he had not had. Was it love? That was what he had thought at first. But the relationship with Esther, his first girl friend, and then Martha showed him it was not quite that – but something else – something special. Love only brought excitement

– he found difficult to cope with its intensity. It did not bring a soothing feeling, a calming influence.

This autumn John felt very different. For once he felt calm and at peace with himself. He often watched Kamala moving gracefully, laughing, singing, doing the household chores which his mother used to do for his father. It was a pleasant feeling, a happy feeling which he had not known before.

As Kamala's confidence in him grew by the day, they teased each other, shared jokes, but above all shared that intimate relationship which two people can only share if they have a strong friendship – an inner urge for the nearness of each other.

'How do you spend your time when I go to work?' John asked one day. Kamala blushed, for if the truth were known, she waited all day for the Sahib to come back. It was him, his image, his gentle talk, his gestures and postures which for the entire day filled her mind. This often made her feel uncomfortable and scared in case her happiness did not last. She knew that the Sahib would soon get married to an English lady, who perhaps would not like her being there at all. She often dreaded that day. While at hospital after the riots she had been resigned to accepting the drudgery of a sad existence; she had even considered taking her life, but at that time she had not known this happiness, this feeling of being completely exhilarated and elated by a man – his voice, his movement, just his presence.

'Why don't you read some poetry?' John suggested, assuming from her silence she had nothing much to do in the daytime. She nodded shyly.

'An idle mind is a devil's workshop, you know,' John teased her. She smiled, thinking if only he knew who that devil was.

John took her to the library and said, 'I have quite a few books here. Shelley, for example; he wrote so much against tyranny and oppression. Read him. I'm sure you would like him.'

Kamala nodded her head again. John was not sure whether she did so just to satisfy him – sometimes it was difficult for him to make her out. Of course he was well aware that he had to be sensitive to her needs. Poor girl! In the last few months she had been through such emotional and physical trauma, John did not want to add to it. He tried to ensure that any suggestion he made even for her own well-being did not bring the slightest pressure on her.

Kamala, however, took the Sahib's wishes to heart. The

following month she spent all her afternoons in the library, reading Shelley and then Keats, Byron, Coleridge, Browning, Goldsmith, Wordsworth – every poet the Sahib liked – almost like an obedient pupil. It surprised John immensely to see how devotedly she read all the poets he had suggested. And when she started asking him questions about various poems, seeking to understand the inner meaning of say, 'the desire of the moth for the star', John's heart filled with delight. He began to take a keen interest in her quest for knowledge and a regular pattern soon started to emerge.

Although Kamala had not had the same kind of education as John, she was bright. She quickly picked up whatever facts and ideas he taught her and then synthesized them in her own mind with her oriental upbringing, coming up with interpretations which were diametrically opposed to his, but equally cogent, equally meaningful, equally penetrating. John was completely taken aback – surprised by her intuitive analytical ability. It had been a long time since he had had so much fun talking to someone – almost like his undergraduate days, when he could discuss poetry with his friends with the same degree of understanding, feeling and intellect.

This relationship with a woman was an unknown experience for John. Both Esther and Martha had been different; their mind wandered every time any subject requiring deeper analysis and penetration came up for discussion. But not Kamala. She eagerly participated and often contributed forceful views: be they on Indian politics, social and economic reforms or literature. In the true sense John and Kamala became friends within a short spell of time.

One Sunday morning after breakfast they both were reading in the library when John suddenly stood up and picked a slim volume from one of the shelves. He brought it to Kamala and said, 'I don't know whether you would like this one – a favourite poet of mine – John Donne. He wrote a long time ago, in the seventeenth century. Let me read this one to you.' Then he took the book and read aloud –

'I scarce believe my love to be so pure
As I had thought it was,
Because it doth endure
Vicissitude, and season, as the grass;
Methinks I lied all winter, when I swore,
My love was infinite, if spring make it more.'

When he stopped, Kamala was completely engrossed. She blushed a little as John caught her eye. He too was embarrassed.

Kamala did not go to the library the following day and for a few days stayed as far away from the Sahib as possible. John had to go on a tour since the cold weather was already back and while he was away, Kamala spent most of her time in the library and read more of John Donne and strangely liked some of his erotic poems. This came as a surprise to her. After her dreadful experience, the idea of love-making had been so repulsive to her that she thought she would never be able to recover from it. But these erotic poems gave her a different feeling, suggested different dimensions – they thrilled her. A strange dream went through her mind. It was only a dream – nothing more. But she did not want to destroy that dream. She had suffered so many nightmares in her life that she indulged herself in this dream, though she knew no credence could be attached to it, for it was so utterly impossible, so totally unworldly that she was even afraid to dream in case she lost the tune, the chord, the music. This was a new experience for her – so very different even from when she was married to Hari. She waited eagerly for the Sahib to come back.

II

John could not settle down properly on this cold weather trip. For some unknown reason he felt that he was being pulled back towards Raigarh. All he knew was that he was bored. The tasks that he had enjoyed so much in past years, talking to local people, finding out their problems, passing judgements on squabbles – all seemed so dreary. His mind almost choked with the routine of administration, for he wanted to escape – escape to Shelley, Keats, Byron and perhaps to John Donne.

He thought of Kamala a lot – the way she wore her sari, put kohl on her wide eyes; the way she tousled her long, black, wavy hair whenever she disagreed with him and argued over the finer points in the interpretation of Shelley or Keats. He had begun to miss her, which made him restless. Soon he was counting the days for his return to Raigarh.

Kamala was waiting eagerly for him when he returned and did not hide her pleasure at seeing him back. She hastened to cook the dishes that she knew he liked best. They talked and talked, giggled, shared jokes, bantered like friends – both were so pleased to see the other.

In the afternoon they went to the library and read John Donne together – feeling the essence of every sentence, every word, every note as they read line after line aloud.

In the late afternoon John suggested, 'Let's take the carriage and go to the hills.'

Kamala's face darkened. She said, 'Sahib, I am afraid for you. People will talk. They are already talking about my staying here. For me, it doesn't matter any more. I was possessed by other men: unknown strangers. My husband, my parents have now left me as a fallen woman. Nothing could affect me. But I'm like a blot of ink – a curse. And I'm scared – scared for you – in case our association brings danger to you, to your career, to your future. I am scared – very scared.'

'Are we on to that destiny business again?' John tried to laugh it off, though he realized that there was a great deal of truth in what Kamala had just said. But he did not want to pay heed to her prudent warnings; he knew in his heart what he wanted and he was not prepared to sacrifice it because of any silly limitations. Trying to fight off his fear, he became expansive and murmured, 'Kamala, I'll take you in front on my horse just as Prithwiraj of ancient India took Sanjukta from her father's palace, daring the world to stop me.'

'Sahib, please! Don't talk like that,' replied Kamala. 'You're frightening me. Be prudent! Be sensible! Let's not spoil your future with my curse.'

John was still adamant. Perhaps he had a devil in him or perhaps he was fed up with all the restrictions which surrounded every part of his life.

At Kamala's insistence John took the *saice* with them. The carriage sped towards the hills. When they had left the town, John bent over and kissed her passionately – the first kiss for Kamala for a long time, as it was for John. She gently held his hand to calm and restrain him and then smoothed out her sari, pressing out all the creases that had been caused by the Sahib's heavy muscular arm. With a glint in her eyes she then put a finger on his mouth and said, 'No more.'

'Why?' John smiled. 'You said nothing would touch you now.'

'No! If the carriage rocks too much, the *saice* will guess.'
Observing her concern, John was amused.

Near the hills they got down from the carriage. John tried to
hold her hand which she did not allow until they were a long way
away from the *saice*. Then she came very close as they held each
other, walking together in even steps in that warm sunshine.

'Can I ask you a favour?' Kamala asked softly.

'What, my love?' asked John.

'Would you do something for me?'

'I will do anything for you, anything.'

'Don't promise so hurriedly. Just come closer.'

John came and stood close. So close, he could feel her shapely
body, her perfume, her warmth.

'Let's hold hands,' said Kamala, 'and walk seven steps with the
sun as the witness.'

'What does it mean?' John asked, tenderly curious.

Kamala held his hand and walked seven steps slowly,
determinedly but lovingly – looking intensely at the bright sun.
Then she turned to John and softly but clearly pronounced, 'It
means – now I am your woman. You can have me if you want. The
sun has given us permission with his strength and power.'

John bent down and covered her face with passionate kisses to
which she ardently responded.

III

It was late evening when they came back to Raigarh. All their
incessant chatting seemed to have dried up now, for they both
waited eagerly for the night to fall. They tried to read something
together but could not concentrate – not even on John Donne.
Excitedly, like a newly-married couple trying to leave for their
honeymoon, they counted the seconds until the evening moved
into night.

Late at night when everyone was asleep Kamala came stealthily
to John's room. He was waiting. Quivering with excitement they
clasped each other close and covered each other with kisses,
drowning in a sea of pleasure and ecstasy as they became one. No
more nightmares for them now, just a sweet dream of love and
care.

When they woke up late the following morning, they were still
in each other's arms.

'I'd better go, darling,' Kamala murmured.

'Umm!' John held Kamala even more closely, keeping his eyes shut.

'All the servants will be up soon. It's for your sake,' Kamala said.

'They perhaps know already.'

'All the same.'

'Do you know something!' John got up and wrapped the sheet round him, looking lovingly at Kamala's beautiful naked body. Kamala, embarrassed, came close to John and covered herself with the same sheet, so that he could not look at her any more – not in the same way.

'You're naughty!' She pulled his nose.

'Eh! You're being rough!'

'Not like you!' She smiled.

'D'you know, I was scared last night,' John confided.

'So was I.'

A few moments elapsed in silence, they were just feeling each other, secure in their unclothed closeness.

'Something you don't know about me, Kamala.' There was a strange seriousness in John's voice.

'I know everything.' Kamala smiled, though she was a little scared and then she continued, 'Please do tell me.'

John hesitated. Seeing his hesitation, she tried to put him at ease and said, 'Only if you want to.'

'I want to but I don't know how,' John said. Kamala waited. John slowly gathered enough courage and then started, 'On the Armistice night when the Great War ended I went out with a girl I knew then, named Esther. We spent the whole evening together, going round jubilant London. The war was over and everyone was happy. We were so excited going from one place to another in the festive city that we missed the last train back and spent the night in a hotel.'

Kamala looked at John – her eyes were melancholy.

'And we made love.'

'Why are you telling me this?' Kamala was hurt.

'Because there's something else I want to tell you.' John paused for a moment, then continued, 'When we came back the following morning I could see from the station that our house was on fire, and I realized that while I was making love to Esther, my mother – alone – was burning to death.'

A strong current of sympathy now filled Kamala's face. 'That's not your fault, darling – you didn't know.'

'Well, in a way I did, you know. Because before that awful tragedy we had a warning – someone scrawled on our door in the middle of one night – "Kill the traitor".'

'Obviously they were cowards to do it in the middle of the night,' Kamala tried to console him.

'After my mother's death I had to go to the morgue and identify her body because my father was far too upset to face seeing my mother in that state.' John paused for a moment and then haltingly said, 'Oh, I will never forget it in my whole life – it was a horrific sight.'

Kamala began to caress his hair to soothe him.

John looked at her intently and then continued, 'Since that evening I have been impotent – I simply couldn't face the idea of love-making, for I had this terrible vision of my mother's charred body chasing me every time I tried. That was until last night.'

Kamala looked surprised and elated, 'Did you honestly not face that nightmare last night?'

'No, darling, no!' John said with a broad smile, full of affection. 'You cured me. You cured me with your love.'

Kamala now pulled him nearer and covered him with kisses as love flowed in abundance.

SIXTEEN

I

Gossip had been going round for some time in the small town of Raigarh that Ratan Banerji's daughter was the Sahib's mistress. At first some people believed it. Many others, however, had refused even to listen to any such nonsense. But now things became rather different. It was no longer Ibrahim's fabrication out of simple jealousy against a Hindu woman gaining the Sahib's favour. It was much more than that. Reliable witnesses started to come forward saying that they had seen the Sahib and Banerji's daughter walking through the hills, holding hands, even kissing and cuddling in broad daylight.

'How could she do such thing?' shouted the older village women. 'No shame at all – absolutely *besaram*. After all the Sahib is a *firingee* – a foreigner – they have strange customs. Unmarried men and women hold each other cheek to cheek and dance wildly to the rhythm of their strange music. Not only that, even married women – and not with their husbands – with other men – drink *sarab*. Everyone knows the *goras* are shameless. But a Hindu, brahmin girl, brought up in the strict discipline of a religious household, offering *phal phul* every morning to gods and goddesses to keep their rage away from our daily living – how could she possibly throw everything away one morning and shamelessly enter into that kind of relationship with a *gora*?'

'She could easily have gone to my cousin in Champadanga and they would have given her a maid's job!' shouted another.

The third one winked, 'You know they'd already had it – had it before even she was married. That's why the Sahib came to the wedding, wearing Indian clothes.'

'Don't you know,' added the fourth, 'Ratan Banerji got his promotion by selling his daughter and then forced Hari to marry her. Poor Hari! Such a shame! He couldn't even marry a virgin.'

Now they all put their heads together and whispered something salacious and burst out laughing.

An elderly woman with a stern face did not want the discussion to end merely in silly giggles. She continued seriously, 'The fact that they are having it in the darkness of night – that's one thing. But in broad daylight, eating together from the same table, reading, laughing, holding hands – that's worse than a *khanki*, a whore. We must tell Ratan's wife. And if necessary, even go to Ratan through the *panchayat* – the village elders. We must make a proper protest. All this *belellami* – shamelessness must stop.'

Everyone agreed with her now, 'Yes! She must leave the Sahib and go away somewhere else. We don't care then if she becomes a *khanki* or *baiji*. But not before our very eyes.'

The anger in the town against Kamala escalated rapidly. She knew the hostility of the locals against her was already at a high pitch; she was, however, protected by staying with the Sahib, because the venom could not reach her with sufficient force to make her life intolerable.

On odd occasions, looking out from the veranda, whenever she caught someone's eye an intense hatred glowed there irrespective of whether it was a man or woman, Hindu or Moslem.

Hari's family had now completely washed their hands of the affair. They even vaguely indicated to their near neighbours that things had not been quite right with her from the start. But because of Hari's pensionable and highly sought-after employment they could not speak out in the way that perhaps they had wanted to, for they did not want to bring the Sahib's wrath upon them. Now they went quietly about arranging another marriage for Hari. As there was no law against bigamy for a Hindu man, this posed no problem and the local community eagerly accepted that under the circumstances the best possible option for Hari would be to marry again. And this time to a decent girl.

The person who had to face immediate punishment from the villagers was Kamala's mother. After the rape she had had to go along with the custom – abandoning her dear child – but it broke her heart. She was so helpless. And she hated this predicament. Many a time she had even suggested to her husband that they should uproot the entire family and take Kamala to some other place where nobody would know about their past. That kind of suggestion, however, did not arouse any enthusiasm in Ratan Banerji, for he knew that to be swayed by his wife's idea and to leave his lucrative, pensionable post in the Raj would be a sure way of bringing total disaster upon his family. And if he asked for a transfer everyone would know the reason and the gossip would arrive at their new destination faster than they themselves.

Of course all these discussions between Banerji and his wife had taken place long before Kamala went to live with the Sahib. Since then Mrs Banerji had been reasonably happy, feeling that even though the Sahib was a *firingee* – a foreigner – he was a kindly man. And the little that she had seen of the Englishman she had liked. If the world had been free from so many complications about race, culture and background, she perhaps would have said that the Sahib and Kamala were a good match. But when you live in society your favoured outcome is rarely possible and she accepted it as one of those vagaries of life.

But the antipathy against the Banerjis in Raigarh had reached such intensity now that Kamala's mother could not go anywhere, see anyone – even her friends shunned her. Banerji was aware of the situation. Things were not much better for him within the community. And then he had the added problem of dealing with the Sahib every day. There had been a time when the Sahib used to seek his advice on almost everything, but now he kept the relationship strictly official – that of a superior officer and a subordinate. On no occasion did he mention Kamala – not even to give the odd piece of news about her. This was a new experience for Banerji – the friendly Sahib he had known before had become an arrogant and stubborn superior officer.

Although Banerji had at first been upset by Kamala's living with the Sahib, in a way he was also pleased. After all, as a father he always wanted the best for his children. Even now he had sacrificed Kamala only in the interests of the other two – at least that was what he told himself. The present kerfuffle, however, made him believe that Kamala's living with the Sahib was improper. But what was the alternative? Banerji realized that letting Kamala live at home would be even worse. After long deliberation he thought of a distant cousin in Calcutta and wondered whether he would be willing for her to stay with his family, perhaps doing the menial tasks of a maid. He immediately wrote to him.

A few months passed before he received a reply. His cousin had not quite jumped for joy at the suggestion. On the other hand he was willing to consider the proposal, provided she was prepared to stay under his strict discipline – more or less of the kind that befitted a widow. And of course he wanted a handsome allowance for her upkeep. With this ammunition in hand, Banerji gathered enough courage one day to make a trip to the Sahib's bungalow, of course during a period when the Sahib was away.

II

For a moment Kamala thought she had seen a ghost, she was so shattered by her father's sudden appearance. Even the servants were surprised. Kamala was polite but distant – asked her father to sit in the lounge and then told Jadu to bring tea for him.

After a brief preamble Banerji started. '*Komu*,' he used the affectionate term which he had not used for a long time, not since she had married, 'I do not think this is quite the right place for you.'

Kamala, not knowing what to expect, did not reply.

'Sahib is a nice man, but he is a foreigner, a Christian with unspeakable habits – he eats beef. This is not really a suitable house for a brahmin girl to live in.'

'Why are you saying this now?' asked Kamala.

'Because I have your interests in mind, *Komu*.'

Kamala could not help pulling a face at this suggestion.

'No! No! Believe me!' Banerji said. 'Ever since you were a child, I have always given your welfare priority over everything else.'

Kamala, though she did not believe a word he said, remained silent.

'You see – people are talking,' Banerji carried on. 'You know what they are like – always fond of gossiping. They are saying all kinds of wicked things about you.'

'What does it matter to you, what they say about me?' Kamala's pent-up feelings came out for the first time.

Banerji did not have the sensitivity to understand Kamala's grief. He was only amazed that his own daughter could stand up to him in that manner. Harshly he now tried to counter her reply. 'Oh *Komu*!' Banerji said, 'You must not speak to me that way. I am your father. I brought you into this world and fed you all those years – do not forget that.'

Kamala realized her father would never understand the depth of pain and suffering that she had had to come through. She curtly replied, 'Tell me what you had in mind.'

'I have arranged with my cousin in Calcutta that you shall stay with him,' Banerji replied. 'You know his wife is unwell. She has been in poor health for years, and now she cannot even move about inside the house. She needs help and they can provide a roof over your head.'

Kamala made no attempt to reply to Banerji's suggestion. This made him nervous. He babbled, 'Of course, I will have to give them some money every month – upkeep is not cheap these days. In Calcutta things are even dearer than here. But I do not mind spending money on you, if it helps you in life.'

'I am happy here. I don't want to go anywhere else.' Kamala's face hardened as she uttered the words.

'You are a mere child! You do not understand all the repercussions of your staying in this house,' replied Banerji. 'People are saying all kinds of things. They are even saying you sleep with the Sahib.'

Kamala could not help blushing at the remark. Banerji, seeing her reaction, became uneasy and continued with even more determination, 'You see you have two sisters. I know you are fond of them, but you also have some responsibility, especially towards their children. Just think how badly they will be affected by any scandal.'

Even though Kamala was upset she was concerned about the welfare of her sisters and their children. Her father's words now weakened her resolve. Banerji, sensing that his daughter was considering his proposal, tried to step up the pressure and said, 'Whatever happened before, after all, that was not your fault. But how can you justify living with the Sahib?'

Kamala could see now why her father had come when the Sahib was away. She was no longer sure what to do and this made her very very angry – angry with herself, with her father, with everyone. But above all she was most enraged by her father's selfish attitude. She blurted out, 'You don't care about me – do you? You only want your own life to run smoothly. You want to show everyone that you have done your duty.' Her face now showed visible marks of pain.

'How rudely you speak, Kamala!' Banerji's enforced mask of affection disappeared fast as he shouted, 'Have you no respect for your father? You have never been like this before! Because the Sahib is my superior officer? Is that it? But you are not his wife, you know!'

'Please go, *Bapi*, before I lose my temper,' Kamala screamed, shaking in rage.

'Do you know what people are saying about you?' Banerji shouted back. 'They are saying you are a whore. You are selling your body to buy comfort!'

'Go! Go! Please go!' Kamala cried frantically.

'Do you know what?' Banerji continued shouting. 'You are spoiling his future, his reputation. People no longer say the Sahib is good. They say he is messed up by your bad influence. You have destroyed Hari, you have destroyed me, and now you are destroying him. You are just an evil influence! I am cursed for fathering such evil!'

Kamala could no longer listen to these accusations. Her father's cruel diatribe pierced her. There was no love, no affection in him now – just undiluted self-interest which she could not withstand even a second longer. She screamed, 'Go! Go!', and ran through the door like a frightened rabbit.

'I am not leaving my daughter in a Christian household – do you hear me?' Banerji's temper had now reached such a pitch that he did not care about the Sahib being his superior officer. Under no circumstances was he prepared to be snubbed by his own daughter. He wanted a showdown – and now. Looking at the door through which Kamala had gone he continued yelling, 'I shall come back soon to take you! No force on this earth, no Sahib can stop me. You are going to live with my cousin – and that is final! Ratan Banerji is not going to be trifled with by a wilful child like you.'

Banerji wanted to follow Kamala through the door but he did not dare. His nerve was fast deserting him. He still showed his rage and stormed out of the bungalow and walked towards the town at a furious pace.

SEVENTEEN

I

When Banerji left the Sahib's bungalow that morning, a sense of extreme terror engulfed Kamala. For a moment she was not sure what to do next. She sat completely numb, worrying over her future.

She knew her father only too well. Not that he was a bad person. Not at all. On the whole he was honest and upright, unless something perturbed him: especially if it hurt his brahminic pride. The issues did not have to be significant – they could be downright stupid and fatuous – but they would still be enough to enrage him. In a rather childish way, he would then seek revenge against those who had brought about his supposed humiliation. At that stage he could be absolutely vicious. He would plot and plan assiduously, in infinite detail, the downfall of his adversary.

Now Kamala started fearing for the Sahib. She knew that her father's rage would fall, not upon her, but on the man she loved.

This very thought made her even more uneasy. After her painful experience, she perhaps would not have wanted to live but for the Sahib. In hospital while she had been recuperating, she had it firmly in her mind that she would not go through whoring to earn her living. But what she had not foreseen at the time was this love. It was an experience she had not known before. She had had a stable married life with Hari. The routine was similar to any other Hindu marriage: Hari would go to work in the morning while she would cook for him. In the evening he would come back, talk to his parents, relatives or friends. After his meal he would sit in the courtyard and smoke his hubble-bubble, while she would read some English novel. It was a firm relationship but there had been no friendship in it, no joy.

Living with the Sahib was completely different. Experiencing togetherness which she had never known before. Never! The sheer excitement of reading, discussing, reciting Shelley, Donne or Shakespeare, going on long horse-rides to the remote hills of the Himalayas, holding hands, watching the sunset in the distant valleys and then trekking back in the twilight along the winding path to the plains, and sharing jokes, mirth and love – that was life in its fullness – life with vigour – life worth living – a sense of purpose, peace and happiness.

The Sahib without doubt, took away her nightmares, and for once gave her life a sense of freedom, a sense of belonging, a sense of equality – not like living in a male-dominated Hindu society, but sharing – sharing meals, sharing pleasure, sharing each other, even sharing dreams. What more could she hope for in life?

Now her father's threat had changed everything. She had no doubt in her mind; she did not want to leave the Sahib. Not for any treasure on this earth or beyond. But could it be that she was adopting a rather selfish attitude – looking only after her own interests? If what her father had said was true, that she was ruining the Sahib's career, even his life, what was she to do? This created in her mind fresh agony and forced her to face another question which for some time she had been trying to put to one side – she was soon to be a mother.

Yes! She was carrying the Sahib's child – a creature conceived in love. But in the world in which they lived, love meant nothing without wedlock. What was to happen to a little Eurasian, an offspring of a Christian and a Hindu, growing everyday inside her, of whose existence even the Sahib did not know? Nobody knew.

No, that was not true. Nobody except Ibrahim. It was not long before his shrewd eyes detected a change in her body and at an opportune moment he made a suggestion.

Under the circumstances it was not really a cruel suggestion, although the very thought created intense revulsion in her. Ibrahim knew an old woman in a remote village who offered abortion at a price – not a significant price, at least not by European standards. The old woman knew that when it was a question of honour, money was never a criterion. And she was right. It was the prestige and honour of the Sahib which was at stake. Leaving aside the awful gossip which no doubt would spread like wildfire, what would the status of the child be? A Eurasian bastard! Born to a loose woman as a result of a night's lust with a sahib! And if the Sahib were to marry someone in the near future, which no doubt he would, what would be the feeling of the new memsahib towards Kamala and the child?

Kamala was now in an extreme dilemma. She could see the wisdom of her father's advice – to run away from the Sahib so that he would never know that his child was growing inside her, saving him from all the embarrassment. But in her heart of hearts, she could not bring herself to accept the final termination of their relationship. So what was she to do? The thought tormented her constantly during the Sahib's absence.

II

Although it was supposedly spring, the weather was extremely hot when John Sugden arrived back in Raigarh. In Bihar, winter was almost over by the beginning of March, the endless scorching sun breaking the soil into clods which soon became stony hard and then finally turned into dust as people, cattle or horse-drawn carriages dragged over them. Storms often came around this time of year, which the locals called violent *Baishakhi*, named after a particular time in their own calendar when thick black clouds covered the sky and endless eddies of dust blew everywhere. Walking or riding then became extremely hazardous.

At the start of the *baishakhi* season John thought he had done enough touring. Moreover, he desperately wanted to get back to Raigarh and see Kamala. He was missing her. In a way she had changed his life. Whereas previously he had been only an intellectual, a theorist, a Balliol product through and through, looking upon the world as it ought to be rather than as it is – now it was all different. Now he was a complete human being: one who could see the problems as they really were. Still impetuous, intellectually arrogant, still believing in his invincibility, there was yet deep down an inner wisdom that guided him to distinguish clearly between right and wrong, not by theories but with empathy, sensitivity and concern for the people for whom he was there to mete out judgement.

He had no doubt it was Kamala's influence that had changed his attitude. Being Indian she knew how the mind of the Indian masses worked – what they really wanted, what concerned them, what agonized them, frightened them. Coming from outside, from an island some seven thousand miles away, with a different culture, different upbringing, different outlook on life, John could never have known the inner feelings of an Indian without her help.

Kamala in some ways was different from others. For all practical purposes she was really a European, for she had a positive attitude to life. At first John found it rather strange living with her as man and wife. In many ways she was soft, beautifully delicate and submissive, but in others, she was strong, direct and definite without a hint of inhibition. In the areas in which most Europeans would be self-conscious she was frank and candid, in others she wanted John to lead the way while she followed, not submissively, more like a disciple whose deep respect and affection made her master even greater than he was.

As he rode back on that hot steamy March day through the landscape already parched by the relentless sun, he wondered what he would have done without Kamala. Before she came into his life he had been beginning to get so bored, so depressed that he could not have seen through even the contractual period in India, let alone made a career of it. But Kamala had changed all that. She brought with her that fresh hope of life, a new dream, a new pleasure, joy and close association. The nightmare of his mother's violent and tragic death disappeared completely as Kamala's perfume, her soft touch, her relaxed, beautiful, golden-brown body holding him at night with love and affection, offered him the security for which he had been searching all these years.

John looked towards the bungalow from a distance. Normally Kamala, whenever she knew John was due back from a trip, would wait on the veranda expectantly, looking along the distant road which met the line of trees near the horizon, waiting for his carriage to appear. With a beaming smile she would wave to welcome him and then run to ask Jadu to pour an ice-cool gin and tonic to be ready and waiting on his arrival. Today John was surprised as he looked towards the veranda, for there was no sign of her anywhere. Unusual! he thought. Perhaps she is ill. This made him highly agitated as various worries jostled in his head. He ordered the *saice* to gallop as quickly as possible towards the bungalow.

Kamala was in her bedroom, sitting rather melancholily, staring at the sky. Her entire world seemed completely distant and different – a world of which John had no knowledge, no perception, no part.

'What's the matter, darling?' John asked anxiously.

Kamala started. Highly embarrassed, she apologized profusely for being so absent-minded. 'Oh, Sahib, I'm sorry. You've travelled all this way through the dust-ridden country and here I am, not even arranging a drink for you.'

Soon she recovered from her melancholy and the usual glint appeared in her eyes as she teased John, 'No doubt, you'll dismiss me now from my job.'

There was a strange sadness even in that teasing remark. Whereas on any other day John would have bantered, saying something equally facile to get his own back, today he stood there stunned, feeling a strange sense of discomfort as if something were not quite right in her. He walked across, came close and held her.

'There's something wrong. Aren't you going to tell me what it is, darling?' John asked.

Kamala sighed and replied, 'No, there's nothing wrong with me, Sahib.'

'There must be something. I know you're not a moody person. Please, please, tell me! Aren't you well?'

'I have been feeling a bit tired,' said Kamala.

'Let's take you to the doctor in Sripore.'

'No, Sahib! You sit down and relax. You shouldn't spend your time worrying about me.'

'But I do worry about you!' John said. Kamala smiled, a wan smile, rather pallid. Her face did not glow in the same way as it would have done a few days ago. 'Darling, you must be ill. I can see you aren't well. If you don't want to go to Sripore, let's invite Father Fallon! Please! You ought to see a doctor. I know you aren't well.'

A thought went through Kamala's mind as she quickly assessed the situation. The priest was a man she had not thought of before, who could no doubt help her in this present predicament. The more she thought, the more it seemed obvious to her that Father Fallon must be the person she should see. No doubt he could guide her in the right direction.

'It would be lovely to see him again,' replied Kamala. 'We haven't seen him for a long time. But there's no hurry.'

'I'll send the *saice* now to go and fetch him,' John said eagerly.

Kamala came close, gave John an affectionate peck and said, 'No, Sahib! Now you sit and relax. I'll ask Jadu to pour you a drink.'

III

'I hear that your father has been here,' John said to Kamala one morning. 'It's about time too. Can't understand that brute. How can anyone treat one's own offspring in the way he has done? I hope he's going to compensate for all his past guilt.'

Kamala remained silent. She was rather sorry that he had heard about her father's visit. Her silence made John uncomfortable. 'What did he have to say? Or don't you want to tell me?'

Kamala remained silent, but her eyes filled and soon they started overflowing, covering her cheeks with tears. John, perturbed, rushed towards her. She almost threw herself into his embrace and started crying tremulously. Much as he tried to console her he felt almost helpless, for he did not know why she was so distraught.

He held her quietly. Her heart pounded for a long time like a frightened sparrow. After a while the flow of tears subsided. John sat down on the bed and took her in his arms.

'Aren't you going to tell me?' he asked, wiping tears from her eyes.

'He wants me to go away from you,' Kamala replied sobbingly.

'What? Is that what he came to tell you?' John said angrily. 'He has the bloody cheek ... I'll teach him a lesson. I'll make sure he never comes anywhere near here bothering you again.'

'But in many ways, what he says is right.' Kamala tried to protect her father from the Sahib's rage.

'Right!' John said contemptuously. 'A man who couldn't protect his daughter! A man who was prepared to let her become a whore because he didn't have the bloody guts to face the world and say unequivocally – "My daughter is innocent; it is I who should be punished for being so spineless" – how could he ever be right?' John paused, choking in anger but soon continued, 'And that bloody parasite now has the gall to come and tell you that you must leave! Wait till I see him again.'

'Oh, please! Please! Don't tell him anything. Please, for my sake!' she pleaded earnestly.

John stayed silent, still fuming.

'But what about your reputation, Sahib?' Kamala got up from the bed. Her voice showed deep concern. 'I know people are gossiping about us. Don't you see what will happen? It'll make your life difficult. Then you won't be able to work here, help the poor. There aren't many like you around. It would be selfish of me to hold you just for my sake and destroy you.'

'Rubbish!' John snarled. 'You would never destroy me. For the first time in my life since my mother's death, you have taken my nightmares away. Oh, Kamala! You don't know how grateful I am to you.'

'Sahib, he's only asking me to go and stay with his cousin in Calcutta.' Kamala sounded distraught even uttering these words. 'Sahib, sooner or later, you'll get married and then your wife obviously won't like me to be here.'

John now got up from the bed and rushed to Kamala; holding her hands he earnestly said, 'I want to marry you, Kamala. Please take me! Please marry me! Don't run away from me! Please! Please! Don't turn me away!' His heart-rending plea overwhelmed Kamala as she found a sense of immense love engulfing her. She was now even more frightened than before, for she could see the Sahib would be destroyed if he tried to do anything as silly as marry her.

'You can't marry me, Sahib. I'm a married woman.' Kamala's voice was full of sadness.

'But you can get a divorce,' John said eagerly.

'There's no divorce among the Hindus.'

John was surprised. He said, 'But Hari's marrying again.'

'Men can marry more than once in India,' replied Kamala, 'but I'll remain his wife until I die.'

'That's preposterous! That's uncivilized! No society could be so callous,' John shouted in rage.

Kamala remained silent; not knowing how to console him.

'I'll find a way to marry you, Kamala.' John's voice trembled with emotion. He paused for a moment and then continued with a strange determination, 'If that means tearing this country apart, I will do it. I will do it, Kamala, I will do it. No force on earth is going to stop me.'

Kamala took John's hand. A slight flutter in her body expressed a strong current of emotion but she calmed herself and asked in a worried voice, 'But what about your career?'

'Yes, I think I have to leave the civil service,' John replied. 'But I don't mind. It's a stuffy place, anyway. I'm sure I could do something different. Stanley and Martha, you know my friends from Calcutta, their father has a booming business. He is eager for me to join him.'

'But will they be so keen if you have an Indian woman with you?' Kamala asked anxiously.

'They themselves are Eurasian,' replied John. 'No doubt they, more than anyone else, will understand our situation.'

Kamala looked at John. Her eyes filled with future uncertainties. Observing her expression John tried to offer her confidence and firmly said, 'Whatever happens I'm not leaving you, Kamala. You're mine and you stay with me.'

Kamala remained silent. She was worried. To ease her tension John rather mischievously said, 'If your father comes here again, I'll break his legs.'

Seeing the Sahib's playful mood Kamala felt easier and smiled – a glowing, refreshing smile. John was now so relieved he embraced her fervently and covered her face with kisses.

IV

Love without doubt had a very lowly status in Hindu society – frowned upon, discouraged, punished. The extraordinary force, vitality and energy of love between a man and woman was seen as a destructive power which could shatter and demolish the basic fabric of society. The Hindus were scared of such a rebellious force within their rigid structure. That was why arranged marriages were instituted to keep a man-woman relationship under control, so that people could participate in society through marriage – a basic, unalterable cell to provide a link with the rest. The strength of love and its inherent isolation was too much for Hindu society to absorb.

Kamala did not know the Hindu view of love so rationally but she had a fair idea of it through her strong intuitive power. She did not believe that the Sahib, in spite of all his strength, would be able to undo this basic framework of the so-called sanctified marriage. Unlike Hari and her father, the Sahib had a strong and persuasive manner which made people believe in his invincibility. This made Kamala more worried, for she could see that the consequences of such a union between her and the Sahib would be disastrous for him.

All these worries were jostling in Kamala's head one morning, when she heard the open, uninhibited Belgian voice bellowing, 'And where's my darling – not waiting outside on the veranda for me?'

Kamala immediately sprang up to greet Father Fallon. It was such a pleasure to see him again, especially now. 'Oh, Father!' she spoke excitedly. 'You haven't been here for such a long time! We all feel neglected. I see – you have no time for us.'

'My dear child, that's the problem with being a human,' the priest replied. 'God has all the time, but we mortals just run around from one place to another, trying desperately to tick. And in the process put all our love and friendship in cold storage, hoping it will survive until we finally come to look for it.'

'Father!' Kamala laughed. 'You're speaking a very complex language – it's beyond me to understand you.'

'My dear child!' Father Fallon smiled affectionately. 'You're one of the most intelligent beings I've ever come across. Moreover, you taught me a lesson – God's basic, prime lesson – how to forgive people – not through cowardliness but with dignity.'

'You're just fond of me, Father. That's why you see things in me which don't really exist,' Kamala bantered.

Father Fallon rolled his eyes teasingly and said, 'Obstinate child! You're calling me a liar!'

Now they both giggled as affection and bonhomie flowed freely.

'So what is it my dear child? I hear from John that lately you haven't been keeping well. Isn't that brute feeding you properly?' Fallon asked in a light-hearted manner.

Kamal smiled – a wan smile. In spite of Father Fallon's presence which always inspired great courage, fear engulfed her once again. Her pale, melancholy face filled the Belgian missionary's heart with sadness.

'Let me do my medical duty first.' He forced a smile.

'Father, I already know the problem. I am expecting his child.'
She murmured the words in a strange, distant voice.

Father Fallon was taken aback by the despair in her. An event
which should have been the most joyful experience for a couple so
much in love, brought her such intense pain that it surprised him.
He could not readily respond to such a complex emotion. Gently
he brought his stethoscope out and examined her – pressed her
stomach, looked at her tongue, checked the pulse-rate and then
said, 'You're right, Kamala. Soon you're going to bring on to this
earth, with God's grace, a wonderful creature!'

'I know,' Kamala sighed. The priest came close and took her
hand. Kamala's eyes filled as Fallon held her hand with paternal
affection. 'I can't marry him father! What can I do?'

'Doesn't he want to marry you?' Concern sounded in the
missionary's voice.

'Oh yes, he does! He does!' Kamala cried out. 'But how could
he? I'm already married.'

'If you both want to marry each other, I see no problem.'

'But Father! I'm a Hindu! I can't divorce Hari!'

'My child!' the missionary spoke gently. 'Under normal
circumstances I wouldn't have advised you to divorce your
husband. In the Roman Catholic church we don't believe in
divorce. A marriage – be it a Hindu or Christian – is between a
man and woman – for richer and for poorer, for better and for
worse, in sickness and in health till death does them part. But your
case is different. Your husband left you through no fault of yours.
And he did it because he himself could not protect you from the
onslaught of the evil forces. And now he has married another
woman. By this very act, he has denied marriage, he has denied a
holy institution which has God's sanctity.'

Kamala was quiet for a while. Then with a sigh she said, 'Even if
I want to, Hindu law will not permit me to marry again.'

Fallon smiled, a soothing smile, full of reassurance and said,
'Years ago when I first arrived in India, I remember a court case
reported in a newspaper. I remember it only because I was both
shocked by it and jubilant at the outcome. Although no European
was involved, their situation was similar to yours. And even today
I distinctly remember the judge's ruling – quoting Trevelyan, the
great exponent of Hindu Family Law, he pronounced – Where a
wife is deserted on the grounds of her conversion to Christianity, a
decree of divorce can be made in favour of that woman and she

can marry again as if the prior marriage had been dissolved by death.'

Kamala remained quiet for a very long time, considering the whole situation.

Father Fallon murmured gently, 'As a principle I don't advise people to adopt Christianity unless they are spiritually ready for it. I don't believe in using religion as a convenient tool. But in your case, child, you have to consider the fact that there is another life involved.'

'I know! I know!' Kamala protested. 'But this marriage won't work. It'll simply destroy the Sahib.'

Fallon looked at her and said solemnly, 'My child, many marriages falter because in a marriage we don't just have two partners – it is not simply a union between a man and a woman, it's a union of parents, friends, neighbours, childhood education, prejudices – everything. It's a wonder how many still enjoy a happy married life. And do you know why? Because God wants us to remain within the sanctity of His institution.'

'But Father, that's why our marriage won't work. We are so different.'

'Why not? You two have had more than your fair share of suffering. You particularly! But I also see – you are in love. Why then will it be impossible to make it work together?'

Kamala was quiet for a long while. Then she shook her head and muttered, 'I know, Father, it won't work. I have a curse on me – the marriage will destroy the Sahib. I know I have to do something else. Ibrahim knows someone who can help me. I don't want to – but I have to. I love the Sahib more than anything. I don't want him destroyed. He will lose his job, his respect, everything, just for me. I will never allow it to happen, not while I'm alive. Oh, please, please, help me, Father!' Kamala broke down, crying. Father Fallon softly put his hand on her shoulder and said, 'I know you are not a Christian but hear out what the Lord has said: "If men strive and hurt a woman with child so that her fruit depart from her and yet no mischief follow, he shall be surely punished, according as the woman's husband will lay upon him; and he shall pay as the judges determine.

"And if any mischief follow, then thou shalt give life for life, eye for eye, tooth for tooth, hand for hand, foot for foot, burning for burning, wound for wound, stripe for stripe".'

Kamala listened to him quietly. It seemed to ease her pain and agony. She desperately wanted the Sahib's love and his child but she was scared, scared for him. The missionary's words soothed the pain that had been within her ever since her father's visit. Now she became overjoyed at the prospect of marrying the Sahib and bearing his child. She could not wait to see him and cover him with kisses of love, of life, of happiness.

'Thank you, Father.' Her face beamed with a smile of gratitude as she addressed those words to the missionary, who was delighted to witness happiness in a girl who had suffered so long.

EIGHTEEN

I

When Banerji came home after that heated exchange with Kamala, his reaction was at first one of fear. He was certain now that there was something between Kamala and the Sahib. The way she had reacted! The way she had blushed the moment he mentioned the rumour! The way she had lost her temper when he suggested going to his cousin! It was obvious. Now it all became crystal clear – it was not that the Sahib, sympathizing with her ordeal during that riot, had given her shelter like an honest, upright man, without a trace of lust. No! No! Not at all! Perhaps the people in the town are right, he thought. Perhaps the Sahib had always had designs on her. The more he thought, the more he became convinced that the Sahib was not the honest and upright man he had believed him to be. A villain – that's what he is, he thought.

Losing faith in the Sahib filled him with paranoia. He could now imagine all kind of evil plots. He even thought that the Sahib had organized this whole nauseating incident by sending men to rape his daughter so that after the ordeal he could show generosity and kindness, and in the process make her his mistress. This sparked off Banerji's brahminic fury. He began to burn with rage and became obsessed with the idea of taking revenge against the man who, just for his lust, was prepared to destroy Banerji's whole life and reputation. Not only that: for his evil purposes he was prepared to sacrifice countless human lives.

But the desire to take revenge was not without its inherent tension. He now suffered from another fear – the fear of Kamala telling the Sahib about his visit. What would happen if the Englishman cooked up a plot and had him dismissed from the job with some phoney excuse of incompetence? He would then be totally humiliated in front of his community, with not just his daughter disgraced, mistress of a *firingee*, but he himself deprived of a prestigious civil service job. This prompted him to face the reality that something, something drastic, had to be done to strike back before the Sahib could destroy him.

II

Anil Saha was a prominent Indian. He did not have the same status as say, Lord Sinha, but by his own standards he was successful. He had taken the same examinations and tests as those taken by European civil servants and was qualified to be engaged in Land Revenue, where most Indian officers found employment.

Saha did not like his fellow Indians as a matter of course. He found them difficult to understand, time-consuming and on the whole a major nuisance to his work. He would much rather deal only with Europeans. In his mind he had no doubt he had been born into the wrong environment. To escape from what in his life he considered as a real tragedy – his origin – he tried hard to rise above it by going to England, competing with Englishmen and qualifying as an ICS officer to demonstrate that his ability was on a par with theirs. This he considered to be his supreme test in life – to prove to himself that he was not truly Indian but just happened to be born with the wrong colour and pedigree.

He always believed that given the opportunity he could qualify as an Englishman. His notion about himself was vindicated when the all-European Station Club had recently invited him to become a member – the only Indian ever to have had that privilege since its inception nearly fifty years before. Saha was proud to belong to this establishment.

Most Indians, however, looked upon Saha with fear because they firmly believed he was capable of causing great damage to their life. This became evident when John one day asked Ghosh, one of Banerji's subordinates, to go to Sripore with a despatch for a land settlement. The frightened clerk in desperation rushed to Banerji for protection. Banerji had been looking for such an opportunity for some time and eagerly offered to take the despatch himself. Ghosh was so relieved he literally touched Banerji's feet to show his gratitude.

Banerji took the following day off. The Sahib was far too preoccupied at work to know about it. Moreover, since his return from the cold weather trip, the Sahib had never spoken to Banerji except on strictly official matters. So the following morning when Banerji left for Sripore, nobody had the faintest knowledge, not even Hari, of what his real mission was.

Banerji arrived at Sripore before midday. Saha in his usual pukka sahib fashion kept him waiting until late afternoon. Under normal circumstances Banerji would have felt humiliated by this insult, but with his own mission in mind he accepted it philosophically.

When Banerji first entered his room Saha ignored him completely. He just looked through some papers, stretching his legs right across the desk. Banerji stood there like a *khitmutgar*, waiting to be summoned. An Indian officer came into the room after a few minutes and gave Banerji a cursory glance. Saha now engaged himself in deep conversation with the officer about something at the Station Club – how he had supposedly been inebriated after a couple of gins and tonic and how much he had enjoyed being there.

The fact of the matter was that whenever Saha went to the club the European community just shunned him. He often sat in a corner and drank alone. If ever he tried to join in the conversation, everyone ignored his comments, as if, just like the waiters, he was not really there. Saha, being a shrewd operator, soon realized that his best course of action was not to join in unless he was specifically addressed, and to visit the club as infrequently as possible so that the honour of being a member was not diminished by his eagerness.

When Saha finished his conversation and the officer left, Banerji tried to catch his attention. But he did not have much luck there as Saha pored over a few documents on his desk. After a while Saha felt it was time to find out the reason for this man's presence. With disdain and irritation he looked at Banerji, who, agitated with this sudden attention, in a nervous, clumsy voice said, 'Sir, I brought some land settlement documents from Mr Sugden.'

'You mean your Sahib in Raigarh?'

'Yes, sir.'

Saha took the documents, looked through them and then in an indifferent tone said, 'That's fine. I shall contact your Sahib if necessary. You can go.'

Banerji, now frightened, decided to drop all his plans and was relieved to dash for the door. Just at the last moment, seeing his carefully nurtured plan was about to collapse, he somehow gathered enough courage to turn back and say, 'There is something else I would like to tell you, sir.'

'What?' Saha was impatient.

'It is about my Sahib, sir.'

'What about your Sahib?'

'There is something wrong with him, sir.'

'You impertinent bastard!' Saha shouted, 'Don't you come here and complain about a European. If you thought I'd be sympathetic – you were wrong. You natives are all the same – the moment you find an opportunity to grumble about a European, you create trouble.'

'No, sir, I beg you. Our Sahib is being seditious.'

'Shut up *ulluk* – you black-faced monkey! You don't even know what sedition means. Just get out of here. I don't want to see your black face again.'

Much to his dismay Banerji realized that his future was now totally doomed. Not only had he failed to rouse Saha's interest, but in the process he had branded his Sahib as seditious. This he felt would soon be reported to the Sahib and he would be suspended from his post for indiscipline and perhaps dismissed. A wave of nervousness engulfed him as he stumbled through the door.

Saha, however, was thinking fast. He was a shrewd operator. He had not reached this lofty position in life, in spite of being an Indian, without considerable cunning. He realized there was no harm in listening to whatever this dolt had to say. Then, if necessary, he could report the bastard for insubordination and have him dismissed from his post. On the other hand who could tell – it might well be that rare opportunity which would give him ammunition to further his promotion.

'You!' Saha boomed. 'Come back here for a second.' Banerji, shocked, clumsily scuttled back. Saha now paid no attention to him, just carried on inspecting other important documents. Then without looking at him, he suddenly said in a cold voice, 'You have ten seconds, no more, to say whatever you want to say.'

'Sir, sir, I beg you. Listen to me! My Sahib is living with a native woman.'

Saha laughed aloud. 'That's no news. Europeans always take native women.'

'No, sir. Not like that – they eat together, they go out together, they hold hands and walk together – they, sir, even kiss each other in public places.'

Saha frowned. He was beginning to sense something. He had never liked John Sugden much – the pompous bastard. Because Sugden had graduated from Balliol, he thought there was no one up to his mark serving in India. And he always tried to dominate people with his clever arguments. But he did not possess one iota of the common sense needed for survival in a place like India. Without Charles Garvey's strong support, Sugden would have disappeared from the scene a long time ago.

'Who's this woman?' Saha asked schemingly.

'A whore, sir, a whore. Many men had her before him,' Banerji blurted out.

'A Hindu or Moslem?'

'A Hindu, sir.'

'Is she a street-woman?'

'Yes, sir.'

'Has she no family?'

This time Banerji stumbled. He knew he would be in trouble if he told lies and was later found out. He kept quiet which made Saha impatient.

'You *ulluk*! Answer my question,' Saha shouted.

Banerji now looked rather spent. With a sigh he stuttered, 'She is my daughter, sir. But she is no good. During the riot a group of men had her. She is desecrated – a loose woman now.'

'Ah!' Saha tried to gauge the situation. 'And you say they walk, holding hands in public! They even show indecent familiarity!'

'Yes, sir.' Banerji was subdued now.

'Do you have any proof?'

'Oh, sir, there are plenty of witnesses in Raigarh who will vouch for everything I have said.'

'Well, Banerji!' There was now a touch of friendliness in Saha's voice. 'Native witnesses do not count against a European.'

I have in my possession water-tight proof, Banerji thought in desperation. But he wasn't sure whether to show it to the uppity officer. A strange sense of loyalty was somehow creating a kind of obstacle which he slowly shook off and then spoke in a determined voice. 'Sir, there is some proof.'

'What is it?'

'A photograph taken during her wedding.'

'What does it prove?' Once again Saha showed impatience. These natives don't understand what's important and what's not, he thought.

'Sir. I believe the Sahib started having an affair with her almost from the day he arrived in Raigarh. During her wedding he came for the whole day, stayed with us and wore an Indian outfit.'

'You mean a native outfit? Loin-cloth and so on?' Saha could not hide his surprise.

'Yes, sir. I have a photograph here – you can see it for yourself.'

Saha took the photograph and inspected it – a picture of John Sugden in an Indian outfit with the bride and groom. The girl looked stunningly pretty. It's not surprising that Sugden should fall for someone like her, Saha thought. But showing affection in public to a native woman is a different matter altogether.

'Can I keep this photograph?'

Banerji hesitated for split second, then replied, 'Yes, sir.'

'What was that seditious business you were mentioning before?' Saha was now more probing.

'Sir, Sahib told me that Gandhi is good for India – better than the British Raj.'

'Did he actually say that?' Saha was dumbfounded.

'Yes, sir.'

'What else?'

'Sir, both the Hindus and Moslems in Raigarh are against the Sahib. Many believe he himself started the riot so that he could have a pretext upon which to possess the woman. The Moslems think he is against them because of his liaison with a Hindu and the Hindus think a Christian should not have a Hindu woman living with him. The whole thing is creating a lot of racial tension which can only help people like Gandhi.'

Saha now felt he had collected enough ammunition! Moreover, he did not think it prudent at this stage to discuss the matter further, for he had not as yet decided his course of action. He had to consider all the options open to him and choose the one which would serve him best. First of all there was the question of Charles Garvey. He and particularly his wife were very fond of Sugden. Garvey was a powerful man with high-level contacts. Rumour had it that he even had the ear of the Viceroy. Anyone trying to do anything against Garvey, without doubt, would be digging his own grave.

The problem though was not so much Garvey as his wife, for she was star-struck by Sugden's Balliol education and intellectual façade. Everyone knew the reason – she had in mind her niece, still at a boarding school in England, but soon to come to India on a cold weather trip. That was why Mrs Garvey lavished so much affection on Sugden.

Saha realized that to mount a campaign against Sugden would be suicidal. He might have to wait a long time. But the ammunition that Banerji provided was invaluable. For the time being the dolt could be a useful ally, as he was burning with rage and desperate to take revenge, provided he did not overstep his limits. This was always a difficult thing to impose upon the natives, as by nature they were anarchic. Anyway, Banerji is no threat to me really, he thought; if necessary I will not hesitate to finish him off. But the question is – could I, with this ammunition, prove enough loyalty to the Raj to secure a worthwhile promotion?

'Oh, by the way, don't mention it to anyone – I mean our conversation and this photograph,' Saha was cautious. 'For the time being, let's say we are just forgetting that this meeting has even taken place.' Saha now looked at Banerji with a sinister smile and continued, 'You understand – don't you? There could be a lot of damage if you break this promise.'

At the sight of that cold, satanic smile Banerji's heart filled with terror. He knew exactly what would happen to him if he ever crossed the man sitting opposite. But what else could he do apart from agreeing to everything that evil man was saying? The rage to take revenge against the Sahib for destroying his family's reputation and making a whore of his daughter was much too much for him to bear. He wanted revenge. Yes, revenge! At any price! Although Banerji was engulfed with immense fear he nodded his head in agreement and hurriedly left Saha's office.

NINETEEN

I

The March sun, though not as hot as that of July or August, was hot enough in Bihar. Even though John had now spent a few years in India, he had not as yet grown accustomed to the heat. It was even worse on the days when he had to go to work, for although in his own office he had an electric fan, the other offices, in spite of the languid efforts of the punka-pullers, were extremely uncomfortable.

In his bungalow, John had installed a couple of electric fans – one in the lounge and one in the bedroom; the other rooms still had punkas. But his biggest pleasure was to sit on the verandah with Kamala cooling him with a wicker fan. John often protested, 'You seem like a slave girl when you do that to me.'

Kamala would smile and say, 'I am a slave girl – your slave – don't you know?'

'But honestly Kamala, you shouldn't fan me like this. I feel awkward! Guilty!'

'You shouldn't feel guilty, Sahib. This is a duty of every Indian wife – to fan her husband. I know you are not my husband in the eyes of the law, but you look after me; care for me more than anyone else on this earth. From a woman's heart of hearts, you are my husband.'

A wave of love engulfed John. He thought how lucky he was to have a woman like her in his life.

It was a Sunday evening; the sun had gone down some time before. The twilight, hazy with the dust stirred from the road by the returning cattle, filled the sky and gave the distant fields a dreamy and picturesque appearance. John was sitting with Kamala on the veranda, sipping gin and tonic, his early evening drink before dinner. As the twilight faded into darkness they heard the noise of a carriage on the path.

'Who on earth could that be at this hour on a Sunday?' John was puzzled.

It was very unusual for anyone to visit, especially since Kamala had come to live with John. Kamala was surprised too. They looked out from the veranda. In the darkness they could see the contour of an Indian gentleman, well-suited and with a trilby hat and a cigar, getting down from the carriage. They had no doubt who it was.

'Good Lord! Anil Saha!' John could not resist voicing his great surprise. 'I wonder what he is up to this time!'

This was Saha's first visit since the time he had come for John's support to ensure a smooth entry to the membership of the Station Club. John at the time had helped him with his application, though he did not know why, for he couldn't say he was particularly enamoured of Saha. Saha's strange, deceitful eyes – cruel and ruthless – gave the impression that he would stop at nothing to further his ambition.

'Good evening! I hope I am not making a nuisance of myself by dropping in at such an ungodly hour.' Saha always had a flowery turn of phrase, especially at the very outset of a conversation when he tried to inject added politeness and managed instead to come out with ridiculous expressions.

'No! No! Not at all! It's always a pleasure to see a colleague, especially since I live in such a remote place,' John was polite.

'I was passing by and thought I would just come and say "hallo" to my friend.' Saha showed his glittering teeth. In the darkness they appeared prominent, focusing everyone's attention on what he was saying.

'Let me offer you a drink. What would you like?' John spoke convivially as Jadu switched on the light and waited for the Sahib's order. Saha did not reply. He was far too preoccupied observing Kamala, which made her uneasy. She rose to her feet. John asked again.

'Oh, gin and tonic, please!' Saha replied. Then looking at Kamala he said, 'John! I don't think I've met this friend of yours before.'

'Sorry, I should have introduced her to you. This is Kamala – Ratan Banerji's daughter.'

'Very pleased to meet you,' Saha stretched out his hand.

Kamala shrank from touching him; not because he was a man and with her Hindu upbringing she was not used to touching other men, but because his concupiscent look made her uneasy. Swiftly she left the veranda on some pretext.

'Will you stop for dinner?' John tried to be hospitable.

'If you insist, my friend,' Saha replied with a cunning smile.

John shouted from the veranda, 'Kamala! Saha's stopping for dinner with us.' Then he led the visitor to the lounge.

Just before dinner Kamala came to the lounge and interrupted John and Saha's heated discussion about the political future of India. Saha was vehemently supporting the British rule and predicting that the Raj would continue right through this century, perhaps for ever. John was no longer so sure.

'Can I have a word with you, please?' Kamala interjected.

'The lady's calling you, John, you'd better go.' Saha, relaxed, sipping his gin and tonic, addressed John with a glint in his eyes. John rose from his chair. Kamala led him outside the door, then rather uneasily voiced her fear, 'I don't want to sit with you at the dinner table.'

'Why not?' John was surprised.

'You see, he's a Hindu. He would then think badly of you,' Kamala replied.

'Nonsense!' said John. 'When he goes to Garvey's, Mrs Garvey plays the hostess.'

'I'm not your wife though, Sahib,' Kamala protested.

'But you soon will be!'

'You don't understand, Sahib. I'm sure he has something in mind. I don't like the way he has been looking at me.'

'That's just his way. Please, Kamala!' John requested earnestly. 'For my sake! Come and play the hostess! I know a Hindu woman would not normally do it. But please! Won't you?'

Kamala looked at the Sahib with great fondness. She knew she could do anything for him, so sitting at the same table with Saha was only a minor matter.

At the table John and Saha discussed various topics, Kamala kept quiet, though attentive to the guest.

'You must be highly liberated, Miss Banerji,' Saha suddenly diverted his attention to Kamala. 'It's rare for a Hindu woman to have your level of sophistication. I know Vijaya Laxmi or Sarojini Naidu have that *savoir faire*, but they are not truly Indian.'

Kamala smiled and nodded, accepting the compliment without uttering a word. 'Your father, Ratan Banerji, came to see me the other day.'

'When?' Kamala asked. There was a distinct trace of anxiety in her voice.

'Oh, about a fortnight ago. He brought a despatch from you, John. One of your land resettlement documents. That's a great job you've done. Very impressive!'

John was surprised. 'But I didn't send Ratan to you.'

'Perhaps he thought others wouldn't be able to speak English.'

'Maybe.' John became thoughtful, wondering what Banerji had said to Saha.

'Yes, he talked a great deal about his personal problems: his daughters, especially you, Miss Banerji. Your father is very fond of you.'

Kamala kept quiet. She felt uneasy now in front of Saha. All the time she had been aware that there must be a motive behind Saha's intrusion this evening; now it became clear. No doubt her father's visit prompted him to make this trip. But what was on his mind? She became anxious.

John, somehow feeling that there was a mute criticism of Kamala's living with him, tried to make the situation absolutely clear to Saha:

'Kamala and I are to be married soon. You're one of the first to know about it.'

Kamala frowned at the Sahib. She was not pleased at all that he had to make such a firm statement about his intention to marry her. She was now even more uneasy.

'Congratulations!' Saha was prompt in his response, although a hint of surprise was written on his face. In a strange voice he then added, 'Your father, Miss Banerji, gave me a different impression. I was told you were already married. Perhaps it was a mistake. The old man did not know what he was talking about.'

John was adamant this time that he would not allow Saha to go out of his house without the Indian knowing the full facts. 'Yes, she was married before. But a stupid custom would not allow her to live with her husband, or for that matter with her parents. Anyway, her husband's married again.'

'Ah! I didn't know that,' Saha replied. 'Yes, some of these native customs are ridiculously outdated for a modern world. All the same, it's very magnanimous of you, John, to help her.'

'There's nothing magnanimous about it,' John retorted. Then he looked at Kamala and spoke in a low voice, 'I love her. We love each other.'

Kamala became really uncomfortable at this. She now hurriedly made some excuses and left the table, extremely unhappy because the conversation was heading in a direction which she would have preferred to avoid.

'But if she's already married, how will you marry her, John? There's no divorce among the Hindus.' Saha was determined to probe further.

'We have a way, my friend. You'll soon see.' John was now eager to end this topic.

'That's wonderful!' Saha still persisted. 'If I can help you in any way, please let me know.'

Saha soon departed. John was no longer sure whether Saha was a friend or an enemy to him. The Indian had a way of camouflaging his real intentions which often created a feeling of insecurity among those encountering him. Kamala, however, was certain that his visit had been preplanned and his intentions were not honourable. There was something evil about him which she could not explain but knew through her sixth sense.

II

It rained heavily in early April that year, which was unusual for Bihar as the monsoon did not start until June. It starts in Bombay on 8 June precisely and then spreads within a week to the rest of the country, almost like clockwork. Although the violent storms of *kalbaishakhi* were normal for this time of year, the rain was not.

It rained for days. Since the roads were inadequate to withstand such a deluge, Raigarh was waterlogged: red, muddy water covered the entire town. John was concerned because unseasonal rain of this kind often brought floods in Bihar. The population, most of the time on the brink of poverty, had very little to spare even during harvesting. Any flood, inevitably damaging the inadequate storage facilities and destroying the whole year's crops, could be disastrous, not to mention the epidemics such as cholera and smallpox that so often followed as flood water turned inadequate sanitation into a nightmare. Although as early as 1796 Edward Jenner, a British scientist, had successfully demonstrated that, by injecting cowpox virus into healthy people, smallpox could be avoided, and the vaccines were now available even in the outposts of the Raj, illiterate villagers were still reluctant to have them. They often feared that a vaccine would bring a curse upon them from the goddess Sitala, the ultimate power behind such disease. Moreover, the early form of inoculation had also produced some side-effects such as ulceration, especially in insanitary conditions. This made them believe that tinkering with their god was an unforgiveable sin and could bring upon them terrible consequences. As the Raj wished to avoid creating any such disturbing impact, the obvious course of action recommended to most district officers was not to enforce vaccination, but to use tactful persuasion – and at least to make the facilities available.

John was totally dissatisfied with this arrangement since he could foresee the likely result of such a low-key approach. To vindicate his fears, within a week smallpox and cholera cases reached epidemic proportions. Literally hundreds died every day but there was little he could do except pray to God, which most Indians did anyway. The situation soon became so acute that he even wondered whether to travel to Sripore and make an earnest appeal through Garvey to the governor, pointing out the dangers of such a short sighted policy.

Surprisingly, at just about that time he received an invitation from Mr and Mrs Garvey. A messenger had been specifically sent to deliver the invitation to ensure its arrival. Mrs Garvey's niece had recently arrived from England and in her honour the Garveys were inviting a few friends to dinner. Eileen Garvey wrote a special note underneath stating that Charles was eager to play a few chukkas with him, for he had in recent months missed John's company. And it went without saying that the Garveys would be delighted for John to stay for the entire week-end, if that was convenient for him.

John's first reaction was to turn the invitation down. Ever since Kamala's arrival he had rarely visited Sripore – unlike last year when he had been there almost every week-end playing polo with Charles at the Station Club and then going on to dinner at the Garveys. Of course, lately he had been so preoccupied with Kamala he had had no time. Moreover, he found the Station Club no longer held the same attraction for him, though only a few months before it had been the main feature in his life for which he had eagerly waited the whole week – just to see European faces and listen to some proper English and not the pidgin that he had to endure all the time in Raigarh.

That frame of mind had changed rapidly when Kamala came to live with him. He hardly went out apart from the necessary cold weather trip. Even that, yes, even that he would have gladly dispensed with if he could. But his upbringing had instilled in him a strong sense of duty. Although he was in love, he did not allow it to interfere with his work. Socializing, however, was a different question and he did not consider it as part of his duty.

'I'm going to turn down that invitation,' John said to Kamala. For a few moments she remained silent, then in a quiet voice she suggested, 'If you do that Sahib, you'll upset them. You have enough enemies already. Perhaps that Anil Saha is spreading rumours against you.'

'But I know why the Garveys are inviting me. They want to lumber me with that niece of theirs and that's no longer a proposition.'

'You never know! When you see her you may change your mind!' Kamala smiled mischievously.

'Never, Kamala, never!' John now came close and embraced her and then looking lovingly into her eyes he murmured, 'Never!'

'But you must go!'

'In that case I'll take you with me.'

'That will not be very prudent, Sahib. Mr and Mrs Garvey will feel insulted, especially if it is for their niece they are inviting you.'

John heaved a sigh. 'You are right. I just don't like this hide-and-seek game. I want to get your divorce settled so that Father Fallon can arrange our marriage as soon as possible.'

Kamala did not reply. She knew he was already agitated and she did not want to add to it.

III

On Saturday it had drizzled since the morning. Once again it was very unusual. Unlike England, it rarely drizzles in India. Either there is heavy rain as in the monsoon, or just the relentless sun. The roads had already taken a battering from the recent *kalbaishakhi* storms followed by the unseasonal rain a few days ago. Not surprisingly it took John quite a while to arrive in Sripore.

Charles Garvey was genuinely pleased to see him. Almost like a father he hugged him affectionately and said, 'I haven't seen you for such a long time, old boy. What have you been doing with yourself – neglecting us like this?'

John felt guilty, especially because he had even considered turning down this invitation. Garvey, without doubt, was a genuine well-wisher, he thought.

In the afternoon they played polo at the Station Club. John did not do all that well in the game – his lack of practice showed.

'You're very rusty, old boy,' Garvey told him after the game. 'You should come here every week-end like you used to do. You have potential; with a bit of effort you could be good.'

'Yes, sir,' John tried to be polite.

'Moreover, I think it's unfortunate – your being stationed in Raigarh with no Europeans for miles. It's not good for your soul. Native company's all right in small doses, but not when you're surrounded by them all the time. We'll change that soon. I've already spoken to the Governor.'

This time John was on the point of protesting, even announcing his plan to marry Kamala. But just in time he refrained, thinking this was not the appropriate moment.

The evening was pleasant; there was no drizzle and the sky cleared. The Garveys had a few friends for dinner, mostly Garvey's old colleagues – all middle-aged married couples. Mrs Garvey introduced John to Edwina, her niece, who until recently had been at Cheltenham Ladies' College. She had passed her matriculation and gained a distinction, rather unusually for a woman, and was offered a place at Somerville College, Oxford. Her parents, however, were not that keen for her to go there. They wanted her to marry and settle down in life. Her father was an old India hand: he had served the Raj all his life, reaching a lofty position before he ultimately retired to a lovely cottage in Sussex. He really wanted his daughter to marry an Anglo-Indian because the old man still had a passion for India. Those officers who served in India, in his estimation, were the highest breed available anywhere in the world.

Mrs Garvey in her letters to them had often mentioned John, a Balliol graduate, intellectual, high flier – just the right sort of person for Edwina. This had sparked off a genuine interest in the heart of the old colonial and he had eagerly sought more information about this extraordinary young man. The idea had been that Edwina would come to India for a year in October, taking the cold weather trip and would spend that year deciding whether to settle down in India or take up the place at Somerville. The Garveys very much hoped that during this period she would be suitably coupled with John Sugden. For Mrs Garvey, that was her biggest dream, to see Edwina and John married.

The plan had been running smoothly until she had heard about this Indian woman in Raigarh. The rumour was spreading fast that John was deeply involved with the woman – so much so that he might even marry her. Liaisons between European men and Indian women were not uncommon. Many men, especially unmarried ones, took semi-permanent mistresses until they found a suitable English rose. From then on, any liaison had to be very casual and well hidden so as not to ruffle the feathers of a contented married life. No self-respecting Englishwoman would tolerate such a situation.

Mrs Garvey, however, was not so certain about John. Unlike other men in India, he had this Quaker streak in him – rather honest, upright and straight-laced – in a way naïve. She had always felt he needed protecting. She tried hard, though the distance between Raigarh and Sripore often prevented her from taking a more positive role.

This time, however, the news had perturbed her sufficiently to make her warn her brother and with great urgency a passage had been immediately booked for Edwina to cross the sea before the summer. Most Europeans with any sense would have avoided coming to India in midsummer, but John Sugden was too good a fish to lose, and Mrs Garvey had not hesitated to emphasise that point to her brother.

Edwina was a young, red-haired, lively girl, slim and very pretty. She had a fresh English skin with a permanent dash of colour in her cheeks. She needed no make-up to add to her beauty, though following the fashion she used it – not to accentuate her prettiness but to tone it down.

That year when she came to India she had already won a music scholarship at Somerville College, Oxford, though music was not her passion. She knew that if she met the right person with whom to settle down in life she would not hesitate to turn down the offer from Oxford.

Her aunt, Eileen Garvey, had been writing about this brilliant scholar from Balliol who was destined for high office and needed someone's stabilizing influence to channel his energy in the right direction. After the Amritsar incident many senior officers of the Raj were aware that a rapprochement with Gandhi was absolutely imperative if the Empire in this part of the world were to survive and for that they needed someone with the right moral fibre. John Sugden with his Quaker background fitted that description.

At the dinner table Mrs Garvey arranged for Edwina to sit next to John so that these two young people would have the opportunity to get to know each other. John, however, was so busy discussing with the other guests the current epidemic in Raigarh that Edwina hardly had any chance to talk to him. But she was impressed by him. In fact more than that. Love at first sight, one might have said. His blond hair carelessly brushed, intense blue eyes and a strong conviction of the righteousness of his arguments made a deep impression on Edwina. Against that the music scholarship from Somerville no longer seemed so attractive.

Dinner was superb. Mrs Garvey had prepared elaborate dishes – some of which she had cooked herself. Everyone offered superlative praise which was well deserved. After dinner Edwina entertained the guests, playing Beethoven on the piano. She was no genius but a competent performer. John could see she was not only pretty but highly talented.

Conversation soon flowed in the lounge. The old-hat Anglo-Indians recounted old stories: of the Afgans, the thuggees, the problems in India – heat, dust, disease, and inevitably Gandhi and his *swraj*. Mrs Garvey knew some of John's strong views about Gandhi. So that the whole evening should not be dissipated by intellectual fireworks, at a suitable moment she suggested to John and Edwina, 'Why don't you two young ones go on to the veranda and let the old ones gossip here.'

Edwina immediately sprang up as if she had been waiting all the time for this very opportunity, which meant John also had to get up – so as not to be impolite.

It was a full moon. The veranda was covered with a soft, luminous, mesmeric glow from outside. The long shadows from the nearby trees criss-crossing the floor and the sibilant sound of the leaves from the gentle breeze of spring made the whole atmosphere dreamy. John had a brandy and Edwina a port. They sat in the soft moonlight.

'I've heard a lot about you,' Edwina said.

'Good or bad?' John smiled.

'All excellent! A great intellectual! A man who can be compared to Nathaniel Curzon! A man with vision who could combat Gandhi's *Swrajists*! My aunt is full of praise for you.'

'That's all exaggeration!' John was already embarrassed by the eulogies.

'My aunt is a shrewd judge of people. It's true she's a fan of yours – but no one fools her.'

'Miss Jones, I think I'm an unworthy candidate for your aunt's praise.'

'Oh please, call me Edwina!' she begged and then asked, 'What do you think of India?'

'Do you really want to know?'

'Please! Although I've heard a lot from many people including my parents, but I would very much like to hear your opinion.'

'It's a strange country!' John replied. 'Full of contradictions! In a way it's a very closed society – stagnant, full of taboos, prejudices, a degenerate caste system which has taken away all the human rights of fifty million so-called "untouchables". They cannot enter into temples to worship, cannot get water from tanks used by others, cannot even walk freely through the street. Then there are superstitions like the one I'm facing now. In spite of the danger of a smallpox epidemic, nobody wants to be vaccinated because they fear it will upset the goddess of smallpox. Just imagine – they even have a goddess for smallpox – such is the level of darkness.'

'Gracious me!' Edwina exclaimed. She suddenly felt a strong wave of attraction for him.

'But then you come across people,' John continued, 'people like Gandhi – and not just him, many others, men and women who have ascended from this prejudice-ridden society to become like prophets, as if they can see beyond – beyond that which you and I with all our education cannot even fathom. They see the whole of human civilization with its endless conflicts, problems, meanness, greed, but above all they see the message of Christ – of empathy, of consideration, of love.'

'You are obviously in love with the country.'

'I am,' John sounded proud.

'Many of us though would not agree with your assessment of Gandhi.'

'I know!' John paused and then continued, 'Do you know, when

I first came to India I saw him in Calcutta – oh, creating such frenzy among people, almost hysteria – burning foreign clothes – clothes from Lancashire. He repelled me then. But I saw him again in Raigarh – in my own town – when he came to a prayer-meeting after the riots and read religious texts from the Hindu, Moslem and Christian prayer-books. It was an experience that I will never forget. He is not a human being – not in the same sense as you and I are. He's deep, sublime and esoteric.'

'That's quite revealing,' Edwina said. 'Perhaps it would be possible in future to work with him.'

'That I don't know.'

'Many people believe you could achieve that miracle, given the opportunity.'

'Oh, I don't know. I don't overestimate my ability.' John was full of humility.

'Perhaps you need a strong support next to you – someone who could stimulate you intellectually, soothe you without putting out the burning flame of your passion.'

John remained quiet. He wanted to mention Kamala, but a strange emotion somehow prevented him.

'My parents know the Viceroy, Lord Reading,' Edwina continued. 'Many senior Anglo-Indian officials, when they are in England, come to our place in Sussex for dinner.'

John could feel the direction in which the conversation was heading. 'Lots of mosquitoes on this veranda!' He stood up in an attempt to change the subject. Edwina stood up and moved towards him. He could smell her perfume, sense her warm body next to him, panting in excitement, a little wet with perspiration. For a moment he was tempted to hold her and kiss her in that romantic moonlight and forget Kamala and all the other problems that were associated with her. But only for a moment. Then he knew what he really wanted to do – what he was now prepared to announce to the world clearly and unequivocally.

He moved a little distance away from Edwina and looked at the moonlit sky framed with the leaves of peepul trees and said rather harshly, 'Perhaps you don't know Miss Jones, I'm soon to marry an Indian woman. In fact I am betrothed to her.'

It was a shock. Edwina had heard a vague rumour but now it was so certain, so pronounced. She was devastated, more than she would have ever imagined. But the human mind is complex. Until now Edwina had only heard of John Sugden from her aunt. Just a notion of a man who was destined for a lofty position in the Raj. This evening, however, had changed everything. Yes, she was in love. Within the last few hours she had built her dreams around him – perhaps foolishly – but she knew she had. The worst part of it all was this feeling of rejection. In her entire life she had never ever faced any defeat. Never! By no one! To think that it was happening here in India! And not even by another Cheltenham-educated English girl! Not by a real competitor! Oh, no! It was a cheap, native hussy who had beaten her to the post. This was too much. Her dreams of a man, a Balliol graduate, an intellectual, a man comparable to Nathaniel Curzon, even a possible Viceroy! And what was she to witness? A man enchanted by a native woman, running after her, trampling upon all the opportunities that with his talent would doubtless have been well within his grasp had he wanted them. What a silly, common man he must be, she thought. But this sense of rejection filled her eyes with tears. No! No! No! She did not want him to have the pleasure of seeing how badly she was suffering from his denial. She was not born that way. She hurriedly ran upstairs to her room, bolted the door and lay on her bed, weeping uncontrollably.

'What happened?' Mrs Garvey, sensing that some trouble was brewing, tried to salvage at least something. If there were to be a misunderstanding of any sort, it should be cleared up in a friendly discussion. She did not want this opportunity to be completely lost through some childish tiff.

'I am not feeling very well,' John spoke with determination. 'I would like to get back home tonight, Mrs Garvey. Please excuse me.'

'It's quite late, John! Over that rough terrain in a carriage! Would you not rather spend the night here and go tomorrow after breakfast?' Mrs Garvey pleaded.

'I would really like to go now if you would please call my *saice* to get the carriage ready. I'll call in another day,' John replied. Mrs Garvey was far too overwhelmed by this unfortunate turn of events to dissuade him. She asked the *khit* to call his *saice*.

The *saice* soon brought the carriage in front of the portico. John hurriedly bade goodbye and disappeared in the darkness of the carriage. The *saice* whipped the horses, rousing them to run through the rough terrain.

IV

At nearly four o'clock in the morning Kamala suddenly heard the noise of a carriage. She had not slept all that well that night, waking up quite a few times. Ever since her ordeal she had suffered from frequent nightmares – a strange, mixed-up combination of half fear and half emotion, such as being chased by a wolf and then devoured. She would wake up and find herself in a pool of sweat, often screaming. When the Sahib was there, especially next to her, just his touch, his presence, made her calm and peaceful. But last night was different. As she tossed and turned that old fear came back again – so strong and vivid that even when she woke up frightened, the macabre images still lingered in more gruesome forms.

At first she was alarmed by the noise of the carriage. Soon she recognized the familiar rhythm – the Sahib! This surprised her, for he was not expected until late the next evening. Anxiously she looked through the window and observed that the horses, after an exhausting journey through the night, were entering through the gate at a gentle trot.

The *saice* parked the carriage under the portico and got down to open the door for the master. The Sahib shambled down and then climbed the steps to the bungalow as if he were in a trance. No, not intoxicated but more like a man in delirium. Kamala, worried, sprang out of bed and put on the dressing-gown which the Sahib had bought her recently.

'Aren't you feeling well? Kamala asked anxiously. The Sahib looked at her as though in a daze and then in a weary voice replied, 'Leave me alone for a while, please!' Then he went straight to the bar and poured himself a tumbler full of Scotch.

For the first time in her life Kamala was frightened by the Sahib. She trudged back to her bedroom and sat on the bed. Then suddenly the floodgates opened and tears rolled down her cheeks. She decided that on no account would she stay there with the Sahib. Her suffering was hers alone. It was her curse, her destiny, written on her forehead on the fourth day after her birth when God had come down to write, 'You will suffer eternally. Happiness will elude you for ever and whoever you touch you will destroy.' No! she thought, I will not allow that to happen to the Sahib. As soon as morning breaks I will go away for ever. Never to see him again! Never!

Fresh pain engulfed her now with the thought of leaving him as she suffered the agony of indecision – stay with the Sahib or leave – both equally painful. The thought of leaving him, never to see him again, rent her heart to pieces. But then again she could not witness him destroyed day by day from her own curse. He was much too kind and gentle with the heart of a real man – a man who was destined to reach great heights. She had no right to steal him away – depriving others of the benefit of his wisdom, his ability, his prophetic power. She had no right to seduce him to the darkness of India. No! She would never allow that to happen. Now she was determined to leave him at daybreak.

Early in the morning, perhaps about six o'clock, the Sahib entered her room. She was still in tears, thinking about the pain and suffering that life had forced her to endure, frightened of what the future might hold for her when she left this kind, protective tower of a man.

She looked at him. His eyes melted in love as he came forward, slowly stretched himself and lay by her and then gently held her hands.

'Promise me, Kamala, you will never leave me,' he implored. There was a strange sadness in his voice.

'Sahib, you will be better off without me. I am destroying you – can't you see?'

'Darling, you took away my nightmares, do you know that? Before I met you, I suffered an awful lot. It was a life of terror. Every night I was frightened of going to bed because I knew what I would see the moment my eyes were closed. No! No! Please, Kamala! Don't force me to go through that life again! Please, I beg you! Don't ever leave me.'

Kamala, once again was plunged into a dilemma. What was she to do? If she stayed with the Sahib, he was sure to be destroyed. On the other hand how could she leave him, knowing this would bring great suffering to the person she loved?

'Sahib, you don't understand – my presence is no good for you. Please, let me go. I am sure you will soon get over your nightmares once you marry a beautiful English girl. You do not know what awful prospect must be waiting for you if you insist on having me.'

'Do you love me, Kamala?' John asked earnestly.

'I do, Sahib, I do. But please, don't make it difficult for me. Please let me go. For your own sake, please!' Kamala begged.

'If you really loved me, Kamala, you would stay with me and not run away.'

'Oh, Sahib!' Kamala held his hand tight. 'I don't know what to do. Please help me!'

John, now more relaxed, caressed her forehead gently and then kissed her eyes. They stayed like that for a long while.

'Is she pretty?' Kamala suddenly asked the Sahib.

'Very!' John had a mischievous smile on his face.

'Is she intelligent?'

'Oh, very!'

'Then why do you not marry her?'

John smiled, full of affection. 'Because you are more pretty and more intelligent.'

'I don't believe you.'

'True! She could organize a dinner party for Lord Reading – or discuss politics – but she could not recite John Donne like you can – not with the same feeling and intensity.'

'You are telling me a lie again,' Kamala's eyes melted in love.

'No, darling! It's true!' John now placed a kiss on Kamala's sensuous lips to seal his love.

PART FOUR

The Trial

TWENTY

I

A week later, on a Sunday, soon after John and Kamala had finished their lunch, they could see dust rising in the air on the distant horizon – a horseman was coming towards the bungalow at full gallop. The way he rode the horse, with skill, confidence and aggressive horsemanship, indicated he was a European. John wondered who could it be at this time on a Sunday. As the horseman approached nearer, he could see the contour of the man – Charles Garvey.

'Oh God!' John exclaimed. He was a little frightened of facing his superior officer.

Garvey was a man for whom he had great respect. Last week when he had turned Edwina down, it was not so much that, but the thought that it could mean the end of a valued friendship with the Garveys that upset him a great deal. But when the choice became stark, there was no possibility of anyone winning his heart against Kamala.

Soon Garvey arrived. His horse, soaked with sweat and dust and absolutely shattered, was foaming at the mouth. It was rather unusual for Garvey not to use a carriage for such a long journey, which would usually have been expected from an officer of his rank. But for whatever reason, Charles Garvey had decided to ride his horse today.

John rushed out to welcome him. 'This is a surprise, sir. I'm honoured. Please do come in!' He politely led Garvey to the lounge.

'I haven't seen this part of the country for a long time. And I thought it was time I visited you,' Garvey replied as he followed the young officer.

'That's very kind of you, sir. Let me arrange lunch for you.'

'No, no, I won't eat anything. But you can certainly offer me a Scotch.'

Seeing Garvey arriving, Kamala stayed away. Jadu brought drinks for the sahibs and they sat in the lounge, trying to chat casually. But they both knew that this was not the main purpose of Garvey's visit, and the conversation was uneasy.

'Let's go for a ride. It's years since I have been to those hills,' Garvey suggested to his young subordinate.

'Certainly, sir.' John knew that Garvey with English politeness would not discuss anything controversial at his bungalow.

They both got their horses and at a canter progressed towards the hills. After a while they rode side by side at a gentle trot.

'I'm fond of you, John,' Garvey opened the conversation. 'And not just I, Eileen's also a great admirer of yours.'

'I know, sir. I'm permanently indebted to you both. Since I've been in India, you two have without doubt, taken on my parents' role.'

'Oh, John, that's very reassuring. I was so fearful before I came here.' Garvey seemed genuinely relieved.

John did not reply. As yet Garvey had not indicated the purpose of his unexpected visit – not that John was unable to surmise the reason – that was far too obvious.

Garvey continued, 'We, the officers of the Raj, have to be a special breed, you know. Only a thousand of us running this vast country of three hundred million people. And they are so different from one another: different cultures, different races, different religions, different habits. Then they have all the superstitions, prejudices, rivalries – and now Jinnah and Gandhi. It's a mammoth task.'

John listened to him expressionlessly. He knew that Garvey would now try to assess the reason for his strange behaviour the other evening but he was not sure how he himself should respond to his superior officer's questioning.

'Do you know what your own Balliol man, Curzon, once said about the Raj?' Garvey continued. 'He said – "To me the message is carved in granite, hewn in the rock of doom that our work is righteous and that it shall endure!".' Garvey paused for a moment and then added, 'But to make it righteous, to make it endure, every officer must ensure that he is treading the right path, the accepted path, the approved path – which we know for certain will not rock the boat.'

John had been listening to Garvey patiently. Now he thought the time had come to respond. 'That would be too regimented, sir. Much though I agree with Curzon's spirit that our work has to be righteous to justify our stay in a foreign country, regimentation is not the answer. One has to explore, analyse, experiment – occasionally even grope to find one's own way – but the right way, the honest way – the way to peace and justice.'

'Of course, you are right,' Garvey replied. 'Our Empire has never been built on injustice or motivated by exploitation. We've never tried to regiment our procedure to such an extent that it's suppressed individual initiatives. You know that's not the British way. We are the proud torch bearers of such names as Nicholson, Sleeman, Napier. They were not regimented officers of the Raj. They were ambitious, independent – they were go-getters. They knew exactly what was needed to make things tick. And don't forget – they were not doing it for their own narrow, personal benefit. They were doing it for a much greater purpose – they were doing it for the Raj – they were doing it for India.'

John was quiet for a while. Then he softly responded, 'What is on your mind?'

Charles Garvey now raised the point that had been bothering him for some time and for which he had made this journey today. 'In many ways, John, I am a liberal person. But I believe in decorum. It is our responsibility to set a standard which Bradshaw years ago pointed out to British officers coming to India – the moral behaviour of all classes of Europeans should be extremely discreet to command the respect of the native community.'

'I suppose you have Kamala in mind,' John tried to bring to the surface the undercurrents that had been flowing between them.

'Listen!' Garvey said. 'I don't mind what you do. But be discreet! It's not uncommon for Europeans to have Indian women. We are not saints. Frankly, we can't be expected to be – living thousands of miles away from home. And very often, as in your case, without a single European in sight for miles. Even the normal feminine touch is missing for many of us in India. But that doesn't mean you flaunt a native woman.'

'What exactly do you mean?'

'I am saying, old boy, that you have the potential to reach great heights. Don't make a fool of yourself.'

'Forgive me for asking you this, sir, but it's not for Edwina that you are upset – is it?' John was pungent in his questioning.

'Good Heavens! No! You're free to choose whoever you like in life. But get this native woman out of your house. People are gossiping; not just the Europeans, but the Indians: Hindus, Moslems – all of them.'

'What do I care about the gossip?' John said rebelliously.

'Stop living in cloud-cuckoo-land, John!' Garvey admonished the young man. 'You have to care about the gossip – because you're a proud officer of the Raj.'

'What you don't know, Mr Garvey, is that I'm going to marry her.' John sounded determined in his reply.

Garvey was shell-shocked by this piece of news. He was a cool, calm administrator who had oiled the wheels of the Raj for a long period. He was not easily perturbed. But hearing John's utterly irresponsible statement made him extremely angry. Now he could not resist shouting at him. 'You must be out of your mind! I know you're a bit eccentric – but not this much. Do you realize what you're saying?'

John was calm and composed, though inside him a storm was raging as he tried to face up to his superior officer's anger. 'Yes, sir. I have given it a lot of thought. Do you think I would make a decision like this lightly?'

Garvey knew this young, headstrong subordinate only too well. Confrontation was not the way to convince him of the irresponsibility of his attitude. He now tried to appease John by his calm reasoning. 'Listen, I know she went through an awful ordeal during the riot and now her family, in spite of her innocence, has rejected her. It's their own inadequacy. Their society is so regimented – it can't cope with exceptions; so it tries to eliminate them ruthlessly. But that's not your responsibility.'

John was not to be spoken to by his superior officer in this manner. He replied stubbornly, 'Sir, if you don't mind my saying so – you are only asking me to follow their example. You are imposing the same discipline, perhaps not so ruthlessly as yet, to eliminate exceptions from your system.'

'Be reasonable, John!' Garvey interrupted him. 'Can you imagine yourself working as a district officer, a magistrate, a man of great importance, commanding respect from thousands of Indians for fair play, peace and justice, while married to a Hindu woman who has already been married, and worse, was subjected, amid a great controversy, to rape and riot? Do you think you would be able to face it out?'

'That I don't know, sir. You may well be right. No doubt it will be difficult. But what I do know is that she is expecting my child.'

'Good Lord!' Garvey, realizing the depth of John's involvement with the Indian woman, could not hide his exasperation. 'That's all the more reason why you should part company at once. Don't allow a potentially explosive situation to explode, for heaven's sake!' He paused for a while and then gently added, 'We'll take care of her and her child, I promise. She will never suffer from any financial problem.'

John was quiet for a moment, then he firmly replied, 'But I love her, sir.'

Garvey could no longer control his temper. He blurted out, 'Do you know what you are doing? Not only are you ruining your own future, but you're in the process of destroying tbe basic fabric of the Raj. If you try to marry a girl who's already married – and there's no divorce under Hindu law – all hell will break loose. A major commotion – perhaps of Amritsar's magnitude – will erupt. The Raj barely scraped through that one. It won't be able to withstand another. The whole place will collapse with riots and strife.'

'But they don't want her, sir!' John helplessly tried to defend himself. 'They left her to be a whore!'

'That's the Hindu way of life and they don't want anyone to tinker with it.' Garvey showed the superior officer's wisdom and his years of experience in India. To ensure that his subordinate understood the seriousness of the problem he added, 'Do you know what her father's saying now? He is saying that you yourself arranged the rape so that you could have her.'

'Who? Ratan Banerji's saying that? I don't believe it.' John was outraged by this accusation.

Garvey looked at the young man with pity and replied, 'Do you know why you don't believe it? Because you have forgotten to keep your eyes open and ears to the ground.' He paused and then continued somewhat anxiously, 'I'm not concerned about that stupid old civil servant, but Gandhi, Joshi, Jinnah – they'll all make major capital out of the incident. And at whose expense? Us – the Raj. Can you imagine the headlines in the newspaper? "A senior European officer, to possess a married Brahmin woman, started a riot and murdered a hundred innocent people". Can you really imagine it?'

'Sorry, sir! My marriage is my personal affair, and I won't accept any official interference.' Though John was upset by what Garvey was saying, he was not prepared to be swayed from his decision.

'I'm trying to knock sense into you, young man!' Garvey spoke in despair. 'Those of us who serve the Raj don't have a personal life. Our life is sacrificed to our king. India is a jungle. An uncivilized, dangerous, ruthless jungle. Your own hero, Kipling, once said about the laws of the jungle, "But the head and the hoof and the haunch and the hump is – obey!".'

'No, sir. On this, I can't.' John was determined and stubborn.

'For the last time I'm asking you, John – don't destroy yourself! And don't destroy the Raj! You have a responsibility towards your king. You can't just shrug your shoulders and deny it.' Garvey still tried to instil some loyalty into this young officer's conscience.

John by now was absolutely clear about his priorities in life. He firmly replied, 'I don't deny that responsibility. But my responsibility to the mother of my child, in my view, is even greater. I'm sorry to have to make this choice.'

'I had high hopes for you, John,' Garvey sounded intensely sad. 'Now I think they were misplaced.' A stern expression covered his face as he murmured, 'If you change your mind, let me know. But soon.'

Then Charles Garvey turned his horse and rode fast in the direction of Sripore. For a while John pondered over the entire question, but he did not alter his decision.

II

The summer was approaching fast. The countryside was becoming increasingly parched. The unseasonal rains and flooding that had created such havoc and started a major epidemic of smallpox had completely dried out within a few days. No longer was there that damp, musty smell of soil, or the wailing of relatives for the death of their near ones, or the constant billowy smoke ascending from the cremation ground – everywhere was now scorching in the relentless sun. The only trace of evidence left by the rain were some of the marks on the road made by the heavy wheels of various bullock carts which had grooved deep into the rain-soaked, miry ground. But the roads, now dried out, gave the impression of an extended field ready for tilling. Whereas previously the wet and soggy road had been a nuisance, now the broken, hardened ground made the journey so rough that it became quite a test of endurance for anyone moving in or out of Raigarh.

After Garvey's departure John spent the next few days in trepidation. Garvey was a good friend but a tough adversary. Like all officers of the Raj, he did not take defeat lightly. John, by refusing his friendly request to leave Kamala, had made it clear that even if the battlefield brought misery for himself, he was prepared to stand firm and fight the issue. It was after all a major issue for him – one of personal freedom – freedom to choose whomsoever he wished to marry. And on this he was not prepared to be dictated to by the Raj.

But the decision to stick to a point on a matter of principle is one thing, he thought, and having to face the battle is another. He knew that if he shared his worries with Kamala it would only cause her anxiety. She might even take drastic action to prevent the Sahib's downfall and in the process bring pain and misery upon herself. John knew that was not the solution he was seeking. No longer. Kamala had become an integral part of his existence. Any future he would be considering now had to be a joint one – his and Kamala's, and of course that of their unborn child.

John did not have to wait long for the Raj's response to his so-called irresponsible behaviour. The hand-delivered note came on the fourth day – telling him to attend Garvey's office at ten o'clock the following morning. A cold official order, with none of the former bonhomie or affection, no little handwritten p.s., inviting him to a game of polo and dinner in the evening which, only a week before, would have been the norm. The message was now clear – there could only be an official relationship between a senior, well-trusted officer of the Raj and someone as anarchic as John Sugden.

III

Garvey, in the last few days, had had to reassess his opinion of John Sugden. Up until now he had been almost star-struck by John's extraordinary brain. Although one gets the crème de la crème – the finest products of British aristocracy to serve in India, he thought, rarely does one come across a person of John's intellectual prowess. He had that uncanny knack of grasping complex problems so easily, so nonchalantly, be they in diplomatic areas, relationships with princes or land resettlement, and then immediately producing a solution, a unique solution, which would be beyond the imagination of almost everyone else.

But like all geniuses, the man had in him the seeds of his own destruction. He simply could not handle the emotional side. A tough situation, no doubt, especially for a man in his mid-twenties, away in a no-man's-land, surrounded by Indians. But his situation was not unique; many British officers had to face the same dilemma as John. And they had never betrayed the Raj.

Garvey in his righteous mood, not only considered his subordinate's obstinacy and stubornness (and he himself was no less stubborn) but was concerned about the destructive element in John. In his assessment of people Garvey often gave credit to those who were prepared to dig in their heels over issues which they believed to be true and honest.

Take the case of Amritsar, Gavey thought remorsefully. No doubt Dyer had rocked the boat by overreacting and killing so many. But in spite of all the blame which could be apportioned to him, there was one thing certain – his patriotism. That was beyond question. He had behaved in the firm, though ill-conceived belief, that his actions had been necessary to keep the Raj safe and intact. If, driven by patriotism, John had been following a similarly destructive course, Garvey would have understood it. But no! It was the narrow self-interest – the lust, that the Raj could not condone. Promiscuity on the side as a sparetime hobby, done with discretion, could perhaps be tolerated, but making it the main aim of life could never be accepted from an officer of the Empire.

Garvey had no doubt in his mind that this whole episode would bring about an enormous furore. Gandhi, Jinnah, Joshi – they would all, like blood-sucking vampires, try to make maximum political capital against the Raj. And who could blame them if an opportunity like this was presented on a plate – a senior European officer of the government, arranging a massacre, killing a hundred, injuring thousands, just to satisfy his lust!

IV

It was a hot, sweaty morning when John came to see Garvey. He was nervous, as could be expected, though strong in his conviction that whatever might be the outcome of this meeting, he was not prepared to sacrifice his principles – Kamala must not be discarded on any pretext. He waited outside Garvey's office with trepidation. Fortunately he did not have to endure this uncertainty for long, because Garvey was prompt in attending to him.

As he entered the room Garvey smiled – a cold smile – friendship was there no longer – not even a trace of affection. He motioned to John to sit down. 'Tea?'

John's throat was feeling so dry with the heat outside and his own nervous tension that he accepted Garvey's offer with alacrity.

The *chaprasi* brought tea. They both sipped in silence for a minute or two. Garvey stood up, walked towards the window and looked outside. Then suddenly in a distant voice he murmured, 'I have unpleasant news for you.'

'I was half expecting it, sir,' John tried to show his courage – a kind of dare-devilry.

Garvey took no notice of his reply. In a measured voice he said, 'The riot in Raigarh has created dismay among various sections in India. Jay Prasad, Khodadad, Joshi – they all are insisting on a full-scale investigation. As impartial administrators of the Raj, we have a duty to ensure that proper procedures were adhered to, prior to and during the riot, and that such sacrifice of human life was not caused by carelessness or negligence on anyone's part. The Viceroy, as a result of the appeal made by various sections of the community, has decided to appoint a commission to conduct a full-scale enquiry. I have been asked to chair the commission. I understand that Anil Saha will also be a member.'

'Anil Saha!' John could not hide his surprise.

'This perhaps would not have happened a few years earlier. But the political wind is changing very rapidly. We have to show our willingness to share power with the Indians, especially after the Amritsar incident. And don't forget that the Hunter commission which investigated Amritsar had three Indian members out of a total of six, and all three came out against Dyer. In that respect you're much better off – only one Indian in a three-man commission, and the member is known to you.'

'I am not questioning the composition of the Viceroy's appointed commission. I have no such impertinence. I was just surprised to hear Saha's name. That's all.' John was calm and composed.

'Initially we approached Lord Sinha,' Garvey replied. 'He would have been ideal – carries so much respect among both the

Indians and Europeans. But he's in poor health these days, and I'm not surprised that he declined. You see, we don't have many qualified Indian administrators to take up an appointment like this. And Saha is a competent civil servant. We feel he will be a major force in the subcontinent in the years to come.' Garvey sounded apologetic about Saha's inclusion.

'I have no complaint against Saha, sir.' John tried to make it clear that he had no personal animosity against the Indian.

'The third member, also a European, is yet to be decided. But he'll be an outsider – perhaps a retired judge.' Garvey tried to impress upon John that the constitution of the commission was absolutely impartial. John made no comment – just listened to him. 'As soon as the commission is formalized you will be notified.'

'Yes, sir.'

'And oh! Unfortunately we have now no option but to suspend you from your duties, of course on full pay, until the commission reaches its verdict. This is not a disciplinary action, I emphasize, only a precautionary measure. John Smith from Nabagram will look after your district for the time being. He will come and see you next week, if you could hand over everything to him.'

'Yes, sir,' John nodded with a pallid face.

Suddenly Garvey blurted out, 'For heaven's sake John, why don't you leave this girl? Can't you see, you're in a bloody mess? The girl's father, your own subordinate, is not only accusing you of arranging the rape but he has now produced a photograph of you in a native outfit. I'm not supposed to show it to you, but there you are – unofficially you can have a look at it, if it helps you to change your mind.' Garvey took a large envelope from the top drawer of his desk and placed it in front of his subordinate.

John was surprised; he had not known of the existence of any such photograph. He took the envelope and opened it – Kamala's wedding photograph – he himself in the Indian costume with Kamala and Hari. Kamali, still very young, looked radiant in her wedding sari and all the jewellery.

'Wearing Indian clothes, I presume, is not a crime.' John was caustic in his reply.

'Under normal circumstances, no. Even then, an officer of the Raj has to be circumspect before indulging in such frivolous but dangerous pursuits. But the worst part is Banerji's claim that even before his daughter's marriage you were having an affair with her.'

John was shocked by this accusation. But he recovered quickly and replied, 'Surely, this photograph does not prove it!'

'True, it doesn't. Neither would you expect a newly-wed Indian woman to be looking fondly at a European DO.'

With immense surprise John picked up the photograph again. It was true! She was looking – not at her husband but at him – and a trace of affection was gleaming in the corner of her eyes.

The photograph only helped fill John's heart with more love and a stronger resolution not to leave Kamala. As he left Garvey's room, he wondered whether the love between them had been there from the very first day they had met each other. That fine afternoon in Raigarh when a young girl had garlanded him was still vivid in his memory.

TWENTY ONE

I

When John Sugden returned to Raigarh, the message to him became loud and clear. The British Raj, which exercised authority and influence over three quarters of the world, was not prepared to accept rebellion from one of its officers. Realizing for the first time the possible consequences of his actions, John became subdued for a few days. The might of the Raj was so immense; only a man of Gandhi's ability and stature could combat that incredible storehouse of power – no one else. Certainly not John Sugden. Moreover, such was his unfortunate predicament that he had now alienated himself, not just from the Raj, but from the Hindus, the Moslems – in fact from everyone in India.

This did not weaken him, however. The Quaker trait in his character only steeled his resolution because he was confident that justice was with him. Persecution had to be endured, he thought. Under no circumstances am I prepared to leave the mother of my unborn child.

* * *

Kamala realized that the meeting with the Burra Sahib that day was not at all one of amity and chukka-playing. She waited patiently for the Sahib to tell her what had happened, but no news was forthcoming. He just brooded over a tumbler full of Scotch. Finally she could stand no more. 'You seem very distant these days,' she commented.

'Just preoccupied with a few things at work. I'm sorry if I am neglecting you,' John tried to reassure her.

'It's not me I'm worried about. But in the last few days you seem to be so quiet. What did the Burra Sahib say to you?'

'Who? Garvey? Nothing much – just a routine discussion – that's all.' John sidestepped the issue. He knew he would only create more anxiety in her if he told the truth. Kamala did not insist, for she knew the Sahib was not in the right frame of mind. And she did not want to add to his anxiety.

II

It was not long, however, before Kamala came to know everything. Not only Kamala, but everyone in Raigarh, everyone in Sripore, everyone in India, even some in England knew that a commission had been appointed to investigate the Raigarh riot.

The Indian newspapers, especially those which as a matter of course supported the government, approved this move. They wrote lengthy leaders which in no uncertain terms considered the responsibility of the Raj for its Indian subjects and their well-being. 'We have a duty to ensure,' they wrote, 'that religious blood baths in the subcontinent do not destroy the basic fabric of harmony. For the sake of peace we implore Mr Gandhi to use his influence and good offices to all sectional interests with the same zest and vigour as he employs against the government for his *swraj* movement.'

The nationalist newspapers, however, took a different view. They asked the government to send Mr Sugden back home forthwith, even before the commission reached its verdict. They warned the government – Do not whitewash the guilt of a British officer by appointing a supportive commission. They also voiced their antipathy to the fact that out of three members only one was Indian – and even he a supposed friend of the accused. Then of course the inclusion of Sugden's senior officer in the commission must raise the question – how independent is it really?

In spite of all these comments by the newspapers the Viceroy maintained his dignity and refused to change the composition except for one minor adjustment – the chairman. Initially it had been announced that Garvey would chair the commission; but now the Viceroy in his wisdom decided that the commission would be chaired by Sir Garfield Evans – a well respected, retired high court judge.

The situation in Raigarh now took a rather different turn. The town did not quite have the civilized tone of the metropolis. Posters soon appeared in Hindi and Urdu, 'John Sugden *murdabad* – death to John Sugden.' Some posters even gave Sugden a pirate's eye-patch with a skull and crossbones to illustrate their view about his role in the riot. Demonstrations were held by the Islamic Front and the Hindu League. Inflammatory speeches were delivered by several leaders, denouncing Sugden and the Empire.

John could clearly see the writing on the wall. He wanted to go to Calcutta to see Stanley Congdon but was scared to leave Kamala on her own.

'Please, go! I'll be all right,' Kamala implored. 'With Ibrahim, Jadu and so many servants around, there will be no danger for me.'

John agreed because he had no other option. He desperately wanted to explore the possibility of a job in Stanley's company. He sent a telegram informing Stanley of his impending visit to Calcutta and had a reply almost by return – 'Please call at my office when you're here.' This reassured John, for he felt that at least his friendship with Stanley, in spite of everything, was still intact.

III

The night before John's departure, Kamala seemed subdued for the entire evening.

'What's the matter? Why are you so depressed?' asked John, somewhat concerned. 'If you're frightened to stay alone, I won't go. Or perhaps you could come with me to Calcutta.'

'No, Sahib. That won't help anyone. You go. I'm just being silly,' Kamala replied. Her eyes were full of sadness.

'Darling, I'll be back within three days,' he tried to reassure her.

'And if things work out, perhaps we could go and live in Calcutta. You wouldn't mind that – would you? Leaving Raigarh?'

'No, Sahib,' she responded politely. John thought she somehow lacked conviction. Perhaps she did not believe he could get a job in Stanley's company.

Kamala, however, was in a very different mood that night. She showered him with all the affection and love he could ever have expected from a woman. If he had not experienced this love, he would never have believed it was possible for any man and woman to love each other as much as they did. Even three days absence from Kamala now seemed too much to bear, such was his mental state.

IV

A hot summer day. The monsoon was still far off. Howrah station was hot and humid. There was pandemonium; people were jostling everywhere – a kind of explosive excitement. One could almost feel the stress of the throng – like the verve of a highly charged pylon, ticking with power. This was unusual even for the hurly-burly of Calcutta.

'What's going on here?' John asked a European who was eagerly making his way to the station.

'Sir Charles Tennant was assassinated last evening. There's a riot in the city.'

'Good Lord! Sir Charles Tennant!' John knew Sir Charles. During his induction programme he had spent a couple of days with him at Lalbazar police station. Sir Charles had a reputation for being a tough police chief and had sent many terrorists to the gallows. His process of interrogation was ruthless, especially if he thought the man was guilty and in possession of information which could lead to further arrests. Most nationalist leaders simply loathed him.

In his short acquainance, John had come to respect Sir Charles. Like many officers serving the Raj, he had scant regard for the Indians, but so had Compton-Smith; and yet he had sacrificed his life to save a little beggar-boy.

The roads gave a clear indication of a riot-torn city – empty on the whole except for groups of people, highly charged, clustered at street corners; some hiding in the back streets, and some on the verandas of near-dilapidated Indian quarters. Pieces of brick, broken glass and blood-stained papers were strewn everywhere. Shops were looted, their doors smashed, showing visible signs of rampaging inside. In places, the charred wreckage of the vehicles which had been burnt by the crowd the previous evening were still there, waiting to be removed. A few people with Gandhi-caps were walking through the streets, apparently fearless, perhaps denoting their non-violent roles. John noticed that helmeted military, carrying guns, not the usual red-turbanned, *lathi*-carrying police directed the traffic at every road junction to ensure that Europeans did not travel through the 'no go' areas.

V

Stanley was at his office when John called.

'You couldn't have picked a worse day than this. Absolute chaos!' Stanley moaned in between his attempts to make numerous telephone calls. 'It's tough to get things done even at the best of times but when Gandhi's rioters are about, you may as well say goodbye to your business.'

'Surely Gandhi's not involved in this – is he?' asked John, surprised.

'How should I know?' Stanley was irritated by his friend's question. 'After all, he's one of the agitators – isn't he?'

'Yes. But there's a difference.'

'What difference? He's just as bad as the rest,' Stanley spoke with bitterness. 'At an exhibition in Bhagalpur, a few months ago, they had the audacity to fly *swraj* flags at six different places. The one Union Jack hoisted was pinned to the pole so that in a breeze you could only see the *swraj* flags flying. That's your Gandhi – cunning and seditious.'

'I know,' John tried to subdue Stanley. 'But our own behaviour, which after all should set an example, is not always brilliant. Think of that stupid major of the 14th Jat Lancers who beat an Indian woman and forced her out of a railway compartment when she had a valid ticket and he didn't.'

'I don't know the ins and outs of all these things. But I do know I have a shipload of goods waiting at the docks and I cannot get them released because of this damn riot.' Stanley sounded highly irritated with this conversation but soon he controlled himself and said, 'Listen, I don't want to fume about my business to you. And I'm pretty pushed for time. Can just about squeeze in a lunch but it has to be brief; I have another appointment at two o'clock.'

They came out. Chowringhee was fairly clear of the rioters, though there was a heavy police presence. They drove to Firpos. There the manager, pleasant and attentive as usual, offered them a corner table.

They made small talk for a while but John knew Stanley did not have much time to spare. He cleared his throat nervously to broach the subject. 'I'm considering leaving the civil service.'

'I know. It's all over the newspapers. In fact both the Islamic Front and Hindu League, given the opportunity, would have you hanged.'

John smiled awkwardly, remained silent for a while, then suddenly mumbled, 'Some time ago your father suggested that I should join his company.'

'Oh, did he? I didn't know that.' There was a trace of jealousy in Stanley's voice.

'What do you think of the possibility now?'

'The problem is,' Stanley lifted his head and looked straight into John's eyes, 'if the Viceroy loses confidence in you as a person, it becomes rather difficult for anyone else to employ you. Let's face it, you won't be an asset to us now, especially if you continue to live with that Hindu woman. People simply won't deal with you.'

John was a bit shaken by his straight and uninhibited reply, but he tried to make a last appeal. 'I thought – being a Eurasian yourself and knowing the problem at first hand – you would at least have some empathy for Kamala and my unborn child.'

Stanley was visibly upset by this reference to his origin. For a few seconds he was mute, then in a bitter voice replied, 'Perhaps you don't know – since the year 1900 we have been officially designated as Anglo-Indian – just the same as all other Englishmen living in this country for generations.'

John realized at once that he had hurt Stanley's feelings. 'I didn't mean it that way,' he tried to ameliorate the situation rather clumsily.

Stanley had already calmed down. In a distant, melancholy voice he murmured, 'In some ways you're right – we are second-class citizens. But that makes it even more difficult for us to have you, because we can't afford to upset the government or the European population. And frankly, we wouldn't survive even a single day if the Europeans were against us.' Stanley paused for a while, turned his face and observed through the window the usual procession of the crowd in the maidan. Suddenly he looked back at his friend and said bluntly, 'You know something, John! I don't feel you would fit in well in a business world. You are much too honest, too straightforward. Running a business requires little intellect but a great deal of ability to get on well with people. I am not sure about you on that score.'

A long silence followed. Stanley soon got up and muttered, 'I must go. I've an appointment. But keep me posted with your news.'

Looking at his face, John knew he did not really mean it.

TWENTY TWO

I

When the Sahib left for Calcutta that day, Kamala was in a dilemma – unsure of what to do. For the last few days, knowing of the appointment of a commission which included that evil man, Anil Saha, she had been at the end of her tether. The writing was on the wall. And she had no doubt in her mind who was the cause of this ghastly turn of events. But even if you knew you were cursed, what were you to do with yourself? She knew she loved the Sahib. Not just love – a lot more than that – an inexplicable bond. But the question was – how to safeguard the Sahib's future?

With all these questions in mind Kamala, soon after the Sahib had left that morning, asked the *saice* to take her to the Hindu quarters. She had not been to her parents' house for a long time – since the night of her humiliation. To her unaccustomed eyes everywhere looked more poverty-stricken than where she now lived, though this was supposedly the most prosperous part of the Hindu quarter. People were surprised to see the Sahib's carriage in that part of the town. Men, women, children – they all crowded outside as she got down in front of her father's house. All the girls and women who knew Kamala from childhood stood round her and then followed her with unabashed curiosity, but distant and unfriendly as if she were from a different planet.

As she went through the gate of her parents' house, one of her sisters saw her in the courtyard and screamed in fearful surprise – Kamala! Hearing her distraught voice they all came rushing outside, but stopped suddenly and stood by the door – looking at her from a distance with a strange mixture of horror and fascination. No one, not even her mother came forward to greet her.

Kamala calmly walked towards her mother and touched her feet to show respect. Her mother's face slowly melted with affection.

'Sit down for a while – your father's away,' her mother said, 'but he'll be back soon. And you'd better go away before he comes, otherwise all hell will be let loose.'

'I am here to see him.' Kamala's voice was soft but determined.

'Why?' Mrs Banerji was utterly baffled.

'I want to leave the Sahib.'

Her mother was quiet for a while. Then her eyes filled with tears. She embraced her daughter with grief and sadness. They both wept, easing the tension which had been building up for a long time.

'Don't you love him?' Mrs Banerji asked soothingly, wiping her daughter's eyes.

'Yes I do! But I don't want him destroyed for my sake.'

Mrs Banerji now looked at her pensively, trying to share the despair of her cursed daughter.

By the time Banerji arrived home the tension between mother and daughter had eased and Kamala was talking to her mother and sisters smilingly. Banerji went almost deathly pale on seeing her there. Slowly his face turned hard and ruthless as he spoke rather mockingly, 'What's all this celebration for?'

Kamala stood up and moved towards her father to touch his feet. He pulled away. 'Don't touch me!' he ordered. She stood still, hurt and humiliated.

'What do you have in mind?' Banerji's voice was cold. 'If you think I'll go to Anil Saha to plead for your lover, I can tell you, Saha is not that kind of person. Very honest and upright he is.'

'I am not here to plead for the Sahib,' Kamala spoke with pride and dignity.

'What then?' Banerji was irritated.

'You mentioned that uncle in Calcutta!'

'What about him?'

'I wonder whether I could live with his family.'

The obvious surprise showed on Banerji's face. He could not believe his own ears. 'Do you really mean it or are you making fun of me?'

'I would never do that – and you know it,' Kamala replied.

Banerji mused for a while, then snorted, 'But now you have a problem. You're expecting a child who's not even your husband's.' Then with utter disgust written all over his face, he muttered, 'Who would have thought there would be a bastard in this Brahmin family – not even a Hindu bastard – but a Christian, half-caste bastard.'

'Do you have to talk to her in such an insulting manner?' her mother interrupted. 'If you don't want to help her, just tell her "no".'

'You shut up, woman!' Banerji shouted. 'It's only because of you, your indulgence, that this family has become so wayward – destroying my status, my honour.' Her mother became quiet.

It took quite a few minutes for Banerji to calm down. He sat in the courtyard, everyone remained silent. Then he looked at Kamala and ordered her to come nearer. Kamala slowly moved towards him and stood nearby. Banerji now spoke rather softly, 'I can arrange it for you but you have to promise me that you won't tell the Sahib anything, or leave any note, or write to him, or see him ever.'

Kamala took a long time to reply. Then she nodded her head in agreement.

II

The following morning John woke up feeling listless. He was now tired of the whole business – tired of his career, tired of India. The only precious thing left for him was Kamala. Without her he would not know how to face life. Now especially, for he could see when the crunch came, everyone had turned his back on him – even Stanley – and he had thought of him as a real friend. Of course John could not blame him; he had to save his own skin. India is a ruthless place, John thought. The apparent lack of pace, the mesmerizing colours, the deep blue sky, the obedient servants and the inflated status of the Europeans could often give a false sense of security. One had only to witness the merciless killings in a riot, the cruelty to someone like Kamala, the miserable conditions in which fifty million untouchables were forced to live, to comprehend the full significance of the medieval punishment still meted out to the vulerable section of society.

But the officers of the Raj were no better off. They also had to conform. Conform! Conform! Conform! The whole universe was one of conformity where an individual had no rights – even if justice was with him. His mother was burnt alive because father refused to kill or be killed for George V. And now not just the Raj – the Hindus, Moslems – everyone was against him and Kamala because their love did not conform to the dictates of society.

The morning was getting hot in spite of the constant circular movement of the fan. John rose from his bed and looked through the window. The bustle of the second biggest city in the Empire was at full throttle. There was no feeling of tension among the crowd this morning as they jostled through the streets in a chaotic mob, pushing, shoving, shouting, screaming – a real Indian *shivaree*! Nothing in the world could be compared with the constant cacophony that this place interminably generated.

John got dressed and went out into the street. The riot-torn city of the previous day was no more. Everything was already back to normal. Even the beggars were back on the street. Droves of the *lathi*-carrying, red-turbanned Bengali police were ruminating upon the events of the day before. The charred chassis of the burnt-out vehicles had been removed so that their presence did not incite people to continue with their violence. The Gandhi-capped *swrajists* were also back, distributing leaflets of one sort or another. British India was once again on the move – obliterating the memories of such skirmishes as those of the previous day.

There were of course newspaper outcries. They decribed in endless detail the riots, the causes, the victims. The pro-British newspapers offered stern warnings to the government against terrorist attacks and advised them to take tough measures to counter every seditious activity. 'The only way the Raj can survive is by maintaining law and order,' they declared. 'If that means bringing back once again the ill-fated Rowlatt Act so that potential terrorists can be put behind bars before they engage in such atrocious crimes, let us implore the government to have the wisdom and courage to take that course. Mr Gandhi should be paid heed to only when he could unequivocally guarantee that the terrorist wing of his movement would not prematurely end the lives of such prominent and effective members of the Raj as Sir Charles Tennant.'

The nationalist papers, however, took a completely different line. They printed on the front page the pictures of those shot dead by the police during the riot and their mothers' grief as they held the blood-stained clothes of their dead sons. With these pictures the nationalist papers warned the government not to resort to violence. Repressive measures would most certainly push more and more young men to take up arms against the Raj, they wrote. If the government wanted law and order, it must refrain from police atrocities.

III

In the late afternoon when the powerful heat of the sun had subsided a little, John decided to go out and buy something for Kamala. This, he felt, would help to lift his spirits. For a moment he wondered whether to buy her some perfume, but then he decided he would like to give her something truly Indian.

In the European quarters of Chowringhee hardly anything Indian was available. The only place where he would find something really indigenous was the Hindu stronghold in north Calcutta. He mused for a while, wondering whether he would be safe to venture through the narrow lanes of Gandhi's territory after the previous day's widespread riot. But the temptation to give Kamala a sari and surprise her was too exciting an opportunity to miss. He called a phaeton and asked the coachman to take him to College Street. The Indian looked at him amazed. He asked the Sahib once again the destination, for he could not believe his own ears.

There were plenty of large sari stalls in this part of Calcutta. As John stepped down from the phaeton he realized that the people around were staring at him – not so much with hostility, more in bewilderment. John felt uncomfortable with so many pairs of eyes on him as he jostled through the crowd, trying to ignore them. In this part of the city the remnants of the riot were still in evidence – broken bricks and stones piled up at street corners, ready for use. The sight made him uneasy, for he was sure that if they knew his identity there would be no chance of his getting out alive from these quarters.

The shopkeeper was highly surprised to find he had a European customer. He gave the Sahib his undivided attention to compensate for his inadequate English. John knew he wanted a sari, but had no idea what kind as he had only the slightest knowledge of Indian attire. The man spread across the floor scores of saris, which only confused John even further. The shopkeeper, not understannding what the Sahib really wanted, soon became ruffled. He called his son who was a little more proficient in English to help him out.

There was an Indian woman in the shop, a customer, who spoke good English. Observing the utterly confused European who was surrounded by scores of saris and two Indian shopkeepers trying to explain to him in their faltering English, she felt rather sorry for him and came forward to offer him help. 'Is it for someone's wedding, sir? Banaras sarees are the best.'

This suggestion appealed to John. He thanked her profusely for her help and decided on a Banaras sari – red with a blue print and sequinned borders. The shopkeeper brimmed with smiles.

'It's bride's sari, Sahib,' he spoke in broken English. 'We use it for our weddings. Your memsahib like it. If you want, Sahib, my wife come and teach her how to put it on.'

John politely declined the offer, smiling to himself – poor old man! Little does he know that this sari is for an Indian memsahib.

IV

It was nearly five o'clock when John came back to the hotel and had a shower to cool himself down. The train was at eight o'clock – the Delhi-Kalka mail. He already had a reservation for it; these days it was impossible to get comfortable enough accommodation on trains without a reservation. With the possibility of further riots still looming large John decided to go to Howrah Station as early as possible. He did not want to take any chances and get stuck at a road block, especially with the rioting mobs still prowling the Indian quarters of north Calcutta.

Fortunately for John, Central Avenue and Harrison Road were fairly trouble-free with the police guarding every street corner. By the time he arrived at Howrah Station he was completely exhausted with the sheer use of nervous energy, worrying about whether he would be able to get to the station unmolested. Now looking back he was rather surprised that in the afternoon he had had the courage to go to College Street. He must have had a real desire to buy that sari for Kamala.

The train was already waiting at the platform when John arrived. He was pleased to see that he had twin-berthed accommodation. His nerves were so jittery at the moment that he would not have liked to travel with too many other passengers.

His European companion in the compartment was an officer in the Indian army. He spoke volubly about Indian politics – Gandhi, Jinnah, even Lloyd George and Baldwin. John listened, barely answering. Only a few days ago he would immediately have grabbed this opportunity and engaged in a heated political exchange, but today he felt distant from the entire spectrum of the Raj. Nothing really touched him, nor sent even the slightest ripple through his conscious mind. All he could think of now was seeing Kamala again and that prospect, after only three days' absence, filled him with excitement.

The *saice* was waiting for him at the station. John noticed his face had a frightened look, as if he were on the threshold of some inconceivable horror. John was slightly amused. The servants all knew their Sahib was in trouble and they were obviously frightened for their own future.

When the hansom reached the outskirts of Raigarh, John felt so relieved, almost as if he were going back to his mother – he sensed that secure, soothing feeling of homecoming where he would be protected from the dangers outside. In a way he was pleased that the job in Calcutta had not materialized. He would rather stay around here and do something to earn his living, though he did not know what – teach at a local school perhaps.

As the carriage approached the path to the bungalow John looked towards the veranda, searching for Kamala with her smiling face. Oddly there was no sign of her – not on the veranda, nor in the windows overlooking the road. When the approaching noise of the hansom still did not bring her eager presence to welcome the Sahib, John became worried. Could she be ill? After a while, feeling concerned, he shouted to the *saice*, 'Where's the Memsahib?'

The *saice* remained absolutely mute. There was a look of dread on his face that made John suspect the worst. Something awful must have happened to her, he thought. Nervous adrenalin flowed powerfully down his spine. He leaped up to the elevated seat where the *saice* was, and grabbed his shoulder roughly, shouting, 'You *badmas*, you rogue, *jaldi bolo kya hua* – speak now, what's happened to her?'

The *saice*, frightened, went deathly pale and began to cry, '*Mera taqleef nahi*, Sahib – I'm not guilty.'

John jumped from the hansom and ran towards the bungalow, calling out, 'Kamala! Kamala!' The sound echoed in the hot, still air of the field.

Inside, in a dark corner of the house, the servants, all of them like frightened rabbits, were huddled together in a cluster, waiting for the catastrophe.

'Where's the Memsahib?' John shouted.

They sat there like dumb clowns in a circus, with only intense fright written all over their faces. Had Banerji come to take her away? Or had something much more hideous happened? John could think no more. He went numb. The scene of that morning after her ordeal was still vivid in his memory.

He went frantically from one room to another, trying to find some evidence to indicate what had happened to her. There was nothing – not a trace. Finally he returned to the servants and grabbed Ibrahim and shouted, '*Kutta* – you dirty dog! Tell me where she is, or I kill you.' Ibrahim started howling. John shook him again which made him cry even louder. John then looked at Jadu who immediately started bellowing. This set all the rest wailing which made John both nervous and irritated.

Finally Albert David, the gardener, came up with the information: the Memsahib, of her own accord, had gone to Banerji the day the Sahib had left. But she had come back yesterday and asked the *saice* to take her to Sripore to catch a train for Calcutta.

John did not have the patience to listen to the rest of the story. He rushed out of the house, then on second thoughts he returned to fetch his gun. He quickly saddled his horse, mounted and galloped fast towards the Hindu quarter. As people saw the Sahib riding with the gun in his hand, they scuttled away, creating a rapid commotion – women screaming, children wailing. But John did not pay any attention. He rode straight to Banerji's house.

A deathly silence fell as he entered through the gate. There was no one in the courtyard. He went to the door and knocked. When nobody answered he started banging impatiently, determined to break it open. Someone finally answered the door.

'Where's Ratan – that son of a bitch?' John shouted.

Now everybody – women, children, the entire household started howling, which for some moments unnerved John. He looked round in desperation and saw one quiet, dignified face among the yelling crowd – Kamala's mother. He rushed to her and in an earnest voice said, 'Mrs Banerji, I love your daughter. We'll be married soon. She's expecting my child. Please let me know where she is! I beg you!'

She looked at him – a deep, penetrating look – the look of a woman seeking, not to preserve decorum, but like a mother lion deeply concerned about her child's welfare. It almost froze him.

She nodded her head and spoke in the vernacular to one of the girls, who went inside and came back with a piece of paper, 'You'll find our auntie at this address in Calcutta, Sahib.'

John was so relieved. Until this moment he had been imagining all kinds of dire mishaps befalling Kamala. At least she was safe. He now looked gratefully at Mrs Banerji. She smiled – a sad, melancholy smile, and then stood up and touched his forehead with her fingers in the same way as she had done to Hari on Kamala's wedding day.

VI

When John arrived back in Calcutta the following day he was completely worn out. This last week had been traumatic for him. First, the news of the commission, then the previous trip to Calcutta and Stanley's refusal, finally Kamala's disappearance and the drama of him riding to the Banerji household with a gun – all had taken their toll. He still shivered at the thought that Kamala's mother could have refused to give him the address.

Howrah Station was much calmer this time compared with the chaos of a few days before. This was a relief for John, especially in his current predicament. He looked at the address given to him by Kamala's niece but he had no idea in which part of Calcutta it could be. Some of the Indian quarters he knew were dangerous for a European to enter. But that was not his immediate concern. He just wanted Kamala safely back with him as soon as possible.

With all these thoughts in his mind he walked along to Wheeler's newspaper-stall and asked the assistant there for help.

'Sir, it's not a long way from here – but it's an awful place – not fit for a European to travel there. The best thing would be, sir, to send your servant. Or if you want something delivered, we could arrange it for you.'

'No! I need to go there personally.'

'Then take a hackney carriage, sir; although I do not know whether it would be able to get there. Some of the roads are awfully narrow.' John thanked him profusely for his help and came out.

The streets were crowded as usual, but not brick-strewn as they had been the other day. The sun was already blazing. He called a carriage and gave the address to the coachman who, although he appeared to be surprised, said nothing, just whipped the rickety horse to get it moving.

The carriage went through narrow lanes – the slums of Calcutta. John had never seen so much poverty anywhere – not even in Raigarh. The ramshackle, dilapidated houses were literally falling apart. Poor, naked children, snotty-nosed, were sitting outside by dirt sewers, sucking their fingers. The sight of this immense poverty, the inhuman conditions in which people had to live, were heart rending. But John's mind this morning was filled with his own problems and not India's.

Soon the coachman lost his way in the maze. John tried to ask a few people but none of them spoke English. They just looked at him with glazed, foolish amazement. At last the coachman found the way, but after a while the road became too narrow for the carriage to pass. The Indian volunteered to bring to him whoever it was the Sahib wanted from there, for he did not think it safe for the master to walk through the narrow lane.

'Thank you, but I have to go personally.' Then with mounting trepidation he walked along the lane which could barely accommodate the width of a normal human being.

Kamala was pulling water from a well by means of a bucket tied to a rope. In front of her a motley range of cooking pots were piled to be washed. Her face looked red hot in the sun. On a raised platform, shaded by a tree, a woman, perhaps her aunt, was leaning languorously on the wall of a rather old house – a cubicle really – with a door at the centre and a small window at each side. The plaster on the house, which at one stage must have been pink, was now so badly defaced with the passage of time and lack of maintenance that its original hue was only a memory.

The old woman who was fanning herself with a wicker fan, seeing the Sahib, hurriedly dropped it, put on her purdah and shouted something in the vernacular. Kamala looked up and her eyes immediately glowed but she did not dare to come nearer John in front of her aunt. The woman shouted for her husband. A bare-chested man, wearing only a loin-cloth and smoking a hubble-bubble, came out. Seeing the Sahib he promptly disappeared and soon came back wearing a shirt and immediately ordered Kamala to go inside. She did not obey him, but moved away from the courtyard and stood not far away from her aunt.

'I am here to take Kamala back with me. Her mother gave me your address.' Hot with the sun and with nervousness, John started sweating profusely.

The man looked at him disbelievingly. Then, shaking with immense rage he said, 'You may be a Sahib, but to us you are an infidel. And no infidel is allowed into a Brahmin household. For us, you are like untouchables. We will have to wash the whole place now with water from the Ganges to purify the desecrated soil on which you are standing.'

'I am here to take my wife,' John spoke those words slowly but firmly.

'She is a Hindu woman,' the man replied. 'Her husband is a Hindu.'

'We shall be married soon.'

'You cannot marry a married woman. Even under British law that is illegal.'

'I am afraid, if you don't allow her to come with me, I shall have to use force.' John's voice was stern and determined as he moved towards Kamala.

The Indian shouted, 'Get out of here! Or I shall call the *swrajists* to throw you out.' John ignored his warning and came to Kamala, who eagerly held John's hand. The Indian now started ranting and raving as he realized his impotence. 'I'll ask Gandhiji to write to the Viceroy that his men are forcibly taking our women from our own homes.'

John did not utter a word now. Holding Kamala's hand he walked straight through the narrow gate, leaving the man still raging.

TWENTY THREE

I

As the days went by, the government was eager to start the work of the Evans Commission. The Viceroy personally requested Sir Garfield to complete the enquiry as early as possible for his review and perhaps for general publication later on to impress upon Gandhi that the Raj had nothing to hide, not even when one of its officers had been involved in a gruesome incident. Justice must not only be done, but it must be seen to be done. A democratic power with great democratic traditions for over a thousand years, who taught the world how to discuss every issue – good, bad, controversial, obnoxious – guaranteeing free speech – synthesizing all contradictions to obtain justice, would not run away now from a paltry incident involving an insignificant officer.

But that was not all. Part of the reason for the government's eagerness was the pressure the Viceroy faced from the political parties. Not only the Islamic Front and the Hindu League, but even Gandhi thought that when over a hundred people had died in a riot, the least the government could do was to conduct an independent enquiry as quickly as possible.

Following the wishes of the Viceroy, Sir Garfield arranged for the commission's work to commence speedily. Although it would have been convenient for him to conduct the enquiry from Patna, the capital of Bihar, he thought it more appropriate to hold the proceedings nearer the site of the riots and so chose Sripore.

The main chamber in the local town hall was selected for the hearing and the decor was arranged to give it the appearance of a court – benches for clerks and secretaries in a corner, three chairs provided behind a large table for the commission members, the witness box, fully supplied with religious texts for taking the oath, the enclosure for the accused (though not needed for the commission's work) and finally the public gallery, in spite of the fact that the whole investigation was to be conducted in camera and the public would have no knowledge of any facts until the report was officially published.

Fearing the possibility of huge demonstrations by the Hindu League outside the courtroom, Garvey imposed PC 144 in Sripore. He was not prepared to take any risk of any kind. He also provided police escorts for the main witnesses.

Observing the government's determination to maintain law and order Joshi temporarily backed down and decided that now was not the time to stage any real unrest, but he eagerly awaited the outcome of the commission's work. He knew that he would have to take action whichever way the verdict went, but for the time being he had decided to save his energy for the impending battle.

Sir Garfield Evans, the chairman of the commission, was a short, stocky Welshman with ruddy cheeks and a flat nose which indicated that in his youth he had been a keen boxer who had compensated for his lack of skill with courage. He was completely bald except for a fringe of neatly cut grey hair at the back of his head and round the ears. In spite of the hot weather he wore a well-cut three-piece suit, perhaps tailored in London. His pince-nez added to the gravity of the man and gave an awe-inspiring impression.

The commission began its inquiry, taking some minor evidence, mainly on four counts – the cause of the riot; its impact; the negligence by senior officers; and the alleged police atrocities. Hari Mukherji, the raped woman's husband, was included among the people they initially interviewed. It soon became apparent to the commission that Hari had no real knowledge of either the alleged affair between the European and his own wife, or the rape. All the men who attacked him that night had had their faces blackened, and he had had no way of recognizing them. And if the Sahib had had an affair with Kamala while she had been living with Hari, he did not know about it; he had no way of knowing; he had not even an inkling. And he certainly held no opinion about the European. But who would – about a European officer?

Hari's was really non-evidence, for it established nothing except a positive affirmation that the British officer was not among the rapists. Although no one in the Raj imagined that an Englishman would be involved in such a bestial act, all the same, there was a sigh of relief when Hari's evidence vindicated their belief.

Now the commission focused its attention on the main characters of this distasteful episode: Ratan Banerji, a civil servant; his daughter, Kamala; and her lover, John Sugden, a British officer, currently suspended on full pay from his duties for alleged corruption and negligence. The final decision on the officer would depend upon the report of the commission.

Of the star witnesses, Banerji was the first to be called. He came in nervously and took his oath on the *Bhagvad Gita*, the Hindu equivalent of the Bible. Sir Garfield politely asked him to sit down. He was relieved. The fearsome aura of justice instilled by the courtroom had filled him with disquiet.

'What do you think was the cause of the riot?' Sir Garfield was clear and precise in his questioning.

Banerji took a sip of water to overcome his nervousness, then replied, 'It was a man-made riot, sir.'

Sir Garfield was irritated by not being called 'Sir Garfield'. He sighed. Having lived in this country for over forty years, he knew that it was extremely difficult to teach these Indians manners. However, he put aside his own feelings for now and framed the question differently to clarify the point. 'You mean, all set up by political parties such as the Islamic Front and the Hindu League?'

'No sir,' Banerji replied. 'The political parties are only a camouflage for someone's sinful activity.'

'What do you mean?' the learned judge asked.

Banerji hesitated for a moment, then said, 'It is an Englishman's work, sir. He arranged my daughter's rape. He started the riot.'

'Who is this man?'

'Mr John Sugden, my superior officer.'

Sir Garfield now asked the reason for Banerji's allegation. Banerji became highly agitated and shouted – 'The Englishman wanted to have my married daughter raped so that he could possess her.'

Sir Garfield seemed puzzled. He looked at Anil Saha for explanation. Anil Saha was waiting for this opportunity to hold centre stage. 'In India,' Anil Saha replied, 'if a woman is taken by a man other than her husband, whether by force or otherwise, the family refuses to take her back. The tradition started a long time ago when Rama, a Hindu god, banished his beloved wife, Sita, for the same reason.'

The learned judge frowned as he absorbed the mythical story. He did not want to be side-tracked, for he had a more important task ahead of him. He said impatiently, 'Forget about the legend! What happens in modern India if a woman is taken by another man – what happens to her?'

Saha was taken aback by the judge's curt way of questioning. But he was highly proficient in dealing with impatient Europeans. He politely replied, 'Very often she ends up as a prostitute, Sir Garfield.'

Sir Garfield shook his head in disbelief. Still frowning he looked at Banerji and asked, 'You believe Mr Sugden raped your daughter so that she would be thrown out from your family!'

'I am not saying he personally did it that night, sir. We could not tell. They all – I mean the intruders – had blackened their faces. But I believe, sir, he arranged it.'

'Surely the victim would know whether her rapist was a European or not, even if his face was painted?' Sir Garfield asserted his authority.

Banerji for a second seemed confused by Sir Garfield's statement, but he soon recovered. 'I agree with you, sir.'

A hint of a sardonic smile appeared on Sir Garfield's face, but only briefly. 'Did you tell the police about your suspicion?' he asked.

'No, sir,' Banerji replied. 'There was not enough evidence. Moreover the police chief is a friend of Mr Sugden.'

'Are you suggesting there was some kind of collusion between the police and Mr Sugden?'

'What, sir? I do not understand.'

Sir Garfield realized he would have to cut down the use of legal terminology to an absolute minimum. The inability of the Indians to speak the language properly never ceased to surprise him. 'Was there any understanding between the police and Mr Sugden?' Sir Garfield shouted in irritation.

'I do not know, sir. I know they are friends.'

'Where is your daughter ...' Sir Garfield looked at his papers to check her name. 'Where is your daughter, Kamala, now?'

'She lives with Mr Sugden,' Banerji replied, disgruntled.

'Do you mean they live together?'

'Yes, sir.'

'As husband and wife?'

'They are not married, sir. He cannot marry her. There is no divorce among the Hindus.'

'Is that true?' Sir Garfield looked at Saha, for he had never in his legal career been involved in Hindu matrimonial cases.

'In a way, yes, Sir Garfield,' Saha replied. 'In a Hindu marriage divorce is only possible if one of the partners takes up Christian faith and the spouse deserts him or her.' He wanted to be absolutely precise. It was only by luck that he had asked John Sugden about his marriage that day. Without the hint from the Englishman, he would never have known about this legal loophole.

'Are they married now – this John Sugden and Kamala?' Sir Garfield asked.

'As far as we know, no, Sir Garfield,' Garvey replied.

Sir Garfield now looked at Banerji and said, 'Your daughter, Kamala, obviously loves John Sugden, otherwise she would not be living with him. Unless, of course, that is the only place where she could find a roof over her head.'

'No, sir,' Banerji replied. 'When the Sahib ...'

Sir Garfield interrupted, 'Can you refer to him as Mr Sugden at this commission?'

'Yes, sir.'

'Continue!'

'He is keeping her by force sir. Recently my daughter managed to escape from his house and came to me for help. I took her to my cousin's place in Calcutta. Mr Sugden then broke into my house with a gun, threatened my wife and extorted the information on her whereabouts. And then he went to Calcutta and dragged my daughter out from my cousin's place by force.'

'That is a serious allegation, Mr Banerji,' Sir Garfield said. 'Did you report it to the police at the time?'

'No, sir. Not much point. We Indians do not get the same justice as the Europeans.'

'I think your remark is out of order,' Saha interrupted.

'Yes, sir,' Banerji replied. He was sorry to have made that slip – accusing the Raj.

Sir Garfield, though annoyed, kept his composure and asked, 'Can you substantiate your allegation against Mr Sugden? For example, would your wife be prepared to support you on this?'

'She is a Hindu woman,' said Banerji hastily. 'She does not talk to outsiders. I can bring neighbours who saw the Sahib – I mean Mr Sugden – breaking into my house with a gun.'

'We want to hear from your wife,' Sir Garfield said and then looking at Garvey he asked, 'Is she among the people we are interviewing?'

'No, Sir Garfield,' replied Garvey. 'But that can be arranged.'

'Please see to it.'

'She does not speak any English, sir,' Banerji shouted. Sir Garfield now looked at Saha and asked him whether he would be able to translate the vernacular into English, to which Saha proudly replied that he did not know any Indian dialect.

'We will have to arrange for an interpreter, then,' Sir Garfield pronounced.

'I'll arrange that too,' Garvey volunteered.

'If we accept the premise that Mr Sugden loves your daughter,' Sir Garfield observed, looking thoughtfully at Banerji, 'it is unlikely then, is it not, that he would arrange for her to be raped?'

Banerji did not know the meaning of the word 'premise' but he did not want to show his ignorance. He was proud of his proficiency in English. Anyway, he understood the gist of Sir Garfield's question and promptly replied, 'There can never be love between a European and an Indian. All lust, sir. Since the very day Mr Sugden arrived, he started on my daughter. To welcome him on the first day, I asked her to offer him a garland, but he took that opportunity and he himself garlanded her.'

'That did not matter – did it?' Sir Garfield was surprised by this allegation.

'Oh, it did, sir! It did!' Banerji shouted. 'In India it is the same as marriage.' Sir Garfield, puzzled, looked at Saha for clarification.

'According to Indian custom,' Saha explained, 'the exchange of garlands between a man and woman could be construed as marriage. The tradition started a long time ago when Lord Krishna, by exchanging garlands, seduced a young woman named Radha, who later became his uncle's wife; but their affair continued because Krishna claimed that Radha was married to him first.'

Sir Garfield did not like Saha's reference to Hindu mythology again, but he was beginning to understand the complexity of this case. He somehow felt that the English officer did not know the custom and he voiced this doubt to the Indian clerk.

"No, sir,' Banerji vehemently disagreed. 'He is a history scholar. He knew it. He did it to bring about a romantic attachment towards him in my young daughter's mind.'

'Why do you say that?' Sir Garfield asked.

'The normal custom for us, sir,' Banerji explained, 'if our children get married, is to present them to the local British officer.

But the Sahib, I mean Mr Sugden, came to our house on the wedding-day, put on Indian clothes and spent the whole day as if he were one of us.'

'Didn't you invite him to come?'

'No, sir.'

'Do you mean he came uninvited?'

'In a way, yes, sir. He made my daughter invite him.'

'Did they know each other well then – your daughter and this John Sugden?' Sir Garfield was puzzled.

'He was always sending her books,' Banerji replied. 'That was how he sent love letters.' Sir Garfield looked at Banerji disbelievingly. 'It is true, sir,' Banerji shouted. 'You can look at that photograph.'

'What photograph is this?' Sir Garfield enquired. Anil Saha passed the photograph of Sugden in Indian clothes to Sir Garfield. He inspected it with great care. 'How are all these incidents connected with the riot?' Sir Garfield was more probing now.

'Sir, some miscreants came to our locality before the riot to start up trouble,' replied Banerji. 'I asked Mr Sugden to arrest them. He refused.'

'Why?'

Banerji was agitated. His voice trembled as he replied, 'They were his men, sir.'

'Are you alleging that a British officer brought those miscreants to Raigarh to start the riot and is now denying his part in it?'

'Yes, sir, as you say – he is denying it now.'

'Do you want to claim that an Englishman, an officer of the Viceroy's Government, is telling lies?' Sir Garfield tried to pin Banerji down.

'Well, sir, not completely unusual,' replied Banerji. 'Robert Clive did it with the Nawab of Bengal.'

'Shut up!' Saha shouted. Both Sir Garfield and Garvey's faces became completely flushed.

'Apologize, you native scum!' Saha boomed.

'Apologies, sir. Many, many apologies. A thousand million apologies. I was carried away. I am under severe stress.'

Sir Garfield, still angry, looked at the clerk and ordered, 'Don't include that statement about Lord Clive in the record. It has no relevance to our enquiry.' He now turned to Banerji and asked, 'Would you like a recess?'

'No, sir; I am happy to continue.'

'So you are saying that in spite of your warning, Mr Sugden refused to arrest the trouble makers.'

'Yes, sir.'

'What were his reasons?'

'He said that as the Rowlatt Act had been abolished, it was no longer legal to hold anyone under suspicion.'

'That is true,' Sir Garfield tried to rationalize the situation.

'But he could see, sir, they were stirring up trouble. The evidence was there,' Banerji tried to defend his position.

Sir Garfield did not listen to Banerji all that attentively because he was eager to bring a new dimension in his line of investigation. 'I was informed that the riot started because of the *holi* festival,' he observed.

'That is true, sir.'

'Then how could it be connected with Mr Sugden?'

'Well, sir,' Banerji replied, 'that gave him the idea. The *holi* incident was only a minor disturbance – very few dead. With tough measures, everything would have been fine. But Mr Sugden took that opportunity and started further trouble instead of putting it down.'

'I understand you yourself were involved in the murder of a Moslem – were you not?' Sir Garfield asked this question pointedly and then commanded, 'Tell me about that incident.'

'I was not involved, sir,' Banerji replied nervously. 'A Moslem friend came to me during the riot. I gave him a police escort to take him to safety. Honest to God, sir, I did. You can ask the Sahib – I mean Mr Sugden. But the local rogues murdered him.'

'Is it not possible that to take revenge against you, some rioters raped your daughter?' Sir Garfield tried to be logical.

Banerji was unhappy with this suggestion. He became agitated and said, 'Sir, even before anyone knew about the rape, Mr Sugden came to Hari, my son-in-law, with the mad Belgian doctor and then he took her to hospital.' This of course was a lie. Banerji himself had gone to the Sahib after the rape to seek the Englishman's help. But he was now confused about the whole incident. Sir Garfield frowned as he sensed a new piece of evidence – the involvement of an alien power. He looked at Garvey and asked, 'Who is this doctor?'

'A Belgian missionary. Not a favourite of ours,' Garvey replied with some reservations.

'You mean – no British doctor had examined her at that stage?'

Sir Garfield was surprised.

'Not until she came to Sripore,' Garvey replied apologetically. Sir Garfield now looked at Banerji and asked, 'Why did you not travel with Mr Sugden when he brought your daughter to Sripore?'

'We were not allowed, sir. He discouraged me. I could not override him. He is my superior officer.' Banerji was convinced he was telling the truth.

'Was that the afternoon when the major riot took place?' Sir Garfield asked.

'Yes, sir.'

'Do you think Mr Sugden started that riot as well?'

'In a way, yes, sir,' Banerji replied. 'Because the news of the rape started the violence and during his absence the whole thing went out of control.'

'So in your view he did not deliberately start the second riot?'

Banerji took his time, then replied, 'No, sir.'

Sir Garfield now started collecting his papers and said, 'That is all, Mr Banerji. Thank you for coming.'

'He is guilty, sir,' Banerji shouted.

Without looking at him Sir Garfield replied, 'That's for us to judge, not you.'

Saha, fearful of Banerji making further blunders, shouted, 'You can go now Banerji.' Banerji fumbled nervously to find the exit.

II

A few days later Mrs Banerji came to give evidence. She was well-dressed in a sari, still a beautiful woman in spite of rearing three children. Although there was evidence of some strain on her face because of recent events, she was calm and composed. An interpreter was brought in to conduct the enquiry in the vernacular. Mrs Banerji sat in a sedate manner. She did not pull her sari right down over her face like a village woman but just enough to show sobriety. Sir Garfield started the proceedings with a polite introduction. 'Mrs Banerji, many thanks for coming over at such short notice.' She nodded her head, acknowledging the thanks courteously.

'Do you know Mr Sugden well?'

'Yes, sir,' Mrs Banerji replied.

'Do you believe the British officer was instrumental in your daughter's rape in any way?'

'No, sir!' Mrs Banerji replied. 'He only came and tried to help us when the rape had already taken place. In fact, when no one was prepared to take her to hospital, he volunteered; when no one was prepared to give her a roof over her head, he kindly offered her shelter. I do not know of such kindness in another human being.'

'Do you believe he is holding your daughter against her will?' Sir Garfield asked pointedly.

'No, she loves him,' Mrs Banerji replied.

'Then why would your daughter run away from him, the moment he was out of sight?'

Mrs Banerji took her time to reply. 'She did it so that he did not have to suffer for her. She did it for love.' Now she glanced at Garvey, then looked at Sir Garfield and continued, 'It is common knowledge that if she leaves him, he will be reinstated by the Raj to his previous position. And that was what she wanted when she ran away from him.'

'But I was informed, Mrs Banerji,' Sir Garfield suggested, 'that Mr Sugden came to you and extorted information at gunpoint – is that true?'

'No, sir,' Mrs Banerji replied. 'I gave it voluntarily, because I knew my daughter would be happy with him. He did not use any force against me or my family. He was very polite.'

'Is it not true that he abducted your daughter from your relative's home?'

'They were treating her badly – worse than a slave. When she saw him there, she was delighted to be back with him.'

'Have you seen your daughter since then?'

'Yes,' she unhesitatingly replied. Nobody had known this before.

Sir Garfield decided not to pursue the questions about exchanging garlands which to his mind were completely irrelevant, nor the matter of Sugden's attending the wedding uninvited, which he did not believe to be true. The invitation, even from the daughter, had to be considered as bona fide. He now changed the subject and asked, 'Do you think Mr Sugden was in any way connected with the riot?'

Mrs Banerji looked straight into Sir Garfield's eyes and replied, 'A man of such kindness could never be associated with any form of violence.'

Sir Garfield smiled at Garvey. 'That is all, Mrs Banerji.' She slowly got up and left the room, upright and dignified.

III

At first John was against Kamala giving evidence to the commission. He thought she was not in a fit state to go through with it – being cross-examined in depth about all her ordeals: the rape; the humiliating rejection by her own people; and then the salacious innuendoes about her association with John. For a pregnant woman, barely twenty years old, it was simply too much.

'I'll make a special plea to the commission so that you don't have to go through the ordeal. It's not fair – you in your condition to be cross-examained by vultures like Anil Saha.'

'No, Sahib, please! Your honour is at stake,' Kamala replied. 'If the commission decides against you, your name will be tarred for ever. Perhaps they'll even blame you for that shameful event. So please – don't do it – don't stop me from giving evidence.'

'I don't care about my career any more,' John said angrily. 'I'm no longer sure that I want to work for the Viceroy. I would much rather work for someone like Gandhi. At least he's doing something worthwhile – uplifting the down-trodden.'

'I can understand your sentiments, Sahib,' Kamala replied. 'Whether you work for the *Burra Laat* in future or not – that is not the question – you should try to clear your name – at least for our child's sake.'

John could see her point of view. She was right – he should try to clear his name, if not for any other reason, at least for the sake of his unborn child.

John's fear was unwarranted. The commission treated Kamala well. They took into account that she had had to undergo terrible torment in this whole tragic incident. And now that she was expecting a child, nothing should occur to her whereby even the slightest blame could be assigned to the Raj. All three members, especially Sir Garfield and Charles Garvey, were particularly respectful and showed her the kind of courtesy which most Europeans reserved only for their own women. They did not ask her many questions, only the fundamental and important one – Was John Sugden, in her view, implicated in the rape? To which she firmly replied, 'I now know this man better than anyone else does. I cannot believe that he would in any way be involved in such a beastly act. When I was in a desperate state and looked for help he was the only person who had the courage to come forward and save me from the humiliation of being a street-woman. He has not only offered me shelter but allowed me the opportunity to lead a normal life.'

This was sufficient for the commission to recognize Kamala's deep attachment to the Englishman. Before departing she left no doubt in anyone's mind about the high pedestal upon which she placed her Sahib.

The very final session was with John Sugden. The commission had already indicated that if Sugden wanted a lawyer to be present with him, they would be willing to consider it; his employer, the Indian government would pay the costs. But John declined the offer.

IV

The mid-summer was fast approaching. Mrs Garvey and many other European women had already left for Simla, Nainital or Darjeeling. For John, the hot weather was the least of his worries.

Sir Garfield was in a sombre mood that day – a little too edgy for a well-experienced high court judge who had meted out justice to many criminals in his life. But then John Sugden was not a criminal.

'Mr Sugden,' Sir Garfield started the interrogation, 'I would very much like to ask you a few questions about your background. I believe they are necessary for this investigation. But you are well within your rights, either for personal reasons, or if in your view they seem prejudicial to your interests, to refuse to answer any or all of them.'

'Yes, Sir Garfield,' John nodded his head politely.

'You are an American by birth?'

'No, Sir Garfield. I was born in England, in High Wycombe. My parents came to live in England before I was born.'

'Do you have personal heroes from American history – such as George Washington or Abraham Lincoln?'

'I have never considered myself an American, so they have never been my national heroes. But as a student of history, I hold them in high esteem.'

'Did you or do you ever think that Great Britain was wrong to have a colony in America?'

'I think the colonization of America was justified,' replied John, 'and similarly the War of Independence – the time was then ripe for the Americans to look after their own affairs.'

'What do you think of Lincoln, his anti-slavery campaign and the subsequent civil war?' Sir Garfield asked.

'That was necessary,' replied John. 'Every human being should be allowed to exercise his fundamental human right – that of freedom which God has bestowed upon us.'

'Even if a man is incapable of looking after himself?'

'Each of us – all creatures – possess by God's grace an instinct for survival.'

Sir Garfield, grim, checked a few notes for the next set of questions. John sat there, calm and composed; his early nervousness now completely disappeared.

'Do you see any similarity between the American leaders such as Washington, Lincoln and Gandhi?' Sir Garfield asked.

'Yes, I do,' replied John. 'Definitely with Lincoln. He has the same empathy for the oppressed, for the poor, for the deprived. Gandhi, like Lincoln, is not just a political leader but a religious leader, a spiritual leader.'

'So you support Gandhi and his activities?' asked Sir Garfield, somewhat surprised.

That did not deter John. He had come here today to tell the truth – the truth about the Empire as he saw it. He said, 'I believe Gandhi is trying to uplift the consciousness of the Indian masses – not just the middle class, educated ones, but even the down-trodden untouchables.' John paused briefly, then continued, 'Ever since Lord Bentinck and the abolition of suttee, we have stopped any kind of social reform in India – mainly to gain an easy passage. We are trying to rule this country without ruffling any feathers. I believe India needs major reforms – and very badly too. Her social condition, superstitions, prejudices and taboos are appalling. Gandhi at least is trying to do something about it.'

'He is also inciting people to burn foreign goods – is he not?'

'Yes, I know,' replied John. 'I believe he is doing it to boost their confidence. He wants the Indians to wear home-spun clothes with pride.'

'So you think this fanning of nationalism is right – the Congress is right to fight the British Government?' Sir Garfield was caustic in his questioning.

It was a difficult question for John to answer. He knew his own feeling about it, but the problem was whether to express it openly to the establishment and invite the wrath of the government. Yes, he thought, he would have to do it. To be honest to himself he would have to discard his long-cherished loyalty to the Raj. 'I think the time is ripe for us to hand over power to the Indians,' he replied.

A current of disbelief electrified the entire room. Anil Saha shook his head in utter confusion. Even Garvey looked dismayed upon hearing his one-time protégé making such seditious remarks. But Sir Garfield was calm and composed as he continued his interrogation.

'Do you have any reason for making such a strong statement, Mr Sugden?'

'Yes, Sir Garfield.' John Sugden seemed determined to tell the Raj whatever he had been holding to his chest for a long time. He continued, 'I have not just one but two reasons. First, we are expecting a great deal of our young officers. They have been given the impossible task of trying to administer a country which no longer wants us. We are making unfair demands on them – pushing them into extreme danger. We no longer have the resources to run a vast country like India.' Sir Garfield now started making copious notes. Seeing this, John Sugden paused.

Still looking at his notes, Sir Garfield asked, 'And the second reason?'

'The second and more important one, I think, is that the Empire has run out of steam. We are no longer a positive force. We are just holding on to power – almost like a father who tries to hold back an adult son to his detriment. The man for the moment is Gandhi – not us.'

Everyone in the room was stunned, almost fearful, listening to such utterly seditious statements from an officer of the Raj. Anil Saha shook his head in complete disbelief. But Sir Garfield remained cool and composed. He continued his interrogation, 'I understand you went to Oxford and there you met T.E. Lawrence.'

'Yes, he came to speak to us once.'

'What was your impression of him?'

'I did not like him much,' John replied. 'He was bitter about His Majesty's government breaking promises to the Arabs.'

'Did he influence you?'

'In some ways, yes,' replied John. 'It was his commitment to the Arabs that impressed me.'

Sir Garfield now went over his notes and looked at John through his pince-nez. 'Your father, Mr Sugden, was against the Great War – wasn't he? Did he not participate in anti-war activities?'

'He was a conscientious objector,' replied John. 'He attended only one meeting organized by Bertrand Russell and put his name as a signatory against the war. But during the war years he worked in a munitions factory to help the government. Towards the end of the war though, when the police investigated him for alleged anti-war activities he lost his job in spite of the fact he was cleared by the government.'

'Is it true that your mother died in strange circumstances?' Sir Garfield continued his probing.

John was exhausted. He breathed heavily, sipped water and then haltingly resumed. 'She was murdered, Sir Garfield. She was burned alive on Armistice night while my father and I were out.'

'Who murdered her?' Sir Garfield's question was ruthlessly insistent in spite of the visible signs of pain in John Sugden's face.

John took a few seconds to recover and then he replied, 'That has remained unsolved to this day. We believe that someone decided to punish us for being conscientious objectors.'

Sir Garfield wrote some comments on a piece of paper and passed it round to Garvey and Saha. He then looked at Sugden and asked, 'Let me ask a few questions about the riot. Why did you not arrest the miscreants who had been stirring up trouble before the riot?'

'We did not have the legal right to do so,' replied John. 'With the Rowlatt Act repealed, there was nothing by which we could hold anyone merely on suspicion.' He paused and then added, 'In fact, even if the Rowlatt Act had been in force, I would not have arrested them – not merely on suspicion.'

'Are you saying – correct me if I am wrong – you are against taking precautionary measures even if you see that a riot could be averted by them?'

'Arresting someone without evidence, just on suspicion, is a fundamental breach of human rights,' replied John. 'It's only a conjecture that they were involved. Even now I am not sure about the role played by those supposed miscreants.'

Sir Garfield now looked into Sugden's eyes and asked peremptorily, 'Were you involved in the rape of Kamala Mukherji?'

'No, sir! Absolutely not!' John replied firmly.

'When you heard about the rape, you called a Belgian doctor who, according to many, is a Gandhi supporter and against the government – Why did you do that?'

'Because he was the nearest doctor – the first person who came into my mind.'

'So you already knew him?' Sir Garfield was inquisitorial.

'Yes, I met him during one of my cold weather trips,' replied John.

'Is he a friend of yours?'

'It wouldn't be a complete lie to say that.'

Sir Garfield took a sip of water to clear the hoarseness of his voice. Though in good health he was over sixty and it had been a gruelling day for him. But he did not have much time in hand, for he wanted to complete the interrogation by the end of the day. He now raised his head and asked the young officer, 'On that day, after the rape, Mr Sugden, when you took Mrs Kamala Mukherji to hospital, the situation in Raigarh was already tense – and she is just one of thousands of people for whose safety you are responsible – yet you decided to spend the entire day with her in the hospital in Sripore, leaving your district unattended. In fact your senior officer had to order you to get back before you moved from Sripore.' Sir Garfield now fixed his eyes on John and posed the crucial question, 'Do you think you neglected your duty by staying away from your station?'

'Mrs Mukherji was in need,' replied John.

'But she had her husband and her father. Or were you already in love with her?'

'No, sir. I was not,' John firmly denied, and then added, 'As no one was forthcoming to take her to hospital, I thought it was my moral duty to do so.'

'Even though you were leaving the entire district in a riotous condition?'

'The place was peaceful at the time,' John emphasized.

'Did you not suspect that the rape of a Hindu girl might be sufficient to spark off a massacre when only a few days previously there had already been a riot?'

'You may be right,' replied the young officer. 'I just did not think of it at the time.'

Sir Garfield's eyes now became intense in the same way as a lion's does when it targets its prey. 'Would you then agree with me,' he asked, 'that albeit for humanitarian reasons, you have been negligent of the duties with which the Viceroy entrusted you?'

John Sugden was quiet for a while, musing over the question. Then he lifted his head, eyes full of sadness. 'Yes,' he murmured in a distant voice.

Sir Garfield started collecting his papers and with a faint smile said, 'That's all, Mr Sugden. We thank you for coming here and giving us your time.'

TWENTY FOUR

I

The interview with the commission made John face life for the first time with total honesty. Until now he had been drifting with the tide, not knowing what exactly he had wanted in life. He had had a few vague ideas from his childhood, when he had heard from his mother the stories about his ancestors. On his father's side had been the Calvinist Dutch adventurer, Samuel. He, with Henry Hudson, the mad sailor, was among the first to enter Hudson Bay in search of a route to the Pacific Ocean, in the ship *Crescent*, carrying the flags of the United Provinces. He and his fellow sailors hoisted the Dutch flag and founded the city of New Amsterdam. When the Duke of York, with the excuse of Hudson being an Englishman, tried to take over the city, Samuel with other Dutch settlers fought a bitter battle. But the English army was far too powerful. They took over New Amsterdam and renamed it New York. When the English soldiers came to take over the sixteen mile tract of land Samuel had acquired under the Dutch regime he died a hero's death.

Then there was was George Fox, the Quaker leader. But George Fox was a different kind of man from John Sugden. He was not one to kowtow to the King's army. He had seen God, had a personal relationship with Him. And George Fox was a hero to John Sugden. But John realized sadly that he had neither George Fox's determination nor his courage.

The few days in Sripore, when he had been cross-examined by Sir Garfield, made John wake up to the reality of the tough, ruthless, unsympathetic world in which he lived. He knew that even if the government gave him back a respected position within the Indian civil service, reinstated him to the coveted post – the distinguished collector and magistrate of the district of Raigarh, a *khas talook*, a major holding of His Majesty George V, King of Great Britain and Emperor of India, it was not what he wanted in life. The Raj no longer gave him a meaningful existence.

While John Sugden had been at Oxford during his late teens and had been still very impressionable, the legends of Nathaniel Curzon – the Balliol man who had been at the helm of the Empire at the turn of the century and had showed what a great intellect could achieve for the Raj – had channelled John's aspiration to join the Indian Civil Service. Then the meetings with Kipling and Lawrence had instilled in him a dream. When they had unfurled the stories of the East, John felt he also had the same mission. Kipling's words were still ringing in his ears. It was Kipling who had made him feel that the Indians had fine intellect, but were vulnerable; that they needed help to overcome their poverty and inadequacy; that they needed someone to bridge the gap between their wisdom and the scientific knowledge and practical ability of the British. And this very thought had stimulated in him a desire, a passion, a dream of a career devoted to service. India's vulnerability had appealed to his idealistic mind. And the obvious vehicle to achieve that dream had been the Raj.

But now the Raj was different. It was no longer the Raj of the nineteenth century when the Europeans and Indians had aimed for a common goal – for the good of India. When Lord Bentinck, appalled by the suffering of Hindu women, sought cooperation from the Indian intelligentsia to halt once and for all the practice of burning alive young widows on the same funeral pyres as their dead husbands, the stalwarts of Hindu society such as Rammohan Roy and Dwarkanath Tagore had come forward willingly, spontaneously, gratefully.

Today the Raj was full of functionaries. Not dreamers! Nor poets! The days of Thuggee Sleeman who eradicated the fear of being killed by rogues and made life safe and secure for the ordinary Indian, had long gone. Now the Raj was full of rigid rules, rigid structures. Adventures? – no more. Nor excitement.

After Queen Victoria the Raj had needed a period of consolidation which required the administrative skills of the Garveys of this world and not the dare devilry of the early settlers. The rules were then formulated, the deviations strictly controlled, enterprise frowned upon. And soon the Anglo-Saxon progressive force ended up in a rut. The Raj no longer had a constructive role to play – it was just trying to survive against nationalist agitation.

But there was a man who could provide the exciting challenge of shaping India to a new destiny. Not Lord Reading, the Viceroy. Nor Edwin Montagu, the Cabinet Secretary. The new star in the otherwise empty sky was, without doubt, Gandhi.

Those among the Europeans who were dynamic, such as Annie Besant, Charles Andrews, Guy Horniman, had already taken sides – not with the Raj but against it. And the very thought that he was actually acting against the progressive forces in the country now depressed John.

'If you really feel so strongly, why do you not join Gandhi?' Kamala was puzzled by his painful self-analysis.

'That's tergiversation. A turncoat, they call it in England.'

'What does it mean?'

'Untrustworthy people. Traitors. I could never do that.'

'Even if you believed in the cause?'

'Yes. Even if I believed in the cause. Because that would be working against the throne, against King George V.'

II

It was not long before Garvey appeared in Raigarh one morning. John knew the reason for his visit. He had been waiting for it since the day when the commission's enquiry had been completed. Garvey sat down in the lounge with John and had a drink – both were uneasy.

'Let's go for a ride,' Garvey suggested.

John had his horse saddled and they both set out for the hills, leaving Kamala in trepidation. She knew why the *Burra Sahib* was here.

'The news isn't good, I'm afraid,' muttered Garvey, riding alongside John on a wider stretch of the path.

'I've already guessed. I wasn't expecting it to be good.'

'You actually asked for it,' Garvey said. 'It was your seditious remarks, supporting Gandhi, which tilted the balance. We would have been prepared to accept even your negligence – but you have broken ranks. We cannot accept that – not from an officer of the government.'

'I know it, sir.'

'Why don't you write a letter of apology to me saying you were under severe stress at the time and said things which you didn't actually mean,' Garvey suggested and then added, 'Incidentally you also have to ditch the girl. Much as I feel sorry for her, under no circumstances can an English officer of the government marry a married Indian woman.'

John said something in reply which Garvey could not hear because his horse had moved away from John's. He stopped his horse and when John closed the gap Garvey said, 'Even if we allowed it the Hindus wouldn't approve of your liaison with a Brahmin girl. Joshi and his Hindu League would never accept it.'

John did not reply.

'What I'm saying is that you still have an outside chance, old boy, if you want to take it.' Garvey's tone was friendly.

'Many thanks, sir. But no.' John replied firmly this time. He stopped his horse for a moment, then as if he were speaking to himself, murmured, 'I don't think I would really like to work for the government. Not any longer. And what's more – I'll never leave Kamala.'

For a brief second Garvey looked worried. 'You're not planning to join Gandhi though – are you?' he asked.

'No, sir. I'm not a turncoat,' John replied with dignity, though a sign of bitterness was visibly marked on his face.

'Thank heavens for that! Otherwise it would be really embarrassing for us.' There was a sigh of relief from Garvey.

'Yes, sir, I know,' John's voice was cold this time.

'The commission has unanimously accepted the charge of negligence against you. Nothing else,' Garvey said. 'They have also recommended that you should be dismissed from your post.'

John listened to Garvey silently, showing no emotion. Garvey continued, 'The report will be sent to the Viceroy. You have a right of appeal. But I think it would be a waste of time.'

'I won't appeal against it, sir,' John replied. There was an air of sadness in his voice.

'Obviously, you must hand over all the crown documents and properties. And I'm afraid you have to vacate the bungalow. Take your time though – a month or so won't matter.'

'Thank you, sir. That's very kind of you.'

'Any idea what you might do?' Garvey asked. His voice betrayed his concern.

'No, sir. I haven't given it a thought yet.'

'I'm sorry, old boy. Things could have worked out differently had you been less rigid.' Garvey was genuinely sorry for the young man.

'Thank you for all your patience, sir,' John replied. 'I'm grateful to both you and Mrs Garvey. You have been very kind to me. Please give my regards to her.'

'Certainly I will. She's fond of you too, you know. She'll miss you,' Garvey said affectionately and then hurriedly added, 'Anyway, I must say goodbye to you now, old boy. May God bless you!' Garvey shook John's hand warmly, then rode away.

III

It did not take long for the world to know about John Sugden's dismissal. He had been punished by the Raj for neglecting his duty – leaving his district while it was in a tense, riotous situation, for a whole day, to take a married Hindu woman, his lover, to hospital after an alleged rape.

The news quickly filtered through in European circles and became a major talking point. Of course it had been known to many for some time, and in various European clubs it was already a source of smutty jokes.

The Viceroy now took the bold decision to publish the commission's report in full, including the allegations about the English officer colluding with miscreants and arranging a rape to possess a married Hindu woman. The report, of course, concluded that this particular allegation, made by the raped woman's father, could not be proven. There was no doubt that the Viceroy showed courage in acting so promptly and decisively to show to the Indian masses, especially to their political leaders like Gandhi, that the Raj had nothing to hide even when the incident involved one of its own officers.

After the publication of the report the national dailies carried extensive coverage of the news – the affair, the gossip, the titbits, and of course detailed analyses of the events. This became a major story for an entire week, capturing the headlines almost every day.

And for many who had been sick of seeing Gandhi's non-cooperation movement as the main news item, it came as a welcome relief, even though most people, Europeans as well as Indians, found the incident disturbing – both morally and otherwise.

The pro-British newspapers praised the Government's courage in openly and publicly handling the situation in spite of its potentially damaging impact on the Raj. The newspapers also showed concern that in recent years the government perhaps was not as scrupulous in choosing civil servants as it had been in the past. Of course during the Great War, the best civil servants had been requisitioned by London to run the war effort, which was understandable as the future of the Empire had then been at stake. But with the war over, the time for reassessing the recruitment policy was long overdue – especially now with the Indianization programme, which would inevitably weaken the entire civil service.

The newspapers also advised the Government that in the choice of officers, the Administration should consider not only the academic achievement of the candidates but their suitability for the kind of trying conditions in which they would be expected to operate – a hot and dusty climate, no other European in the vicinity, disease, race riots, not to mention Gandhi's continuous agitation to unsettle the government. Sugden in their view had been a bad choice.

The pro-nationalist newspapers did not allow the event to pass without some tub-thumping. They thought the commission had not tried to explore fully Ratan Banerji's allegation of a possible collusion between the Englishman and the riotous elements. The fact that over a hundred lives had been lost through negligence, a hundred families had lost their sons, or husbands, innocent children had been orphaned by this abominable event, bread winners had died, leaving entire families destitute – and the only punishment meted out was a mere dismissal, had to be a gross miscarriage of justice. In their view the Englishman should have been convicted of murder.

The pro-Hindu newspapers brought into play a new factor – the Englishman's impending marriage to a married Hindu woman. They were shocked that under the British law the marriage would be valid, nullifying her previous Hindu marriage. This particular point stirred up the belief among the masses that to the British,

Hindu marriages were not sacrosanct – could be undone at the whim of any Englishman who wanted to elope with a Hindu woman, whether by force or otherwise.

Joshi had long been waiting for this opportunity. His Hindu League now took up the cudgels on behalf of the nation and decided to organize mass demonstrations against a law which demeaned such a holy Hindu institution as marriage. They proclaimed that no foreign power should be allowed to tamper with the three inescapable events in a Hindu life – birth, marriage and death.

Joshi's indomitable energy was deployed to organize demonstrations in Calcutta, Bombay, Delhi and many other cities. The Hindus, distressed by the supposed attack on their religion, supported the Hindu League's stand on this issue. To fan their emotion even further, the Hindu League committed its storm troopers to take direct action. Their orders were: Demolish the marriage.

The Congress, however, showed a more tactical attitude. They deplored the event which had caused so many deaths. But they noted that the civil servant was a sympathizer with Gandhi and his nationalist movement. They wondered whether the whole thing was a real cock-up by the Raj and Sugden happened to be the scapegoat. They even considered the possibility that the adminstration had deliberately put the officer on the spot so that they could conveniently get rid of a Gandhi sympathizer.

For John and Kamala, the bitter experience came not from the national uproar but the demonstrations held in Raigarh itself. The local leaders openly declared their abhorrence of the depraved example set by the woman living in sin and about to give birth to a bastard, and the man who had led her up the garden path, so to speak. Obscene leaflets, issued by anonymous persons, showed sketches of Kamala in compromising postures with many men and then the caption – 'a local whore is about to give birth to a half-caste bastard'.

Public meetings organized by the Hindu League, in comparison, were much more sedate. They invited Ratan Banerji to speak. He came and denounced his daughter in public, causing extreme pain to his wife. This upset Kamala more than anything else.

John fumed helplessly. He wished he could do something against this public humiliation. He did not mind so much about himself, but the emotional impact of all these demonstrations on Kamala began to wear her down.

TWENTY FIVE

I

The birth of a newborn child in India was always celebrated with dancing by the local eunuchs. Very often the dancing reached extremes of vulgarity. The Indians somehow accepted it with a sense of light-hearted humour. But for John Sugden the experience of the local eunuchs dancing in front of his bungalow brought bitter humiliation. That was the day when he really lost his cool; the locals aroused him to such frenzy he could have done anything, even kill someone.

The place, just outside John's bungalow, was teeming with people – men, women, children, Hindus, Moslems – everyone was there. They all were in fits of laughter as they watched two *hijras* performing what could be called the infamous affair between a European and a married Hindu woman.

'Ma, why is that man's face painted white?' a little boy in the crowd asked his mother.

'Because she is meant to be a Sahib.'

'Is she a woman?'

'No, a *hijra*.'

'What is a *hijra*?'

'Neither a man nor a woman – a eunuch.'

The boy did not seem satisfied but he did not want to ask any more and show his ignorance.

The *hijra* who was dressed as the Sahib with a painted face and a hat, swung his hips and clapped his hands rhythmically, smoking a cigarette to impress upon the crowd the supposed wealth and status of the Sahib. The big, dark *hijra*, with protruding teeth stained from betel leaves, was dressed as a woman. A small, emaciated *hijra*, stooping in a corner, played the drum and at the same time yelled out a song in a shrill voice.

The big *hijra*, holding the end of her sari to the crowd's delight, danced coyly and shouted something obscene. Everyone roared with laughter. She now stood up, went across to the drummer and pulled a dirty, torn piece of loin-cloth from a bundle. She put it inside her sari to make her stomach bulge and then proceeded to dance, swinging the bulging stomach to the rhythm of the beat. The *hijra* with the painted face sat down in the middle, twirling a rod.

The big woman stooped in a corner and pulled her sari up and started mock contractions, yelping, 'This is my first baby. Oh, dear! Oh, dear! I am having so much pain.' Then she picked up a doll and put it inside her sari. The little *hijra* drummer beat her drum frantically to create a mood of suspense. The man with the painted face now stood up with his rod and started dancing in a quicker rhythm. The big woman yelled and the drummer banged her drum as the woman produced the doll from her sari. The crowd was now delirious with laughter.

'I'm not putting up with this,' cried John.

'Darling, what can you do? So many men are there, they'll beat you up.'

'Let them. I don't care. They are not coming to my house and insulting me. This has to stop. Even if it means the end of my life, the end of everything – I don't care.'

Kamala was frightened at seeing the Sahib taking his gun. She wanted to stop him, but he was so incensed she did not dare utter a word.

John went outside. The sight of the Englishman brandishing his gun immediately stirred many people who decided to scuttle to safety. A few organizers maintained a brave face and stood their ground. John went to them and shouted, 'If within five minutes you don't clear out from the front of my house I'll shoot the damn lot of you.'

That did the trick; whatever brave face the Indians had put on before now dissipated quickly as they accelerated out of sight.

II

The hot weather continued that year because the monsoon was delayed. Normally when the rainy season starts, the weather cools down, except for a few hot days when, because of high humidity, life becomes unbearable. Fortunately autumn soon comes, ending the tribulation as fresh breezes blow from the snow-bound Himalayas.

After the heavy rainfall in early April, the relentless, hot, scorching sun, like a violent, unruly force, went about its task of drying up everything on the earth. The ponds, the wells, the tanks – they all dried up. *Vistis* – the water carriers now had to walk miles to fill their leather bags and then had to carry their heavy load across the burning land, often with bare feet – the price of even a cheap pair of shoes being beyond their means. Peasants, waiting to till their normally fertile land for the second crop, were in panic, not knowing where to find fodder for the cattle to keep them alive until the rain came. The price of rice and wheat moved up rapidly as the black marketeers, spotting the opportunity, came and bought whatever was floating spare in the market. Moneylenders had a field day, for they continued to give cash advances to the poor farm workers at an extortionate rate of interest, secured of course against what little land they possessed. A situation like this would have sparked off great passion in John in the past and he would have rounded up the black marketeers and moneylenders, cautioning them in no uncertain terms. But now he viewed it as an outsider with only a vague academic interest.

III

After the fracas between the Sahib and the local gang, John's servants became alarmed by the entire situation. They knew the Sahib's predicament. Queen Victoria, most of them firmly believed, was still the Empress of India, though the Sahib refuted it strongly, even to the point of showing them the image of the present king, George V, on the coins. They were certain that Her Majesty, Queen Victoria, the ruler of three quarters of this world, would never accept a Sahib living in sin with an Indian woman. With the Sahib no longer a strong force, it became difficult for them to side with him against the local youths, especially as Gandhi was gradually extending his influence in the countryside, many thought it was only a matter of a few years before the entire Raj had to leave the so-called 'golden shores' of India. On the other hand, the servants did not feel happy siding with outsiders against their master. *Nimakharam* – they could never be.

Ibrahim was the first to find a reason to leave. He came from a dusty, mountainous village in the Punjab, where money was hard to come by. He had a wife and children to maintain there. Normally he went there once every two or three years. Even then he did not stay there long, for he liked the life in Raigarh much better, where, unbeknown to his wife, he had a close relationship with a local woman. However, he had learnt that his wife was unwell and he wanted a couple of months' leave to look after her, he told the Sahib.

Next in line was Jadu. He came from the other side of the province – Orissa. He was not married, but his parents were still alive. His mother suddenly became ill and he had to go.

Finally it seemed that everyone had something or other happening to their families and desperately needed to leave. The only exception was Albert David, the untouchable Christian. For whatever reason, whether out of loyalty or the thought that for him the outside world would be much harsher than being under the protection of the troubled Sahib, he decided to stay put. And much to John's relief, the untouchable proudly took over a fair proportion of household duties.

The hot weather made it increasingly difficult for Kamala to move about comfortably as it was only a matter of weeks before the baby was due. John wanted to help her but Kamala would not have the Sahib doing any menial work, servants or no servants. And no amount of protest made her change her mind. So John finally gave in to her inevitable rule.

Occasionally they went out in the carriage but the uneven, parched land made the journeys very exhausting and unbearable for Kamala. Seeing her condition, John advised her to stay at home. But sometimes when he felt restless, being cooped up within the confines of four walls, he went out alone, riding.

The hills were now dry everywhere, but still beautiful. The sunset broke almost blood red in the sky, and the reddish yellow earth, reflecting the light, turned the deep blue distant sky to a mellow saffron. John felt strangely alive amid that barren yet colourful landscape.

But the problem that preoccupied John's mind most of the time was the question of marriage. There was not long to go before the baby was due and he did not want his child to be born a bastard. Kamala, though equally keen to be married before the birth of the child, did not quite have the courage to face the inevitable demonstration from the storm-troopers of the Hindu League. She was afraid. Whatever might or might not happen in the future, she did not want her unborn child to die in a stampeding crowd. John understood her concern and shared the fear. All the same he was not happy, watching the days passing by with no immediate prospect of marriage.

IV

One Sunday afternoon John was sitting on the veranda while Kamala was doing something inside the house, when suddenly he saw the dust blowing on the distant horizon – a horseman galloping towards the bungalow. Who could it be? He wondered. Surely not Garvey! As the horseman drew nearer, he could see the mane of a white beard blowing in the wind and the unmistakable ruddy cheeks of the Belgian priest.

'Father Fallon's coming, Kamala,' John shouted in excitement. Kamala came running out with a beaming smile. They had not seen the missionary doctor for a while because he had been fully occupied by a local cholera epidemic. They waved at him fervently. It had been a long time since anyone had been to their place. Even before Father Fallon had had a chance to come through the door, Kamala almost threw herself into his embrace. 'Father you have been neglecting us,' she cried feigning anger, but her eyes were full of affection for the old man.

'My child, if I had it my way, I would spend all the time with you. I feel jealous of this Sahib of yours.'

'That doesn't sound like a Catholic missionary,' John teased.

'Please, don't talk like that,' Kamala was serious. She never enjoyed this kind of joke.

Father Fallon smiled now – the graceful smile of a man steeped in religious conviction. 'I'm afraid I won't be seeing you for some time after today,' he said somewhat sadly.

'What do you mean? Where're you going and why?' Kamala asked almost possessively.

'I have received my marching orders.'

'Who from?' Both John and Kamala were surprised.

'From the government.'

'Why?' asked Kamala. She could not understand why someone as dedicated to helping the poor as the priest, had to go.

'Perhaps they think I'm like a bad penny,' Fallon replied, 'turning up everywhere and exerting a seditious influence upon their civil servants.'

'How long do you have here then?' John asked anxiously.

'Only a couple of days.'

'Oh God!' John was visibly upset. He said, 'I was hoping you would be able to deliver the child. In the current political climate, I'm scared to take her to an Indian hospital.'

The priest was quiet – anxiety written all over his face. Suddenly his eyes sparkled. 'Why don't you both come with me?'

'We can't go to Belgium. What would I do there? And I don't want to leave India.' John sounded despondent.

'No! No! I'm not going to Belgium,' Father Fallon replied. 'My home is here. Until the dust settles, I'm off to Pondicherry. It'll do me good – speaking French again. Oh I miss it so badly!'

'But what would I do in Pondicherry?' John asked.

Father Fallon was full of constructive ideas. 'You can teach English,' he said. 'With a bit of luck, I might be able to fix up something for you over there.'

'That's not a bad thought,' John looked at Kamala for approval.

Kamala, opening her large and beautiful eyes, asked, 'Do they have the Hindu League in Pondicherry?'

'No,' the priest assured her, 'you won't have that kind of trouble there.'

John jumped up in excitement and shouted, 'Hurray. We are definitely coming with you. When do you go?'

'The day after tomorrow,' Fallon replied. 'Would you be able to get ready by then?'

'Perhaps we can follow you in a few days,' John said. 'We have to arrange for the entry permits.'

'Leave that with me,' said Fallon. 'It will be easier for me to arrange them.'

'In that case we'll come with you,' Kamala interjected. 'I'm a bit frightened of the Hindu League. And as the government is turning you out I'm sure they will keep a watchful eye on you until you get out of the country. I'd much rather go under the government's eagle eye than be hounded out by the storm-troopers.'

'How right you are, darling!' John was delighted with Kamala's down-to-earth suggestion. Even Father Fallon looked at the young girl with real admiration.

Kamala, embarrassed by this attention, murmured, 'Why are you both looking at me? Don't you agree?'

'You're a real gem, my love!' John moved forward to kiss her.

'Not in front of Father Fallon, please!' Kamala pushed him away.

'Yes! Not until you're married,' the old Belgian uttered the words with an impish grin.

They all laughed, free and easy. The young couple had not laughed in such a spontaneous, relaxed way for a long time.

TWENTY SIX

I

On Monday morning both John and Kamala were very edgy. They had hardly had any sleep the previous night, tossing and turning with anxiety. There was simply so much to worry about now, especially with a newcomer soon to arrive in their family. Most of the morning they spent on the veranda, eyes glued to the distant horizon, keenly observing even the slightest speck of dust blowing in the air. Their eager waiting was rewarded around midday when they finally saw a horseman galloping at a distance. Kamala had only gone inside for a few moments just at that time. With eager enthusiasm John shouted from the veranda, 'Kamala! Fallon is coming!'

Kamala immediately rushed outside. There were traces of little petals in her hair which indicated she had been praying to her Hindu gods and goddesses for their safe journey to Pondicherry.

The beaming face of Father Fallon soon appeared at the door. Just by looking at his smile both John and Kamala knew that the news was good. At last! At last! Lady Luck was really turning for them. They had waited nearly a year for Fortune's smile – perhaps here it was at last.

As Fallon entered through the door he spoke excitedly without any preamble, 'Everything's set for us now.'

'When do we go?' John and Kamala asked eagerly.

'Tonight! By the Toofan Mail! I have already booked the tickets.'

'What about our entry permits to Pondicherry?' John asked. This question was also foremost in Kamala's mind.

'We have a six-hour stop in Calcutta. We will arrive there at about two tomorrow afternoon. Once we get there, I will go to the French consulate and arrange them.' Father Fallon seemed highly optimistic.

'Suppose we don't get our entry permits – what then?' Kamala was nervous. She knew Joshi had his biggest stronghold in Calcutta. For Kamala and John the most dangerous place in the world at the moment without doubt was that large sprawling city – the epicentre of the Hindu League's activities. It was there in the Bengali heartland that people took Kamala's impending marriage as a threat to the existence of Hinduism.

Fallon, seeing the nervous concern of the young girl, tried to reassure her with his calm demeanour. 'I believe God is with us, child. Do not fear!'

These few words of courage were enough to remove any doubt which both John and Kamala had had in their mind. Now they looked forward to their journey that night.

II

Just before ten o'clock that evening Father Fallon appeared holding a small suitcase containing his worldly possessions, which consisted mainly of medicines, a stethoscope, a hypodermic syringe, a few changes of clothes, toothbrush, tooth-paste and some basic necessities. The world for him was nothing more than the place where he was needed to help people. And he was always prepared for it. Kamala and John were surprised, however, to find that he also had a big bundle with him, because it was so unusual for him to carry anything apart from that small suitcase.

'What have you got there, Father?' they both asked, almost echoing each other.

Fallon smiled somewhat awkwardly and then looking at Kamala he said, 'I'm afraid this is a punishment which, my child, you have to face until we reach Waltare. After we reach the southern heartland I don't foresee any problem from Joshi's storm troopers.'

Before John and Kamala's gleaming eyes the father now started to open the bundle – it was a nun's outfit!

'Oh God!' Kamala started giggling. 'You mean to say we would be able to fool people with this nun's dress – they would immediately spot my bulging stomach and wonder what sort of a nun I must be.'

Fallon smiled. 'You are a small person. I am confident you will be able to get away with it. And with your pale skin and me with my dog-collar there wouldn't be even the slightest suspicion.'

Father Fallon was right. When Kamala finally put the outfit on there was no chance of anyone suspecting that Kamala was other than an ardent follower of the Catholic priest.

'I am feeling very nervous now!' John could not help throwing in a bit of light-hearted banter. 'When your wife becomes a nun what is left for you in life?'

'We aren't married yet!' Kamala warned him. 'Let's pray to God that we can be married in future.' Those words were enough to put into everyone's mind the fear of the risks ahead of them.

III

The plan that Father Fallon, John and Kamala had worked out for their journey was that Albert David would take them to Sripore station in John's carriage and would then come back to Raigarh. He was told not to tell anyone about their departure for at least a week. By then of course John was supposed to have vacated his bungalow. He had already taken the inventory of crockery, cutlery and furniture and submitted the list to the government confirming that nothing was missing.

When Albert David realized that the Sahib was going for good he cried, for he knew that he would never find another master as kind as the Sahib. John gave him quite a bit of money to see him through before he could find a job. The life of an untouchable was not easy in India and nobody knew it better than John.

Kamala, earlier in the afternoon, had been to her mother's to say goodbye. She knew it was not safe to tell anything to her father or sisters. John did not go with Kamala to see Mrs Banerji, although he wanted to, for that would have created immediate suspicion in everyone's mind. Moreover since the tribunal, although Kamala in spite of Banerji's annoyance had visited her mother from time to time, there was never any question of John going there.

In the afternoon when Kamala went to see her, both mother and daughter wept for a while but faced this parting with a mixture of sadness and hope. They knew that they would not meet each other again for a long time. But Mrs Banerji was pleased that at last Kamala was going to a safer place. She wished them both well in life. While blessing her daughter she said, 'Let the name Kamala be really truthful this time.' In the midst of all her crises Kamala had nearly forgotten that her name represented the goddess Laxmi – the provider of wealth, grace, good living and happiness. For the first time in her life her mother's wish offered her a promise of hope. But she was far too scared to dream any further until the journey through Calcutta was over.

IV

In the darkness of the night when they finally came out of the bungalow Kamala shed a few tears. So much of her life, so many memories revolved round that bungalow, right from the time when she and Hari had first come to tea with the Sahib soon after their wedding. And then the time when she had found shelter there when nobody would have her in Raigarh, or for that matter anywhere else in the world. Only one man had had the courage to embrace her whole-heartedly and in the process accept dire consequences. She also remembered the happiest period in her life in that bungalow – all those evenings reading Shelley, Keats, Byron and especially Donne. And then that extraordinary night when she and the Sahib had for the first time made love. She would never in her life forget that night. That was the night when she had passed the stiffest test of her life: had not just accepted but eagerly invited another man to replace her husband. That was the night she had crossed the threshold from being a Hindu to a human being – that was the night when she had experienced love, affection, commitment and responsibility. But above all that was the night when she had embraced life for the first time and the sheer joy of that living had been with her ever since.

When they arrived at Sripore station it was nearly two o'clock in the morning. There was hardly anyone in sight except a handful of passengers. However, to remain on the safe side they stayed in the hansom and came out only when they heard the whistle of the approaching train. John pulled down his hat to cover his face and so did Father Fallon. Kamala with her nun's outfit looked so foreign that even with the most fertile imagination nobody would have guessed her true identity.

Father Fallon could not get a coupe for the journey to Calcutta. There was only one other European passenger in the compartment. Luckily he slept right through the night and for the better part of the morning. He woke up around midday when the train arrived in Burdwan. He hurriedly put on his tie and hat and called a porter to take down his luggage.

Kamala could never sleep in a train. The constant rhythmic noise always induced her to go through a song or a poem with the sound of the train. Lying in the darkness of the carriage she went through Donne's poems one after another while Father Fallon snored and John tossed and turned and only occasionally, realizing Kamala was not yet asleep, asked her whether she was feeling all right and then dozed off again.

When dawn broke and the sky became pale and clear Kamala sat on her seat and looked through the window to watch the ever-changing landscapes. Later John came to join her but carefully sat at a distance so that no suspicion would be aroused about their relationship.

V

At about two o'clock in the afternoon when the train approached Howrah station Kamala felt acutely nervous. Her stomach started to churn and she became sick, though she did not tell anyone so as not to add to their agony. She managed to regain her composure after that – the jangling nerves somehow became calmer.

The station itself was filled with posters. Joshi's demon face was everywhere with a slogan, asking people to stop the marriage of a married Hindu woman to a disreputable British officer. John was tense when he saw the posters. They hurriedly made their way through the crowded station to the first class rest room, reserved for European passengers only. Fortunately the rest room was empty. They made themselves at home on the comfortable seats and switched on the newly-installed electric fan. And when Father Fallon went out to the consulate John locked the door so that no one else could come in. Kamala soon fell asleep – she was utterly exhausted after that sleepless night in the train. John, however, stayed awake – anxiously awaiting Fallon's return.

It was nearly five o'clock when Fallon came back. By then Kamala was already up, eagerly waiting for his return. The anxiety of both John and Kamala showed through the prominent veins on their otherwise very young faces.

'The news is good,' Fallon exclaimed. 'I've got the permit for myself and John. They could not issue one for Kamala straight away, but they will telegraph it to the border post tomorrow. The chargé d'affaires assured me personally, so there will be no problem.'

Kamala looked tense again. She was scared in case everything went wrong. These days she always expected things to turn out against her.

Seeing her anxious face Fallon tried to reassure her. 'Don't worry, my child! If necessary I will ditch my Christian principles and bribe the guard to get you through.' Then he smiled impishly and to lighten the atmosphere added, 'Nuns have a special place in Catholic countries – they would let you through just seeing that outfit.' That comment seemed to ease Kamala's tension.

VI

The train from Calcutta to Waltare was much more comfortable. This time they had a coupé to themselves so they were more relaxed. At least at night Kamala could take off her headgear and let her black wavy hair fall freely on her shoulders.

'What sort of a nun is that?' Fallon teased the young woman to keep her spirits up. She smiled, but didn't reply. Once the Bengal Nagpur Railways train left Kharagpur the priest spoke with relief; 'We are fairly safe now – we've crossed the Bengal border.'

Nearly thirty hours later the train stopped in Waltare. It was a long stop – nearly two hours – mainly used by passengers as a stop-over for lunch. John, Kamala and Fallon did not go out to the restaurant but stayed in and ordered some lunch. At this stage they were not prepared to risk anything and their safest bet was to stay in the compartment and keep the door firmly locked.

Of course since the morning Kamala had put her headgear back on so that not even one speck of suspicion could be aroused in onlookers from outside the train, though she was beginning to feel that at last perhaps all her ordeals were about to be over. But she did not want to daydream, for she knew that she did not have an entry permit yet. Anything could still happen.

When the train started from Waltare Station Kamala shouted

out in dismay, 'It's going the wrong way – we are going back to Calcutta!'

'No, darling! Don't panic!' John tried to calm her down. 'They have just changed the engine. The Southern Railways have now taken over the train from the Bengal Nagpur Railways and the engine was shunted to the other end of the train.'

Kamala was not totally convinced. She looked anxiously through the window to see whether she could catch sight of any familiar scenery they had already passed on the way to Waltare from Calcutta.

Observing her anxiety-ridden face Fallon said, 'Trust your man, my dear. He is right. You are not going back to Calcutta.' Then to divert her mind from her worries, he suggested, 'Come on – let's have a game of cards.'

Both John and Kamala were pleased with this suggestion.

'But we don't have a pack,' Kamala said rather disappointedly.

'I have,' Fallon said with a grin. The young couple were surprised that in his small suitcase Father Fallon was carrying a few tricks other than his medicines.

'What shall we play?' John asked as Fallon brought his pack of cards out from the suitcase.

'How about a game of whist?' There was a playful look in the Belgian priest's eyes.

'That's a gambler's game,' John teased him.

Fallon smiled and replied, 'We won't gamble with money but with love – we shall see who can give how much. In our game the loser will be the winner. The more love you give, the better you are.'

'All right, I accept your rules,' John said smilingly.

'I will be the loser then,' Kamala seemed to have perked up now from the fear of the train going back to Calcutta.

The priest replied with great affection, 'My dear, that's what makes you the winner.'

VII

The following day when the train arrived in Madras Kamala was much less tense. Even the worry about her entry permit to Pondicherry seemed to have disappeared from her mind.

From Madras they had to take a narrow-gauge train to Pondicherry. The train was very small, moving slowly now through the lush fields of the Madras Presidency. The landscape was very different from the rugged hills of Chotonagpur. Everywhere was beautifully green, framed by an abundance of coconut trees.

It was nearly twelve hours before the narrow-gauge train came to the border post. Father Fallon went with some trepidation to enquire about Kamala's permit as John and Kamala held their breath, hoping to goodness that they would have a smooth passage through the post. They had no idea what they would do if the French guards refused to let Kamala enter into their enclave. But Fallon was confident about the French chargé d'affaires' promise.

Well, as one might have expected there was no permit waiting for Kamala. For a period there was panic all round. Fallon, red-faced argued in French with the border guards. They had a good look at the nun which made Kamala highly agitated and nervous but she somehow managed to keep a calm expression on her face. Finally the chief of the guards nodded his head and all three of them felt an immense sense of relief. Fallon had been absolutely right in his prediction: in a Catholic country they wouldn't stop a nun, especially when she was travelling with a priest. Because that was what finally gained the favour of the police chief.

TWENTY SEVEN

I

It was a bliss such as Kamala had never known in life before. Pondicherry was so different from Raigarh – no parched lands between enclosed hills, rutted by the relentless sun – nor the excavated mines of mica, reflecting the parody of life. Here on the Coromandel coast the deep blue water of the Bay of Bengal washed the golden shore. A little further up, the green, prodigious land was abundant in coconut trees, not all tall, straight and thin, but some bending, almost in a semicircle, touching the ground as if whispering in some foreign dialect, unknown to anyone but themselves, only themselves.

Looking at the distant horizon where the blue sky touched the even bluer sea, Kamala felt relaxed for the first time after long years of suffering. The air was so free and boundless, the vision not restricted by even the smallest obstacle, only the sea, asking relentless questions – what's life all about? Is there a purpose? Or is it just a cosmic cycle – a union between vitality and splendour, science and philosophy, man and woman?

As Kamala stood by the shore, looking at the countless small waves breaking – momentarily white and then disappearing into the deep blue of insignificance – she felt life itself perhaps was just as transient. But she wanted this happiness – the happiness between John and herself to continue like a star, timelessly transmitting light through the dark universe.

Yes, for the first time, here on the sun-drenched shores of Pondicherry, in this freer environment, with neither the rigid discipline of the Raj nor the religious strictures of Hinduism playing their overzealous roles, she felt John was no longer the Sahib, the master, the lord, but the man in her life – a partner to whom she could relate without feeling the pressures of society.

She wondered why they had had to run away to Pondicherry to relate to this pristine language of life – that between a man and woman – that of love. They had to escape from India, from the Raj, from Hinduism, the League, the Congress, Gandhi and Jinnah before they could, without inhibition, hold hands and walk along a crowded avenue. Nobody in Pondicherry batted an eyelid on seeing them together – not even out of curiosity – as if it was not a scandal, not news, not even a surprise.

During the first few days, which they spent in a local guest-house, they found Pondicherry very different from India. French characteristics were imprinted all over the place. Wide tree-lined avenues, cafés in the street with chairs spread out on which Frenchmen, mulattoes, Indians, sitting next to each other, chatted endlessly.

'Is Pondicherry very much like France?' Kamala asked John with intense surprise in her voice.

'There's a feel of Paris in Pondicherry. It's the Frenchness, the smell – so different from the rest of India.'

'What I like most is this intermingling of different races.'

'You see, in France, unlike England and India, class is not

determined just by your birth. The French attach a lot more importance to intellect. In comparison, we, in England, are mere philistines. But many would say, the French may read more books but they also have more revolutions – and some violent ones too. We are more staid. We dislike change because it brings ripples which, our worldly experience has taught us, could be destructive. That's why we distrust unworldly intellectuals.'

Kamala listened to John's sagacity which was too far removed from her world. 'What I like most here is that you and I can go out together and nobody cares – no agitation, no demonstration, no newspaper headlines. I feel so close to you, which in spite of all my love I never could in India.'

'Do you know, I feel coming to Pondicherry is the best thing that could ever have happened to us,' John smiled lovingly at her then added, 'And soon, with Father Fallon's blessing, we will no longer have to live in sin, as they say.'

Kamala now moved closer to him and said, 'Would you really like to marry such an ugly Hindu woman? One with a past?'

John embraced her, giving a soft kiss on her forehead, then added, 'You're beautiful! More everyday!'

'With this?' She touched her heavily pregnant, bulging stomach.

'That makes you more serene, more lovable.'

'In that case, we have to have plenty of children so that you find me lovable all the time.'

'Not too many please! Otherwise you won't have any time for me. And I wouldn't like that.'

'My love! Even if we have a hundred children, I'll always have time for you.'

'Make it ninety nine, please!' John teased her. She pouted her lips and feigned disappointment and widened her eyes. John caressed her rich, luxuriant, black hair and said, 'If you allow me to hold you like this from time to time, I don't mind.'

'Would you feel jealous, if I love him?'

'Of course I will. How can I not feel jealous if you love someone else?'

'I have to love him. The little baby will need love. But I promise I won't take it from my love for you.' She smiled.

'As long as you promise,' John said teasingly.

'Darling, my love for you is growing all the time. And I don't know how it can still grow.' Kamala paused for a moment and then asked, 'What are those lines from John Donne?'

'I don't know which lines you mean.' John feigned ignorance.

'You do! Please, stop teasing me,' Kamala pleaded.

'This is the real test of your love. Let's see whether you remember them.'

Kamala now raised her large brown eyes and softly murmured, 'Methinks I lied all winter, when I swore, My love was infinite, if spring make it more.'

John looked at Kamala and thought even if he had to sacrifice everything in life, everything he ever had, all tangible or intangible wealth – he would have done it without a speck of hesitation, just to savour this very moment.

II

A few days later John was surprised to find Kamala looking depressed.

'What is it, darling?'

'I am so happy, I am scared.'

'What for? There's no reason to be scared in Pondicherry. No Joshi, no Gandhi, no Jinnah – not even your father.'

'That's what scares me. I fear happiness is not for me. I fear losing you.'

'Why should you lose me?' John was surprised. 'You're not planning to run away again – are you?'

'No, darling, no! Of course not! I am just scared because I love you so much.'

'Let's not talk about silly things,' John tried to change the subject. 'What would you like me to give you for a wedding present?'

'You have already given me a present. A child. Your child. Growing inside me. Kicking me every now and then, like a restless European.'

'Did you think it would be a sedate Indian?'

'No, darling. I didn't. I want our son to be strong, powerful and upright – like his father.'

'How do you know it's a boy?' John asked her curiously.

'I can tell from his kicks. Do you want to feel him?' Kamala took John's hand and spread it over her stomach. 'There you are. You see how hard he kicks?'

John did not feel anything but he did not want to contradict her. He was just happy to see her happy. After all the ordeals and sufferings she had had to endure in life, it was such a pleasure to see her happy.

III

Father Fallon moved out from the guest house after a couple of days and found accommodation in a hospice, tending the old and infirm. John took an apartment in the rue St Honoré, near the Avenue Napoléon. It was small – only two bedrooms, one of which Kamala had already designated for the newcomer. Coming from such a spacious, luxurious bungalow, John was a bit concerned about the smallness of this apartment.

'Only two of us, darling. We don't need a palace.' Kamala was well aware that John no longer earned a princely civil service salary.

'But soon we shall be three. Moreover, you need servants to help you with the household chores, even if we don't have as many as twenty-four.'

'Darling!' Kamala called to him affectionately.

John looked at her, not knowing what was on her mind.

'Will you promise me something?'

'What, dear?'

'Please, promise me first!'

'A blank cheque?' John teased her.

'I won't rob you. Please!'

'All right, I promise.'

'I do not want a servant staying with us all the time. I just want you. No one else. Of course, except our little baby.'

'But you'll need a servant. You'll need somebody to look after the baby.'

'I'll be able to look after our child. I am good with babies. You will see!'

'Then you'll neglect me and I'll be jealous.'

'I won't neglect you, my love.' She now came nearer and showered him with kisses.

IV

John's happiness with Kamala now reminded him more and more of his childhood, especially of his mother. No longer was it the dreadful memory of that horrific image – a charred face in the morgue – but the warmth and affection of his early childhood, when his world was just his parents, mostly his mother. This, in a strange way, prompted him to think of his father. He had not written to him for a long time. In his first year in India, he had written home regularly. Then the flow had simply dried up as there had been less and less news to give. Of course there was the news of his relationship with Kamala. But that he had not wanted to share with anyone. It was so personal and fulfilling that no one outside, he thought, would be able to understand the depth of the relationship; very likely they would misconstrue it on a purely factual basis.

But now that the wedding and the birth of his child were no longer far off, he wanted to share his happiness with his father. He gathered enough courage one day to write a few lines about Kamala – her background, the ordeals she had had to suffer – and also the good news about the imminent arrival of his grandchild.

It was not long before he received a reply. Not hostile. Not that he would have expected it from his father, but a little distant. In many ways, almost prophetic. It read:

Dear John

It's news for which you should be congratulated. Though deep down I feel nervous at the prospect of the battle that you have decided to take on. All my life I have tried to fight for the ideals that I have believed in; and the end result was that tragic event – losing your mother. Me being me, I don't think I could have acted any differently and you have the same genes in you.

Marriage is a strange institution. It requires an awful lot of sacrifice and compromise from both parties. So many marriages end in divorce even though the partners come from the same background, same locality, same culture. Many people believe adversity makes a strong marriage stronger and a weak one weaker – the ultimate test. However, it seems your relationship with Kamala has crossed at least the initial hurdle and survived during a very trying time for both of you. That's a good omen.

Finally a piece of advice. As long as you try to look for the inner light, all outside problems will disappear into oblivion.

We wish you both happiness.

Father.

A little note from Joyce, his stepmother, underneath. 'Pleased to hear your news. Congratulations! Look forward to meeting you all in the near future.'

John was somehow disappointed. Perhaps he was looking for a more positive note from his father. Though rereading it, he could see nothing to cause this disappointment.

Through Father Fallon's contacts John soon found a job, teaching English at a local school. It was a new experience for him since he had never taught before. The pleasure of seeing young children with enthusiastic eyes, bubbling over with questions, took him back years to when he himself was at school.

Then his mind turned towards his own soon-to-be-born child, and a strange feeling engulfed him. Another Sugden coming on to this earth – inheriting the adventurous spirit of the Dutch sailor, Samuel, who had crossed the sea with Hudson; and the empathy of Tom Lloyd, the rebel, humanitarian Quaker; and perhaps all these, blended with the wisdom of the East, would provide a real cross fertilization; not just of ideas but seeds – the new world merging with the old – to bring harmony in which colonizers and colonized would seek the same goal, the same objective – the enhancement of every-one, irrespective of race, colour and creed. The new one perhaps would be a proud torch-bearer of this new world. Not a Eurasian – but a man who could represent everyone – East and West – because he would understand them, identify himself with them – not as an out-side observer, but as part of global civilization. Let's hope he can, John thought joyfully, for he so wanted it to happen.

V

As John gradually settled down to his teaching job from Monday to Saturday – Saturday only a half day: there were no classes after the lunch-break – Kamala suddenly found she had quite a lot of time to spare. Over the last few months in India when John had had to give up his job and had stayed at home all day, she had become used to his company. But here, with John going to work once again, she started missing him in the daytime. Moreover, looking after him was the easiest of tasks. He was not a demanding person. Very easy-going. Not pernickety in any sense of the word. All he needed was a meal in the evening and even then he did not really mind what was offered to him. His only concern was Kamala's health and happiness.

To while away the long days alone in the apartment, Kamala started making the soon-to-arrive infant's clothes – all for a boy.

'Suppose we have a girl – what will you do then? Make her wear all these boy's clothes?'

'Did you not feel the kick that day?' Kamala replied, greatly surprised, 'It could never be a girl.'

'But how do you know? You've never had a baby before?' John asked, mystified.

'Women know these things. They don't need to learn them. Just as you didn't need to learn how to teach.'

'At least when I was at school and university I observed the teachers. It's not really new ground for me.'

'The same with me. I saw my sisters' children grow up,' Kamala replied.

John now gave up, realizing he could never win this argument. He was pleased to see how confident Kamala had become since they arrived in Pondicherry.

Apart from clothes, Kamala also started making little items of bed-linen. Here she did elaborate embroidery, following Indian tradition: each with a picture – not even just a picture, more like story-telling – such as the Sahib riding a horse with a gun pointing at the sky.

'That's unfair,' John said. 'You have never seen me riding like that with a gun.'

'I can imagine how you looked that day.' There was a mischievous smile on Kamala's face.

'Dear, that was for you. No wonder, I was raving mad. I didn't know where you were. You didn't even bother to leave me a note.'

'I know!' replied Kamala. 'You see, I promised father I would not write a note. I thought if you did not hear from me, you would soon forget the native girl.'

'Stop calling yourself a native!' John shouted. 'I don't like it. Anyway, you should know me better – as if I would really forget you.'

'I'm sorry, darling,' Kamala softly replied. 'I shouldn't have done it; just a spur of the moment decision. You see, I did not want you to lose your job for me. But now that I know your love and this happiness, I would not miss it for anything – not even for your career with the Raj. Selfish – aren't I?'

'No, darling, not at all; you're just responding to my love.'

'And you to mine.'

On another day Kamala embroidered a story about the Sahib

dancing with a European woman.

'That can't be me!' John exclaimed. 'To make it truthful, at least you should put yourself there.'

'But I don't dance,' Kamala replied. 'I have never been to a dancehall.'

'That's all the more reason why you shouldn't make it – because it's so unreal.'

'But I can imagine how you look, dancing with a European woman,' Kamala teased.

'Nonsense!' John said. 'You've never even seen me with a European woman.'

'Yes I have. Don't you remember that friend from Calcutta who came to Raigarh once. Oh, we were so curious. We thought she was going to be our new memsahib.'

'Good Lord! You have a memory! Anyway she didn't become the new memsahib – so there!' John paused and then with a twinkle in his eye asked, 'Why don't we make a pact, dear? You change that European woman into an Indian and I take you to a dancehall.'

Kamala with mock fright in her eyes shouted, 'Never!'

'Never what?' John asked with feigned innocence. 'Go to a dancehall or change the picture?'

'Both,' Kamala replied, smiling.

'All right! Let's make a compromise. You don't have to change the picture but let's go to a dancehall one evening.'

Kamala, putting a look of horror on her face, replied, 'What would people say, if I go? A woman with a bulging stomach, wearing a sari, dancing with a sahib?'

'But that's the Sahib's wife. Who else could he dance with, if not with her?'

Kamala kept quiet; her eyes gleamed at the thought of dancing with the Sahib.

'Come on!' John implored. 'I'm sure you'll enjoy it.'

Kamala, rather embarrassed, but curious all the same, replied, 'Maybe, after the baby is born.'

'Hurray!' John shouted. 'Is that a promise?'

Kamala smiled indulgently and replied, 'Only if you promise to keep any other wild ideas out of your head.'

VI

It was only a fortnight before the baby was due that Father Fallon finally arranged the wedding. The reason for the delay was that under French law, all marriages including church ones had to be registered. And there was quite a waiting list for the registrar. The registration was to take place in the town hall on the morning of the wedding-day and, following the French custom, Father Fallon would solemnize the marriage in church in the evening.

The morning was lovely and warm. Early November: but in this part of the world you could even go sea-bathing since the temperature still soared into the seventies. Kamala put on the red Banaras sari which John had bought in Calcutta and which she had been saving hopefully for this very day. John wore a long coat and a top hat and the traditional rose in his button hole, and so did Father Fallon, deciding that a priest's robe would not be suitable on this occasion. The other witness was the headmaster from John's new school. Being a Frenchman and a bachelor he knew the value of romance and was eager to be associated with this marriage.

The ceremony itself was short, austere and very businesslike. When they came out, Father Fallon with adolescent enthusiasm brought out confetti from his pocket and showered the newly-married couple, shouting, 'According to French custom, you're not really married until the priest solemnizes it this evening. So children, you must behave.' They all laughed except Kamala who blushed.

John replied with a glint in his eyes, 'Yes, Father, we will.'

In the evening Fallon took them to a small chapel, quiet and peaceful, surrounded by a garden full of flowers: roses, bougainvilleas, hollyhocks – and a lawn, neatly mown. The place had the ambience of a quiet French town – very European.

The inside was small, with room for only a couple of benches and the altar. Father Fallon stood there in his priest's robe and read the vows. John took them aloud, Kamala softly. At the end Father Fallon pronounced them man and wife.

The French headmaster was also there for the occasion. 'Let's go and celebrate,' he shouted as they came out.

Fallon, no longer priest-like, said mischievously, 'When an Englishman marries a Hindu, perhaps they celebrate with lemonade.'

'Not in Pondicherry,' the Frenchman boomed.

They went to a restaurant in the Avenue Foch – beautifully

decorated with vine leaves shaped into an arbour to provide sunshades under which chairs and tables were spread out.

They ordered a meal and champagne. Kamala was so happy, she even drank a little champagne. John, not wanting to lose this opportunity to tease her, shouted, 'Now that you're drinking, let's go to a dancehall and dance, like that picture in your embroidery.'

Kamala tapped him under the table to shut him up. They all saw it and laughed. The bachelor Frenchman appreciated this gesture from the bride and shouted, 'Bravo, Madame Sugden! Your marriage is now complete.'

They all roared at this comment as happiness flowed from all directions over the newly-married couple.

TWENTY EIGHT

I

On Friday, exactly six days after his marriage, John Sugden, with the headmaster's permission, left school early to go to the bazaar and buy something special to give his wife a big surprise. He wanted to celebrate this weekend. Perhaps this would be the very last on their own. Not that he was feeling jealous in any way about sharing Kamala with the baby, but he realized that life could no longer remain the same. She would have to pay a lot of attention to the newcomer, and seeing how motherly she had already become before the baby was even born, he had no doubt in his mind that she would pour a great deal of devotion and love on to the new arrival.

This last couple of months, since they had come to live in Pondicherry, had been a time of unmitigated bliss and joy for John – having Kamala so intensely, so passionately – with no one to intrude in their life. Now and then he felt sad about the arrival of the baby but he soon recovered from that feeling. He wondered though whether he had the maturity to take on the responsibility of fatherhood. A bit too late to think about it now, he thought. But he would try to be a good father – not like his own, who had not really guided him; left everything for his mother to do. He would take the father's responsibility seriously – be more positive in shaping the youngster's interests and ideals.

The afternoon was getting cooler as the sweepers had already watered the roads. The red dust had settled, giving an earthy smell. He took a tonga and asked the dark Tamil to go to the bazaar. Being a Friday afternoon the roads were already crowded with people starting to relax at the thought of the weekend ahead.

The bazaar was bubbling. Everyone looked at John with curiosity. Even in Pondicherry, the sight of a European shopping in a bazaar without a servant was unusual. This was quite an experience for John. All the years he had been in India, he had never known how it felt, jostling through a crowded bazaar. The hawkers outside the main market hall were shouting with their produce on the pavement. They all knew the Sahib – even those inside the market hall: the stall holders. They were all intrigued by this mad Englishman, and when they learnt that the Sahib was married to an Indian woman, it aroused in them both an affection and a desire to protect him from the hurly-burly of the bazaar. Keen to sell him their produce, they slashed their prices, vying with one another to gain his custom.

John bought some fruit and vegetables and then went to the fish market where a throng was waiting just outside as a boat-load of fresh fish was being unloaded. People were screaming, shouting, pushing, jostling to get the best bargain, but as soon as they saw John, they stood back showing respect and gave way to him. The fisherman that John went to was eager to give him the best possible fish at the lowest possible price. He shouted, 'This would be good for your madame.' Perhaps he had already seen John and Kamala together in town. John was pleased with the purchase, for Kamala was fond of fish; since she had become pregnant, she had developed a passion for it.

Before leaving the bazaar, John went to the flower seller – an old mulatto woman who always spoke to him in French though she knew English. Unlike others in the bazaar, she did not try to practise her English on the Sahib. John bought a bunch of red roses, his favourite flower. The old woman asked after Kamala – how she was keeping; whether she had given birth to the child yet. Then she took a bunch of freshly-cut jasmine and gave it to John.

'This is for your madame from me.' John was overwhelmed by this goodwill and thanked her profusely.

When he left the flower-seller he took a tonga. A thought suddenly went through his mind. He realized, that preoccupied with all the worries, he had forgotten to find Kamala a wedding present. He asked the tongawallah to stop in front of a jeweller's shop. He had just received his salary and wanted to splash out on his wife.

He found a necklace he liked but the price was more than the money he had with him. While John was musing over it, the jeweller, sensing his indecision, said, 'I know you are Father Fallon's friend. Don't worry about the money – pay me next month or whenever you can.'

'No, no, I don't need that long. I'll pay you early next week.'

The man put the pearl necklace in a box and said, 'They are pearls of Coromandel – taken from the sea-bed near here. Your madame will love them.'

As he sat on the tonga, John pictured Kamala's face and started planning how he would make it a real surprise for her. He would perhaps ask her to sit in front of the dressing table and then stealthily bring the necklace from his pocket and put it round her neck. The imagined picture of Kamala's excited and surprised face gave John immense satisfaction.

The tonga went through the narrow streets of the old town and finally arrived at the rue Saint Honoré, near the town centre, where John had the apartment. He was already late. Kamala would have been expecting him for about an hour before. Still he was hoping to see her gleaming face, waiting for him on the balcony which overlooked the road. Kamala, ever since John had started this job, did her hair in the afternoon, put on a special sari and waited on the balcony for him to come home. Her eyes would glitter as he turned the corner and entered their road when she would wave with a broad smile and rush inside to put the kettle on for tea.

When the tonga turned the corner, John looked expectantly at the balcony. There was no sign of her. A cold shiver went through his spine. No, no, she would not run away now. Of that much he was sure. Then what?

He asked the tongawallah to wait in case she had gone to hospital. It is unlikely, he thought. She had not given even an inkling of it this morning. He took all the shopping and hurried to the apartment. Everything was clean and tidy. There was a note on the table, neatly folded. John eagerly took it and read –

'Darling

Sorry about it. Not me – it's your son who has been giving me trouble. I should have told you this morning but did not want to worry you as I thought I would be able to wait until you came home. I am going to hospital. Do not rush. Take your time ...'

John did not read the rest. He darted out of the apartment and jumped on the tonga and shouted, 'Go to the European hospital. Hurry.'

The tongawallah whipped his horse and creaked into a hasty start. John sat in the tonga, worried. Then to control his nerves he opened the letter again and read on –

'*Your dinner, all cooked, is in the kitchen. Please eat everything. From tomorrow I have arranged with Madame Dubois, next door, that you would eat with them. She is very pretty. I would be jealous if you looked at her more often than is necessary. Eat properly. Look after yourself.*
With all my love.
Your Kamala.'

The tonga stopped in front of the European hospital. John jumped down and eagerly ran to the reception.

'My name is Sugden. I believe my wife was admitted here today.'

The receptionist looked through the register. 'Oh yes. That's the Indian lady. On the third floor, monsieur.'

John climbed the stairs quickly and came to the third floor. He eagerly scanned the ward for Kamala but there was no sign of her. He asked the matron.

'Oh, yes, the Indian lady. She's in the labour room. Went there some time ago. Should have been back by now.' She looked at the clock. 'Please, wait here, monsieur, I'll go and check.'

John waited impatiently. He paced the floor up and down to control his nerves. The seconds ticked away. His heart started pounding with unknown fear. He did not know what pain Kamala had to go through to have the baby. Why hadn't she said anything to him this morning? He would have taken the day off. He had already mentioned about it at his school and his headmaster wouldn't have minded. The Frenchman was eager to see John and Kamala settling down properly in Pondicherry. He had taken a liking to them both. Especially Kamala. On the wedding day when his headmaster had met Kamala, he had told John afterwards, 'Mr Sugden – you are a very lucky man. All my life I have been waiting to find a wife like yours. But I am unlucky in love – if you know what I mean.' The Frenchman must have had some bad experience with a woman.

But where was the matron? Why was she taking such a long time to come back? John was becoming a nervous wreck. Oh women! Why hadn't she told him this morning that she was having contractions! As if his going to work was more important than making sure she was all right. This, John could never understand. She was normally so sensible. What had come over her? Did all women get so foolish when they were about to give birth to a child?

The matron was coming. John could see her through the glass panel of the swing door. He eagerly rushed forward.

'How is she?'

'Your wife has given birth to a boy, monsieur. He's fine.'

'How about my wife? How's she?' John's loud anxious voice echoed on the hospital wall.

'You can come with me, monsieur, and see her.'

John followed the matron through the corridor. His heart was pounding like cannon fire. At least she is all right, he thought. Or is she? Surely if there is such a thing as God, nothing should happen to her. All the punishment God has made her go through in life – surely even God has a sense of justice! Or hasn't He? No, no, he could think no more! She is so pretty, so young, so beautiful! They have been so looking forward to this child! And happiness! Suddenly something went through John's mind. He nearly shouted – I don't believe it. No, he didn't believe God would be so callous as to come down on the fourth day after her birth to write on a pretty young baby's forehead such a cruel thing as *all through your life you will only have pain, humiliation and suffering*! How could he be so heartless! No. John did not believe in that kind of God. His God was merciful!

The matron was well ahead of John now. She was walking quite fast. A few other doctors and nurses in their white aprons were rushing round. The groaning noise of women in labour and infants bellowing from a nearby room filled the air. The matron turned left towards the end of the corridor. On the right was a green door, marked 'Cas Urgent – Silence'. The matron opened the door. Yes, John could see Kamala. She was lying in bed. Very pale. Whatever was the matter with her? Why did she look so pale? Almost like a sheet of paper. There was absolutely no colour in that pretty face. Oh God! Whatever had happened to her?

He was relieved when Kamala turned her face to see who was coming through the door. Her eyes lit up as she saw him. John rushed towards her.

'How are you, darling?' John asked. 'Why didn't you tell me this morning? Oh, why didn't you?'

For a moment Kamala's eyes looked sad.

There was a doctor in the room whom John had not noticed before. He was a Frenchman with ruddy cheeks and a big, thick, bristly moustache. His skin looked so incredibly healthy compared to Kamala's. The Frenchman signalled John to go to him. John held Kamala's hand for a brief period. Oh it was so cold. Almost deathly cold. As if there was no blood left in her. 'I will be back in a second, darling,' John told Kamala and anxiously followed the grim-faced Frenchman.

The French doctor took John outside the room and then in broken English he said, 'We had to do a Caesarian on your wife, monsieur. Before we operated on her we tried to contact you but you had already left school by then. We didn't know what time would you be here. Your wife was eager that we operated on her. She gave us permission. It was an emergency, you see.'

'What was the matter?' John asked, almost petrified with fear.

'Umbilical cord – you see – the cord was trapped round the baby's neck. Of course, we didn't know that at the time, but we knew that if we didn't operate immediately he would die. Your wife, you see, was adamant that the baby's life must be saved. We followed her wish. I am sorry, monsieur. We tried to contact you before we operated on her. We did our best. There was nothing else we could have done.'

'How is she now?' That was all John wanted to know. He had no interest in his son. He only wanted his wife to be alive.

'She has lost a lot of blood, you see. It's touch and go. She might pull through with God's grace. I don't know. I don't want to give you any false hope. You see, she was already very weak when we operated on her. But we had no choice. You see, your wife wanted it. She wanted the baby to be safe.'

For a moment John felt absolutely numb. He wanted to hear no more. Anyway what was there to hear? He came back to Kamala.

A tired, pallid smile appeared on Kamala's lips when she saw John but her eyes were lively. He held her hand.

'Have you seen him? Have you seen your son?' she asked enthusiastically.

'Not yet. He's fine, I've been told.'

'Go and see him. Go and see your son first. I am all right. Please, do!' Kamala implored.

John went reluctantly. The boy was kept next door. A lump of flesh – little eyes, little hands, little feet and plenty of dark hair like Kamala's – hard to imagine he had been in her stomach all this time.

'He is fine, monsieur,' the mulatto nurse tried to cheer him up. 'A big boy! Nearly four kilogrammes! He was saved just in time. I was in the operating theatre, monsieur. That umbilical cord hasn't done any damage to him. He is perfectly healthy. He will be a strong boy, monsieur.'

John was no longer interested in his son. He wanted to come back to Kamala. Nothing mattered to him but Kamala's life. Oh God, please save her life! Please! His desperate plea went round and round his head. If there is any justice in this world she should live. Of all people in this world she should live and enjoy at least a little happiness in her life. No, no, John did not believe in reincarnation! And even if he had, there was nothing on earth, no sin, she could ever have committed in her other life for which this punishment would be due. If anyone deserved happiness it was she. She deserved her husband, her son and a tiny speck of happiness. Oh God! Please see to it. Even if you punish me, don't punish that young, beautiful, innocent girl any more. Please God, please!

John did not want to stay in that room with his son any more. No, he did not hate him. If anyone was guilty, it was not him. Yes, Gandhi, Jinnah and the Raj – they were guilty, but not him! God was guilty, but not him! Not him! John was eager to go back to see Kamala.

When he came back, Kamala's eyes were closed. An expression of pain registered on her face. As he came in she opened her eyes and signalled him to come nearer. He came and held her hands.

'Please, kiss me, darling.'

John could see the white sheet covering her body was fast becoming red. Frantically he shouted, 'Doctor!'

'Please, do not call anyone. Do not bring anyone now between us.'

'Kamala, please! Let me call someone.'

'No, darling, no! Not now! Not any more!' Her face twisted in pain. But only momentarily. She smiled again. 'Isn't our son lovely? Handsome – just like his father.'

John did not reply.

'Will you promise me something, darling?'

'Anything! Anything!' John cried.

'You won't take revenge on our son, if I go – will you?'

'You will not go.'

'Promise, you won't take revenge on him.'

'I promise.'

'Promise, you will make him as strong, as idealistic, as powerful as his father.'

'I promise.'

'Tell him about his mother. Just good things.'

'There is nothing but good in you, Kamala, there is nothing but good. The world is bad, but not you,' John said haltingly, overwhelmed with emotion.

'The world is good. That is why we have this happiness.' Kamala was calm.

'Kamala, don't leave me! Please, don't leave me! It's so unfair. So unjust.'

'Oh, darling,' Kamala said, 'if you marry again, don't let her beat our son.'

'Darling, I will never marry. I will never have anyone else. Please, don't go away.' John's voice croaked.

'No, you marry again. You need a woman to look after you.'

'Please, don't talk like that. I'm sure you will be all right.'

Kamala paused for a while, trying to control her pain. Then she asked, 'Darling, can you recite Goethe's "Sweet remembering" for me?'

John, tearful, cleared his voice and then started –

Angedenken an das Liebe
Glucklich! wenns lebendig bliebe
Angedenken an das Eine
Bleibt das Beste, was ich meine.

Kamala repeated, '*Angedenken an das Liebe Glucklich! wenns lebendig bliebe* – Remembering what is dear will be happiness if it remains alive.'

A sudden pain now came on her face but she ignored it. Her eyes lit up again, lively and young – just as they had been when John had first arrived in Raigarh, that afternoon when they exchanged garlands.

'Do you know something?' Kamala asked.

'What, love?'

Kamala paused for a moment and then held John's hand tight to control her pain.

John started crying. Kamala raised her weak hand to wipe his tears. John tried to control his emotions.

'Come nearer!' she whispered. John sat even closer and held her tight. She indicated with her hand for John to come even closer. He took her in his arms and placed a kiss on her dry lips. She looked at him lovingly and then softly murmured, 'Methinks I lied all winter, when I swore, my love was infinite, if spring make it more.' And then she smiled for the last time.

John gently placed her head on the pillow. She was peaceful and serene.

TWENTY NINE

After Kamala's death the next twelve months passed uneventfully for John Sugden. That year was also a period of political inactivity for the Congress, mainly because the party could not decide whether to share power with the British under the new reform or stay away. This indecision divided the party. Those who wanted to share power, called themselves *Swarajists* and attacked the negative attitude of the others – the 'No-Changers'. Gandhi did not want to participate in this squabble and devoted more and more time and energy to social reforms, especially to trying to uplift the status of the *Harijans* to ameliorate the abominable conditions in which these untouchables had to live. 'We must not create conditions in which our foreign exploiters are replaced by much worse Indian ones,' he warned.

Without Gandhi's energy and vitality in the political struggle, the Congress found that they made no headway into the general consciousness of the Indian public. This impasse within the Congress provided an ideal opportunity for Lord Reading to solve the Indian problem amicably. But according to historians, he lacked the creative imagination to initiate a constructive settlement.

After nine months in Pondicherry, Father Fallon became increasingly restless and wanted to return to Bihar. The charm of speaking French all the time had now worn off and he wanted to get back into action among the down-trodden, whose lives were riddled with disease and suffering.

Through diplomatic channels he made an application to the Indian government. This became successful, though with one proviso – he would not become involved in any political activity, especially with Gandhi. Fallon agreed, albeit reluctantly. He simply could not stay away from India.

Before leaving he asked John to come with him, mainly because he thought John, without him, would feel lonely in Pondicherry. Also since Kamala's death Fallon felt a strange kind of responsibility – he was worried about the young Englishman since within such a short spell of time he had had to face problems and sufferings of great magnitude.

John, however, declined to go. India did not hold any attraction for him. Not any more. If anything, he became increasingly critical of all the weakness and inefficiency, both of Indian society and the Raj. The only reason for going to India would be to join Gandhi and help him to improve the social status of the ordinary Indians. This he could not do even now, for it would be tantamount to going against His Majesty King George V.

Fallon's departure, however, allowed him the time to reflect on his own future and that of David, his son. He had promised Kamala on her deathbed he would look after David – protect him from any outside danger. The more he thought about David and his future, the more he felt he ought to move out – move out from even the shadow of the Raj. He did not want David to face humiliation because of his parentage. The very fact of being a Eurasian in India was a problem in itself. On top of this, David would have to contend with his mother's past which Hindu society would never forget, nor would the Raj forgive John for marrying Kamala against their wishes.

John started taking more interest in the news of England. The fact that he had had to leave the civil service had meant forfeiting his right to a furlough. Over five years had gone and he had not seen England. He was now longing to get back and show David to the boy's grandfather.

Also there was something else – the emergence in Great Britain of a new party for the working-class. Ever since the Russian revolution in 1917 when for the first time the proletariat had enjoyed the taste of power, all over the world, especially among the liberal intelligentsia, this victory generated great enthusiasm. In England, because of the strong democratic tradition, the intelligentsia felt that the best way to gain power for the working-class would be through the ballot box. In this, they achieved almost overnight success, especially as the constraints on eligibility to vote had been gradually lifted to allow the voice of the ordinary people to be represented in Parliament.

Ramsay MacDonald, the charismatic leader of the new party, though born illegitimate and in poverty, had already established his influence in the country and, during a brief spell as Prime Minister, shown his potential. Many people firmly believed that in the years to come he would become a major force in the Empire and change the destiny of people in the English-speaking world.

Although previously John had supported the Liberals, after spending a few years in India he found his allegiance really lay with the down-trodden, and the ideologies of the Labour Party appealed to him. What he liked most was that it did not blindly follow Marxism, denying the existence of God. With his Quaker background he could never support materialistic atheism. That was why he could feel no enthusiasm for Lenin's Russia.

On 15 November 1926, exactly a year after Kamala's death, John Sugden with his son, David, boarded the SS *Bristol* in Bombay bound for Tilbury, expecting to find a new Britain of social equality where they could settle down in relative peace and tranquillity.

POSTSCRIPT

The boat had stopped a while ago. David Sugden was so engrossed in his father's diary that he had no idea of the time and place. He could see each event in that diary vividly as if it were he who had gone through that traumatic experience. He looked through the porthole of his cabin. The sun was dazzling over the greenish shallow water – the end of the Arabian sea. A long queue of ships was waiting patiently outside Bombay harbour. Nearer the coast there was a hazy mist through which India, the jewel in the crown, looked mysterious, even ethereal. The yellow sandstone of the Gateway of India where George V, the Emperor of India, first marched through to receive millions of his subjects looked distant and unreal. So this is India, the land of my birth, he thought. He now became excited at the prospect of fulfilling his mission.